NOTHING NORTH OF DELMAR

ALSO BY ELLEN BARKER

East of Troost

Still Needs Work

The Breaks

NOTHING NORTH OF DELMAR

a novel

ELLEN BARKER

SHE WRITES PRESS

Published in 2026 by
She Writes Press, an imprint of The Stable Book Group

32 Court Street, Suite 2109
Brooklyn, NY 11201
https://shewritespress.com

Library of Congress Control Number: 2025920901
ISBN: 979-8-89636-118-3
eISBN: 979-8-89636-119-0

Interior designer: Katherine Lloyd, The DESK

Printed in the United States

To everyone living north of Delmar,
including the Delmar Loop in University City,
and to Washington University.
My time there made everything after possible.

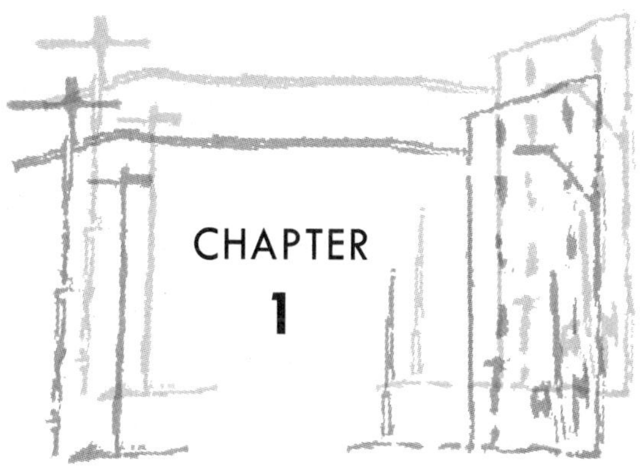

CHAPTER 1

Welcome to Saint Louis, I tell myself. I'm on a city bus headed for University City and, fingers crossed, a waiting apartment. Before this bus, I was on a Greyhound bus for five hours. I'm tired and anxious and very sweaty.

Across the aisle, a boom box is playing the Lovin' Spoonful's "Summer in the City." A teenager sporting an Afro and beads is sitting halfway into the aisle and dancing to the music, as well as you can dance sitting on a bus seat. He doesn't smell so great.

I ooze away from him, pressing into the duffel bag in the seat next to me. My T-shirt is stuck to my back and pulls away as I move. Ick—I'm the one who doesn't smell so great. After twenty-four hours of sharing marginally air-conditioned space with smokers and families packing fried food, I really need a shower. It's midday and the bus isn't full, so I'm hoping the duffel bag and backpack will ward off potential seatmates. I look up and see the boom box kid is looking at me, grinning.

"S'cool, I'm friendly," he says. He must have noticed me oozing away. I lean forward, shift in my seat, pretend that's all I was doing. I smile at him ruefully.

"It's definitely summer in the city," I say to him.

"Cool song, gotta love them oldies," he says. He closes his eyes and hums with his boom box. Funny, the song is ten years old but doesn't seem like an oldie on this particular day. I'm guessing it gets a lot of airtime in the summer. In the city, or anyway cities like this one.

"Is it always this hot here in May?" I ask and then think I shouldn't be giving away the fact that I'm new here and possibly vulnerable.

"Don't know where you're from, but it's June in this town." He goes back to humming.

I sigh. Of course it's June, June 1, 1976, the day my lease starts. It's just that it was May when I last slept somewhere other than the seat of a Greyhound bus. The song ends and the DJ informs us that we're listening to KSLQ and that it is indeed hot in the city: "It's eighty-eight outside, but we're stayin' cool on KSLQ."

I look out the window, check the cross street, look at the map in my hand. I've got a lot of luggage, and I don't want to miss my stop.

"You goin' a WashU?" The kid's talking to me again.

"Yes. Well, going to University City right now."

"That's cool. U City's cool. You live there?"

I don't know how much I want to tell this guy, but he's the most pleasant person I've run into since boarding the Greyhound.

"I plan to. I'm supposed to pick up my key by three o'clock." I look at my watch. It's only a little after two so I don't need to worry, although I will anyway.

Worrying is what I do, and I come by it naturally. Way back in my bassinet, I must have seen that no one else in my family worried about much of anything, so it was up to me. My father didn't worry enough to even come around all that much. He would drop in for a day, a week, a month. He'd treat every kid on the block to Popsicles from the ice cream truck. We'd go to the zoo or the amusement park. And then he'd be gone. Mom was happy when Dad was around and just as happy when he wasn't. She cut hair in a makeshift salon in the garage, and if she had customers, we had food. If she didn't have customers, we'd poke around the back of the cupboards looking for forgotten cans of beans or packets of spaghetti. If Dad came around at Labor Day flush with cash, Mom would sign us up at St. Joseph's school and pay our annual book fee, twenty dollars for me and seventeen for my little sister. If Dad didn't come around before school started, we went to Hope Street Elementary.

So, I worried for the whole family. I worried about whether Dad would be home for Christmas. I worried when the milk carton or the peanut butter jar was almost empty. I saved my milk money and drank water from the drinking fountain, then gave the nickels back to my mother for groceries. I begged the nuns to let me be one of the two seventh-grade girls who helped in the cafeteria and got a free lunch. On Saturdays I swept the floor and handed out capes in my mother's makeshift salon in hopes of tips.

Worry never did any good, but I did it anyway. For all I knew, the milk and peanut butter would disappear entirely if I didn't worry about it. Schoolwork, on the other hand, was the one place where worry could be translated into success. So I worked hard in school, and my grades showed it. I liked math best, because I could do the problems and know they were finished and they were correct. I loved English and social studies too, but it was a lot harder to be sure of an A on a writing assignment. I did all the extra-credit homework, just to make sure. I finished eighth grade at the top of my class. That year was a St. Joe year, so I had taken the exam for St. Stanislaus High School. I won a scholarship, ensuring four years at the same school. I breathed a sigh of relief. I would have a uniform, so I wouldn't have to worry about my clothes, which were mostly hand-me-downs from Mom's customers.

The first week of high school, we had an assembly in the gym to meet the teachers who were new that year. Among the new staff was the school's first-ever college counselor, who worked three mornings a week. In her short introductory speech, she told all the seniors that they were required to sign up for a meeting with her before the end of the first quarter, even if they were not interested in college. This was almost certainly the first time I had thought about college. I knew nothing about college whatsoever, but I decided at that moment that I was going to go.

By that time, I had started babysitting for neighborhood kids. I opened a savings account at the parish credit union. My mother had to sign the form, and I gave her a long look when she handed it back to me. For the first time in my life, I had a shred of distrust. I hedged and put half my earnings in a book that I hollowed out, bit by bit. It was a book of poems. I was pretty sure no one in my family would ever open it.

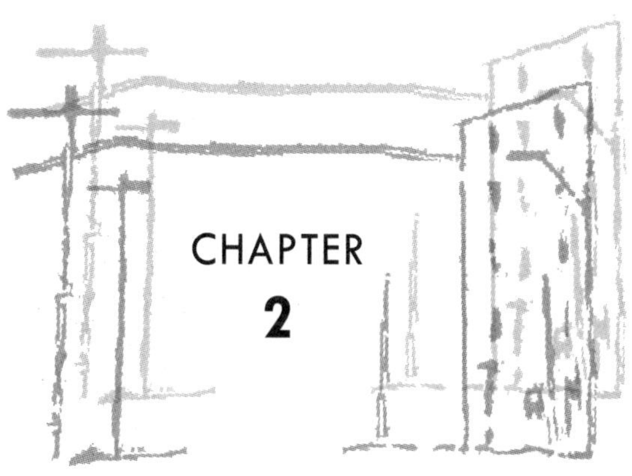

CHAPTER 2

"Nice talking to you."

I look up and realize the teenager is speaking again. He is standing up, ready to get off the bus.

"Oh! Yes, you too. I think I zoned out for a minute there."

"This is my stop—I work at Talayna's. The Loop is just another few blocks. I'm Lamont, by the way. Stop by Talayna's sometime." He reaches over and shakes my hand.

Lamont waves and is gone, and I realize he's turned off the boom box and the cool-guy attitude. He's walking down the street like a college student. I wonder what the Loop is and then wonder what Talayna's could be.

I'm not actually going straight to my new apartment on Wingate Avenue; I have to pick up the keys first. I've been given an address on Delmar and told to ask Mr. Lipschultz for them.

It's all I can do to heave my luggage out of the bus before it roars away, diesel fumes spewing. As if I'm not smelly enough. I check the addresses on the storefronts, cross Delmar, and walk slowly down the street, looking for something that could be a real estate office. Instead, I find myself standing in front of a dark, dingy storefront, very small. LIPSCHULTZ AND SON it says on the door, JEWELERS. The number and the name are right, so I heave the door open and drag my luggage through. It's hot and dusty inside. And dark, after the glaring sunshine outside.

"May I help you?" I make out the shape of a man behind the counter. Short, thin, and rather elderly, I'm guessing. His voice is formal with a trace of accent. I don't know enough about accents to place it.

"Yes, I'm Novelle. I'm here to pick up keys to my apartment. Mrs. Marzello said you would have them."

"Oh yes, Novelle. I am pleased to meet you." He reaches across the counter to shake my hand. "I have the keys for you." His voice sounds sad to me.

He turns around, and I see that the shop is more a repair shop than a jewelry store. On the counter under a bright work light is a watch in what looks like dozens of pieces. I look at my own watch, my grandmother's watch, which has been running fast. It's not three o'clock yet; I didn't keep him late. He turns back to me.

"Here they are," he says. "The outside door, the apartment door, and the mailbox. I am sorry, I do not know which of the door keys works in which door." I reach out to take the keys. The sleeve on the arm he has extended has slipped toward his elbow, and I see a fraction of a tattoo in the wrinkled skin. He doesn't look like a Marine to me. He pulls back his arm and tugs the sleeve down.

His smile is friendly enough, but it's clear that he has nothing more to say. I have a lot of questions about the apartment and the neighborhood, but I can tell that this is not the place to ask them. I thank him and escape to the slightly fresher air of Delmar.

I consult my map. Only a block or so to Wingate. I struggle along with my luggage, which seems heavier, as if it has absorbed pounds of smoke and dust and humidity. I cross the street, check addresses. I'm not sure how far down Wingate I have to go, and I'd really like to stop in the Dairy Queen and cool off. But most of all, I want to drop my duffel, wash my face, and find out what my apartment looks like.

This will be my first apartment ever. I spent my four undergraduate years in dorms, the last two as an RA for the sake of a free room. Those last two years I had a single, but it was tiny, barely big enough for the built-in bed and desk. And both years I was supervising first-year floors, with all the energy and angst and noise of teenagers away from home for the first time. I loved the job, and the kids, but now I am more than ready for a little more space, a little less noise, and a lot more privacy.

All the buildings on Wingate are brick, mostly three-story apartment buildings. Mine is two blocks down. The key to the outer door works and I haul everything inside. I take a moment to catch my breath and check the mailbox, not that I'm expecting anything. The key doesn't work.

My unit is on the second floor, Apartment 2B. I like the sound of To-Be. The key doesn't work. I pull out the rental contract, which clearly says 2B. I look at the paper key tag. It says 3D. So now what? Do I have the wrong contract, the wrong apartment, or the wrong key, or even the wrong building? I leave the luggage and trot downstairs to check the address, in case I belong in the mirror image building next door. Nope.

Back at 2B, I knock and no one responds, not surprising on a workday afternoon. I try upstairs at 3D. No one answers there either, but the key works. I open the door slowly.

"Hello? Is anyone here?" A black cat zooms in from the hallway, leaps onto a sofa, and sits looking at me as if he had been there all the time. Why am I looking at a cat and a sofa?

"Hello," I call a little louder. The apartment has the empty, airless feel of a vacant space. I've entered enough empty dorm rooms to know. Once I'm all the way into this one, it's pretty clear that the cat and the couch are the only inhabitants. That, and a phone on the floor. I lift the receiver and get a dial tone. Thank you, Previous Tenant, for not shutting off the phone. I dial the number on the contract.

After six rings, I'm trying to think of a Plan B, but I can't, so I let it keep ringing.

"Hello?" A sleepy voice.

"Hi, my name is Novelle. Is this Mrs. Marzello?"

"Yeees."

"I'm the new tenant on Wingate. I'm a little confused. My rental agreement says Apartment 2B but the key says 3D. Did I get the wrong key from Mr. Lipschultz? Or . . . or something?"

Silence on the other end, and then some throat clearing.

"Do you want my daughter-in-law?" she finally says. "Wait up." She sounds more awake now.

In the background, I hear muffled conversation. The phone has a long cord, and I walk around investigating. The tiny bedroom has a bed with no bedding. The closet has a winter coat, a down comforter, and a few flannel shirts, plus a very small and completely empty chest of drawers. No one lives here.

I wander into the kitchen, which has a fork, a plate, two glasses, a bag of sugar, two cans of tuna, and an almost-empty Cheerios box at the back of a cupboard. No table, no chairs. And if not exactly barren, everything left has the air of discards.

I'm startled when I hear Mrs. Marzello again.

"She says to tell you she isn't here, but you can call back later." This time there is a note of mischief in her voice.

"She's actually there, isn't she?"

"Yes, she says you can call, what, after five?" The last bit is indistinct, as if she's turned away from the phone. I hear more muffled conversation and then a different voice comes on.

"Hello, this is Mrs. Marzello. I'm sorry, Mother is a bit confused these days."

I'm not interested in the Marzello family drama. Well, a little interested, but mostly I want to resolve the apartment question before dark. I have no backup plan if I can't sleep here. I'm almost regretting the phone call. I should have just moved into 3D.

"Well, my rental agreement says I'm in 2B, but the key says 3D. I'm in 3D now, and there is some furniture and a cat."

"No pets! That's in the contract!"

"Right, and I don't have a cat. But there is a cat here, along with some furniture. Is this the right apartment or is someone else still in 3D? Am I in 3D or 2B? The building on Wingate."

"Oh, in the Loop." Her tone changes slightly. "I can rent you that furniture." I picture Mrs. Marzello's mother-in-law in the background, rolling her eyes. Which is what I would be doing if I weren't starting to wonder how quickly I can find another apartment and whether I can get my deposit money back on this one.

"No, thanks," I say. "I just want to know which apartment is mine. Should I stay here, in 3D, or if I'm supposed to be in 2B, like my contract says, can you bring me the keys? Right now?" I add because I'm losing patience. I'm looking at the bathroom now. They took the toilet paper. Definitely moved out.

"Oh, well, you said you're in 3D, right? So that's fine." I'm beginning to think she's well into happy hour and the last thing she wants to do is leave her martini to deliver keys.

I pull the shower curtain aside. There isn't actually a shower. It's a clawfoot tub with a shower curtain on a ring suspended from the ceiling.

"Hey, there isn't a shower here. The contract says there's a shower."

"Oh, I'm sure there is a shower. I remember seeing a shower curtain, so that's all right. You just call back if you need anything."

"Wait!" I really want that shower; I was very careful reading the ads. I only called about apartments that specified showers. And now I'm racing to the kitchen to make sure the promised refrigerator and stove work.

If they don't, it's too late—she's hung up. I'm not completely reassured, but I've come to the conclusion that 3D isn't *not* my apartment, and that I'm staying. The living room is a comfortable size and the bedroom and kitchen are big enough for someone who just moved out of a dorm room. It's got a lot of windows, and I throw them open to let in fresh air and find that the day is cooling off. I inspect the bed, which is just a mattress and box springs sitting on concrete blocks. It's unstained except for a shoeprint in one corner. I look at the sofa and matching chair, which appear to be borrowed from someone's solarium. They have bamboo frames and thick tropical-print cushions. They look comfortable. But I don't get too close. One of my RA tasks was treating every mattress on my floor for lice just before move-in day and just after move-out day. A task not on the official list was telling my freshmen about crab lice and other uncomfortable realities of dorm life. And besides, I need toilet paper. I take one more look at my showerless tub, get my wallet and keys, and walk back to Delmar.

The hardware store has lice spray, and I look at the plumbing while I'm there, then throw myself on the mercy of the clerk at the counter. I explain my shower situation and ask if they have something I can attach to the spigot and use to at least wash my hair. It seems I'm not the first person to ask. He says that most of the apartments in the Loop are like mine and brings me a device made from a length of hose, a hose clamp, a shower head, and a bracket. He shows me how to attach it to the wall with mollies, and I leave happy. I stop at the 7-Eleven for food and toilet paper, thinking I'll have to figure out where the real grocery store is soon.

On my way back, I check the mailbox for 3D. The key works. Inside are a phone bill and a postcard addressed to David Black. I leave them for the moment and head upstairs.

While the lice, if there are any, are suffering their fate at the hands of the bug spray, I dig through my duffel for the little toolbox I had used to solve all kinds of problems at my dorms. When I get ready to install the showerhead, I see that this isn't the first time one of these handmade devices has been screwed into the wall. Apparently, David Black decided to take it with him. But I'm only out four dollars and I have my shower, my apartment, and a bed. I spread out my sheets and sleep.

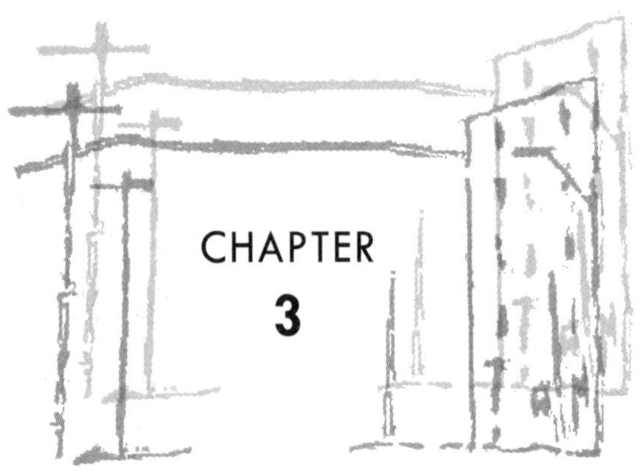

CHAPTER 3

Bells rouse me at six o'clock. Soft and almost familiar, but what is it? I get up, stretching my neck, which is sore from sleeping without a pillow. I look out the north window, which seems to be where the bells are coming from. Ah, church bells—the morning Angelus.

The sun is up, and now I'm up, on my first day in my first apartment. While I shower away the crick in my neck, I think about priorities. High on the list is a pillow. I didn't even try to pack it along on the Greyhound, but now that I'm sure of my address I can tell my mother to go ahead and mail the boxes I left with her. Not only a pillow or two, but also my typewriter and books. I've also boxed up my winter coat and quilts, but those can wait a few months. I just need to call her and have her change the apartment number on the labels from 2B to 3D. It's seven thirty at her house and still night rates in Saint Louis, so I go ahead and call her.

"Novelle, you made it!" It doesn't occur to her that I could be waylaid; I'm supposed to be in Saint Louis, so I am in Saint Louis.

"Yes, I made it. No problems at all." Another mother would

want to hear about the trip, but mine didn't expect problems and she was right.

"Of course not! Did you find a job yet?" She's not worried about me finding a job; she's assuming that one has already materialized.

"Not yet, but soon." If I focus, I can be as positive as she is. "I mostly wanted to let you know that you can send the boxes now."

I explain about correcting the labels without going into why. Another mother would have wanted to know all about that and probably advised me to get the contract corrected. Another mother would also have asked me for my new phone number. But not my mother, so I didn't have to explain that I was making a call that would probably be charged to someone named David Black. There are days when I miss the kind of parents that other people have, but all in all it saves time and a lot of eye-rolling to have the kind that don't worry.

Now that Mom has mentioned it, a job is also top of my list. I've moved to Saint Louis directly from my undergrad dorm with the plan of stockpiling some cash before I start grad school at the end of summer. Since I don't have a car, I need a job nearby or on a bus line. I'm hoping for something on campus. I've got a couple of copies of my resume, but I need a phone number to put on them, and I need my typewriter to put them on with.

It seems early to call the phone company, but I do anyway and arrange to have service turned on in the apartment. I make an appointment for the next morning. I get out my map again and trace a route to the Washington University campus. Maybe on the way, I'll get a newspaper and see if there are any job ads in the weekday edition. I walk west as far as the library and make a mental note to get a card as soon as I have some proof of my address, something with the correct apartment number. I pass three bookstores, two movie theaters, a diner called the Maryland Café, and Blueberry Hill, which is a bar and eatery with a lot of memorabilia from the '50s. Also a bike shop and the 7-Eleven and hardware store I've already patronized. There is a sort of open space on the north side of the street, with posters announcing that the farmers' market is on Thursday afternoons. I'm pretty psyched about the whole downtown.

I'm in a friendly mood and say hello to several people, asking one of them if Wingate is the best way to WashU. They send me to Melville, which ends in a walkway that connects to a pedestrian bridge over Forest Park Parkway and directly onto campus. I love the walkway, which passes along behind the backyards of some large houses on shady lots. Some of them are growing tomatoes on the walkway side of their back fences. I don't see any trash or graffiti. And even today, weeks after graduation, there are other people walking and biking in my direction. It looks perfectly safe in the bright morning sun. I'm not going to worry about going back and forth to campus alone.

I walk up the steps of the overpass and realize that no one else has bothered—they've all just run across, dodging traffic, and are now working their way up the driveways on the other side and through gaps between buildings. I like the view from the overpass and take a moment to look back the way I came. The walkway separates the big houses on the east side from apartments on the left. Maybe I could have found one of those and been that much closer to campus.

I dig through my backpack for the campus map that came with my acceptance. I head for SUPAC, which includes the student union, the performing arts center, and the bookstore. Maybe I'll find job listings there. On the way, I'm bowled over by the red granite buildings, the shady green spaces, and the ancient trees. Skirting the one blot—a rather ugly Olin Library—I peek into

Graham Chapel and then let myself into SUPAC. I don't see anything that might be a student union, but then I'm not sure exactly what a student union is anyway. I wander through the bookstore and resist buying a WashU T-shirt just yet. Instead, I get a notebook and ask the clerk if he knows where campus job listings might be posted. He hands me a copy of *The Record* and tells me that it's the faculty and staff paper. *Student Life* is the student paper and would be better, but he doesn't think they publish it in the summer.

"You could also ask at the Y," he says. "They have a lot of student programs all year round."

"The Y?" I can't picture a YMCA gym on a campus with its own gyms and pools.

"Campus Y, they have volunteer programs and yoga, that sort of thing."

I don't make a connection between yoga and job listings, but I let him tell me how to find the basement of Umrath Hall and go off in the direction he points. It's not far. I look at the narrow stairway going down the outside of the building, ending at a solid metal door. Not very inviting. But they've installed a large glass-front bulletin board at the top of the stairs, and I begin to see what he meant. Kinloch Tutoring, Peer Counseling, Leadership Development—a mix of volunteer programs and classes just outside the academic realm. I'm here and the sign says it's open, so I head down the stairs and through the metal door.

After the new and open atmosphere of SUPAC, the Umrath basement is very . . . basementy. I don't see anyone, just a sort of lounge and a hallway.

"Hello?"

"Back here, just keep walking!"

I follow the voice down the hall and reach a sort of office, with a couple of desks, typewriters, and a ditto machine labeled

"Hal." I wonder if they are *Space Odyssey* fans. I wonder if they'll let me borrow a typewriter to add my phone number to my resume, once I have a phone and assuming the type size matches.

A female body unfolds from the floor behind the large desk facing me.

"Hi. I'm Betty. Excuse the mess."

"I'm Novelle," I say cheerfully. I'm still working on my relaxed, be-like-Mom campaign. She'd charm this Betty into giving her a job on the spot. "I'm new on campus and I'm . . . well, this is my first stop, really. I start grad school in the fall, in Economics, and I am looking for a job on campus, a summer job, although maybe I could work in the fall some too." Out of breath, I stop.

"Well," Betty says with what seems like unnecessary caution, "I don't think we're actually hiring for summer. Unless you can type, then maybe. Part time." She looks me over.

"Let me get an application for you."

"Oh, sorry. I meant I'm looking for job listings, I was hoping someone could tell me where to find them. Someone at the bookstore thought maybe you would know."

"Tall kid, long hair, probably in a Campus Y T-shirt? Like this one?" she points to her own shirt, which sports a logo of a tree with spreading branches and roots.

"Yeah, that sounds right. Black guy, Afro, chatty."

"Arlo. He heads up the Kinloch tutoring program here. Designed the logo, too—that's why he wears the shirt all the time. We paid him in T-shirts." She's unearthed the application she was looking for and hands it to me. It has the same logo at the top.

"Oh, I like the logo. Is he an art major?"

Betty starts to tell me about Arlo, but we hear the door bang down the hallway.

"Becky! Are you in?"

"I'm back here, come on in, Adela," Betty says, and then to me, "Board member. She's amazing except she can't remember names. Just watch."

"Hi, Adela," she says as a large middle-aged woman teeters into the room lugging a box. I leap up for the box. "Adela, this is Novelle, she's new and—"

"Oh, thank you, dear. Noelle, is it? So nice to meet you. Always great to have new people." She turns to Betty. "Becky, the news isn't good. Ray isn't going to be back in June after all. Maybe not . . ." She glances at me, and her voice trails off.

Betty glances my way too, and then sort of comes to attention.

"Novelle, why don't you start on that paperwork?" She looks meaningfully at the application she handed me a minute ago. "You can use that desk." She motions toward a desk tucked into the massive stone foundations that define the entire underground office.

"Good," says Adela, looking at Betty. "We'll talk in here." And she picks a notebook out of her box and walks into the office behind Betty's desk as if it were a corporate corner office and she owned the company. The door closes firmly behind them.

I sidle over to the desk and sit down, wondering whose space I'm invading. There are pencils and notepads in the desk, but nothing personal on top. The giant blotter-style desk calendar has a lot of notes, obviously the work of many hands. The desk is no one's, I decide. Or everyone's. Something about the place appeals to me, and it would be a massive relief to get a job today, without time-consuming interviews and worry about clothes. I have never had a job that required dressing up, and while it would be a good idea to head in that direction, I'm a bit short of cash and clueless about fashion.

I've barely written my name and new address when I hear the outside door slam and flip-flops slap down the stairs. I hear the footsteps coming toward me and debate with myself—turn around and say hello, or ignore whoever it is because I can't help them anyway? I mentally cross my fingers and hope that it's someone who comes here often and knows what to do.

"Hello?" A young woman, clearly a student, appears next to me.

"Oh," I say, trying to imply that I didn't realize anyone was there. "Can I help you?" I say that without thinking. It just comes out.

"I'm taking a summer course and I just thought I would stop in and see about using the gym."

I'm pretty sure there is no gym in this cave-like setting. I stand up so I can face her and look around desperately for information. I know I should just admit that I know basically nothing, but I don't.

"Oh, it's not that kind of Y," I say as if I knew that for sure. I try to remember what was on that glass-front bulletin board at the top of the stairs. "We have tutoring programs and things like that." That's not quite right. "I mean programs where students can volunteer to tutor children, that sort of thing." That's the only thing I can remember. I spy a rack of brochures on the wall.

"Here, let's take a look." I walk her over to the rack and find mimeographed brochures for leadership training, volunteering, yoga classes. "I'm not sure what's available during the summer, but take a look. If it's really a gym you want, though, that would be in the university facilities." I have no idea what WashU has in the way of gym facilities, but there must be something.

She thanks me and I go back to my desk. I'm just finishing up when the outside door slams again and three women burst in, talking all at once. They breeze past the girl at the brochure rack and present themselves to me.

"I'm getting married in Graham Chapel in August," one of

them says. "And they told me that this is where the bride and bridesmaids get dressed."

"So we want to see what's here," another one, apparently a bridesmaid, says. Both of them are friendly but firm.

I should say, "I'm so sorry, but I don't work here," but it seems a little late for that.

"Well, take a look around," I say instead. "The lounge is back near the door." I walk them in that direction and see the ladies' room sign. "And the ladies' room is there." It's under the stairs, so I'm guessing that it's not spacious. "And of course there is a little kitchen space here." I know this because I have just looked in over their shoulders. We go in and I see that the sink and refrigerator are at the end of a large room with a very large worktable. "Lots of space to get organized here," I tell them.

What am I doing? I don't even know if they are in the right building. I leave them chattering and scoot back to the brochure rack hoping for something about weddings. I hear Betty and Adela, who are now back at Betty's desk. Adela appears to be leaving.

"So, for now, you are in charge," Adela says to Betty. "Noelle can take over your job, can't she?" Adela turns and sees me. "You're doing great work here, Noelle. We're lucky to have you."

Again, it's the wrong moment to announce that I don't work here. I look at Betty. She gives me a Cheshire cat smile and bats her eyes, then rolls them. I take that to mean I should just go with it for now.

"Oh, thank you!" I say. "Do you need any help with that box?" It's not my place to shoo her out, but I don't know what to say.

"Oh no, that stays here. I've just got this one folder, but thank you." She turns to Betty. "See you both next week." And she's gone, passing through the bridal party with smiles all around.

The bridal party!

"Betty, those girls are asking about a bride's room. Is that something the Y does?"

"Yes, hold on." She rummages in her desk and pulls out a folder. "Give them this and show them the contract. They need to pay at least two weeks before the wedding."

I take it and look through it as fast as I can, and then go back to the lounge, where the girls are now pretending to flounce around in wedding finery. I pick out the one who said she was getting married and hand her the folder.

"Here is some information for you," I tell her, and they all crowd around. "The contract is there too. You can look it over and let us know. We need at least two weeks' notice." I know I should ask if they have any questions, but I have no answers. I hope they'll just take the folder and come back later when someone is around who knows more than I do, since I know exactly as much as they do at this point.

They thank me and leave, and I look around for the girl who wanted the gym, but she seems to have slipped out at some point. I turn to Betty.

"Welcome to the Campus Y," she says. "You've got a job."

"But."

"You heard her."

"But."

"Look, she seems a little wacky, but she's also really, really sane. Let's sign you up while we have the chance. If it doesn't work out for whatever reason—you don't like it here, or we find out that you are an ax murderer or something—then we'll figure it out. Deal?"

"Deal!" I say, because why not. It's air-conditioned here and the work doesn't involve serving burgers or working until midnight. Unless I end up babysitting that wedding party. I hand over the employment application, telling her I've left the phone number blank but should have that in a day or two. She looks at me, eyes narrowed.

"How long have you been in town?" she asks me.

I look at my watch. "About twenty-four hours, if you count from when the Greyhound got in downtown."

She slaps the top of her head.

"Jesus H. Well, at least you seem to be able to get things done. Can you start tomorrow by any chance? Seeing as how you seem to have started today?"

I tell her that I'll be in as soon as the phone guy leaves and write down the Y phone number so I can let her know.

I retrace my steps toward home with only a little help from the map. My head is spinning but I am elated about having a job, even though I don't know how many hours it is or how much I'll be making. I decide not to worry about that until tomorrow. I don't actually have to take the job, or I can take it and look for another one if it's not enough. I hope it is enough. I hope I can actually do whatever Betty's job is. I did grab a few fliers on the way out, so I can read up a little on what exactly the Campus Y is and does.

My euphoria wanes a little as I unlock the door of my building. What if David Black has come back and found my stuff in his apartment? I check the mailbox—no one has removed his mail. That's a little reassuring. I tell myself I'll see if he's there, then knock on my neighbors' doors and see if they know anything about David Black.

I knock, then unlock the door. Again, the cat swoops past and perches on the sofa. No one is there and everything is as I left it. With relief comes hunger. It's well after noon. I check the date on the cans of tuna in the kitchen cupboard and use one of David's forks to eat David's tuna. The cat rubs against my leg and I let him finish the can.

Then I get out the University City telephone book and look up grocery stores. I learn that University City is better known as U City, which I now remember Lamont saying. I also learn that U City is fairly large. I work out the street numbering and find that most of the groceries are farther west, beyond walking distance. Schnucks seems to have more than one store. Who would call a grocery store "Schnucks"? The closest store isn't a national brand, but I set out to investigate. J&G is a little run-down but it's a real grocery and close enough that I can manage two bags of food, one in my backpack and one in my arms. I'm sweating and wishing I lived on the first floor when I get back, but once upstairs I unpack and feel like I'm really on my own now. I shower and lie down on the bed. From this position I can see only sky and the tops of sycamore trees. A little breeze floats in. It feels good. I like this place. And "3D" is almost as good as "To-Be."

After dinner, when it's cooler, I set about cleaning. I rummage in the broom closet for supplies and find a bucket and sponge. I get to work, musing about David Black. I'm amused that he has, or had, floor wax, unopened. Did he buy that and not use it? Did his mother buy it, expecting him to use it? And what about a toilet brush? Surely he didn't choose to move that and leave his toaster. Maybe he threw it away when he left. Maybe he never had one. I'm finding out odd, intimate things about someone whose larger life is a total mystery. I don't even know if David Black is actually the former tenant. I'm basing that strictly on the fact that there are two pieces of mail in the mailbox labeled 3D. For all I know, those things were put in the wrong box. And then I think: For all I know, David Black is the tenant moving into 3D, and he just isn't here yet. Maybe the mop and the coat and the toaster belong to someone else entirely. I finish cleaning the bathroom floor, which is an appealing pattern of small, unglazed blue and white hexagonal tiles. I take another shower, make sure the chain is on the door, and go to bed.

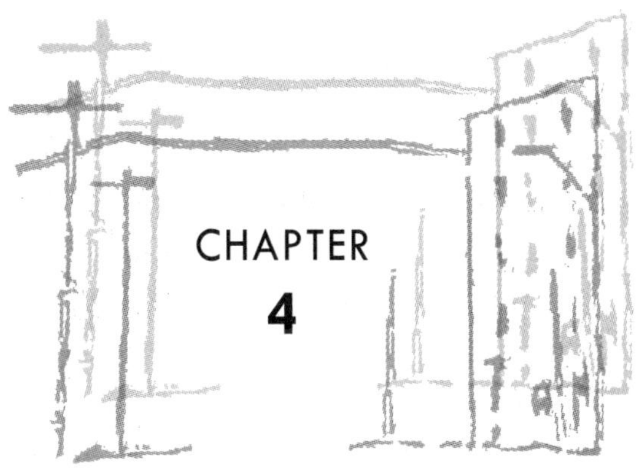

CHAPTER 4

When the church bells ring at six the next morning, I'm already half awake. It's windy and cloudy. I look through my duffel for my radio but don't find it. It must be in one of the boxes that I hope my mother has mailed by now. Oh well, I'll take my rain jacket, assuming it's in the duffel. I decide to unpack instead of rummaging every time I want something.

I immediately discover that I should have packed a few hangers, since the closet has none to spare. I fold up David Black's coat and shirts and put them on the top shelf, then hang everything that can be hung on the three hangers. I hesitate about using the drawers, in case he shows up today and wants his furniture, so I stack the rest of my clothes on the shelves and the floor and mentally give him a deadline of one week to show up before I start using the dresser.

I'm stuck now until the phone guy is due, so I clean kitchen shelves and drawers and rearrange the few kitchen items I've unpacked. I put all of David Black's things on the top shelf, then put them back within easy reach and make a list of what's his. Next, I tackle the stove and find a skillet in the oven. Scrubbing it takes until the doorbell rings and I run downstairs to let the phone man in.

Only it's not the phone man, it's a meter reader. I have no idea where the meters are and neither does he. We find a door that might go to the basement, but my keys don't work. I tell him I'll contact the landlord and find out. He says not to worry, they'll just send estimated bills. I close the door, then open it again and ask him why he rang 3D.

"Started at the bottom and rang them all. You're the only one who answered."

I walk back upstairs slowly, pondering that. I'm the only person in the building. Not entirely weird; everyone is probably at work or school. Or home for the summer, if they are the sort who can afford to pay rent on a vacant apartment. Maybe David Black is one of those. I've got to stop thinking about David Black. The phone guy finally shows up just before noon. I use my new phone to call Betty and tell her I'll be in within the hour. I have Cheerios for lunch, find my rain jacket, close the windows, and saunter off to campus and the first day of my new job.

Betty is alone when I get to the Y, absorbed in paperwork. She gives me a distracted smile and hands me a new employee form, which is basically the same as the application I filled out yesterday. This time I can fill in the phone number space. Then she tells me that she wants to run my paperwork through manually so she's going to Brookings Hall. She gives me some thank-you letters to type, tells me to answer the phone and take messages, and gathers up her purse and papers.

"Do you want me to lock the door, or are you okay here by yourself?"

Somehow locked in is more frightening than being alone, so I tell her I'm fine and she leaves. The letters are basically form letters thanking donors for contributions. There are only a few, so I make sure they are perfect. After four years of writing college papers, I can type easily, and the electric typewriter is much nicer than my old manual one. I finish and wander around looking at posters and brochures and exploring the public areas, which include a meeting room in addition to the big workroom and lounge I saw yesterday. There are a few more cubbies like the one I used the day before. I use the ladies' room and make a note to ask Betty about the brides. Then I'm at a loss. I'm getting paid to do nothing, and I don't even know yet how much I'm getting paid. I think about investigating Ray's office and the ones I can see through a door next to Betty's desk, but decide that if I do, Betty will come back and I'll be embarrassed. So I sit in the lounge and leaf through magazines.

Betty bursts in a few minutes later, bringing the smell of rain. She leans over and shakes water out of her hair.

"Where is my brain—I didn't take an umbrella. It's raining cats and dogs out there! Did you hear the tornado sirens?"

"I had no idea. I guess it's soundproof down here."

"Well, the basement is the place to ride out a tornado, so I guess it's all right. We should turn the radio on."

Betty drops into her chair and wipes her face with a tissue.

"Sorry about running out like that—the personnel office closes at three in the summer, and I wanted to get you set up so you'll get a check next week. I just barely made it. Here's your temporary employee card."

She hands me a card and I wonder what I've signed up for. Answering a phone that doesn't ring and typing form letters in an empty basement isn't feeling quite as exciting as it did yesterday. I stare at the card.

Betty must sense my apprehension. She heaves a big sigh and looks at her watch.

"We're not getting off to a great start today, are we?" she says.

I shrug, give her a weak smile.

"Okay, what about this? I'll show you around, and maybe you could do some filing while I finish up this thing I'm doing for Adela. And then at four we'll close up shop and go have a beer and talk about the job. Or better, we can go over this thing for Adela and get your thoughts. It's a plan for the rest of the summer. Anyway, your job is in the plan. Sound okay?"

"Sure, that sounds good." What else am I going to say?

Betty shows me the basics of the filing system and I can see that she really wants to get back to whatever she's working on for Adela, so I don't ask many questions. I'll file what I can and stack the rest to worry about later. We work in silence for a while. The phone rings twice, and I answer it and take messages. At 4:05, Betty rolls a page out of her typewriter and puts it in a folder.

"Ready?" She's standing up. "Let's see if it's still raining." She disappears through the offices I haven't seen yet and I wonder if I'm supposed to follow. She's back immediately, though.

"All clear," she says. "Oh—there's a back door. I haven't even given you the tour, have I? Well, let's go and I'll explain things." We exit through the front door and she locks it with a key, then hands it to me. "This is an extra. You can keep it. There's a wedding on Saturday, and if you're available you can handle it, so you'll need a key. There's at least one wedding every weekend in June. We can split them up. I mean, if you're willing." She heaves another great sigh. "Sorry, I'm a bit frazzled. Shall we go to The Rat? Or no—how about we go to Blueberry Hill? Have you been there yet? I want to get off campus."

I don't know what The Rat is, but I know Blueberry Hill is on Delmar, so it's fine with me and we start off across campus toward the walkway to U City. She points out landmarks on campus and shows me a different way to get to the walkway. We take the pedestrian bridge, and she shows me the Women's Exchange on the other side.

"Good place to look for used furniture, if you need anything. For other stuff, though, there's a resale shop on Skinker, just around the corner from Delmar. Kitchen gear, even some clothes."

We talk about the weather and the private neighborhood we're passing through. No mention of the Y or my job.

"Hi, Joe," she calls out as we enter the bar. "We're dying of thirst." We sit in a booth, and I look around. I'm amazed. The bar is a monument to the 1950s. I see my sister's first-grade lunchbox and the cowgirl hat I got for Christmas when I was three.

"Cool, huh?" The beers arrive and although I'm not a big beer fan, its icy coldness tastes great. Betty turns back toward the bar.

"We're starving, too! We need burgers here." She looks at me. "Burger okay?"

I nod.

"And bring us some fries!"

Once the food arrives and we've had a few bites, Betty gets down to business.

"Ray won't be coming back," she says, and I see a tear slide down her face. "Ray's the director of the Y—did I even tell you that?"

"Oh no," I say, suddenly sad about someone I barely knew existed. I don't even know his last name.

"He had a heart attack two weeks ago, but we thought he was getting better. Then he had another one last night, and he's in a coma. The doctor gave him hours, or at most a day or two." She stops, blows her nose, swallows hard. "Campus Y was his life. Everyone loves him."

I'm not sure what to do or say, so I just wait. She blows her nose again, starts to talk, sips her beer.

"Anyway, your timing is either perfect or terrible." She smiles through her tears. "As you saw, Adela thought you already worked at the Y, and it seemed easiest to just go with it. So, let's talk about that." She has another sip of beer and takes out her folder.

Between bites, we go over the plan she has laid out for Adela, who chairs the board and is therefore responsible for dealing with a crisis like this. Betty will step in as interim director, and I'll take over as interim administrator. The two program managers are off for the summer and will be back in mid-August to get ready for the new school year. Summer is a slow time at the Y, except for weddings and a yoga class that is popular with summer students.

"Lots of kids come in for coffee and to hang out. We're kind of a low-rent alternative to Holmes Lounge. On rainy mornings the place is full, but we don't need to worry too much about them. Just shoo them out when it's time for yoga."

Her face falls.

"Oh no, Ray taught the yoga class. How am I going to find a yoga instructor?"

"Advertise on campus?" I ask. "Maybe a summer student would be interested in making some extra cash."

"Oh no," she groans again. "We don't have that in the budget. Ray just did it as part of his director job because he loved yoga."

"But without his salary . . . won't there be a little extra?" I know that sounds cold-hearted, but economics is my field after all.

"Oh. Oh. Right. Right. That's why we can pay you full time." She leafs through her plan and gets to the budget page.

Now I know that I'm full time, at least for a while. Next I

need to know how much I'll make. I wonder if I can get a look at the budget page without seeming too crass.

"Here," Betty says, turning the page around and handing it to me. "You're right. Now let's try to figure out what else we need to backstop."

I see that I'll be making more than minimum wage, so I'm happy and focus on the budget. She's done a nice job of listing responsibilities, both hers and Ray's, with names next to each task. She will take on most of Ray's work, with Adela handling the executive parts. I'm down for most of Betty's normal workload. Program planning, next year's budget, monthly financials for the board. Mostly numbers—I'm comfortable with all that.

"Unfortunately, there is still the typing and filing and weddings." Betty seems apologetic. "But the typing and filing does let up from mid-June to mid-August."

"And I've got no weekend plans, so I don't mind the wedding duty," I tell her, wondering if that will change by August. Will I know anyone by then to make plans with? And will it be safe, walking home afterward? Will I be cooling my heels while the wedding guests dance at Holmes Lounge, assuming that's a reception-worthy hall?

"What time are the weddings, normally?"

"Oh, they can be at eleven or two or five. A few weekends we're booked for all three. They are usually out of the Y and off to the reception by six. So 10:00 a.m. to 6:00 p.m. is the outer limit for us. We can share. And all you do is make sure they don't drink, because we're technically part of the YWCA, and they don't allow drinking in their facilities. It's in the contract, but you know how brides can be. You don't have to police them too carefully, just nothing obvious and make sure they take everything away when they go."

"Sounds like my RA job."

"Yes, I saw that you were an RA, even went back for a second year of it. I called early this morning to check you out. You were a popular RA—with both students and staff."

I'm pleased by that and pleased that an RA gig has value in the job market. I'll need to touch that up on my resume. I'm even pleased that she checked, that the whole place isn't as scatterbrained as it seems at the moment.

"Well, I need to get home. It's been a day and a half," she says to me. She turns toward the bar and raises her voice. "Thanks, Joe—see you later." She waves at Joe as we leave. "Joe's the best thing that could have happened to the Loop. See you in the morning."

I start to ask her what exactly the Loop is, but let it go. I drift home feeling bad about the Ray I never knew but also feeling good about having made a friend in Betty. Or something like a friend, even if she is my boss.

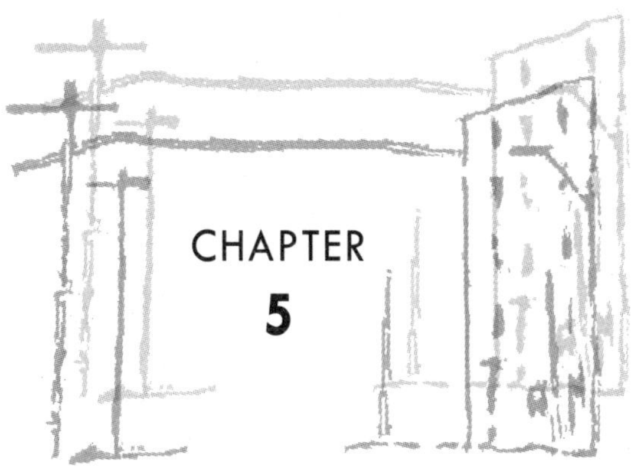

CHAPTER 5

Although it's cool after the rain and I'm exhausted by nine o'clock, I'm not sleepy. The day was full and I am slightly troubled about many things, including David Black, my new job, and further out, graduate school. From there, I can worry about finding a professional job, choosing a city to live in, and the general shape of my whole life. I even worry about being alone in the apartment building, not that I even know if I am alone or not. I get up and make sure I've put the chain on the door. I switch off the lights and sit in bed gazing out the window at the night sky, aware of the sycamore leaves moving in the light breeze. After twenty minutes or so, I'm calm and relaxed and I fall asleep.

I wake early feeling rested and hopeful. I pack a lunch, check the sky, close the windows just in case, and head for campus. The walk feels different today in the cool after the storm. Roses are blooming on fences along the walkway. I'm happy until I get to the Y and find Betty standing at her desk, talking on the phone.

She's not crying but she has been, if the tissues on her desk are any indication. It seems obvious that Ray has died.

"Yes, I'll let you know. Of course I will. But I need to take another call now." She half smiles, waves at me, and punches a button on the phone. "Campus Y, this is Betty."

The phone rings again and I pantomime answering it, a question on my face. Betty nods and turns away from me, telling the person on the other end of the line that the funeral will be on Monday.

I pick up the phone, punch Line 2, and mimic Betty: "Campus Y, this is Novelle."

"Oh. Ah. Is Becky there?" asks the voice on the other end. It must be Adela.

"Betty's on another line. The phones just keep ringing this morning. Can I have her call you?"

"Oh right, you're Noelle. Just tell her I'll be in around eleven. No need for her to call. I'm so glad you're there." And she hangs up.

I find a pink message pad and write down the message. When Betty gets off the phone, she fills me in on Ray's funeral plans, which she's typed up for me. The funeral is Monday at St. Roch.

"He lived in Clayton, but he grew up in the city and went to grade school at St. Roch and just kept going there. They let you go to whatever parish you like now. The neighborhood's a little iffy; I bet some people won't go even in broad daylight."

"Where is St. Roch?" I ask. And I wonder who was St. Roch. I've never run across that one.

"Over by Talayna's." That rings a bell, but I can't place it. "The pizza place just off campus." She points vaguely northeast. *Oh. Talayna's, where the guy on the bus works.*

"You go north on Skinker a couple of blocks past Talayna's, and then it's around the corner on Waterman."

"Got it." I don't really, but I have a general idea.

"If you could just deal with the phone today, that would be great. And maybe work on a draft of a letter we can send out today to our general mailing list, letting people know. Most of them won't get it in time for the funeral, but we'll do it anyway. I'll make a list of people that we absolutely have to call, preferably today."

This isn't how I pictured my first full day on the job, but this isn't an ordinary day, so I find a tablet and start the draft and work on it between answering calls. No one asks who I am. One woman does ask about St. Roch.

"That sounds Catholic," she says, suspicion in her voice.

"I'm not sure, let me check." I spin around in my chair, locate a Saint Louis phone book, and look up St. Roch.

"Yes, ma'am. St. Roch is Catholic. It's on Waterman just east of Skinker."

"Is that north of Delmar? I don't go north of Delmar." She's less worried about it being Catholic now.

"No, it's a little bit south of Delmar," I tell her. I've worked that out on the map.

"But it's Catholic? I never knew he was Catholic. I don't think I can do that. And not that close to Delmar." She hangs up. I want to call her back and tell her that I'm Catholic and I live north of Delmar and what does she think of that, but of course I have no idea who she is, and I wouldn't do that anyway. Besides, my apartment is barely north of Delmar and not in the city proper and I'm not properly Catholic these days. But I'd still like to tell her off.

A little before eleven, Adela arrives. She's written a letter, so I can abandon my pitiful draft. Hers is written from the heart and by someone who knew the man and can also tell the readers that there will be a search committee and that she and Betty will continue Ray's work until the new director is hired. She even mentions me as interim administrator. It's perfect, and I tell her so and ask Betty if she wants me to type individual copies or use the ditto machine. I eye it warily. It has a name—someone has put a "Hello, my name is Hal" tag on it. Underneath is a smiley face with an evil look.

"Neither. Hal is mean and ugly, and we don't have time to type a hundred and some-odd letters. Have you ever used a mimeograph? There's one upstairs in the student union."

I haven't, but I take the stencil she gives me, along with a bottle of blue correction fluid, and carefully type the letter. I notice that Adela has correctly spelled Betty and Novelle even though I've never heard her call us by those names. There's more to her than meets the eye. I have to type it twice, and when we have all read it carefully, Betty gives me directions and I go off armed with a charge code and the hope that someone will be there to show me how to use whatever a mimeograph turns out to be.

It's not that hard, as it turns out, mostly because in the process of showing me how to use it, the clerk pretty much does it for me.

"Do you want those folded? The folder is really easy."

I make an executive decision to fold them, and I am amazed at how fast and how loudly the job is done. I return to the basement with two new skills that I hope will never go on my resume. Adela and Betty are hard at work addressing envelopes, Adela by hand and Betty using a typewriter. Adela is bemoaning her lack of typing skill and her writer's cramp.

"I'll take over," I tell her, and she hands me the address list and starts signing the letters. I wish I had waited to fold them, but she doesn't seem to mind having to unfold each one.

"Gives my signing hand a moment to rest," she says.

We finish up and I ask about stamping and mailing, and they send me off to the campus post office in Brookings. I let them go out for lunch while I answer the phone and eat my peanut butter. It's eerily quiet and I wonder where the radio is but don't want to go looking for it. When they return, they set about making phone calls, which takes so long they finally recruit me to help. They give me a script and I work out how to explain who I am. It's easier for me than for Adela and Betty, who are having a hard time having the same sad conversation over and over.

By three o'clock, people are starting to drift in to console and be consoled. Most of these are university staff who worked with Ray. I offer to finish the phone calls, and Betty sends me back to one of the program manager's offices, where it's completely quiet. Everyone I talk to is shocked and sad. Most of them want to tell me a story about Ray, and a few more are concerned about the location or the denomination or both. I reassure them that it will be fine and eventually start saying that we would miss them if they didn't show up. I want to point out that the church is approximately four blocks from the northeast corner of campus. I want to say that the Ray they admired so much went there every Sunday for decades, with no apparent harm to body or soul.

"But he taught *yoga*!" one of them wails. *Yes*, I think. *A Catholic yoga teacher. Cool.*

By the time I finish the calls, only Betty and Adela are left in the office. I tell them about the people who are afraid of the neighborhood or the fact that the church is Catholic.

"Why do they keep asking if it's north of Delmar?"

They look at each other for a long moment and then back at me.

"Well . . . Delmar is . . . kind of a line," Adela says slowly.

"Between Black and white," adds Betty. "It's not legal, but there it is. Black people north, white people south." And she goes on for a minute or so about redlining and white flight and then trails off, looking at the floor. "White people got to thinking that there's nothing worth anything north of Delmar."

The room is silent for a beat, and then Adela speaks up. "In the end, those folks will probably show up for Ray. Curiosity if nothing else." She picks up her purse, lifts her chin, and takes a deep breath. "Why don't you both come to my house for a drink. I'm sure I can scrounge up something to eat, or I'll order a pizza. We need to unwind."

Betty demurs, pleading pressing family commitments. Adela turns to me.

"You'll come, though." She says it as a thing decided. "I'd like to get to know you, and I know students can always use a free meal."

I'm not dressed for dinner with the chairman of the board, and I'd really like to sit down and close my eyes for five minutes, but I'm also curious and charmed, so I agree.

We go in her car, once we've established that I'm on foot. She lives just west of campus, in Clayton, and I'm relieved that I will be able to walk home from there. At her house, she points me to a powder room where I can "freshen up" and tells me she'll meet me in the kitchen in about ten minutes. "Very civilized" springs to mind. The powder room has a small upholstered couch, and I get my five minutes of silence. I'm careful to give her the full ten minutes, plus a bit, before I go in search of the kitchen.

She offers beer, wine, or cocktail, and I am momentarily stuck. I got through both high school and college without consuming much alcohol, mostly because I obsessively saved all the money that came my way for college. And because I was not particularly social. I just never quite understood the thrill of meeting a crowd of teenagers in a park, in the dark, for illegal drinking. I heard all the stories on Monday morning, and I just never got it. I felt like a freak on Monday mornings, but I didn't really want to be whatever the non-freaks were either. So I mostly pleaded work, which was true because I accepted every babysitting job that came my way. In college there were more non-drinking students, mostly pre-meds obsessed with getting A's, and once I took the RA job, I knew that it wouldn't take much to lose it, so I had another lame but useful excuse. All of which got me to where I am now, in Adela's kitchen, having to choose between Chardonnay and Cabernet—or Budweiser, or maybe a screwdriver, which is the only named drink I can think of.

Adela seems to understand. She's grinning. "Most people like beer with pizza, but I prefer a nice dry red." She pours herself a glass of the Cabernet. "Red for you too? The pizza will be here shortly."

"Yes, that's great," I say. "I'm not much on beer." I may not be much on Cabernet, either. I haven't had enough to know. She pours me a glass and raises hers.

"To Ray, may he rest in peace," she says.

"To Ray." I take a sip and think that I could really learn to like Cabernet. "Nice." I nod knowingly, and she laughs.

"Not much of a drinker, huh? I didn't think so, but it's good to have an answer ready when people ask. And now you do." She lifts her glass again. "To the Campus Y's newest employee! You did well today."

I decide I like Adela.

We eat the pizza and she gives me a lot of background on the Campus Y, and Ray, and her own role, and I start to feel like a real employee. She doesn't ask much about me, but she listens carefully to everything I say, and I get the feeling that she's learning more about me than I realize.

At seven, I get up and tell her I really need to get going, mostly because I am sure she has more to worry about than a temporary employee. She offers me a ride, but I insist that I'll enjoy the walk, and she doesn't press me.

"You're in the Loop, right?"

"I guess so. Everyone talks about the Loop but I'm not really sure what it is."

She explains that the commercial district on Delmar grew up around a streetcar turnaround, or loop, adding that some of the tracks are still visible if you know where to look.

"All that talk about Delmar? Don't worry about it. The Loop is as safe as anywhere. Just stay alert."

I tell her I'll be careful and head back to campus and on to my usual route home. Crossing Delmar, I see that the weekly farmers' market is just closing up in the open area that must be part of the streetcar turnaround. I'm in time to get some last-minute bargains on peaches and tomatoes.

As I'm struggling with my bags and keys to the outer door, the cat zooms in out of nowhere. I don't try to stop him. He's not my cat. Upstairs, he does his usual race to the sofa, where he stops and paces back and forth a few times. He meows and walks in and out of all the rooms. I follow him, but nothing seems out of order. I tell myself that cats are born actors who enjoy perplexing humans, and I go back to lock the door. The doors of all the apartments in the building have an outer louvered door that can be swung closed and latched on the inside, allowing air to circulate. The jalousie window at the end of the hall is open and a nice breeze is flowing through my doorway. I fasten the louvered door and leave the solid inner door open. The cat scoots through the gap at the bottom of the louvered door and disappears. I get out the battered copy of *Emma* that I brought to read on the bus and sit down to finish what must be my third or fourth reading of it.

I'm nodding off when I realize the cat is back, snuggled up next to me on the sofa. I get up to lock the inner door and go to bed. He doesn't take the hint, and I don't have the energy to force him to leave, so I pretend I don't see him and drift off to sleep.

CHAPTER 6

Friday morning is hot and I'm glad to go underground at the Y for the day. Adela appears again at eleven, and the three of us commence planning for the inevitable influx of guests following the funeral. The family is hosting a reception at the church hall right after the service, but Adela and Betty are sure that some people will either skip the service and expect a wake of sorts at the Y, or they will go to the service but still want to pay their respects here. We order a dignified sort of cake and plan a grocery run to lay in a lot of cookies that can be frozen if they aren't eaten, plus the peanuts that Ray always loved, and coffee.

"Should we set up a little memorial or something?" I ask.

"I wish the students were here—they would be dreaming up all kinds of things that would be weird if we did them but charming if the students do them."

"Ummm, is Arlo a possibility?" I offer. "I could go to the bookstore, see if he's there, thank him for the job lead, see if he knows about Ray. Maybe not in that order. Or maybe not at all." I can't picture this working out. Silence reigns.

And then we hear a slam, followed by "What happened?

This did not happen," except in all caps in a very loud, very undergraduate male voice. Arlo. Did I just conjure him out of thin air?

Arlo is hugging Betty, pacing, waving his arms, and talking all at once.

"We need to do something!" he wails.

Eventually he calms down, and we tell him about the funeral and the cake and cookies and peanuts. He doesn't seem to recognize me, and I don't try to thank him for anything. That can wait, possibly forever, since it would be weird to say anything right this minute and weirder to say anything next week and weirdest of all to say something someday in July. I think he just sees me as another adult with dull adult preoccupations. I can see that he is thinking that cake and cookies are not going to cut it, with or without peanuts. I can see us disappear from his consciousness. He is pacing again, looking at the ceiling. Or at the huge pipes that hide most of the ceiling.

"I'll be *back*!" he says and runs up the stairs. The door slams behind him.

We look at each other with "what just happened" faces, and then one of us giggles and we all end up laughing until the tears run down our faces and our sides hurt.

"He'll be back," I say, nodding emphatically, and we all start laughing again.

"I needed that," Betty says when we are finally and truly calm again. "God knows what he'll come up with, but we can check that off our list."

"Whatever 'that' is," says Adela, and we start laughing again, but it doesn't last long this time. We're back to the reality of the day. The phone is still ringing every few minutes. People have started asking about contributing to a memorial, so we talk about that. Betty thinks we should know what it will be, something like a bench or even a scholarship, before we accept contributions. Adela says that people want to give now, as part of grieving, and won't give later, so it's okay to accept them now. We can deposit them in a separate account to make sure the books are clear. She gets on the phone and makes some calls to Brookings to get the proper paperwork going. Betty suggests we replace Hal with a real photocopier. Or get a real cassette player with separate speakers so people can actually hear music during yoga and hear recordings made during other classes. I say that machines like that are temperamental, and we'll end up kicking them and that's hardly an appropriate memorial. They smile thoughtfully; we're laughed out. Then I feel like I've overstepped; it's still my first week and I never even met Ray and I should shut up and file something.

"Any typing I should be doing?" I ask. They look at me like I've suggested painting the ceiling purple.

"Who knows? Who can even think right now? Let's make sure we've got cups and plates. Maybe rearrange chairs or something." Betty says.

Adela suggests we get a book so people can write memories of Ray. Or a binder, and they can bring in stories.

The door bangs and suddenly the room is full of students and noise and poster board. A boom box appears and Chicago starts singing "Old Days." We back off and watch as Arlo lays out poster boards on the big worktable and starts drawing a life-size cartoon of Ray. At least I assume that's who it is. I've not even seen a picture. Chicago moves on to "Harry Truman" as the kids start making speech balloons of Ray-isms. They are laughing and arguing and singing along with Chicago and running in asking for scissors and tape. I volunteer for phone duty and move myself to the back office where it's almost quiet.

By four o'clock they are gone, shouting their goodbyes and

see-you-Mondays and taking Chicago with them. They leave the entire hallway lined with Ray—standing, sitting, upside-down in a yoga pose, up in a tree, every place the kids can picture him. They've filled the space around him with Ray-isms, but left room for others to add their favorite sayings. And they've cleaned up after themselves.

I tell Betty I'll come in and answer the phones during the funeral, since I'm kind of a fifth wheel, but they both object. The board and staff will sit together, they tell me, and I need to be seen as part of the staff. To make sure I get it, they tell me it's part of my job and I am required to be there.

"I mean, unless it's totally freaking you out or anything like that. I know some people have never been to a funeral before and it scares the heck out of them."

I assure them that I have a huge extended family and have been going to funerals since before I could walk. I don't tell them that I have nothing suitable in my closet. I've got the weekend to fix that. We turn out the lights and agree to meet here Monday and walk to St. Roch together. I take a long route home and go by the church. It's huge and beautiful, red brick with a great tall clock tower. I'm in awe. And I have nothing to wear when I walk through the door on Monday.

I go back to Skinker and walk north to Delmar, cross Delmar, and keep going. I'm looking for the resale shop Betty told me about. I get a few catcalls from carloads of young men driving by with booming sound systems. I don't make eye contact. I do find the store, but it's closed for the day. Open Saturday at ten. I peer in the windows. A few clothes, a lot of household items. I'll try to get here early, since it doesn't really seem like the place for funeral clothes. But it should definitely fit my budget.

I go home and remember to check my mailbox. David Black's mail is gone and there is a flier advertising pizza. Plus a phone bill. I go upstairs with some trepidation. Is David Black up there?

I knock on my own door, feeling ridiculous, and then unlock it and go in.

"Hello?" No answer. Also no cat. I look around and there is no sign that anyone has been here. I close the louvered door and leave the inside door open, suddenly missing the cat. It's not my cat, but he's almost always been waiting when I got home.

I decide that I need to mark my territory in some way. My name on the door, or a wreath. Is there such a thing as a summer wreath? Maybe a flag—the Fourth is coming. But I'm not keen on flags, they seem so self-righteous. I mean, who is going to see a flag on a house in America and think "Oh, a patriot lives there"? But something. Something op-art-ish, maybe. I'll try to think like Arlo. A tree would work, something like the Campus Y logo. A door-sized tree. Something to tell David Black, if he comes back here, that someone else has moved in. Then maybe I'll stop worrying.

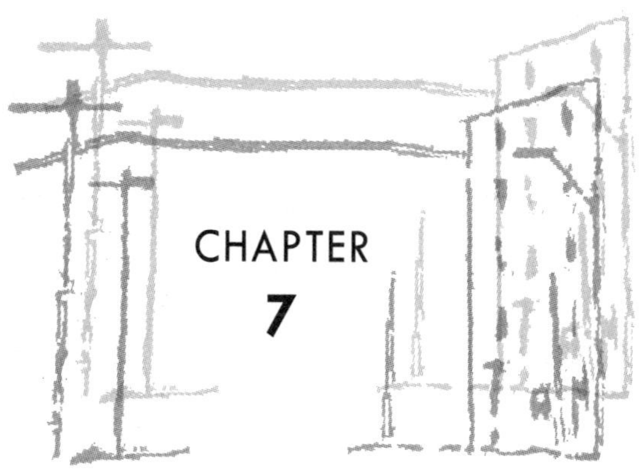

CHAPTER 7

On Saturday morning, I'm at the bank when it opens and leave with temporary checks, which I can use if someone doesn't want to take my out-of-state checks. Next stop is the library, where I present my checks, my rental agreement, and my phone bill as proof of residency. I've got the pizza flier in reserve, and luckily I don't need it. I leave with Studs Terkel's *Working* and two novels and drop them at the apartment before trekking down to Skinker and the resale shop. It's already hot and I'm not very excited about trying on clothes, especially used clothes.

I slip inside and wander around, closing in on the clothing section, afraid of getting stuck talking to a clerk who is determined to find something for me, something that fits but that I hate. I'm not good at clothes shopping. But the shop owner is there and comes over to help. Instead of saying "just looking" and running out into traffic, I tell her that I've just moved here, my boxes haven't arrived, and I need something to wear to a funeral on Monday.

"Ray Nesbitt's funeral? You're a WashU student, aren't you?"

How could she know that? How small is this town? Isn't Saint Louis something like the twentieth-largest city in America?

"Well, actually, yes. I'm starting grad school in the fall."

She laughs. "It's not that hard to figure out. You're white and in your twenties, and we're about a hundred yards from WashU, so that means there's about a 90 percent chance you're a student. And if you're new in town you probably don't have friends or family, or you wouldn't be shopping here—they'd be taking you out to Clayton. So it's not a relative who died. And everyone on campus knows Ray Nesbitt. Or knew him. I went to grade school with him, that's how I know him. I never left the neighborhood."

I'm staring, speechless.

"So, let's find something for you. There must be a black skirt somewhere that we can make work. Maybe a midi length so you can get away without stockings—too hot for that, but it is a funeral. At least St. Roch is air-conditioned now. Do you have shoes? Maybe a simple shell?"

I don't have either of those things, but she does.

"Your timing is good—when school lets out, a lot of kids can't be bothered packing up and taking everything back to New York or Chicago. Sometimes they bring it over here and sometimes they just toss it—even fairly new stuff. Sometimes the RAs rescue things from the trash and bring it all to me."

She flips through a rack and comes up with a gray skirt.

"This should do—you don't need to wear black to funerals anymore, especially not when it's this hot. And we can pair it up with something cream colored and you won't look like a maid in black and white."

She doesn't find the right sort of cream-colored top in my size, but she finds a pale blue shell that I prefer anyway.

"You might need a little sweater, in case they crank up the AC in there. Sometimes they do."

We don't find the right sweater, but I'm pretty sure I won't need it anyway. The shoe situation is more worrisome. She doesn't have very many to begin with, and nothing I'd even consider wearing. Plus I'm going to have to walk there and back, so they have to be comfortable as well as funeral-worthy. She ponders.

"Okay, this is a bit off the wall," she says. "What about Dr. Scholl's sandals? Everyone wears them everywhere. They definitely come in black, and you might find them in that shade of blue even. I think it will look great, and you're young enough to get away with it at a funeral. Especially this one—people are going to be so sad they won't do their usual catty commenting on what everyone wears. Just keep your chin up and look calm and collected—you can definitely pull that off, since you really are calm and collected."

I'm thinking that dumbfounded is a more accurate description, but I'm flattered anyway and say I'll do that. She asks me which way I'm going and I confidently say "the Loop" and she says that I should be able to find Dr. Scholl's on Delmar. I pay and then remember my hanger situation and ask if she has any for sale. She gives me a skirt hanger and a regular hanger and says she'll see me on Monday. It takes me a second to realize that means she'll be at the funeral too. I feel like hugging her, but I just thank her again and leave.

"I'm Molly, by the way," she calls out as the door is closing.

"I'm Novelle!" I shout back with a wave.

On the way home, I duck in and out of almost every storefront, unsure where I will find shoes among the headshops and bookstores. About halfway to Wingate, a headshop that seems to be moving from the psychedelic '60s into whatever the '70s are becoming has what I am looking for. The only pair in my size is black, so that settles the color question.

It's even hotter when I get home, so I take my backpack to the grocery and spend a long time walking up and down every aisle, absorbing the cool through every pore. By the time I get back to my third-floor apartment, I've sweated through my T-shirt and the ice cream I bought is softening. I put the groceries away and take a cool shower. I eat ice cream for supper and wish for a fan. I write my mother a long newsy letter, going light on the funeral parts. She'll want to hear about new clothes and the new job, so I focus on those and include a cartoon drawing of me in my new outfit. It makes me realize that I don't really know how I look in it, since the only mirror I have is on the medicine cabinet. I end the letter with a reminder about the boxes, disguised as a thank-you. "Looking forward to getting my boxes next week—thanks for taking them to the post office!" I know it's possible that she's put it off from day to day. In her mind it's at the top of her list, but in her reality it might not have quite happened yet. At sunset, I walk slowly to the post office and mail her letter and a shorter one to my grandmother. The cat is waiting when I return.

CHAPTER 8

When the six o'clock church bells wake me on Sunday morning, it's already hot. I haven't slept well but I'm not going to be able to sleep now. I drink ice water and eat cold cereal and wonder how I'll get through the next twelve hours without melting. I take a library book and go downstairs, where it's marginally cooler, and cross the street to a playground. I find a bench in the shade and pass an hour or so. The sun finds me and I move to a swing. The church bells ring again and I look at my watch—it's nowhere near noon, when the Angelus will ring again. It must be the five-minute call to one of the morning Masses. I wonder if All Saints is air-conditioned. I haven't been to Mass in years and I don't want to go now. But it might be cool in there. It might also be very hot, as my childhood church was in the summer, with sun pouring in the east windows and the oscillating fans high up on the walls powerless against the heat. I feel sticky just thinking about it.

I read a little longer. The Studs Terkel book is engrossing but the sun has swung around and sought out all the benches and swings, so I go home for more ice water. I sip it, looking out the kitchen window at the people leaving Mass at All Saints. They don't look like they've just been parboiled. One woman is taking off a sweater. It must be air-conditioned over there. Cars are leaving and more are arriving, so I assume another Mass is starting soon. I'm desperate. I rinse off and put on my new clothes. Might as well take the new shoes for a test drive too. When the bell rings, I'm clattering down the stairs.

It's so cool inside, it's all I can do to stay awake. If the church weren't so full I might not be able to resist stretching out on a pew and falling asleep. But I'm also feeling an unfamiliar sophistication in my new outfit, so when the service starts, I sit up straight and pay attention.

I've accidentally chosen the guitar Mass, so the music is upbeat and everyone is singing. I don't have a great singing voice, but I like to sing, and this is one place where marginal skills like mine are fine. The songs are mostly familiar from my high school Masses, so I don't even have to struggle reading the music. After the closing song, I breathe in the last of the air-conditioned coolness before facing the outside heat. I wonder if there is some dark corner where I can sit through the rest of the day's Masses unobserved.

I leave with the surge and feel a hand on my shoulder.

"Noelle, is it?"

Adela isn't the only person who gets it wrong, but I assume she's at the other end of the hand. But it's Molly, from the resale shop.

"Molly, good morning! It's Novelle, but I do answer to Noelle. It's just easier sometimes."

"I see you got the shoes. You look fantastic!"

"Yeah, I thought I'd test it out this morning, make sure there are no surprises tomorrow. I'm not used to dressing up anymore." I pause and then add, "Okay, I'm really here to get out of the heat. I'm thinking about coming back for the eleven-thirty Mass just to stop sweating. I'm going to have to rinse these clothes out again anyway."

She laughs at that and says, "Ah, that explains why you didn't go up for communion. Somehow I thought you were Catholic."

"Well, I am. Or was. I guess I'm on a break."

"Breaks are okay," she says. "How can you have belief without doubt?" She gives me an understanding smile.

Someone comes up and claims her attention. She touches my arm lightly to say goodbye, then turns to the new conversation.

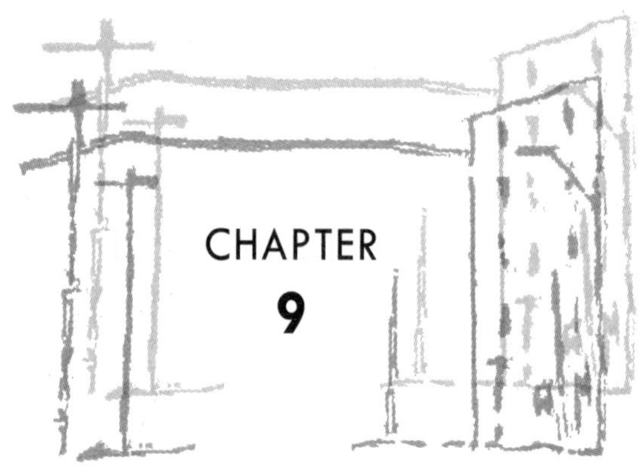

CHAPTER 9

Monday morning, I take the first of what will probably be three showers, if recent history is any indication. I pack my funeral clothes and shoes carefully in my backpack and set off for the Y. I get raised eyebrows from Betty when I walk in wearing shorts and a T-shirt, but I hold up my backpack to indicate that I've come prepared to change. She's on the phone and just nods.

I change in the ladies' room and finally get a good look at myself. I'm not as dowdy as I thought I might be. The new wooden sandals somehow save me from frumpdom. I'm not sure about the hair, which is long and straight and suddenly seems stuck in the '60s. I pull up the front into a barrette and wish I knew how to put it all up, off my sweaty neck. But I know it would make me self-conscious, so it will have to do as is.

Betty smiles and gives me a thumbs-up. The phone is ringing and she's still talking, so I answer it and assure the caller that the funeral is at the Catholic church on Waterman, not Graham

Chapel on campus. I tell her that she will be welcome, whatever faith or lack of faith she professes. "They don't check IDs, so please come," I tell her, trying to act as adult as I feel. "It will be good for you, and for everyone else who loved Ray, to have you there." I consciously don't roll my eyes and do my best to mean what I'm saying.

After a second call asking me where to park to get to Graham Chapel, I ask Betty if we should put a note on the door directing people to St. Roch. She agrees and asks me to type it on a three-by-five card and make another one for the office door, including a notice that we'll be closed during the funeral.

"Don't put a time on it, who knows how long it will go."

As we are setting up for the post-funeral reception, I notice a new poster board with a banner across the top: Ray's Memorial Ideas. I wonder if it's Arlo's work, or Betty's, or even Adela's. I feel like I should write something on it to encourage others. But "photocopy machine" and "bench" sound so lame, I can't do it. And from what I saw of the Y kids yesterday, it's unlikely that they'll hold back.

We arrive at the church early, but it's already pretty full. The air-conditioning is, in fact, cranked, as Molly put it, but it's barely keeping up with all the warm bodies in there. Everyone is talking, creating a roar, which surprises me. I've never been in a Catholic church that wasn't quiet. I wonder if things are different in Saint Louis, or if things are different in other denominations and there are a lot of non-Catholics here. Or maybe it's just nerves making people chatter. I keep still, and so do Adela and Betty.

The organ starts up and the talking stops and we all rise. The service is long but engrossing, and I find the incense and the familiar ritual calming. I gaze at the stained glass soaring behind the altar. The priest clearly knew Ray well and gives a heartfelt eulogy, which leaves even me in tears. At communion time, Adela and Betty nudge me along and I give in to peer pressure. If I don't believe, it can't matter anyway, can it?

We go to the reception in the church hall, but the din is deafening, and I have no one to talk to and no story to tell, so I let Betty know that I'm going back to open the Y and she nods me on my way. As soon as I'm back on campus I take off my sandals and walk in the grass. At the Y, I turn on the big coffee percolator and find the first aid kit. I need a couple of Band-Aids if I'm going to wear the new shoes for the rest of the day. After that, I just sit in the cool quiet and wait and try to let my mind rest.

Betty and Adela were right about the Y people needing more time to grieve after the funeral. By the time the coffee is ready, the Y is bursting with board members and students and what Betty calls FOYs for friends of the Y. Arlo's tape has expanded beyond Chicago and is now playing "Goodbye Yellow Brick Road." I'm sure we'll hear "Candle in the Wind" and "Funeral for a Friend" and wonder if he's included "Daniel" or "Rocket Man." I know I'll find out.

When the crowd thins, Betty tells me to go on home. I change into shorts and a T-shirt and put on my old sandals. I angle across campus to Skinker, though. I'm desperate for a good night's sleep and have my fingers crossed that Molly's shop is still open and has a fan.

She's open, still in funeral attire but barefoot and leafing through the Sunday newspaper. I ask about a fan, and she says she almost never takes used electrics, as she calls them, unless they are new in the box.

"There are signs all over the place saying everything is sold as-is, but with electrics, people keep returning them if something is wrong. So it's just not worth it. And anyway," she says pointedly, "you can get a new one at Kmart for less than ten dollars." She rustles the newspaper looking for the Kmart ad and spins it around.

"Six bucks on sale, and it's new." She doesn't realize that I don't have a car to get to Kmart. Oh well, I'll see if the hardware store has anything. I thank her again for helping me with the funeral clothes.

"You looked great, by the way. I saw you, but I was way over on the other side. My guess is that the skirt was a Christmas present from a mother thinking her daughter needed interview clothes, but the daughter thought differently and it ended up here. It's kind of fun to make up stories about some of these things. Kind of sad sometimes, too, though."

"You should write them down, the stories," I tell her. "I'm reading *Working* by Studs Terkel, and it's all these little stories about people's jobs. Nothing spectacular, but very interesting reading. Eye opening, really. Of course yours would be fiction." So it's not the same at all, but her face lights up and she makes an interested-but-noncommittal sound.

"Oh, that reminds me—I saved this in case you wanted it." She bends down and brings out a straw hat with a wide brim.

"I got a box of these from an importer. Only eighty-eight cents—such a deal." She tries on a New York accent. "Here, try it. It would have been great this morning, but it's good with the shorts too."

I put it on and see what she means. It dresses up my long, straight hair, which I'm starting to think is looking a little too '60s.

"Get yourself a wide grosgrain ribbon, maybe dark pink or black."

I'm not sure I'll ever wear it, but I like it, so I dig out the eighty-eight cents and start down Delmar into the late-afternoon sun. The brim shades my face, relieving some of the heat, and I think I might wear it after all.

I stop at the hardware store, but the fans there are much more expensive. They look heavier than those in the Kmart ad, which might be good, but I want something I can easily move around. So I walk on down Delmar to the library and look up the nearest Kmart and then check the bus schedules. I take the schedule I need and also one for the Delmar bus downtown, the one I arrived on just a week ago. I'm tired, but I really want that fan, so when I see the bus to Kmart coming, I get on it.

I bring home a box fan, which would be unwieldy if it didn't have a plastic suitcase handle on the top. I feel a little ridiculous getting on the bus with a fan in hand. I'm still wearing my hat and carrying my funeral clothes in my backpack. If I had been voted "Most Likely to Be Totally Uncool at Age Twenty-Two," I'd be fulfilling that prediction right now. But I remember Molly's advice and keep my chin up and smile at hand. Kmart had hat-suitable ribbons, so I get them out and tie on the black one. I'm sitting in a sideways seat to accommodate the fan, so I'm facing other riders, who watch me, amused. When the ribbon is in place, I sweep back my hair and put on the hat, pulling it down as far as it will go. The other riders are watching, so I strike a few poses and get several laughs and a few compliments.

On the way upstairs, I check my mailbox hoping for a package slip, but the box is empty. I wonder if whoever took David Black's mail also took my package slip and is now unpacking my books and typewriter. For today, lugging the fan up the stairs is enough. I put the fan in the north window of the bedroom and turn it on low, letting it blow full on the bed. Heavenly.

CHAPTER 10

The next few days at the Y seem quiet after the drama of my first week. We're still fielding calls but not so many visitors. I get a handle on the summer schedule, which includes a few classes, including yoga if we can come up with a teacher. Betty takes on that job and eventually finds a grad student who has never taught a class but has taken yoga for several years.

"Her only teaching experience is being a TA for freshman calculus. Think that counts for anything?"

"Not really, but it doesn't mean she can't. Why don't we have her give us a class, just you and me, as a try-out?" I have an ulterior motive here: I'm interested in taking the class but don't want to commit until I know what it's like.

"Me?" Betty says. "At my age?"

I have no idea what her age is, but I'm pretty sure she's not past forty.

"You're a lot younger than Ray, and he could stand on his head," I say, pointing to Arlo's cartoon of Ray doing just that. "Besides, no one will see us. And I'm a little nervous about it too. I'll look ridiculous in a leotard." I've seen photos—most of the students wear tights and leotards, which seem both hot and revealing to me.

"I'm not wearing tights! God, Ray never wore tights—see!" She points to the cartoon again, which shows cartoonish bare feet and legs sticking out of pants that have slid to Ray's cartoon knees. "He wore a sort of judo suit." She sighs. "I better confirm that the judo teacher is still on."

"Sooo . . . we'll do the yoga but we'll wear shorts and T-shirts?"

"All right, you win. I guess the interim director has to try new things. *If* the maybe-teacher is willing."

And so on Wednesday at five o'clock, we lock the door and put out three yoga mats and walk through Ray's syllabus with the potential teacher. She's anxious and we're nervous, but after we all get the giggles doing the lion pose, we relax and decide that we've found our teacher. Betty tells me that staff can take classes for free, so I sign up for both yoga and judo. I'll make up the hours on wedding duty.

Meanwhile, I spend a lot of time typing thank-you letters for all the memorials that are pouring in. We get a few suggestions, which I add to the poster. None of them excite anyone, but we tell each other that we need to wait until at least October, when students are back and the word has gotten out to Ray's far-flung fans and we know how much money there is. Scholarship and park bench bracket the possibilities.

On Thursday evening, I finally find a package slip in my mailbox, and on Friday, I leave work early to pick it up. I worry that there is only one slip, since I had two boxes packed and ready.

The box doesn't look like one of the ones I packed, but it is from my mother, and it's heavy. I untie the string and pull off the brown paper. A pillow, books, clothes, no typewriter. I glance at my watch, pick up the phone.

"Mom, where is my typewriter?"

"Well, hello to you, too! I'm fine, how are you doing?"

"Sorry, Mom. I'm fine, just hot and tired. Are you all okay?"

"Your granny is a little peaked, but otherwise we're all just peachy here."

I wait for her to mention the typewriter, but she doesn't.

"Lulu's good?" My younger sister was looking for a job when I left and I'm hoping to hear that she has one now.

"Yes, she's working at one of the banks downtown, I forget which one. Just a clerk job, but potential!"

That sounds good to me; my sister will like dressing up and talking to customers all day. But I want to get back to the typewriter, although with a little more diplomacy than is usually necessary in my family.

"Hey, I got the box today—thanks for sending it. I can't tell you how glad I am to have a pillow at last." I tuck the phone under my chin and pick up a raspberry-colored dress. "Whose clothes are these, by the way?"

"Oh, Lulu bought some things for work but she's not supposed to wear sleeveless, so she sent you some things."

"Okay, well, I'll try it on later. Are these all my books?" I'm building up to the typewriter.

"Of course. Well, most of them." She doesn't elaborate, and she is obviously not going to mention the typewriter.

"Wasn't my typewriter packed up to send?" I know it was, and so does she.

"Oh, it's so heavy, it would cost more than it's worth to send it. Besides, you don't need one now—you said you were typing at work, so you can use one there."

"Mom, that's just a summer job. And anyway, I have to have one in my apartment. I mostly write papers at night."

Silence.

"Didn't I leave enough money for the postage?" This isn't like my mother. She never worries about spending money as long as she has any.

"Oh, here's your sister! Lulu, come talk to Novelle."

I congratulate Lulu on her new job and don't mention the clothes, since I'm not especially happy about getting her rejects. She tells me about work and the boy she's got a date with tonight. I wait her out and then ask her what's going on with my boxes.

"Hey, I really need my typewriter. It wasn't in the box I got today. Mom didn't seem to want to talk about it."

I hear a door close, which in our house means she's taken the phone into the bathroom for privacy.

"She's teaching herself to type. She got one of our old high school typing books and is pounding away when she thinks I can't hear. I think she wants to try to get an office job. She doesn't have so many hair clients now that all the women in the neighborhood have jobs—they go downtown on their lunch hours. I think she feels left out."

This is more insightful than I expect from Lulu, and I remind myself that she's grown up now, finished with community college and working full time.

"Okay, I guess." I want to pout, but I really am happy for my mom, and she did buy the typewriter for us when I started high school. "Why don't you tell her that you know what she's doing and you'll help her learn and that you told me and I'm all for it. I'll figure out something here. It shouldn't be that hard."

Lulu offers to send me money to buy a new typewriter, feeling flush with her first paycheck. I am touched to the point of tears but tell her I'm working now too and I'll be okay. I'm really warming up to the idea of Mom teaching herself to type.

"But tell Mom she still has to trim my hair for free."

We say goodbye and hang up without my talking to Mom

again. I don't want to embarrass her. Lulu is much more attuned to Mom's moods and will jolly her out of any discomfort.

I'm thrilled to have a pillow again and glad to have the books, even though I now see that she sent textbooks but nothing literary. Maybe she wants to read those. I'm feeling gracious and don't mind—I can get anything I want from the library. I hold up the raspberry dress. It's a shift in linen-like fabric, with little flippy cap sleeves. Not something I'd wear. But I try it on and see immediately why Lulu rejected it—it's too long for her. She probably thought she'd hem it, or get Granny to hem it, and then just passed it on instead. I wonder what Mom meant by Granny feeling peaked—she's the one who would have done the hemming. Well, it's longer than I would have worn just a few months ago, but maybe it's okay. I can't really tell without a longer mirror. I picture myself on the bus, bringing home a long mirror from Kmart. Even after the fan adventure, I can't picture the mirror on the bus and then walking down Wingate.

My robe is also in the box—I must have forgotten to pack that the morning I left. I can't remember what else was in the box with the typewriter, but I'm happy right now for what I got, including Mom's secret adventure with the typewriter.

CHAPTER 11

Saturday morning brings a sense of freedom and possibility, along with cooler temperatures and a morning breeze. I'm free until wedding duty at four. I go through the box from home again and stack up the books. No place to put them except an unused shelf in the eating side of the kitchen. In the bottom of the box is a crumple of newspaper. I take it out and find it's heavy. My radio at last! I turn it on and spin the dial until music comes on. Now maybe I can keep up with the weather forecast.

I count up—Day Twelve in the apartment. Time to claim it. I wipe out the chest of drawers and put in all my folded clothes. I contemplate David Black's posters. I like the Beatles and the Grateful Dead as well as anyone, but I'm kind of over album posters. On the other hand, what do I have to replace them with? Nothing, nothing at all. I take them down anyway. I move David Black's kitchen things and mingle them with mine. I reconsider the front door and open it, hoping for inspiration. The cat whooshes in and meows. I haven't fed him for days, so he's obviously someone else's cat, but he's making it clear that today is my day to feed him, so I open a can of tuna and give him a blob, along with a bowl of water. He eats up and settles on the sofa, watching me with interest. I examine the door again and try to picture something there, something not cute or weird, just something to say it's mine. As I'm squinting, I see a little metal object about two inches long attached to the right-hand door frame, tilted slightly to the left. I look closely and see that it's made to look like a tiny scroll. It looks vaguely religious although certainly not Catholic. *Interesting*, I think. Maybe I'll put a little cross below it, or a less-obvious dove, or even a Chi Rho. I must have a medal somewhere. I'll put it up and we'll have a history of who has lived here, at least who lived here in the past few months. But first I'll find out exactly what the little thing is.

I go back inside to report my findings to the cat, who seems interested but doesn't comment. Maybe he wants a cat on the door, or a tuna. He gets up and walks over to the vase of flowers I brought home from the Y yesterday, when we decided that all the funeral flowers we've received are just about gone. We left the best to welcome today's bridal party and divvied up the rest among ourselves, including Arlo, who had stopped by to admire his posters and look for additional Ray-isms. He seemed flattered and not at all embarrassed to walk out with a huge vase of slightly wilted lilies.

My vase includes some catkins that have dried out rather than just wilted. I pull them out and eye them critically. I snip a bit of hat ribbon and tie the bunch to one of the louvers on my outside door. That will do for now. I still want to make the door-sized tree, but that will have to wait until I can figure out how.

I spend some time with the phone book, looking for someplace to buy a typewriter, preferably a sturdy one, even if it's used. I expect to put a lot of miles on it in the next two years. I listen to my radio and work out which stations play rock music.

I enjoy the breeze and the feeling that I've moved into a more adult phase of my life.

At three I get ready to open the Y for the wedding. I take Lulu's dress along so I can see how it looks in the long mirror the Y has for the brides. Then I think, *What the heck, I'll just wear it*, and I add the hat because it looks great with the dress, at least the little I can see in the bathroom mirror.

I leave in plenty of time and detour from the walkway, taking the parallel Wingate instead. This part of Wingate is shady and green, lined with large houses, well cared for. I feel elegant instead of student-ish.

I open the Y and turn on the lights, rearrange the flowers a little. I move two of the Ray posters into the office area and close the doors to the areas that are off-limits to brides. I check my instruction sheet to make sure I've done everything, take a look around to make sure the floor is clean and that no cups or plates have been left in the lounge, and then look at the contract for today's bride. I memorize her name so I can greet her and check the times she has agreed to. I think that a little music would be nice and wonder about the radio Betty mentioned when the storm hit last week. I don't find it, and it feels like snooping to look too far.

The bride and her mother arrive at ten past four and the bridesmaids appear soon after, one of them complaining about having to walk from the parking lot and another, who is in high heels, complaining about the steps. The bride is in sneakers and ignores the complaints, so I do too. Her hair is gorgeous in a simple braided chignon that I momentarily envy. She takes her dress out of its zip bag and I am entranced. It looks like ivory linen, ankle length, with a square beaded neck and a wide beaded waist and bracelet-length sleeves. No lace, no chiffon, no butt bow. I'm glad I wore a dress instead of shorts and a T-shirt, although I've forgotten to see how the dress looks in the long mirror. The bride doesn't seem to be concerned about makeup until her mother hovers with a lipstick and she lets her apply it. After that, she goes from one bridesmaid to the next, adjusting bobby pins and helping with buttons and zippers. The dresses are all in shades of pink linen and are similar but not identical. I gradually realize that they are all relatives and younger than the bride. They are polite to me but self-sufficient and mostly they ignore me.

A knock on the outside door and the photographer asks if they are ready. He takes a few pictures and they all troop out, the bride glowing and shepherding the younger ones from the rear.

I tidy up a bit and take a look at myself in the mirror. I like the dress, especially with the hat. I try braiding my hair but can't get the knack of the chignon, even borrowing all the bobby pins left on the sink. Maybe there's a book in the library. I leave the braid hanging over one shoulder. Back to business, I get out the checklist. I should have locked the door in case they've left purses, and I'm supposed to wait at the back of the chapel so I can open the door again when the bride or her mother or some other designated person comes back to gather up the street clothes and tissue paper and makeup kits.

I slip in the back door of Graham Chapel and watch. Someone who might be an aunt is just finishing a reading, and the officiant calls the couple to make their vows. Sunlight streams in through the stained glass. I see why this place is booked up all summer for weddings. It's big but not huge. It's old and elegant and speaks of seriousness befitting wedding vows.

The bride and groom exit and form a receiving line, and by then I'm back at the Y, reading the outside bulletin board and keeping an eye out for whoever is coming back. I can just hear the cheerful babble and the organ music still playing inside. I wish I had asked who was responsible for pickup, and I make a mental note to ask the next time.

The bride herself comes back with two young men in tow.

"These are my cousins," she says. "They'll take everything away to the cars." She thanks me more than is necessary and sends the boys inside. "If you wouldn't mind, just check before they leave. They're boys, you know—they miss stuff."

I smile the smile of the insider. As an RA, I know all about boys missing stuff. I assure her that I'll check carefully and call her mother on Monday if we do miss anything. She strides off confidently in her beautiful hair and dress. I want to be like her when I grow up, even if she is only a year or two older.

The boys are sweet and on their most grown-up behavior. I check carefully and send them on their way. The taller one runs back and pounds on the door.

"I forgot, this is for you," he says. He hands me an envelope and runs back up the stairs and away. Inside is a twenty-dollar bill. A tip. I'm flabbergasted. It can't be for me, it must be for the Y. I leave it on Betty's desk and lock up. I'm relieved that this was so easy. No booze, no tears, no demands, no complaints. And everyone out in good time.

It's a beautiful evening, and I walk slowly past Graham Chapel toward home. The last of the wedding guests are leaving and one of them comes up to me and asks for directions to the reception. I tell him I don't know, I'm just passing by.

"But you look like you were part of the wedding! You look just—" and then he stops, embarrassed I guess. Another young man calls to him—he's got the directions.

"Hey, would you like to go anyway?"

I give him an amused but perplexed look.

"Oh, I guess that's weird. Well, thanks. Or, um, have a good evening."

I wave goodbye and meander home. The dress must look better than I thought. It can't be the Dr. Scholl's.

CHAPTER 12

Sunday morning I put on the dress again and catch an eastbound bus. I tell myself I want to see the cathedral because I like cathedrals, but I've timed the bus for the eleven o'clock choir Mass. I like to sing, I tell myself, and it's easy for a marginal singer like me to sing along with an overpowering organ and choir. Also, choir Masses take longer, so I'll have more time in the air-conditioning.

It's a breezy day, almost cool, and I decide to walk the three or so miles home. I've got a map and I'm wearing my old comfortable sandals. Forest Park is inviting, but it's a little out of the way and it's already going to be a long walk. I head west on Lindell, admiring the big houses on very large lots. At Union, I go north to Pershing, looking for a quieter street. It looks a little rough, but it's noon on a Sunday and I march on. At DeBaliviere I come across what looks like an abandoned business district. What's going on? I'm south of Delmar and only a few blocks from lovely Lindell and probably only a mile from home. Everyone I see is Black. And friendly. Everyone says hello or at least nods in my direction. I turn northwest on DeGiverville and eventually find myself at Delmar, not much east of Skinker. But it's a whole different Delmar. I cross Skinker and am back on familiar ground. Every face is white.

On Monday, I wake to a headache, cramps, and a damp, rainy day. I drag myself to campus and make a cup of tea. Betty asks me about the wedding, and I tell her how well it went, how beautiful and composed the bride was.

"And she left us that," I point to the envelope with the cash. "I guess it's a tip. She'd already paid, right?"

"Yes, she's paid up. It's a tip for you, not us. You're the one who took time out of your weekend for her convenience."

"But I get paid for that."

"Nevertheless, tips are on top of pay."

"We should put it in the Ray memorial."

"No, we should not. You take this and you keep it. That bride was chair of the student cabinet here, and she sometimes did bride duty during her senior year. She knows the drill. And she's a class act. Even as an undergrad. She meant it for you. Besides, she's a lawyer now at that big downtown firm, something Cave, I think it is. She can afford it."

That makes me feel like I'm not a class act, even as an almost-grad student. So I change my tune.

"In that case, thank goodness, because I need a typewriter by the time classes start." I would have gone on and told her why, but the cramps are worse now and I don't have the energy. I'm not sure I can pull off a funny version as opposed to a pathetic version.

"Hey, are you all right? You're looking a little pale."

"Just cramps. They'll pass."

"Yeah, like maybe by Wednesday. You take anything? Not that anything helps."

"No, Midol is useless and aspirin might just make me throw up."

"Did you eat anything?"

"Tea."

"Bah. Take yourself over to The Rat and get yourself a bagel and eat it really slowly. And a Coke. Not a can, get the kind in a cup with ice. Sip that and then get an Excedrin or whatever we've got in the first aid kit and go lie down on that ratty old couch in the back office."

I feel like I should protest, but I don't. I do what she says and an hour later I really do feel better. I'm still on the couch with my eyes closed when a door opens and a voice shouts, "Anybody home?"

I jump up and see a vision of color floating down the back stairs. It's a woman a little older than I, with black, very curly hair standing out all around her head. She's wearing loose, filmy pants and a straight, colorful tunic shot through with gold threads. Gold bangles on her arms jingle.

"Oh," she says. "Sorry. I wasn't thinking. Are you okay? Of course you're not, or you wouldn't be on the sick couch."

"I'm feeling better now."

"Good. I'm Jackie, by the way. I work here." She points at the desk.

"I'm sorry, I didn't know this was your office."

"It's not. I only work during the school year. It's a two-year deal, last year and next year. I'm home in Chicago for the summer doing theater. So it's not my office right now. And anyway, the sick couch is for anyone, anytime. Mostly girls with cramps."

"Well, that's why I'm here. But I'm better now."

"I'll bet you had a bagel and a Coke over ice, right?"

I nod and a voice interrupts.

"Jackie, are you back there bothering Novelle?"

Betty appears and hugs Jackie enthusiastically.

"I guess you two have met, but what brings you here? I know you couldn't make it for the funeral."

Tears well up in both their eyes.

"No, and I feel terrible about that. But I did come down for the wedding Saturday and stayed over to pay my belated respects." She turns to me abruptly.

"Were you at the wedding? Did I see you there in a dark pink dress with a hat?"

"I was just bride-sitting, but maybe you saw me lurking at the back."

"Well, you looked smashing."

I want to protest that she looks smashing on a Monday morning, which is a much bigger feat. I'm pretty sure she always looks smashing. But she has an arm around Betty and they have moved away. I hear Jackie exclaiming over Arlo's caricatures of Ray.

I lie back down for a minute or two and then get back to typing thank-you letters.

Jackie and Betty go out for lunch. They invite me, but I insist that someone needs to keep the office open and that I'm better but not that much better. It's a fine line, but they accept it and leave. I type away, sipping the remains of my Coke and nibbling the last of the funeral cookies.

Betty comes back alone, saying that Jackie wanted to get back to Chicago before dark. We work quietly the rest of the afternoon. When we are leaving for the day, she tells me to stop at the liquor store on Delmar on the way home.

"Buy yourself a bottle of red wine; it doesn't matter what kind. Cheap is fine. Have an inch or so if the cramps come back. It's better than Coke, but you can't be drinking wine in the middle of a workday. Midol, what a racket. If only men got cramps. Then we'd see some decent meds."

I've never bought a bottle of wine, but I'm twenty-two so it's about time. I take Betty's advice and get a couple of Cokes, too. I wonder if I'm the only woman in America who doesn't know this already.

CHAPTER 13

The next few weeks are uneventful. I get a few more kitchen items from Molly. I sleep well at night thanks to my pillow, my fan, and an occasional glass of wine, which I drink from one of David Black's juice glasses. I've taken to calling the cat David Black and don't think about the human David Black very often. I take his posters down and roll them up, and then later toss them in the trash.

One Saturday, I get all my clothes out and lay them on the bed. The shorts and T-shirts go back in the closet. The bell-bottom jeans go into a grocery bag. I think their time has passed. When I started wearing them around 1968, it seemed like that was the future of clothing and would last forever. But now it looks dated. I need something different for grad school. Two peasant blouses go in another bag. They are pretty bedraggled at this point anyway, as is the shirt with wide sleeves gathered into long cuffs. I'm left with not much beyond the summer shorts and T-shirts and the raspberry dress. I shoo out the cat and take the bus into Clayton.

I don't really plan to buy anything, I just want to figure out what I want to look like. There's an intimidatingly large Famous-Barr store at the end of downtown Clayton nearest campus, and I start there. I start there, and I end there. It's overwhelming. Mostly I find what I don't want: bow blouses, dressed-up denim, belted sweaters, and anything made of polyester double knit. And please nothing suitable for disco. I decide that wider pants will work, as will turtlenecks once the temperature drops below fifty. I search in vain for something like the raspberry dress. I return home with nothing but underwear and notes.

I'm overdue for a trip to the Laundromat, so overdue that I have to take my duffel. Saturday night at the Laundromat feels absolutely pathetic, but I take a book and treat myself to a Dairy Queen milkshake. The Laundromat is full enough to seem festive and empty enough that I don't have to wait for machines. I strike up a conversation with two women, roommates who share an apartment on the campus side of Delmar. I envy them their shorter walk and they envy my lower rent. It feels good to talk to someone my age.

When I get back to my building, I see lights on in a second-floor apartment. I try to remember when I've been out after dark to even notice lights. I've gotten used to the idea that I'm the only one in the building, other than David Black the cat, whose name has now been shortened to DB. I wonder if his real home is the lit-up apartment on the second floor.

Maybe not; he's waiting and follows me to the third floor. I've given in and bought a small bag of cat food, guiltily, since I know pets aren't allowed. But he's not my cat, and I don't have a litter box. He seldom stays overnight, although I can't really be sure about that. He's a stealthy one when he wants to be.

Once the busy-ness related to Ray's death dies down, Betty and I focus on what she calls the Summer Sweep, which is her annual clearing out of the previous school year's detritus. This is the first year she's had someone like me to help, and we go at it with gusto. She wants things to be as slick as possible for the new director, whoever that is. She's hinted that she's applied for the job, but she doesn't talk about it. Adela, on one of her regular visits, has said that the board is getting ready to begin the official search process. The two of them spend a lot of time closeted in Ray's old office, so I'm sure Adela knows about Betty's desire. Meanwhile, we sort and sweep and sneeze.

One day we take on a storeroom that Betty says hasn't been touched in years. She unlocks the door and we go in. A lot of posters and papers from old projects greet us.

"Straight to the dumpster," she declares, and I haul load after load to the rolling bins she has borrowed from the maintenance department. "Don't even look at it or we'll never get through it."

I've got no history with any of it, so I toss with abandon.

After a morning of tossing, we find tables and chairs.

"I remember this. One of the board members was moving and thought we could use these. We put them in here and never touched them again. See anything you want?"

I do want the yellow kitchen table and its two black chairs with yellow vinyl cushions. I've eaten every meal so far sitting on the sofa and I'm tired of it. I want to sit at a table and prop up a book. So I say yes and we move them into the lounge and wipe them off. I picture myself carrying it home bit by bit, a chair today and a table leg or two tomorrow. I don't want a car, but then I do want one. Still, I know I can get this home eventually, so I don't have to worry about it today. We push on and find more furniture, probably the lounge furniture that predates the current collection.

"Maybe we can have a garage sale when school starts?"

"No, I want it out of here before then. I'll call the Women's

Exchange. They'll take what they want and haul the rest to Goodwill for us."

I find a lamp, which I desperately want, and then another one. Betty laughs at my excitement, but she's clearly happy to find someone who actually wants these castoffs. I'm starting to think that instead of the girl in the hat, people are going to start thinking of me as the girl in the hat carrying furniture. But that's better than being the girl in the hat who doesn't have a table, so I'll take it.

Betty looks thoughtful.

That afternoon, she casually mentions that one of my jobs is to check students out before they borrow the Campus Y van. I didn't know we had a van, but we do, and students can use it to drive to volunteer sites like Kinloch. I've finally worked out that Kinloch is a mostly Black suburb where students do after-school tutoring. Betty tells me that students have to take a test drive with a staff member before we let them sign out the van, and that I'll need to have a test drive before I can do that.

I see through this, because by the time students are back I won't be working here, at least not for very many hours. But I can see what she's doing, so I agree.

"We could take a break and do it now," I suggest.

"Okay, let's go. We can take this stuff to your place and get it out of my way while we're at it. Two birds."

So, the Loop is spared the spectacle of me trudging down the walkway and across Delmar with a table balanced on my head.

Betty is kind about the apartment, saying she loves the big windows and the view through the waving sycamores. Seeing the place through her eyes is a little embarrassing—it looks so stark with the bare white walls. She looks at the one big wall thoughtfully.

"We should get Arlo to do a class on giant cartoon drawing. We'll get rolls of brown paper and black Magic Markers. You could do some wild stuff on this one long wall. If you get tired of it, just rip it down and do something new."

"Is it too late to add it to the summer program?" I ask. Not because classes are free to staff and I won't be staff in the fall. Only because the bare walls need something soon.

"I'm the director for the summer," she says, "and I just approved it. But you make the arrangements with Arlo; that's in your job description."

I negotiate free yoga for Arlo if he teaches three two-hour sessions of the art class. We're both excited about it, and I tell him he has to draw up a syllabus for the director to approve. He gives me a raised-eyebrow look and I tell him that we're all about personal growth at the Y and this is a job skill he'll thank me for someday. He and Betty both laugh at that, but Arlo gets into the spirit and writes up a very good syllabus. We work through a few drafts, mostly because we're both new at this, and we're proud of the final result. Betty tells me that promoting the class is my responsibility, and I write up an announcement for the paper. Arlo makes posters and puts them up on campus. In the underpass that students use to get from the main campus to the dorms, he paints a section black one night and goes back early the next morning to paint a white poster on the black background. It's so impressive that I hear students talking about it when I cross campus that evening, and the next day Betty and I go over to admire it. We take the Y camera and photograph it for the permanent record. Betty says this one may last for a long time. The underpass is in constant flux as students paint silly, serious, and mysterious messages. The more interesting ones last longest, but nothing is sacred. Arlo likes it so much he goes back and paints a complex memorial to Ray. That will last even longer, although eventually it, too, will disappear under something more timely and more pressing.

CHAPTER 14

The Fourth of July is a holiday, of course, and this year it's even bigger because it's the bicentennial. An all-weekend festival is scheduled for the grounds around the Arch downtown, with fireworks after dark on Sunday. For the first time since I've arrived in Saint Louis, I miss the boyfriend I said goodbye to in May. We were good friends, but we weren't really attached to each other and parted without tears. Now I really want to go to the Arch with him. I know it isn't really him I miss, but someone like him who will be thrilled by the fireworks and will eat cotton candy and hot dogs and sing along with the bands. He'd probably find a goofy hat to wear, just because I have a hat. And I wouldn't have to ride the bus home alone in the dark. I'm not really afraid to do that, not much anyway. Still, I'm going. But it will feel awkward going alone.

Arlo solves the problem for me. He organizes an official Y trip and signs out the van. The Friday before, the signup sheet is almost full, but there is still a spot, so I sign up. At least I'll go with a group and have a ride home.

It's a perfect day, and the slope from the Arch to the Mississippi River is a perfect grandstand for watching fireworks that are set off on barges in the river. The Y group separates and reforms throughout the afternoon and evening, and I end up with some of them when it's time for fireworks. Afterward, though, we get separated in the rush. Arlo's instructions were that the van would leave for campus at ten-fifteen and anyone who wasn't there by then he'd assume had found another way home.

I push my way toward the parking lot, but when I get there, I see it's the wrong lot, and by the time I find the right one it's ten-thirty and the van is gone. Downtown is clearing out quickly, but I find a bus stop and board a bus for U City. It's packed and everyone is in a party mood, so I stop worrying about missing the van. When we get past Kingshighway, though, I realize that the bus isn't going toward the Loop; it's quite a bit north of there. I try to picture the map I don't have with me and ask my seatmate if he knows exactly where the bus is going in U City. He says he doesn't know; he gets off at Skinker. At least I know how to get home via Skinker, so I get off there too. I look for a bus stop that will take me south on Skinker, but I'm scared and have no idea if there will even be a bus after eleven on a holiday Sunday. So, I start walking.

Street traffic is light and foot traffic is nonexistent. Streetlights are far apart and some are not working. There are no houses and few businesses, all closed either for the night or forever. I'm north of Delmar but technically in U City since I'm on the west side of the street. Or almost in U City anyway. A car races by heading north, and then another, this one with horn honking and passengers whooping it up. I'm guessing they're on their way home from the fireworks. Brakes squeal and I hear the car coming toward me again, backing up at high speed, then slowing as they draw even with me.

"Hey mama! Lookin' good."

I ignore them and walk on. I'm not sure how much farther it is to Delmar and not even sure that Delmar will offer much safety. I wish I'd had more than one judo class. What do I know about self-defense that will be of any use? Be aware of your surroundings. Keep your knees bent. I'm aware, and my knees are fully engaged in forward propulsion.

When I don't respond, the car drives off again, but a minute later it's back, this time cruising up next to me in the same direction. I'm crossing a street, and the car swerves up close and a hand reaches out. I leap away but my hat is gone. The car roars off, my hat waving from a rear window. I'm relieved, a little. Just joyriders in high spirits. I'm okay, just missing an eighty-eight-cent hat. I'm almost to Delmar where I'll at least find a bar open.

Then the car comes back and veers over the center line toward me. I stifle a shriek as an arm reaches out again. The car swerves away and my hat comes sailing toward me. I grab it and run.

"Happy Fourth!" I hear as the car roars away to the north.

I flee west on the first side street, without knowing what it is or where it goes, if it goes anywhere. When I can't run anymore, I slow down, look around me. I'm in a neighborhood of apartment buildings like my own, although they are mostly dark. I hear voices, but they sound friendly. And I smell something wonderful. Baking bread.

The voices and the smells are coming from a bakery in among the apartment buildings. Pratzel's Bakery, it says above the door, although I see it as Pretzel's. The store is all dark, though. A human form appears around the corner, and there is enough light to see that it's a student-aged human with a brown bag in the crook of one arm. The other hand is busy with a bagel.

"They just opened the side door," he says as one insider to another. I nod as if I know what he means and turn around the corner. Now I get it. The side door of the bakery is open, and a small crowd of mostly young adults are lined up and buying bread and bagels right off the cooling racks. I crowd in like a lost puppy returned to her litter, soaking up the warmth of a safe haven along with the aroma of people and bread.

"You gotta try this." A man about my age shoves a bagel in my face and I take a bite. He takes a bite and moves on to someone else. "You gotta try this," he says to the next person.

I linger until I'm calm and buy a half-dozen bagels. I look out the door into the dark street and try to get my bearings. When I'm sure which way is west, I follow a group of people heading that way. They are talking and in high spirits and don't notice me, so I can follow them easily down Clemens and practically to my door. DB the cat walks upstairs beside me. I toss my hat on the kitchen table and see that it has a tiny American flag, the kind attached to a toothpick, stuck under the ribbon. I have a sip of wine and a cool shower and go to sleep, although it takes a long time. The cat curls up on a corner of the bed.

CHAPTER 15

I don't tell anyone at the Y about the incident with the car on Skinker. I'm no longer frightened by it and I'm not sure exactly how I feel about it, although I've thought about it a lot. I realize that I don't know for sure if the boys were Black or white. I thought at the time that they were Black, but now I can't be sure.

At work, we are back to clearing out the storeroom and musing about what to do when it's all cleared out—should we keep it as usable storage and call it a resource area, or make it into something else? A quiet space? An all-day yoga room? A noisy study room? One thing we are sure about is that it will be the Ray Nesbitt Room. That, we hope, will keep it from becoming a junk room again.

Dotty drops in from time to time. She is the other program director and is spending the summer as a camp counselor. She has every other weekend off, including Friday, and stops by to pick up her mail and have lunch with us. Dotty is the least dotty person I know, all seriousness and solid colors, not a dot in sight. I ask her about it, and she says she's tried to be Dorothy, but all kids, both her schoolmates and now the campers, will insist on saying "Dorky," so she's resigned herself to Dotty. Or Dots, which is what her family has called her ever since she gave her brother a black eye, when she was ten and he was twelve, for calling her Door-key one time too many. We offer to call her Dots and she says we can call her anything that doesn't start with d-o-r-k.

When the old storage room is almost empty, we take Dots on a tour. She likes all our ideas but has no preference, commenting only that we get more and more students through here every year, so whatever we do will be good. She asks us what's in the cupboards that were inaccessible before we hauled off everything stacked in front.

"We don't know—we can't find a key that works," Betty tells her.

Dots hmms and then goes back to her office and we hear drawers opening and closing. She comes back with a key ring.

"This has been in my desk since I started. Let's see if anything fits."

And so, we open a time capsule of files, photo albums, and all kinds of things that might be useful someday but apparently never have been needed. A coffee urn, platters, an ancient adding machine, a telephone headset. And a typewriter, a manual one that appears to be made of iron. I know that if I say anything, Betty will tell me to take it, but I already feel like I've taken more than I should, including the table and chairs and lamps and then the free-to-staff classes and the morning off sick on Jackie's couch. I sigh, maybe louder than I realize.

"Novelle needs a typewriter," Betty says, ending my qualms. "I wonder if we can get that thing to work."

We haul it out, and it's heavy but manageable. Dots looks it over without touching it.

"I had one of those in high school," she says. "And I'm not getting near it in this white blouse." She says goodbye and takes off. The phone rings and I go off to answer it and enroll two summer students in Arlo's art class. When I get back, Betty has a sheet of paper in the roller and is tapping random keys.

"It seems to work. None of the keys stick. The ribbon's dried out so I can't tell if the letters line up properly." She reaches the end of a line and the bell dings. She gives the return lever a smart flick and it smoothly moves to the next line. Another flick, another line.

"The paper guides are still there," I say and shove her aside and start typing. "The shift key works, and it's got a cap lock. It even has a number 1 key—I had to use the L key on mine. My old one." I turn to Betty. "My mom wanted it back. She's teaching herself to type so she can get an office job. She raised us by doing hair at home, so she could take care of us at the same time, but we're gone now and she wants something new, I think."

"Well, good for her. She sounds like a go-getter. Good example for her kids."

I've never ever thought of Mom as a good example; I've thought of her as irresponsible, but I see what Betty means. She was responsible, just not as careful with money as I thought she should be.

Betty hands me the typewriter ribbon and tells me to run over to the bookstore and see if they sell one that will fit.

"And then you can take the van out—I'm sure it needs gas." She looks at the typewriter, at me, and at the typewriter again. I give her a hug and run up the stairs.

The bookstore does carry the right ribbon, and I'm deciding between all black or red-black combination when Arlo sidles up to me.

"Sorry about Sunday night, leaving you downtown," he says, and I see that he's both sorry and concerned.

"Oh no, that was fine," I tell him, and I realize that it was. "That was the deal. The van was leaving at ten-fifteen. And I'm guessing you waited as long as you could."

"Sure, but still, that was for the others. I didn't mean I would leave anyone there alone. But they were closing the lot and everyone wanted to get back for some party in the Loop."

"Really, it was fine. I caught a bus. I didn't even have to wait more than a minute or so."

He doesn't need to hear what happened at the other end of the bus ride. I suddenly feel like it would be good to discuss it with him, or with someone my age, but he would only see that he caused it, so I know I'll never bring it up.

"Let's talk about Big Art instead. I'm determined to cover the one blank wall in my apartment with giant art."

Arlo takes the bait and says he's now thinking that poster paint would be better than Magic Marker, and we go back to the Y together and go through the stack of things we're still deciding on to see if there is any. There isn't, so I remind him about the supplies budget and the supply list and tell him to figure it out. He looks thoughtful and leaves.

CHAPTER 16

The next weekend I'm on bride-sitting duty again and get to the Y in plenty of time, feeling like an old hand. The bride is waiting and not happy about it. I check my watch.

"It's not quite three o'clock," I say. "Doesn't the contract say three o'clock?" I scramble to unlock the door and dig the folder out of my backpack at the same time. It's not there and I picture it at home on my kitchen table. I wonder if my watch is correct.

"It's three-o-five!" she says. "And how am I supposed to get ready in one hour anyway?"

The Graham Chapel clock chimes the hour, and one of the bridesmaids rolls her eyes. I feel a little better and rush down the stairs, turning on lights and talking too much, pointing out the ladies' room and telling them that the men's room is at their disposal too and that it was cleaned after we closed on Friday. Two of the bridesmaids giggle and open the door a crack, as if the men's room was something slightly dangerous. I don't see anyone who could be the mother of the bride, so I ask if anyone else is coming before I lock the outside door.

"Who knows," the bride says. "The almighty step-bitch might deign to show." She smiles a bit wickedly. "But you can lock her out."

The eye-rolling bridesmaid gives the bride a look that I recognize as an older-sister look. She whispers to the bride, puts an arm around her, and nudges her gently into the lounge.

I see that my previous bride-sitting experience has not made me an expert. I try to lighten the mood a little by making a general statement that they all look great and that their dresses are beautiful. I should have known better. I've been to enough friend and cousin weddings to know that bridesmaids' dresses are always despised by their wearers.

"Butt bows," one of them comments, and they all glare in the bride's direction, which means they all face away from me and I see that they are right. The bows are enormous.

I hear the bride's voice say "They hide your . . ." in an exasperated tone, but her sister has her in hand and she stops mid-sentence.

I feel the giggles coming on, but someone is pounding on the door, so the giggles are forgotten and I race back up the stairs.

"I told you to lock her out" floats up from the lounge and "What's going on in there?" can be heard from the other side of the door. I open it slowly so that I don't further upset the stepmother or whoever is on the other side. A very red face appears and a bridesmaid detaches from the group below, sighs audibly, and glides up the steps in her kitten heels, skirt held just off the concrete.

"Mom! Everything is fine, we're almost ready—just come in here and sit down for a minute."

So, this one must be a stepsister of the bride, although she seems to be playing the big-sister role to her mother today. She shepherds her mother into the workroom, keeping herself between her mother and the bride. The bride's sister has the bride at the far end of the lounge now and is unpacking an enormous white dress behind the tri-fold screen we set up for these occasions. Another bridesmaid approaches tentatively with a shoe box, sets it down near the big sister, and retreats.

I suggest that they all sit down and relax. If it were me, I'd want to sit down and kick off the stilettos for as long as possible. Interesting that only the stepsister has chosen, or been allowed to choose, the lower kitten heels.

"We're not allowed to sit," the youngest bridesmaid whispers.

"Because of the damn butt bows," another one says, not quite whispering. I think about taking them into the workroom to get them farther from the bride's ears, but I don't know what the stepmother situation is, so I don't.

Instead, I offer to make coffee. Usually, they specify coffee in the contract if they want it, and they didn't—I checked before I left, which is why I left the folder on my kitchen table. But I'll make coffee if it will help keep this situation under control.

"No coffee either. We're not trusted. Might spill it on someone's butt bow."

I bite my lips and wonder if I can get away with running into Jackie's office and laughing my head off. Instead, they all get the giggles and I have to go find a box of tissues. I expect the stepmother to come out and demand to know what's going on, but her daughter has closed the doors firmly and they stay closed.

The bridesmaids then take turns checking their makeup. They clearly arrived ready to go, with hair and makeup and dresses and shoes all perfect, so I'm not even sure why they are here. Even the bride is completely ready except for dress and shoes, so I can't understand why an hour is not enough. I decide that it's just bridal nerves and she was allowing for traffic or parking problems or who knows what, and I mentally cut her some slack.

By now, the dress and shoes are on, and the older sister leads the bride out into the center of the lounge. She seems calm and happy now, and the dress is beautiful if excessive. I wonder if it will fit through the door and if I should run up and give the doorway a wipe. The older sister is holding a white shopping bag and nudges the bride, nodding her head. The bride takes a deep breath.

"Thank you all for being with me on my special day," she begins in a sing-song voice. Then she stops. Tears run down her face and she turns red and sobs. The bridesmaids seem to take this as normal and say nothing. One of them hands her a tissue. She takes it and mumbles a thank-you. Her sister whispers to her. She whispers back and the sister gives her a long look, then seems to come to a decision. She looks around.

"Where is Cecily?" she asks. The bridesmaids, still silent, look toward the closed workroom door.

"Shall I get her?" I mouth to the sister. She nods and I crack open the door. I assume Cecily is the daughter and not the older woman, and I realize I'm in a jam because I don't know if the stepmom is wanted or not. But it's not up to me, so I just say "Cecily?" to the room in general, and the younger woman comes to the door. She looks back at her mother, who is sitting. She's also drinking from a flask. *I didn't see that*, I tell myself. No way am I going to invoke any rules—well, unless the daughter seems to want me to. I step into the room, though, and the daughter steps out.

She gives her mother a sharp look and goes out to meet the others with a smile that is almost believable, closing the door firmly behind her. I hear gentle murmuring; it sounds friendly through the door at least.

I turn to the woman, wanting to leave but feeling like I need to supervise her, based on her earlier outburst and her daughter's obvious concern. She looks at me and says "Hmmph," and I just smile and pretend to be busy straightening chairs. There isn't much to do, so I move around behind the woman so she can't see that I'm doing nothing. I open and close a few drawers.

Out in the lounge, the voices are calm and I hear a "thank you" that sounds sincere enough, so I take it that all is well. I check my watch. Five till four. I wonder if I should give them a time check. Betty has told me that it's a good idea, although she said that some brides want the first bridesmaid to start down the aisle on the dot and others plan to be fifteen minutes late, "for no reason that I can discern."

I speak softly to the stepmother.

"It's almost four—did you want to go on ahead? I will unlock the door whenever you're ready."

"*She* doesn't want me there now, or ever." She's slurring just a little, but at least her voice is fairly soft.

"Well, still, you'll need to be seated." I decide not to say that her husband will be expecting her. It seems unwise to bring up any family members.

She sighs and heaves herself to her feet.

"Keep this for me, will you?" She hands me the flask. I take it and nod. Anything to keep the peace here.

She's out of the room before I can move, and I have to rush to unlock the door and let her out. Several tuxedoed young men are waiting at the top of the outside steps, nonchalantly talking among themselves and looking like nothing in the world concerns them in the least.

"Mrs. Dugan," one of them says, holding out a hand and bowing slightly.

She allows herself to be escorted in the direction of Graham Chapel.

Back downstairs, the mood has lifted, and the girls seem more excited, checking each other's hair and dresses. No one checks anyone's butt bow. I try to keep "butt bow" out of my head.

"The groomsmen seem to be ready whenever you are," I say. "They look great too."

The older sister gets the others in line, and the stepsister leads them up the stairs. The older sister walks the bride all the way up the outside stairs and turns to face me.

"Sorry," she mouths, and then says aloud, "Cecily and I will meet you back here as soon as we can."

The bride turns and gives her a sharp look but allows herself to be coddled into place and they disappear. I go inside, lock the door, and heave a sigh of relief. The giggles are gone, and not even "butt bow" can bring them back. I feel sorry for every single one of that crowd. There will be no tips from this bride, I'm sure, but I don't mind. I didn't expect a tip the last time, and I'm getting paid well for the little bit of work this requires.

There isn't much to clean up, but I pick up tissues and fold up the bride's street clothes, leaving them neatly next to her street shoes. The other girls have left purses but nothing else, so I leave them where they are. Next to each one is a framed photo of the bride, each with one of the girls. They are sweet photos, snapshots taken at birthday parties, the beach, a graduation. Maybe she is nicer than she seems today. There are also jewelry boxes, all open and empty, so she must have given them each a necklace that they all chose to wear. Or maybe they'd been told. No one seems to have left a necklace they took off. I check the restrooms and pick up stray bobby pins and tissues. I leave one bobby pin in the men's room to amuse whichever guy goes in there next.

After fifteen minutes I lock up and walk the thirty feet to the door of Graham Chapel to see how it's going. Betty has warned me that some services don't take any longer than that, which puzzles us both. She guesses that the reception must be the real reason for all the flurry over dresses and shoes and hair. "Or maybe it's just the photos, for some of them."

This is not one of the short services, but it's not very interesting either, and I gaze at the stained-glass windows. A rustle in the pews rouses me to the end of the service, and I scoot out and retreat to the top of the Y stairs. I'm there for another thirty minutes waiting for someone to show up. The wedding party is out of my sight, but it's clear that there is some trouble with the receiving line at the church door. Finally, the bride and groom take their leave, and I see Cecily and the bride's older sister coming in my direction.

"Oh my God," Cecily says.

"What a—" They see me and pause. "What a butt bow." And they collapse against each other laughing.

I help them gather up the bride's clothes. A groomsman arrives with boxes for the purses and photos. It's clear from their conversation that the sister collected the photos and framed them and wrapped them and even presented them to the others today. I wonder if she made one for herself. I decide she did, otherwise the ruse would have been a failure.

To my surprise, they both hand me envelopes and apologize for the hysteria.

"Oh no, it's not necessary," I tell them. "And it wasn't that bad." Maybe it was, but I try to pretend that I've seen worse.

"Oh yes it was," they say in unison and start laughing again.

I lock the door behind them and then remember the stepmother's flask. I pause for two seconds, wondering if they'd rather it be forgotten, and then open the door and call to them.

"Hey, your mother—or whoever—left a . . . um . . . something. I'll get it."

"Wait! Is it silver and looks like this?" Cecily says, pantomiming a furtive drink from a flask.

I nod and give her a sympathetic look.

"We didn't forget it. You can have it—or put it in the dumpster," the sister says.

"Yeah, it's not like it's her only one."

I wave them off and go back to retrieve the flask. I think about donating it to Molly's shop, but in the end I put it in a paper bag and toss it in a dumpster on my way home. I think I won't even tell that part of the story, or maybe I won't tell this story at all.

When I get home I remember the tips and open the envelopes. One of them has a hastily scribbled note. "Sorry you had to see that. It's not as bad as it looks. PS: If you ever have a wedding like this, please God no butt bows." Each envelope has a twenty-dollar bill. I warn myself not to get used to this. And then I think about my sixty-dollar tip, which gives me a little cushion in case of emergency. I can stop at the Women's Exchange next week and see about a desk, now that I have a working typewriter.

CHAPTER 17

The first Big Art session starts Monday at four. I'm the staff person assigned to supervise and lock up when class ends at six, which means that I get paid for an extra hour as well as getting the class for free. I tell Betty that seems excessive and she sighs and tells me to come in late the next day if I'm going to be all moralistic about it.

"There's a word for that—scrupulosity," she says and looks at me pointedly. I register surprise and she gives me a self-satisfied look. "You need to take some philosophy along with all your economics. Do you good."

I'm chagrined, but she's smiling kindly. I know she means it, though. I again feel the sharp need to find some cohorts my own age. I love all the new adults in my life, but I need some equals to sit around and rap with, as we said a few years ago. I'm used to having long discussions about everything and nothing, right and wrong, morality and immorality, life and death and fear and courage. I resolve to get out more.

At three-thirty, Arlo shows up with piles of newspaper, which turn out to be the small-print want-ad pages from the

Sunday paper. He covers the entire work surface in the workroom with multiple layers. It seems excessive, since those tables are very well worn, but I admire his caution in protecting them from our Magic Markers. Then he lays out the markers.

"Where is the brown paper? I thought we were working on that."

"It's here, you'll see." He has a mischievous look, so I back off, get a clipboard, and sign in the students as they arrive. Everyone seems excited and most seem a little nervous. No one comments on the want ads, but then they haven't been in on the planning. Arlo climbs up on a chair, clearly for effect since he's perfectly visible to all, and gives a little speech.

"We are here to *make* art! Art is what we *make* it! End of speech."

He hops down, grabs a marker, and tells me to stand on the chair. This wasn't in the plan, but I climb up and parody him, both arms in the air, then on my hips, then one foot on the table.

"Perfect, let's all draw that!" Arlo grabs a marker and draws a stick figure of my pose. It takes up a full spread of want ads. No one else moves a muscle.

"See, it's all about shape. We're doing a version of caricature, so feel free to exaggerate a little." He looks around. "Ready? Go to it!"

People slowly pick up markers, jostle a little finding space, and look at Arlo's drawing. He snatches it off the table, tosses it in the trash, and hops up on another chair. He strikes a pose, then another, then gives me a "Now you" look. I fake a ballet position, then cross my arms and glower.

"Save the face for next class," he says to me. "Today, we want big shapes. Now you get down and draw."

People have picked up markers and are starting to get into it, but the pictures are small.

"People!" he says. "Newspaper is free! Use it all! If you don't like it, toss it and start over. Let's use up all this newspaper."

I take a deep breath and draw a head as far away from myself as I can reach. I add a stick for a body, then a leg. I look at it critically, shift my eyes to the drawing next to me, and draw a leg that reaches out and kicks the nascent sketch next to mine.

"Hey!" The girl whose drawing was kicked by mine turns sharply, sees me smiling, and laughs. She rips her drawing off the table and quickly starts over. Her stick figure now has two hands grabbing the ankle of mine. I rip mine off and draw a hopscotch jump over hers. It's barely discernable as human, but now everyone is watching us. Two spaces down, a pond appears for my hopscotch figure to land in. On the other side of the table, a volleyball game takes shape, and the ball ends up on our side of the table. A foot is drawn kicking it back. Arlo is ecstatic and Betty comes in to see what all the racket is about. I give her an all-under-control look and I see her eye a marker for a moment but then back away and return to her office. Once Arlo is satisfied that everyone is engaged, he calls a halt and sweeps all the drawings off the table.

"Okay, warm-up is over and everyone gets an A. Now we are going to be serious for a while."

For the next half hour, he points out features of his Ray drawings, how a stick figure was made into a cartoon drawing, and how to get proportioning right—or right enough for giant drawings on old newspapers, anyway. He makes sure that everyone is drawing every minute, and everyone's shyness about displaying their efforts vanishes.

About the time we all feel like we have something we're willing to take home, Arlo sweeps them all off the table, to loud protests.

"Don't worry, they'll be right here—you can take them when you leave. But now we move on." And he lugs out an enormous roll of brown paper and starts cutting six-foot sections. Most of the walls in the Y are the huge granite stones of the building foundation, but a few interior walls are smooth, and we help him hang the strips. Some students elect to spread theirs on the floor. I use the back of the outside door.

"People! Pair up and draw each other! All's fair in Big Art!"

The others all pair up with the closest person, leaving me the odd one out since I am at the top of the inside stairs, taping my paper to the door.

"I'll draw you and you'll do me," Arlo says. "Turn around and get started."

I start to protest that I need him to model, but everyone else is drawing quietly, so I decide to beat him at his own game. I draw him wide-eyed and wild-haired, standing on the table and gesticulating wildly with four arms. I turn around to see if he is amused and see him kneeling on the floor at the bottom of the steps. He is finishing up his drawing of me. His drawing catches me in the act of drawing him, right down to the fourth arm. The drawing of me is painted in broad strokes of poster paint, and my drawing of him in the background is lightly sketched in marker. From the shoulders up, I am hidden behind the hat, which I am not wearing at the moment. He turns and gives me a Cheshire cat smile, then leaps to his feet.

"People! Let's see what we've all done." He sweeps us together into a tour of all the drawings. Sometimes he pretends to be horrified at first glance, but he always makes some suggestions, and he always ends with "What do you all think? Does this get an A?"

We get to his drawing last, and he tells us that next week we will be adding poster paint, which we can use or not, depending on what we want to achieve. That starts a chorus of questions about color and subject matter, but Arlo just closes his eyes and holds up both hands, a gesture that I immediately want to draw for the sake of the laughs it will get.

"All will be revealed in seven days. Class dismissed. Take home anything you want; the rest is going to the great beyond."

It's after six, so the space clears quickly. I help Arlo clean up, which mostly involves stuffing newspaper in the trash and corralling the markers.

"Well done, Maestro," I tell him as we leave and I lock the door. "I think your class is a winner. The newspaper was brilliant, much less intimidating than a big sheet of clean new paper. No one was afraid to screw up drawing on last week's newspaper."

"They were afraid anyway, but they got over it quickly, didn't they? Thanks for taking your cues and jumping in there. I was pretty nervous until you drew that kick and Sue, or whoever it was, took the bait."

"You, nervous? Not possible."

"Yep, me. Nervous. See you soon." And he kisses me lightly on the lips and turns toward the dorms. I put my hat on and drift home, exhausted and happy.

My mellow mood lasts until I get home. A woman about my age is sitting under the sycamore in the little bit of yard in front of my building. She's leaning on the tree and looking up into the branches. I've been admiring the tree myself, wondering if I could use it as a model for Big Art, and I don't see her until I turn onto the little walk up to the door. Her face is not familiar.

She hears my footsteps and looks around as if she's been miles away. She rises in a single motion like a dancer and picks up her backpack, which is the kind backpackers use, not the kind students use to go back and forth to class. She follows me to the door and waits as I unlock it. I look at her.

"Lost my key," she says. "I mean the outside door key. You'll let me in?" The tone is friendly and light and assumes that I will let her in. I'm not sure what to do.

"Oh, sure." I can't imagine slamming the outer door in her face. "Do you live here?"

She hesitates just for a second, half a second.

"Yes." It's a bit tentative. "Yes!" more confidently.

I don't check my mailbox, I just unlock the next door and start up.

"Well, it's nice to meet you. I haven't been here long and don't know too many of the other tenants."

I don't know even one other tenant, but I don't want to tell her that.

She follows me up to the first floor without comment. When I turn to continue up the stairs, she follows, making a few comments about the weather. At the next landing, she lags behind. I assume the backpack is heavy, but I'm a little suspicious about the lack of chatter. No small talk about the building, or how long she's lived there, or which apartment is hers.

At the top floor, I walk past 3A and 3B and open the louvered door to 3D. I turn and see that she is following slowly, looking at the numbers on the doors. She glances at the 3D on my door and then at my face, and then at her own hands.

I haven't unlocked the door yet, the key is still in my hand, which is in my pocket. I wait, a little tense, remembering to bend my knees slightly. The hall is dim, but I think I see a little color rise in her cheeks. I wait.

Finally, she squeaks, "You live in 3D?"

I put my drawings down and face her, hands out of my pockets. I'm worried. She doesn't look dangerous, but something is wrong. All I can come up with is that she's just moving in today and she got the wrong building. Or maybe the landlady is confused again. That must be it. I relax just a little.

"Yes, I live here. Which apartment is yours?"

She sighs. "I thought it was 3D." She starts going through her pockets.

I start to tell her it's okay, the same thing happened to me, but something stops me and again I stand still and wait. Once she finds her rental agreement we should be able to straighten this out. But she doesn't have a rental agreement, she just has a scrap of notebook paper with an address. My address, apartment 3D. She looks at the paper, at my door, at the paper again. I hear her take a deep breath and then she turns and walks quickly away.

I'm tired and I want to let her go, but my RA instincts kick in and I call out.

"Wait up!" She stops. "Just give me a second here." I open the door and shove my backpack and artwork in the door, then close and lock it. I follow her down the hall.

"Do you want to get something to eat?" I ask when I'm close to her. This was my usual opening when presented with an angry, crying, or frightened freshman. Sometimes I let them in my room and made tea, fed them animal crackers. Sometimes we went to the communal kitchen and got something from a vending machine. Sometimes we went to a nearby ice cream shop or farther, to the student dining hall, assuming it wasn't a midnight meltdown. The bigger the issue, the farther I would take them, because walking is calming and sometimes it's easier to talk if we're both facing the same direction. This seems fairly big.

"How about the Maryland Café on Delmar?" That's several blocks and as far as I want to go tonight.

She nods, and I wonder if she even knows what that is or where it is. We start off and I tell her my first name. She sighs and seems to struggle internally, and finally says she is Ruth.

"I'm not usually like this," she says, not specifying what "this" is. I've worked out that she must have been planning to stay with someone and was bluffing about losing her outdoor key. Now I need to find out if it was David Black, but I want her to say it.

"You don't really live in my building, do you?" I ask, as kindly as I can. We walk on.

"No." Her voice is very soft, and again I wait. I think about asking her where she *does* live, but we wouldn't be having this conversation if she lived anywhere near the Loop, so I don't ask. I'm becoming aware that this little jaunt is different from my RA walks. I'm not responsible for where she sleeps tonight, but every step takes me closer to that reality.

"My boyfriend said I could stay with him," she says finally. "At least, he said I could stay there."

That's pretty vague, but we're getting somewhere now.

"Who is your boyfriend, Ruth? What's his name?"

Another wait and another sigh.

"Dave. Dave Brown."

I think about that. My first impulse was to correct her, to ask if she means David Black. But I keep that knowledge to myself, for future use, and I spare her embarrassment, at least for the moment. We've arrived at the diner, and I ask if this is okay or would she rather go to the Dairy Queen across the street. It occurs to me that the Dairy Queen is easier to escape, since we'd probably end up outside at a picnic table. She might feel safer there. If things get uncomfortable, there won't be any awkwardness about the check, one or both of us can just say goodbye and walk away.

"This is fine." She actually perks up a little, and I choose a table as far as possible from anyone who might listen in. I make sure it's a booth so I can look her in the eye. The walking and talking phase is over.

We talk about the menu, which is cheap and extensive, until we've ordered and are drinking iced tea. Then the RA takes over again.

"So, Ruth. Tell me what's going on." I keep my voice even, kind but also the adult in charge. I duck down a little to catch her eye and get her to raise her head. She'll feel better that way, and I can assess things a little more easily. I've had a lot of training in the signs of drug use, depression, malnutrition, and prevarication.

She sighs yet again, but this time it's a resigned sigh, the opening to the story of Ruth, the girl with the backpack who was going to stay in an apartment that may or may not be occupied by David Black or David Brown, or David Green for that matter, any of whom may or may not be or have been her boyfriend.

The story comes out. To her credit, she admits that showing up on Wingate was an act of hope more than anything else. She met David on spring break and she thought he really liked her. They slept on the beach at Padre Island for five nights and she asked if she could write to him and he wrote down his address. That was about the extent of her relationship with Dave.

Our food comes and she eats all her fries and then starts in on her BLT.

"You want this coleslaw?"

I take it because it feels like a little act of kindness on her part, although she probably just doesn't like coleslaw. She eats her pickle and I fork over mine.

"Do you know anything else about Dave? Maybe we can find him. Did he go to school in Saint Louis?" I don't say "at WashU," again wanting to make her say it. The RA code says to avoid yes-or-no questions unless the kid is not talking at all.

"Saint Louis U?" she finally says. I don't take that as meaning anything other than that SLU is the school most often associated with Saint Louis, for obvious reasons. Half the people I know think I'm going to SLU, no matter how many times I've told them it's Washington University, which is in Saint Louis. She doesn't know anything much about Dave.

"That's a few miles away from here," I say gently and change the subject. The Dave theme isn't going to get us anywhere in the few hours left of today.

"What brought you to University City?" I ask. "Other than Dave, I mean." Maybe I can move her on to whatever her real path is, since it's clearly not Dave.

She seems to reach a decision. She sits up straighter and reaches into her backpack for her wallet.

"It doesn't matter anyway," she says. "But thanks for listening."

She opens her wallet and I see that it's not empty, she's got cash. She gets out a credit card and lays it on top of the check. I object, but she insists.

"I shouldn't have come, I probably scared the daylights out of you," she says. "I don't know what I was thinking."

And suddenly I do know what she was thinking.

"Are you pregnant?" I watch her closely and see that she is.

"Maybe."

Spring break is too long ago; there is no maybe about it. The waitress brings the charge slip and while Ruth is signing, I take a quick look at the name on it. George Mehlman. So, she has parents, or at least a father, who has given her a credit card, probably for emergencies. Food may be an emergency he expects to cover, but a pregnancy is probably not. I wonder how old she is. Could she be underage? Surely she was at least a freshman in college last spring break. The RA Novelle knew exactly what to do with a pregnant freshman, but this Novelle isn't at all sure.

"So, what next?" I ask her, hoping she has a Plan B.

"Oh, I can catch a bus; I'll be fine." She looks up and sees that I don't believe she'll be fine. She lowers her voice but not her chin. "I'll go to my mom's. She'll be mad as anything, but she'll just have to get over it."

That sounds like a solid plan, and the bitter detail tells me it's what she'll probably do. But it's too late to let her get on the Delmar bus to downtown, where she'll probably end up sleeping on a plastic chair until sometime tomorrow, when the bus to Mom leaves. Nothing about that seems safe to me.

"Okay, that sounds good," I finally say. "You can do that tomorrow. Tonight, you can sleep on my couch."

The look on her face is completely open and the tears that appear tell me she can almost certainly be trusted.

"Let's go then."

On the short walk back, she becomes more animated, commenting on the bustle along Delmar, the ubiquitous brick buildings, the amount of green in the landscape, and the evening's heavy, fragrant humidity. I wonder if she's from Texas. The desert part of Texas. I don't ask. I'm mentally thinking through hosting my first houseguest, about whom I know almost nothing. As long as my wallet is in my bedroom with me, there isn't much she can steal, other than food. Certainly not my one-ton typewriter. I picture her sneaking out the door with it and almost laugh out loud. Most likely she'll sleep like a log and I'll have to wake her up and shoo her out before I go to work.

"I need to leave by eight o'clock tomorrow morning," I tell her as I unlock the door. "Will that work for you?"

She nods and I think I should have made it more clear that she has to leave by eight also.

"You'll be okay then? I'll walk you to the bus stop and you can get to the Greyhound station downtown. Sorry I don't have a car, or I'd drive you."

We go in and I pick up my backpack and drawings. Did I really make those just today? I put them in the bedroom and get out a towel and washcloth for Ruth. I don't have extra sheets to put on the couch, but I could offer her my pillow. I take the towels into the living room and see that Ruth is curled up on the couch, her head on a jean jacket she's pulled out of her backpack. She's asleep or doing a good job pretending to be asleep, and DB the cat is curled up with her. I put the towel on her backpack and turn out the light. I very gently lock my bedroom door and lie awake reading for a long time, too overwrought to sleep. A little after midnight, I hear Ruth get up, run water in the bathroom, and flush the toilet. I listen hard, willing her not to leave the apartment in the middle of the night. But I don't hear anything at all, and eventually I fall asleep myself.

When I wake up in the morning, the sun is high and I know I've overslept. My first thought is that I'm late for work, which seems slovenly and embarrassing to me. Then I remember Ruth. I open the bedroom door and see that she's not on the couch. She's also not in the bathroom and not in the kitchen. Her backpack is gone and the towels I left for her are folded neatly on the couch.

I quickly dress and grab my backpack, run down the stairs. Maybe I can catch her at the bus stop. But then I think no, she's chosen to go forward on her own. I open the mailbox and find that she's stuffed a note through the gap at the top. "Thanks for everything. You are a kind soul, and I am grateful. Ruth Mehlman." There is also a postcard addressed to Dave, no last name. "Hi," it says. "Hoping to see you soon. I've got great news!! Rutheroni." I cringe. Poor Ruth. Maybe her mother will be kinder than she expects. I start toward campus, then turn around and walk into All Saints, where I light a candle for Ruth. That's the only thing I can think of doing for her now. Or maybe I just do it for myself. I hope DB walked her to the bus stop.

CHAPTER 18

The Y is quiet that week, and Betty tells me that this is normal for summer. Donations are still trickling in and I'm keeping up with thank-you notes and filing. We finish clearing out the storage room and tentatively start going through Ray's office. I help when asked and otherwise hang back, again feeling out of place dealing with what is a tragedy to Betty but has very little meaning to me, other than that I just missed out on something wonderful in Ray Nesbitt.

Betty has me take over all the business related to bride-sitting. Sometimes that involves a lot of phone calls and sometimes it takes almost no time at all. That particular Saturday, the bride is incensed when it starts misting just as she's ready to walk the thirty feet or so to the chapel door. She hasn't brought an umbrella, but I find one and offer it to her. She balks and insists that there is a tunnel from the Y to Graham Chapel. I assure her that there is not and urge her toward the umbrella and the door. She stamps her perfect satin slipper and tells me there is, that she used it once before when she was a bridesmaid for her best friend. I tell her I'm sorry again, and she demands to use the phone. I get her an outside line and she calls the friend. She talks for a while in low but insistent tones while I wonder why her best friend isn't here. In the hospital having a baby? Moved to China? It can't be that, only local calls can be made from our phones. She hangs up and stomps to the door, where her maid of honor holds the umbrella over her head and suggests that she take off her shoes for the sprint across the wet grass. The bridesmaids follow. The last one turns to me and whispers, "The friend got married at SLU. And she's not her best friend, she's a sort of step-cousin-in-law. Sorry about all that." I get a lot of "sorry" in the bride-sitting business.

My mother calls late Sunday night and I realize that I haven't had a letter from her for a few weeks. I find out why. My grandmother has fallen and broken both arms and is having trouble breathing and "thinking," according to my mother.

"Mom, what does that mean? Do you mean she can't remember things? Mom?"

My sister Lulu takes over, and again I'm reminded that she is older and more mature now.

"Mom means that Granny had a stroke and fell and broke her arms and bumped her head. She can't talk and she's mostly asleep. It's been two weeks now. Mom didn't want to call you until she had better news, but I insisted. The doctors don't think we're going to get better news any time soon."

"Oh Lulu, not Granny! What happened? Or what's going to happen now?"

"She fell in her bathroom and probably hit her head on the tub or the sink." I hear Lulu sniff and I give her a minute. "They don't think she's going to die or anything, but she's going to have to go to a nursing home."

"Ooh no. You don't think she'll get well enough to go back home?"

"Mom says she will, but Mom knows better. Granny's not been well all summer. She'd already fallen once or twice, but she just got bruised before. Those might have been mini strokes, the doctor said. Anyway, home is a long shot. Actually, home is just not possible anymore."

I groan a little and tell her I wish I lived closer.

"Now that you mention it," Lulu says, "the real reason Mom called is to see if you could come home for a couple of weeks and see Granny and help with arranging a nursing home and going through some of Granny's things."

I try to think how I can make that happen. School is still a month away, but I need to work. On the other hand, what is more important than family?

"But if you could just come for a weekend, that would be fine. Just see Granny, hold her hand. I can help Mom with everything else."

Tears fill my eyes.

"Oh Lulu," I start.

"No, don't say it." Lulu is firm, grown up. "You were there for me all those years, through all the freaky times. I can do this. I know I can. You need to be in Saint Louis."

And I see that she can, and that she needs to be the one in charge this time.

"But a weekend, can you do that?" And I see that she's still my baby sister and I suddenly want to be there more than anything.

"Yes, next weekend. I'll get there Friday and leave Monday, or something like that."

We hang up and I call Greyhound and find that a bus leaves late Thursday and arrives very early on Friday. I'll figure out the return later. I write a note and run down to the post office to mail it.

— — —

The next morning, I ask Betty if she can take care of the next Saturday's double-header bride fest, and she says of course she can and asks me about my mother and sister and grandmother. She seems to know better than to ask about my father, and she doesn't tell me any stories about other grandmothers who have fallen or had strokes or moved into nursing homes. For that I am grateful, and I tell her so.

"Grieving people are like brides. Not much space in your heart for other people's sorrow." I'm a little puzzled about the implications that brides have sorrow, but I take her point and let it go.

I'm impatient for the weekend and pack and repack my backpack, not sure what to take. I realize that things could change and I might have to stay longer. I work a few extra hours at the Y, making sure all the brides are as ready as possible, that Arlo is set for the next session, and that all the thank-yous are typed and the filing is filed.

Betty tells me to calm down, that it's the slow summer season still, and if I'm worried about the money, I can make up some hours when I get back, either on Saturday or in the evenings.

"Things will pick up in August and you can work all you want then."

On Thursday I finish packing and take my overstuffed backpack to the Y with me so I can leave directly from campus. I realize that I don't have a book for the long bus ride and wonder if I can run over to the library at lunchtime. But I get distracted and forget about it until I make my afternoon pass through the lounge checking for forgotten books and stray cups. When I take a pair of sunglasses to our lost and found box, I find a copy of *Zen and the Art of Motorcycle Maintenance*.

"Betty, how long has this book been in the lost box?"

"Since before graduation, so I don't think anyone's going to claim it, at least not until fall semester. Anyway, everyone on earth has already read it. Take it if you want it."

I guess that makes me unearthly. I leave a note saying it will be back next week. Maybe that's overkill, but at least I don't agonize over it.

I'm hoping to sleep on the bus so I'll be fresh for Friday with my family. I sit in the front seat, right behind the driver and as far as possible from the smoking rows in the back, and also far from the creepy guys who seem to prefer the back of the bus. It's dark when we leave, so there's not much to see beyond lights in farmhouses. I turn on my reading light and open *Zen*. It's absorbing and I read for an hour or so, until I come to the line: "Sometimes it's a little better to travel than to arrive." I slap the book shut. In the eerie darkness of the bus that has become completely quiet, it feels like a premonition I don't want to hear. I switch off the reading light and lean back, trying to relax and let go of my worries and fears for the next few days. I listen to myself breathe for what seems like hours.

I wake up as the air brakes are squealing, dreaming that I'm in a factory and late for work. This isn't my stop, but the next one is, about thirty minutes away. I run out and use the ladies' room, wash my face, and buy a bag of chips. Back on the bus, I brush my hair and try to psych myself up for meeting my sister, or mother, or both, at the bus station. The book is on the seat beside me, and I pick it up. It opens at the page where I left off. There is that line again. This time I notice that it's only a little better to travel than to arrive. Anyway, it's just a book and it's just one line in a book, and Robert Pirsig is admittedly a little out there anyway, isn't he?

CHAPTER 19

Mom and Lulu are both waiting. Lulu is dressed for her bank job and I feel frumpy and smelly. They insist that we go to the hospital, which scares me at first, but they assure me that Granny is no worse and that they got permission from the nursing staff to stop in as soon as I arrived. When we get to her bedside, she's sitting up with her left eye wide open. The right side of her face is droopy.

"Granny!" Lulu rushes to her, and Mom tells me that this is the first time she's been sitting up since the stroke. I get in on the hugging and Granny gives us half a grin.

"Eye oo girls," she whispers, and we squeeze her hands, both the one that squeezes back and the one that can't.

We don't stay long. The nurses want to bathe her and they tell us to come back during regular visiting hours.

Lulu goes to work, and Mom and I head home. She scrambles eggs while I shower, and then we sit down at the kitchen table. I don't usually drink coffee, but she puts a mug in front of me and I sip. It tastes almost good and I drink a little more. We're both starving and I'm glad Mom is not too upset about

Granny to eat. Not that she's ever been too worried to eat. We make small talk about my job and various friends and neighbors. I ask how the typing is coming along, even though she's never mentioned it. She pretends that it's been an open topic all along and says she's pretty accurate now, but only types thirty-six words a minute. The precise figure tells me she's serious about this, and I think back to high school and tell her that thirty-six words a minute is pretty good for a beginner, especially if she's not making mistakes at that speed.

"What's your goal?" I ask, afraid to be more specific. I don't want her to just blow this off as a lark when it's clear to me that it isn't.

"I don't know, what do you think? Sixty?"

I wasn't expecting a typing speed, I was expecting to hear that she wants to work at a law firm or an advertising agency or something. I shift gears mentally.

"Sixty would be really good for almost any job," I say. She must be thinking about a job, not writing her memoirs, if she's timing herself and counting her typos.

"Unless you were going all out for court reporting or something—then you'd need to go way up, eighty or ninety." I had a pin for ninety, but that's just because I was bored silly after the first two weeks and had to go for speed to keep from falling asleep in class.

"Of course, you'd need to learn shorthand too if you wanted to be a court reporter. Probably even a private secretary, although I don't know—I think they mostly use Dictaphones now."

She frowns.

"There is probably a shorthand book in the attic, but if you really want to work in an office, just start with the typing part. Call Kelly Girl and see what typing speed they expect. Then you'll know what your goal is."

We're only talking about this to avoid talking about Granny, and I'm here for Granny and want to move on.

"So how is Granny really?" Kind of abrupt but I'm feeling a little weird, maybe from lack of sleep and the coffee. Somehow, my mug is empty.

"Well, she was a lot better today, but Lulu is sure she's not coming home and that we have to find a nursing home. I think she's wrong. What do you think?"

I ignore the question and ask her what the doctors say.

"Oh, doctors, they don't know." And she starts to tell me about a friend's mother who had a stroke.

"Okay, they don't know everything, but what have they been saying?"

"That she won't be able to live by herself anymore."

I can tell that she hasn't said this out loud before. She doesn't want it to be true. No one wants it to be true.

"And she can't stay here, of course. Not with all these steps. You'd work yourself to death." I want to let her off the hook right away because it's likely that her brother is expecting her to do just that.

"That's what Lawrence wants me to do," she says, so I know I was right about her brother.

"Is he going to come over here and help? Or pay someone to help you?"

"Pfffft. Girl's work. Not his responsibility, he says."

"So, we're going to look at nursing homes today? Just in case she can't come home and can't come here? Do you have any in mind?"

"Lulu got a list from the hospital of the ones that have a unit for stroke rehab, or whatever they call it."

"Well then, let's go. Or should we wait for Lulu?"

"She's off at two today, so we'll start then. Don't you want to take a nap or anything?"

I don't; I'm revved up on nerves or coffee or the need to do something.

"Not really. Should we be doing something else?"

"Well, Lulu made me promise that I would talk to you about Granny's car."

I feel a flush of anger on top of the nerves and coffee buzz.

"You mean the car that Granny gave me four years ago in payment for taking care of her all summer after she fell and broke her hip? That car? The blue Chevy that I was supposed to take back to school for sophomore year?"

"We've been over all that," Mom says, her voice as loud and angry as mine. Then she slumps down in her chair.

"Oh honey." Tears slide down her face, and to my astonishment, I find myself crying too.

The fact is that I hadn't really wanted a car. I wanted Granny to be well and driving it herself, and I didn't want to have to worry about gas and oil and flat tires and friends wanting to borrow it. But Mom and Granny had promised it to me if I would come home and stay with Granny while she recovered. And then at the end of the summer, Granny had miraculously stopped needing a walker and found she could drive just fine, and nothing was said about me taking the car. My nineteen-year-old self was incensed, even if I was also secretly relieved that I didn't have to take on the burden of car ownership.

"Didn't you know that was just a ploy to get you to come home for the summer? We knew you'd be gone for good after that. We just wanted you here one last summer."

"I know, Mom," I say, and I suppose I had always known. I get up and wash my face, blow my nose, and get a glass of orange juice. No more coffee for me.

"So, what about the car, Mom? Do you need it? Does Lulu want it? Should we sell it?"

"No, no, not that. Now it really is yours, absolutely positively."

I'm skeptical but I don't want to argue, so I don't say anything.

"Really," Mom goes on. "Lulu had the title changed and everything." She puts on a wry grin. "I don't think she trusted us."

"Lulu knew? About the car?"

"Of course she did. She was what, sixteen or seventeen? She was not the baby sister you thought she was, even then. She paid attention when we thought she was just zoned out listening to the Monkees or whatever that horrible music was. Bubblegum, wasn't it called?"

So, Lulu knew, and now she's making sure I finally get the car. I'm not sure I want it any more than I did four years ago. It's got to be fifteen years old by now, and I still don't have the money to lavish gas and oil and tires on it, never mind insurance and license plates and whatever else a car demands.

"She even took it to Bob's and had him check it over. New belts and whatnot. It's ready to go."

I can see that it won't be easy to say no to the car, and I'm embarrassed about my earlier tantrum. I give in without a fight. At least I won't be going back to Saint Louis in the smoky confines of a Greyhound bus.

"Shall we go take a look at it then?"

The car is spotless, literally. It's been washed and waxed and vacuumed and emptied of whatever Granny might have allowed to accumulate in the glove box and trunk. There is no sign of rust, and I remember that the car has spent every night of its existence in Granny's garage, and most days too. She liked to take the bus downtown and she liked to walk to the shops and church, which were near her little house. She mostly took the car on drives in the country or to visit friends in the hospital or the suburbs, and she only did that in nice weather. It's likely that the car never tasted road salt. Unfortunately, its new life in Saint Louis is going to be a shock.

"Maybe I should take your car, or Lulu's, and let you have this one. It would be a shame to let this one sit out in the rain and snow at my apartment."

"Ha! You think either of us could coddle it like Granny did? Nope, it's yours and you're taking it. Besides, you'll need it to take some things back with you."

"What things?"

"Well, obviously we're going to have to start clearing out the house. There's no use pretending. I mean, I know I'm the one who's been saying that Granny will be back, but I know she won't. And I bet you can use a few things for your apartment. No point just selling it all or giving away things you can use."

She's right, and I'm a little excited about having some of Granny's things, but I'm instantly ashamed, too. The tears start up again.

"Stop it, let's just go inside. We don't have to do anything about any of it today."

So that's what we do, and we are still there, just looking and touching, when Granny's phone rings and Lulu is looking for us. We agree to meet at the first place on her list.

We don't like the smell in the lobby and turn right around and walk out.

"Do you think they're all going to be like that?"

No one can answer that question.

The second one smells better, but alarms are beeping the whole time we are there.

"It's just the call buttons," the director tells us when we ask about all the beeping. "They push the buttons and forget why. Sometimes they don't even know they pushed the button."

We exchange glances and leave.

"Mean, mean, mean. Even if it's a little bit true."

The third place is more promising, so we check on availability and rates. There are two rooms open, but they are both on the back side, facing into trees, she tells us with an apology in her tone.

"Is that bad?" we ask.

"Well, no, not really!" She goes into selling mode. "It's just that most of our residents want to watch people coming and going in the front. The rooms in the back are larger and cheaper because people say there is nothing to see."

Granny loves trees and birds, so we don't see the back rooms as a problem, and we put a hold on one of them.

"Let's ask for the corner one," I say to Mom and Lulu. "Granny's hearing is still good and it might be quieter." I know that I'm the one who wants quiet, but the place is rather noisy and I don't think she'll like having to listen to someone else's TV programs. She's not used to watching daytime TV, and all the rooms here seem to have the TVs on.

"Okay," Mom says as we walk out, "I say we go with this one. I don't think I can keep looking."

Lulu and I are glad she said it so we didn't have to. We go back to the hospital and find Granny napping quietly. I take her hand and she opens her left eye and smiles her half smile. "Elle," she whispers, and falls asleep again. We tiptoe out and go home to talk about what to move to Granny's room and what to store or sell or give away. We agree to store some things, just in case, but sell the house, which has too many steps, with the bedroom upstairs and the laundry in the basement. Maybe an apartment, we tell each other. One with an elevator. We're kidding ourselves, but it's the best we can do. I am yawning by seven and they shoo me off to bed at eight.

On Saturday, we visit Granny off and on during the day. Once she's sitting up; the rest of the time she's lying down, sometimes asleep and sometimes just drowsy. She seems to be at peace but rouses a little when we arrive. In between, I test drive the car and thank Lulu profusely for making all the arrangements. She insists that it was nothing, but I can see that she's proud that she got it all done before I arrived.

Going into Granny's house without her there is the hardest thing we do. Lulu and Mom are insistent that I start making a pile of things to take home with me.

"Don't you want the sewing machine?"

I don't see sewing as part of the life of an economist, but I remember Granny teaching me to sew on her Singer Featherweight, and it seems like the sort of thing she won't be using anyway, so I say okay.

"What about the toaster, the waffle iron, the Hobart mixer?" I put them in the pile.

"You only have that one set of sheets, right? And one pillow? Take these." I let them add to the pile too.

I'm aware that they are slipping in other treasures, and I let them. They are going to have to bear the burden of emptying the house, and if this makes it a little easier, I'll let them do it.

On Saturday night, Mom announces that we're going to the nine-fifteen Mass, so I appear at eight-thirty in my raspberry dress. Lulu sees me and her eyes open wide.

"Where did you get my dress?" She's accusatory, a teenage sister again.

"Your dress? You sent it to me, in that box with my books and my radio!" I'm a teenager again too, but I bite back a comment about the typewriter that was not in the box.

Lulu turns on Mom. "You sent her my dress? I've looked all over for that dress."

"Well, you never said anything. And anyway I thought you said you couldn't wear sleeveless to work."

Lulu takes a deep breath, but not so much to calm herself as to prepare for shouting. "That didn't mean I didn't want it."

"Hey, Lu—it's okay, you can have it. I didn't even want it at first, although I've gotten kind of fond of it. I can see why you want it. I'll take it off. Really."

I don't have anything else to wear, but I'm more than happy to take the dress off and give it back.

Lulu returns to her twenties.

"You know, it looks great on you. It really does. You keep it." I try to think of some way to make it up to her, but nothing comes to mind.

"No, it's okay. I've worn it so many times I think people are sick of it. Maybe we can trade. You wear this and I'll wear something you're getting tired of." I'll miss the dress, but I am wondering if people think it's the only dress I own. They'd be right, but still.

Lulu decides that might be the best solution, and we go through her closet and dress me up in a skirt and blouse that I would like a lot if they weren't polyester.

After Mass, we visit Granny again and find her sitting up and cheerful but not talking at all. We don't stay very long, and she doesn't seem to mind when we leave. We go out for brunch and don't talk about how Granny is doing.

In the afternoon, we load up Granny's car so I can leave early Monday morning. We're all aching inside, but we get through it and I realize again that as hard as it is for me to leave, it will be harder in the long run on the ones who are staying.

Over dinner, we finally talk about the typewriter again. "I want to work sitting on my butt like the rest of you, instead of standing on my feet," Mom confesses. I tell her I'm proud of her and don't need the typewriter anymore. I tell her to practice by writing a book on it, *Memoirs of a Garage Hairstylist*. So, we are able to go to bed on a light note.

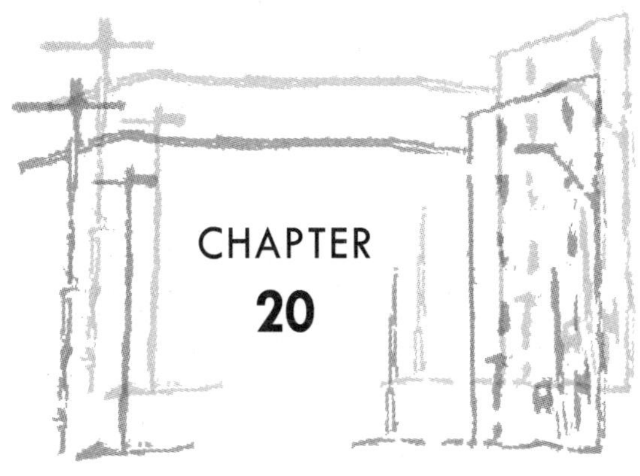

CHAPTER 20

Before dawn on Monday, I say goodbye to Lulu and Mom and drive by the hospital without stopping. "Bye, Granny," I say with a wave toward her window. I cry until I'm out of town and back on the interstate, driving too fast. I slow down. I don't want to talk to the Highway Patrol and explain why I'm crying while speeding in a car jammed with old-lady things. By the time the sun is rising behind me, I've got the radio on and have even started singing along.

I pull into the little parking area behind my apartment building in late afternoon, pleased that the car ran well and I've made it before the afternoon sun started searing my lap. The lot only has six spaces for twelve apartments, but it's nearly empty, as it usually is. I back into the space closest to the door, get out, and stretch. I start with the box in the front seat and pull out a box with a blanket spilling out the top. I manage to hit the horn with the corner of the box, and a loud beep startles me. I kick the door closed and turn, but the blanket is caught in the door and also stuck under something in the box. The box thuds to the ground, digging an edge into the top of my foot.

"*Damn!*" I shout and hop around on one foot. "Damn it."

I pick up the box and make it to the door, where I have to put it down and fumble for the key. It doesn't work, and I realize that I'm trying to open my door with Granny's house key, which is on the ring with the car key.

"Damn again," I say to myself but out loud.

"Hold on, let me help you." I hear a voice from above, literally from above. I look up. God isn't female, or maybe she is.

The door opens and a woman my age appears. She stands back and holds it wide open.

"I'm Marianne, in 1A." She pronounces it "wunna" and it takes me a minute to decipher.

"Oh, thanks." She must think I'm a nitwit, between the honking and swearing over a single cardboard box. "I'm Novelle, in 3D."

"Nice to meet you—you have more stuff to carry?"

"Yes, but it's a lot more. I can get it."

"Don't be silly, someone helped me move in. It's the least I can do."

We haul it all into the tiny lobby, and I explain that I'm not really moving in, I'm just moving more stuff in. I find myself telling her all about my trip home.

"But enough about that—are you new here?" I ask.

As we shift the boxes and bags to the third floor, along with the Featherweight sewing machine that weighs a ton, she tells me that she moved in a year ago last May, after graduating from WashU. She's starting grad school in the fall.

"You've been here all this time? I've never seen you."

"I went to New York for the summer with a boyfriend," she says. "Didn't work out, so I'm back." She seems perfectly okay with the end of the boyfriend.

"We're not supposed to sublet, but you probably know how

clueless Mrs. Marzello is. I just told my friend Jake to lie low. He probably never even turned the lights on. And he spends his days with his own true love, the big computer in Sever Hall. So, I'm not surprised that you never saw him. Pleased, in fact!"

I give her the highlights of my own experience with Mrs. Marzello and the mix-up in apartments. The name David Black doesn't ring any bells with her.

We've got it all upstairs now, so I open the apartment door and Marianne waltzes in.

"Look at all this open space," she says, spinning around. "I've got too much junk in mine. And look at your view!"

I'm standing still with my mouth open. She should not have room to waltz. My sofa and chair are gone. I look in my bedroom. The bed is gone too, although my sheets are in a heap on the floor. I open the closet door. Everything is there, even David Black's coat and shirts. I check the kitchen. My table and chairs are gone. My mind races. Okay, maybe the couch and chair weren't really mine, and maybe David Black came back and Mrs. Marzello let him in to get them. But the table and chairs are mine. And the typewriter, where is that? Where are my lamps?

"Novelle, what's wrong? Is something wrong?"

I take a deep breath, and then another one.

"My furniture. It's gone. I had a table and two chairs here, and a couch and chair there, and of course the bed. There was a bed when I left, not a pile of sheets." I explain about the bamboo couch and chair and bed. "But the chairs and table were mine for sure. And how could someone come in here and just take it without a note? Who even has a key other than Mrs. Marzello?"

We look around to make sure there is no note, then go through my mailbox, and finally inspect the door for signs of forced entry. We find nothing.

"Wait a minute," Marianne says. "You said bamboo, right? Did the cushions have a green tropical sort of print?"

I nod.

"There was a chair like that in the parking lot, sort of by the dumpster, when I got here on Friday. I assumed someone was throwing it out and took it over to that charity shop on Skinker."

"Molly's shop?"

"Yes. Let me call her and see if it's still there."

Marianne looks up the number and calls and tells Molly that she needs the chair back, that it wasn't abandoned after all. She hangs up and tells me that we can pick it up later today or tomorrow. Marianne is feeling responsible even though she's actually saved me—or saved my one piece of furniture anyway.

"So that can wait. Now, we'd better call the police."

I do, but they are not very helpful. No sign of breaking and entering, they say, makes it hard to prove a crime. Did anyone else have keys? Did I contact the landlord? They tell me I should be more careful with the keys to my apartment.

I give up on the police and tell Marianne that I'm calling Mrs. Marzello. Marianne looks at her watch and rocks her head back and forth. "Maybe not too late in the day. Kinda on the edge."

I look at my watch and say, "What? I'm supposed to be at work by three-thirty."

"Go ahead and call, and then I'll run you over to campus. I'm assuming you don't have a parking sticker yet. Actually, I don't have one either, but I'm heading out to Maplewood to do some shopping, so I can drop you off. I'll go get my keys. Or better yet, I'll wait—a call to Mrs. Marzello is always an experience. If you don't mind?"

I call and get the older Mrs. Marzello, who doesn't seem sleepy. This time I tell her my whole story instead of asking for her daughter-in-law. She listens and chuckles.

"Hold on, let's see what we can do." She sounds like she's planning some mischief. I cover the mouthpiece and tell Marianne that I got the mother-in-law this time. She nods and smiles, mischief in her face too.

Meanwhile, I'm not hearing anything on the phone. Maybe they have an office phone with a mute button, or maybe she's had to go in search of her daughter-in-law.

After a minute or so, I hear voices, first far away and then louder. I strain to hear. They are talking about keys.

"So, you take that stuff right back over there, all of it, right now!" At this point, she's close to the phone and I can hear every word.

"Mom said it's not hers so I could have it. I already sold it to a guy."

Old Mrs. Marzello's voice comes back to me, kind and grandmotherly. "My grandson made a mistake, he, um . . . got the wrong apartment."

I hear "no I didn't" dimly in the background.

"And he will be over tonight to return it," she says, very firmly, so I assume she's giving her grandson a stern look. "Will seven o'clock be okay?"

"Yes, thank you. Seven is perfect." Before she hangs up, I hear further protests in the background, ending with Mrs. Marzello saying, "Well then you can just take her the money."

"You should have told them to have the locks changed," Marianne says. "Sorry I didn't think of that ninety seconds ago."

"One thing at a time. I'll do that tomorrow. Or maybe not. Do you think I could just have them changed myself and deduct it from the rent?"

Marianne thinks about what she knows of the Marzello family. "Worth a try, but call and tell her first. Just tell her, don't ask her. Call during cocktail hour. If you get the old one, she'll tell the young one while she's drunk. The young one will forget but the old one won't."

I make sure I have keys and we lock up and leave. Marianne turns back and looks under my doormat, then feels along the top of the doorframe. "Well, look at this. Better call the locksmith right away." She hands me a key that looks suspiciously like my door key. "There was one under the mat when I moved in."

CHAPTER 21

My mind is full of the past weekend when I get to the Y, but Arlo's class finally clears my head. He shows us how to exaggerate facial features to comic effect, using himself and Abe Lincoln as examples. We want him to do Richard Nixon, but he says he's been done to death. Then he does it anyway.

In the second part of the class, he has us try the poster paint, although he only brings out the black bottles. Some kids choose to stick with the markers. I like the way the brush can swirl the paint, and I'm glad I don't have to figure out colors. I make a single six-foot tree, a caricature of the sycamore outside my window.

"Interesting," Arlo says. "You're looking out on it, not up at it. Interesting." This week he's gone before I finish closing up. I walk home and find a note from Marianne sticking out of my mailbox: "Stop in 1A for a second."

I knock on her door and say "Wunna?" when I hear her "Yes?" from inside. She opens the door.

"First tell me—what's 'Wunna'?"

"Oh, it's 'Won a,'" and she spells it for me. "As in 'You just won a trip to Kalamazoo!' I'd rather have 'To-Be,' but this is all that was available."

I tell her about my travails with 2B, finally settling for the second-best 3D. "Or maybe third best—'Won a' is pretty good too."

We agree that 2A is for alcoholics, 3A is a shoe size, and 4A, if we had a fourth floor, would be "for a what?" I feel like I've finally found a friend and hope it's true.

She offers me a glass of wine and I sip it, knowing I'm dead tired, sleep deprived, coming down off the high of Big Art, and facing the possible if not certain arrival of a Marzello at almost any minute, an event that could go well or end with another call to the police. We imagine various scenarios, most of which are preposterous, and the laughter feels therapeutic.

At eight o'clock, I'm yawning and tell Marianne I'm going to give up on the Marzello grandson showing up tonight and go to bed. She says she'll keep an eye out, and we exchange phone numbers.

"Oh my God, Novelle. We got so involved I forgot why I told you to stop in. Molly dropped your chair off. She said it's too big for my Squareback, which by the way it is but we could have tied it on top, you know? You didn't tell me you knew her! She was so upset. Anyway, she's keeping an eye out for new furniture for you, but meanwhile you should be able to make a sort of bed out of the chair cushions. Or you can stay here, but it's a bit of a tip, as the Brits would say."

"You got my bamboo chair back? Where is it?" I look around the "tip" and don't see it, but it's pretty full in here.

"Oh, it's upstairs outside your door. I was pretty sure no one would get it past me since I can see the front door from here. That's a blessing and a curse."

I'm not as confident as she is, having lost the chair once, but I thank her and take myself upstairs, where the chair is sitting in the hall just as she said. For a moment, I think I see DB sitting in it, and it occurs to me that I haven't seen him for ages. Maybe not since Ruth spent the night. I hope she didn't take him, and then I hope for her sake that she did. It's hard to imagine her getting him on the bus, though.

I wrangle the chair through the door and examine it under the bright ceiling light. It seems no worse for wear, in spite of its adventures. I give it a little spritz of lice spray anyway. Thirty minutes and one shower later, I truly give up on getting my furniture back. I put the cushions on the floor end to end, spread out my sheets, and go to sleep.

CHAPTER 22

The next morning, my neck aches from sleeping on a two-part mattress that parted ways in the night. Marianne calls to me as I am walking out the front door of the apartment building.

"God, I feel like I'm spying on you. I hope you're not creeped out. I just wanted to let you know that the kid didn't show last night, so I waited until eleven and called Mrs. Marzello. I told her to get a check for a hundred dollars over here by eight o'clock this morning—which it almost is. *And* to have the locksmith here today. Sorry to be such a nosy nobody, but she is so annoying. Usually I just work around her, but this was just too much. Feel free to tell me to shut up and mind my own business. Really. Want some coffee?"

Somehow it seems rude to say no, so I say yes and she brings it outside just as a black Lincoln rolls up.

"Mrs. Marzello," Marianne whispers to me. "Just pretend you already met her. She won't remember."

"Hi, Mrs. Marzello!" I say as cheerfully as I can manage. "Thanks for coming by so early."

That sounds horribly fake to me, but she takes it at face value and walks over and shakes my hand.

"Here is the check," she says, curt but not overly so. "And the locksmith will be here after lunch. I'll be here to let him in."

"That's okay, Mrs. Marzello," Marianne chimes in. "Locksmiths can let themselves in. Besides, it's your regular locksmith, right? So, he already has a key. He can just leave the new key in Novelle's mailbox. Or better yet, he can leave it with me. I'll be here all afternoon."

I'm not sure I should trust Marianne with a key to my apartment, but she seems more trustworthy than the Marzellos and she'll at least make sure the locksmith works on the right apartment.

The Lincoln glides away and I thank Marianne again.

"How did you get her to do that?"

"I may have mentioned something about Legal Aid." She smiles. "Take the coffee, I'm sure you need it."

I stuff the check in my pocket, wondering if one hundred dollars is enough to replace everything that is missing, and walk slowly toward campus, nursing my headache and my coffee. Again, I find the mug empty before I know it.

At the Y, Arlo is talking and waving his arms, so I don't have to figure out how much to tell Betty about my weekend, the missing furniture, and Marianne.

"We'll call it 'The Big Draw'—get it? It's drawing and it will draw people in." Arlo is explaining a new idea for freshman orientation.

"I get it, I get it," Betty says. "But I think freshman orientation is all set by now."

"Well then, let's do it for WILD. Or both. It can even just be sort of ad hoc."

Arlo stops enthusing for long enough to fill me in on his idea, which is giant paintings to encourage people to check out the Y's programs.

"I know, let's draw it on the side of Umrath, pointing down our steps." He draws a sketch on a slip of paper.

"We'll never get that approved—once the university lets people start painting buildings the whole campus will look like the underpass."

"But tempera!"

"Nope. It's a great idea, but keep thinking. And work it out with Novelle; she's in charge of . . . that."

Arlo gives me a smile that is half pleased and half secretive and leaves. I give Betty the short version of the weekend—Granny is stable, Lulu and Mom are coping, and I am back with a car. I give her a little more detail on the missing furniture and Marianne's help. I tell her what I didn't tell Marianne, which is that I feel scared and violated and angry and helpless.

"Treat yourself like you treated your freshmen when you were the RA," Betty says.

"I did—I called the police, just like I would have called the police for one of my freshmen. Only the campus police would have done something!"

"I didn't say to treat the situation, I said treat yourself like you treated your freshmen."

"But this is my home, it's my whole life," I say, realizing as the words come out of my mouth that I'm repeating what dozens of freshmen wailed to me when they saw their boyfriends kissing other girls or when they got a C on a pop quiz because everyone else in class cheated and the professor graded on the curve and then just smirked when the student protested.

Betty raises her eyebrows but doesn't say anything.

"Okay, it's not my life. It's just some furniture. Furniture I didn't even pay for, now that you mention it."

"I didn't mention it."

"You just didn't say it out loud." I toss my hat on the coat rack. "They got the typewriter too, and the lamps. And I don't know what else."

"Now that's just mean," Betty says. "We'll come up with something. Why don't you make a poster, with those little tags at the bottom with your phone number? Something like 'Looking for used typewriter, manual okay, must be cheap.'"

That's better than anything I can think of, so when I take a break for lunch, I draw a cartoon of my old typewriter and print WANTED across the top. Below, it says "Used typewriter, preferably manual, the cheaper the better." When Betty gets back, she tells me to put the Y number and my home number on it. I put the first one on the Y bulletin board at the top of our steps and plan to make more at home that night. When Arlo stops in later with his latest, slightly less preposterous idea for The Big Draw, he's carrying my poster.

"Is this yours?" he asks.

"Yep, I need a new one." He doesn't need the whole story.

"Hmm." He tells me his new plan for The Big Draw, which involves bedsheets instead of painting directly on buildings. I tell him he can't use purloined sheets from the South Forty dorms, but that if he has legitimate sheets we can sew them together and make a really big draw. I say "we" instead of "I" because owning a sewing machine suddenly feels frumpy and old.

I roll up the drawings I forgot to take home on Monday and leave the Y in time to stop at the bank and deposit Mrs. Marzello's check. On the walk across campus, I pass a poster board tied around a huge tree trunk. The entire poster is a drawing of an old manual typewriter with a sheet of paper rolled most of the way out the top. The paper says WANTED—DEAD OR ALIVE in huge letters. The word "dead" is lightly Xed out. The typewriter keys are labeled with "C—A—L—L" in the top row and my home and the Y phone numbers on the second and third rows. The space bar announces REWARD. I am still laughing when I come across Arlo tying a second one to a fence on the U City side of the pedestrian bridge. This time I give him a kiss on the lips and he returns it. I tell him I want to see the proposal for his latest Big Draw idea by the end of the week and scurry off to the bank.

When I get home, my new key is in the mailbox and Marianne doesn't answer when I stop to thank her. I don't see her until Wednesday evening, when she knocks on my door to ask if everything is okay and see if I have made progress on replacing my furniture. The phone rings as we are talking, and she walks around looking at my Big Art drawings while I answer.

"Hey, are you the person looking for that typewriter?" It's a young male voice but not familiar.

"Yes, do you have one for sale?"

"Oh, I thought you were looking for that particular one. The poster says there is a reward."

"Do you have it?"

"How much is the reward?"

I wonder if the caller is someone Mrs. Marzello's son sold it to. Or even the son himself, although surely he wouldn't be stupid enough to try to collect a reward.

"It depends. I'd have to see what kind of shape it's in."

"It's fine, just fine."

"Does it work? Did you try to type anything on it?"

He finally admits that it doesn't work at all and that he bought it "from a guy." I tell him I'll meet him at the Dairy Queen in five minutes and hang up.

"Did you do these?" Marianne asks before I can tell her about the call.

"Yes, it's for a class at the Y called Big Art. It's just a three-session summer thing. A kid called Arlo is teaching it, I think it's just kind of a lark for him."

"Oh, Arlo. He's a fun guy." She turns to me, then looks at me closely.

"Everyone loves Arlo," she says pointedly, "and Arlo loves everyone."

I know it's a warning and I'm pretty sure my face is turning red. She turns back to the art.

"These are really interesting. Maybe you could do one for me."

I'd like to do something for her in return for all she's done for me in just three days, so I say I'd love to and we move on to talk about the poster and the phone call.

"Yikes, I'm late—I'm supposed to be meeting the guy right now!"

"I'm coming with!" Marianne says, and we race outside and run down Wingate.

I forgot to tell him that I'd be the one in the hat, and I'm not wearing it anyway. I know nothing about the guy we're looking for other than that he's male. He's not hard to find, though. He's leaning against the Dairy Queen with a typewriter at his feet. I'm sure it's my typewriter and I'm resolved to take it home no matter what. I kneel down and look at it closely and see that the lock is on that holds the keys in place and prevents it from typing. That's why he thinks it doesn't work. I leave the lock on.

"I'm Joe Ellis." I look up and see that he's introducing himself to Marianne.

"Mary," says Marianne. I wonder why the alias. Is it because this guy may be a thief, or because he's Black? Or is Mary actually a nickname?

"And I'm Novelle," I say, although it seems to come out as Noelle.

We all seem to be at an impasse. I decide to come clean. Prevarication is too hard for me.

"This looks like my typewriter," I finally say. "Mine was stolen from my apartment sometime in the last week." I gesture vaguely in the direction from which we came, which covers at least a hundred apartments.

"We're not saying you stole it, though," says Marianne. "But she'd like it back." Her tone says, "And we're not leaving here without it."

"How much did you pay for it?" I ask, hoping it's not much so I can just give him his money back and go home.

"Ten bucks. But if it's yours, you can just take it. I don't want any trouble." His voice is low and earnest. I think of all the boys I know who would be demanding a reward, insisting they bought it legitimately.

"Would you tell us who sold it to you?"

He thinks about that.

"I think you deserve ten bucks for bringing it back," Marianne says softly. I was hoping for five bucks, but I'm okay with ten, since a new one will cost more than that. Marianne is just hoping to get him to give up the name. We all wait silently.

"Uh, I don't know his name, but he had a bunch of stuff in a pickup truck on DeBaliviere. You know where those stores are? Around there."

"Is he there often?"

"Most Saturdays. Hey, don't say anything, okay? He thinks he's Sylvester Stallone or something."

"You look like you could hold your own." This from Marianne, who is looking him up and down.

"Don't work that way," Joe says, voice still soft.

"Our lips are sealed," I say, handing him two five-dollar bills. Marianne picks up the typewriter and puts it down again with an "Oooph."

Joe ignores the money and picks up the typewriter easily. "The least I can do is carry it for you." He looks at us. "Or maybe you'd rather I not."

I could run back and get the car, but that would be awkward all around.

"That would be great, if you wouldn't mind," I say, and glance at Marianne. She looks concerned, then shrugs, and we start down the street.

I've still got the bills in my hand, and Marianne takes them, making a shushing face. When we turn onto the walk that our building shares with the one next to it, Joe puts the typewriter down and says, "I'll let you take it from here." I realize what he's doing. This way, he can't know which of the twenty-four apartments belong to us. He's sparing us the embarrassment of letting him know that we are afraid to let him into our apartments.

"Here," Marianne says, shoving the two bills into his pants pocket. I giggle; that's something I can't imagine myself doing. "She got her typewriter, with free delivery, and you still have to buy one."

Joe protests, but he's laughing too and I heft the typewriter for the short walk to the door. Marianne opens the door for me and then runs back down the street. When she returns, she's got Joe's phone number.

"I'm going to find that guy a typewriter," she says, "for less than ten dollars." And I have no doubt that she will.

CHAPTER 23

On Thursday, I take down the posters and tell Betty the story of the typewriter. Arlo arrives with his latest plan and two brand-new bedsheets. They are light blue, so they can't be confused with dorm sheets, and he's neatly printed "Sheets purchased through the Ray Nesbitt Memorial Fund for Outrageous Art" along the hem in small letters. His almost-final drawing is of a hand coming up out of the door to the Y. The hand is printing "The Big Draw" in giant letters. He has a neatly typed proposal that includes getting permission to hang it on the side of Umrath Hall. I tell him that permissions are his department. I also tell him that the hand is a little too ghostly.

"Make it a strong hand," I tell him, as though I am now the art expert. "Exaggerate the knuckles a little."

He snorts, but fiddles a bit with the small drawing. Then he sees that I've brought his posters back and I tell him the typewriter story and thank him for his help.

"So, Marianne promised him a typewriter?" He says her name in an easy way that tells me he knows her.

"I don't think she promised. I think she said she'd look around."

He ponders that and puts one of the wanted posters on the desk. He borrows Betty's Wite-Out and changes "Reward" to "$10 or less."

"I'm going to go get permission for sheeting," he says. "You can put the posters up this time." He runs backward down the hall toward the door. Thirty seconds later, he's back. "You two are going to look for that guy on DeBaliviere on Saturday, aren't you? Are you sure you want to get into that?"

"I'm just going to cruise by and see if my table and chairs are there," I say. "Or my lamps. If they aren't, I'll just keep driving." I see his puzzled face and add, "I brought my grandmother's car back last weekend. I'll be totally incognito."

"Okay," he says, and turns to leave, then turns back. "But what if it's there? Your stuff, I mean."

"I might buy it back."

He leaves, but more slowly.

Betty has been quiet, and now she says, "You probably shouldn't do that on Saturday, but I guess Marianne will be with you." She says it as a question, but I don't answer. Marianne has already told me she's going away camping for the weekend.

Thursday is farmers' market day, and I stop on the way home. I'm wondering how to cook eggplant when I hear a language I don't recognize next to me. An elderly woman dressed in black is haggling over a flat of tomatoes using a lot of hand waving. A young man comes over and leans down, talks to her for a few seconds, and then works out a deal with the woman running the stall. They move on and I look up to ask the woman about eggplant and see she's watching the old woman and the guy, who must be her grandson. She turns back to me.

"Russians, I think. Must be Russian Jews—refugees, you know. I guess they have to live somewhere."

A customer next to me speaks up. "Of course they do, and why not here? They pay their way. And they've suffered enough, haven't they?" Her tone is more exasperated than strident. I turn to her.

"Sure, of course," I said. "I just didn't know."

"No one knows, that's the problem."

She moves away and I drag my attention back to the eggplant, which seems pretty boring at this point. I buy tomatoes and peppers—I know what to do with those, at least.

CHAPTER 24

On Saturday, I have second thoughts about bearding the thief in his den on DeBaliviere. I got my money, after all. On the other hand, I like my yellow table with its black-and-yellow chairs. On the other hand, I don't even know what time he'll be there. I can't drive around all day. On the other hand, he needs to learn a lesson. On the other hand, it's stupid to take any risks. That neighborhood is pretty rundown, and those shops are mostly boarded up. On the other hand, four fingers and a thumb. I set off at ten. I'm just going to drive by.

But when I see my table and chairs on the sidewalk, I park and get out. He doesn't know me, after all. I'm just someone passing through.

"How much for those?" Someone is asking the guy who seems to be selling. Joe is right, he looks tough. "I'll give you ten bucks."

Tough Guy says, "Can't do it for less than twenty."

The first guy hesitates and turns to a woman who has just walked up. "What do you think, honey?"

I want her to say no, but then I decide that my best chance is with witnesses.

"I'll take them," I almost shout, although my voice quavers a little. I clear my throat. The couple turns to look at a kitchen stool. I pick up the chairs and head for my car.

"Hey, you have to pay first!"

"I'll pay. Just help me with the table."

I know how it comes apart, so I'm able to get the table into the trunk quickly and fit the chairs on top.

"You a dealer or something?" he asks. "I've got some other stuff too."

I start to ask about lamps, but he might not be as stupid as I think, so instead I say, "Like what?"

He's got a station wagon full of small appliances and I look for my lamps. I only see one of them, but I pick it up. The other couple asks him about the side table. I shove the lamp in my back seat, jump in the driver's seat, and close the door as quietly as I can. I turn on the ignition with one hand while I lock the door with the other. I stomp the gas pedal and pull away just as he reaches for my door handle.

"Say hello to your grandmother for me," I yell. He chases me on foot for a while, but of course he can't catch me. When I slow down, I look in the rearview mirror and see him waving his arms at his other customers. He's trying to get the back of the station wagon closed. I take that as my cue to disappear before he can follow me. I speed a little getting to Skinker and then drive south. I go past campus and then turn randomly left and right until I'm deep in a residential neighborhood. I park for a while, until my pulse stops racing and I come to terms with what I've done, which is steal back furniture that Mrs. Marzello technically paid me for last Tuesday, a small moral quandary. I could have paid him with her money, I realize, but I'm still out a couch and a bed and one more lamp. I give up the moral question and worry about him recognizing my car. I don't have an answer for that, but I drive slowly home, watching at every turn, and take the furniture up to my apartment. Then I drive to campus, park in the reserved wedding spaces, and face my next bride. At least he won't be looking for my car here.

The sky has turned dark, with a greenish cast. I unlock the Y. It's early and the bridal party hasn't arrived yet. I find the radio on Jackie's desk and turn it on. Only FM works down here, but that's enough. I dial around for a while until I get a weather report. There is a tornado watch for the entire Saint Louis bi-state area. I hear laughter and go meet the bride. They are a cheerful group, with no undercurrents of family strife. We probably won't need the copy of *I'm OK—You're OK* that I've taken to leaving out.

I remind them about alcoholic beverages and retreat to the back to check the weather. The tornado watch has been upgraded to a tornado warning, which means take cover. We are already taking cover, so I don't have to move the bridal party, but this could disrupt the wedding. I slip up the back stairs and crack open the door. The tornado sirens are wailing. I close the door. There's nothing in my fact sheet about this situation, but surely a former RA can cope.

I take the radio into the lounge and tell the bridal party that we are under a tornado warning and remind them that we're already in a tornado shelter.

"What about the guests? They should be in Graham Chapel by now."

Graham Chapel can surely withstand a tornado, but all that stained glass is a big problem. I'm pretty sure it has a basement, but I don't know if it's habitable or even unlocked.

"You all stay here, let me go investigate. I'm sure everything will be fine." I'm not sure, but I can't tell a bride that on her wedding day.

I walk outside into utter stillness and sprint across to the chapel. The officiant, who today is a school chaplain whose face is vaguely familiar, has everyone crowded into the lobby, which has fewer windows than the chapel. I try to think—could we get them across to the library? It has two levels below ground, so that would have to be safe. I ask the chaplain. He cracks open the door and peeks out. The stillness has been replaced by furious winds.

"Too far," he says. "Too many trees, too much glass. Can you get them all in the Y?"

"It's all we've got," I say.

He gets everyone's attention and tells them to follow me. He'll go last.

I race toward the Y, then stop at the top of the stairs as I realize that many of the guests are elderly or in high heels and can't keep up with me. The bride's face appears in the door and I tell her to go downstairs and clear the way while her maid of honor holds the door open and I wait at the top of the outside stairs. I hope someone is alert enough to whisk away any of the lingerie that often gets left out when the bridal party leaves for the chapel.

Someone who looks like he could be the bride's father marshals the groomsmen and they practically carry several older women to the door. The wind howls. I realize that we'll never get them all down the steps and through the one door. I squeeze through the crush and race up the back stairs, then start yelling and waving. The chaplain sees me, or hears me, and starts redirecting some of the guests in my direction. I leave the first person in charge of holding the door and station the next few to help the high-heeled ones down the stairs.

The hallway fills up quickly and I start pulling out chairs and moving people away from the doors to let more people get through. I draft the bridesmaids to kick the kids out of the chairs in the lounge and seat their older aunts and uncles and grandmothers. The lights flicker and I wonder if we have any flashlights. A crowd has formed around the radio and I ask for an update, but no one hears me.

Eventually everyone is in and the doors are closed. I stand on the front stairs and look around for the chaplain.

"You're in charge," I tell him. "And we need a plan for if the lights go out. I don't know if we have any flashlights."

"Okay, you look for flashlights while I talk." Thank goodness he's up to the challenge. I can deal with a lot of things, but I don't know how to keep this crowd calm.

The chaplain starts clapping his hands slowly and gets the attention of the people nearest him.

"Hands up, everyone. Hands up." He holds both hands in the air and gets those around him to do the same. Gradually all hands go up and the entire space gets quiet. I reappear with one flashlight, and he calls me up beside him.

"This is . . ." he looks at me and I whisper my name. "This is Novelle, and we're going to get through this just fine. First of all, I want you all to say a silent prayer that the power doesn't go off." He says this cheerfully, but then he closes his eyes and bows his head. I can feel the room calm down.

"Thank you. Now Novelle is going to tell you about restrooms and first aid and so on."

We're next to the restrooms, so I point them out and tell them that I've got two flashlights if we need them, which we won't. I smile at the chaplain, and he nods.

"There are a few more chairs in the workroom, and if anyone is feeling unsteady, please ask me or one of the bridesmaids for help. We can find you a seat or get you a glass of water." I'm thinking the bridesmaids are the most likely to know where the sink is. "Water is in the workroom too. Now, who has the radio? Can you turn it up for us?"

The crowd around the radio leans in and turns up the volume, and we all listen to the tense voices of the announcers. I'm grateful that everyone is engrossed. I don't have any other ideas at the moment. I really, really hope that no one decides it would be a good idea to pass the time by singing. An image of the Y full of slightly windblown party guests earnestly singing "Kumbaya" comes into my head and I know I'm going to get the giggles, so I turn and go up the last few steps to the door and crack it open. I'll face the storm if I have to. I can't imagine what will happen if I start laughing uncontrollably in that nervous crowd. They'll either have hysterics and we'll need a squad of ambulances, or they'll be appalled and all stare at me stone faced while I make a fool of myself, and then they'll report me to the provost, and I'll be expelled before I even enroll in classes. The idea of a stern provost pronouncing sentence makes me relapse and I slip outside and let myself go.

Before I've regained control, a groomsman opens the door with a worried look. He sees me red-faced with tears running down my cheeks and gets the wrong idea. I tell him that I just had a vision of everyone down there singing "Kumbaya" to keep themselves calm. He looks at me like I'm a raving lunatic, and then the corners of his mouth turn up and he starts to laugh, which just sets me off again.

"Stop it," I say, shoving him as though he were an old pal. "Go back in there—they'll think you've blown away in the tornado."

"You go, I can't."

Another face appears in the door, and we try to explain but can't.

"It's okay," I finally choke out. "And look, it's clearing—no sirens."

The chaplain comes out and more people crowd onto the stairs.

"I think we've lost control," I tell him. "What is the radio saying?"

"The main part of the storm is across the river now," he says. "But there is still a watch until midnight. Let's get this wedding started while we can."

Any thought of an orderly exit is abandoned. The elderly and highest-heeled seem to have the sense to wait for the rush to abate. When everyone is gone, I race around putting furniture back where it belongs, picking up tissues, and washing glasses. I forget to watch for the bride, but it doesn't matter. Two of her friends find their own way in, and we gather up everything they need to take away. I lock up, checking both doors twice, and saunter home.

CHAPTER 25

I'm the first one in on Monday morning and am flipping the calendars to August when the phone rings.

"Campus Y," I say into the phone, voice a little raspy from lack of use.

"Campus Y? I was calling about a typewriter. Is this the right number?"

"I don't think so. We've got typewriters."

"Okay, well, your number was on a poster. It was kinda off the wall, so I guess the number was wrong."

The fog clears.

"Oh yes, a typewriter. We are looking for a typewriter. Or someone here is anyway. Sorry, it's early." I'm babbling, so I get back to the point. "Do you have one for sale?"

"I'm not sure we can sell them, but we do have some old ones that we don't use anymore. If you want one you could borrow it. I thought you were looking for a prop for a play or something. The one on the poster looked really old."

"Oh, right, we were using mine as a model." That's at least 99 percent true. "What happened is . . . well, a typewriter was stolen. A student's personal typewriter. So, we were trying to find a replacement for cheap. An old manual is fine, as long as it works. Just something for this student to write papers on."

I realize that I don't even know if Joe is a student, or if he still needs a typewriter, or if Marianne still has the number.

"In that case, I suppose we can just give you one of these. They're just gathering dust. Do you want to stop by today and choose one?"

We decide on one o'clock and at the last second I remember to ask where he is.

"Sorry, Economics. I'm Professor Pound. Edward Pound. Just talk to the receptionist. And you are?"

"Novelle. See you at one."

Great, I've been a total fool in front of someone who will as likely as not be my adviser. I find a staff directory and look him up. Department chair, even better. *How did this happen?*

Betty arrives and I tell her I have to run home and change my clothes. She laughs and tells me to stick my nose outside and tell her if I see one single student who is wearing anything at all different from the jean shorts and T-shirt I am wearing.

"And you're at least wearing a bra," she adds.

As it turns out, I worried for no good reason. The secretary is expecting me and walks me down to the basement. I had thought this through enough to have typing paper with me, and I try a few of the old manuals that are gathering dust. I check all the keys and choose the lightest one.

"I'd love to get these out of here," she tells me.

"If I run into anyone else who needs one, I'll send them to you," I tell her and get myself back to the Y. I don't take it home that night, though. I want to make sure Marianne still has the number and Joe still wants the typewriter. Maybe he has a car and can meet me here.

Today is the last day of Big Art and Arlo isn't there at a quarter to four, so I get out the roll of brown paper and the markers and poster paints and wonder what to do if he doesn't show. I can certainly let them draw, but they are here for the drama and outrageousness and ideas of Arlo. Maybe I'll reschedule for the next Monday. At four o'clock, I tell the group we'll give him until four-fifteen and meanwhile we'll talk about The Big Draw. I hope that Arlo didn't consider that a secret. At four-fourteen he arrives, winks at me, and mouths "I got permission," which I interpret as permission to hang the Big Draw sheets on the side of Umrath. He then rolls out huge sheets of brown paper and shouts, "Final exam in Big Art today!"

The final consists of Arlo shouting questions—"What is the number one purpose of Big Art?"—and waiting until everyone, including Arlo, has shouted an answer: "Impact! Drama! Entertainment!" The last question is: "What grade do you get in Big Art?" He gets a chorus of "A!" followed by a "Q!" and then a "Who frickin' cares!" and the exam is over. The rest of the session is only a little quieter as we switch to a free-for-all of horizontal drawings that results in cartoons of people lying down, an alligator, a line of giant ants, and a tree broken off near the ground and lying on its side.

"That's the tree outside my bedroom," the artist says grimly. "On Friday I was up in the leaves playing my recorder and on Saturday it looked like that."

On that somber note, everyone rolls up their drawings and most of them hug Arlo and tell him they love him and wish him luck on The Big Draw. He turns to me sharply.

"Did you tell them about that?"

"Might have done that." He looks hurt and I say, "I had to do something when you were late. Besides, you'll need help putting it up if nothing else. They'll help you. People love to be insiders."

"Okay, you're right and I was late." He seems mollified but doesn't say goodbye, he just disappears. I notice that the few sketches that we did before he got there are gone. I roll up my horizontal drawing, a life-size bamboo sofa with a cat curled up, asleep.

Marianne doesn't answer my knock that evening, so I slip a note under her door telling her I have a typewriter for Joe and walk upstairs reading my mail. I've got bills, so I write checks for those and walk to the post office just to enjoy the cool evening air. No lights are on at Marianne's when I return.

The trip to Economics and the act of flipping the calendars to August make me realize that I'm only a few weeks from starting grad school. I read through everything in my packet for the fourth or fifth time. I see that "A few TA positions will be available." I write down the name and phone number of the contact person. I look, but it doesn't say how much it pays and how many hours it takes. If that doesn't work out, I don't know if I can work part time at the Y, so I make a note to check on that. I'm still in a quandary about clothes. Plus, I need a couch and a bed. Or at the very least, a bed. I need to take care of these things before school starts.

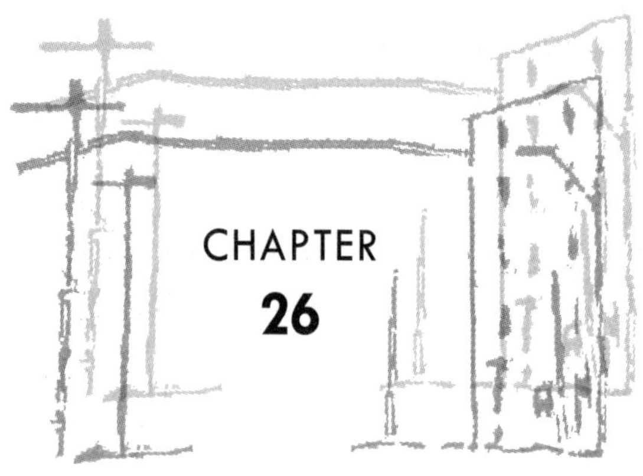

CHAPTER 26

On Tuesday I call Economics and am told that I need to apply in person for a TA job. I look at my shorts and T-shirt and decide it can wait a day. Betty seems distracted, so I put off asking about working part time. Just before I leave for the day, she tells me that the search committee for the director position has been formed and they want a student member. I suggest Arlo, for the simple reason that he's one of the few students I know. I also think he would be a hoot in a meeting with the staid board members.

Betty says, "I was thinking of you."

I say, "But I'm not a student." I roll my eyes. "I mean I'm not a Y student. I'm staff here."

"You'll be a student by the time they start meeting," she says. "And besides, you're taking yoga and Big Art, so you are a Y student."

I hem and haw and she finally says, "Novelle, just make my life easy and say yes."

I've never heard that tone before.

"Yes, then, of course I'll do it. But what's wrong?"

She tells me that no one from the committee has approached her about the job and she only found out about the application process because Adela called and told her.

"We aren't even handling the paperwork here. I don't know who is doing it for them." She looks at me as if to make sure they haven't been giving it to me behind her back. "You don't . . . you haven't . . . ?"

"No, no way. I would never keep a secret like that. Is Adela on the committee?"

"Yes."

That's all she seems to want to say, so I give her a hug and tell her I'll support the best candidate and that she will be that candidate. I barely get a smile. On the way home I take down the typewriter posters, which are pretty damp and bedraggled at this point, and put them in the trash.

In my mailbox is a note from Lulu saying that she's coming for the weekend, driving in Saturday morning and leaving Sunday night. I wonder if there is something she wants to talk about away from Mom, or if she's just feeling the freedom of earning money on her own. I think about taking her to the Arch and maybe the zoo, which I've discovered is free. I am a little concerned about losing the whole weekend, but maybe she'll help me with the clothes quandary.

Wednesday morning, I present myself in the Economics department at lunchtime and ask about TA positions. The secretary gives me a form to fill out. She doesn't know anything about hours or pay. She says I'll need to come back later when the real secretary is there; she's just filling in during lunch. I get busy in the afternoon with September brides and don't have time to get back to Economics before they close for the day.

Marianne knocks on my door that night and shrieks with excitement when she sees my chairs and table. I haven't told anyone else the story, and it feels good to share it with someone.

"I wish I had been here," she says. "And I never thought you would go there by yourself."

I tell her about moving my car around, trying to make it sound funny and not creepy. She tells me not to worry about it, surely he has bigger problems than me and my table. She muses about getting the sofa back, but I discourage her. I don't want any more trouble to keep me awake at night.

"Anyway," I say to change the subject, "what about Joe? I got a typewriter for him; do you still have his number?"

I tell her about the call from Economics and the motherlode of manual typewriters. She's brought the number and leaves it with me, saying she's exhausted from sleeping or not sleeping in a tent and is going to bed.

It's not that late, so I call the number, but no one answers. I try again a little later and Joe picks up the phone. I have to remind him about who I am and how he knows me. When I say, "the two women at the Dairy Queen," he finally places me.

"I came up with another typewriter if you'd like it," I tell him. "This one is free. The Econ department at WashU has some old manuals they don't need anymore."

"You didn't need to go to all that trouble," he says. "Although I appreciate it, I really do. But I was able to get a corporate sponsor, so we got all we needed."

"Oh, I thought you wanted it for yourself."

"No, I guess I didn't explain. I was collecting typewriters for the Boys and Girls Club afterschool program in Kinloch, if you know where that is. I thought it would be good to teach the kids how to type this summer, and then they can use them to practice their writing skills. If I let them use a typewriter, they get more excited about writing. They come up with some pretty cool stories."

I'm excited about the program just listening to him.

"After that fiasco with your typewriter, I realized I'd never get them one at a time. I got busy and made some calls and got Mallinckrodt to help us. They wanted to write us a check, but I convinced them to put out a call to their employees for old manuals. I felt better about giving a bunch of active kids the manual kind. They can pound away all they want. I really liked yours because it was so sturdy. I hope you got it working, by the way." Now he sounds concerned, and I feel guilty for not telling him that it wasn't broken at all, it was just that the lock was on.

"It turned out okay," I tell him. "There's a lock on some of the old manuals. I just had to shift the lever on the lock."

"Good to know if I run into one that doesn't work."

I want to ask him if he's the director or a volunteer or what, but I can't think of a polite way to do that, so I wish him luck and hang up and think about all those typewriters gathering dust in Economics.

On Thursday I take my TA application in and find myself facing the secretary who gave me the typewriter. I tell her I might have a home for all of the others, but I'll need a few weeks.

Then I hand her the TA application and she looks up in surprise.

"I thought you worked at the Y," she says, recalibrating.

"Just for the summer. I got to Saint Louis at the beginning of June and found that job the next day." That sounds like I was a little haphazard, but it's too late to revise the story now. "It's been great, though. Lots of different responsibilities." Sure, typing letters and babysitting brides.

"It's on the application there." Dressed up as overseeing student programs and preparing for the next semester, which really isn't a stretch.

She smiles, recognition dawning. "Did you have anything to do with that Big Art thing? I saw the posters."

"A little. We've got another one coming for freshman orientation, but that's still a secret." *Although not as secret as Arlo would like*, I add to myself.

"Well, I'll watch for that. It sounds like you've gotten right into things here. I guess you really miss Ray over there, though."

I say yes and leave it at that. It's too complicated to explain that I do miss him but never met him. So, I try to get back to the TA job.

"How many TAs do you hire?" I ask her.

"Five, usually, and there are twelve incoming master's students. We've only got two applications so far, but it's early. Most of them will come in next week or even the week after. And now I'm sure you're going to ask about your chances, which are x divided by five, times y, and about the pay, which is minimum wage times 1.55, and the hours, which are five to ten hours a week, plus or minus the unknown. Does that about cover it?" She raises her eyebrows, but she's smiling.

"Just about. I guess I do have one more question, but you probably shouldn't answer it."

Her face says "try me" although her mouth says nothing.

"The application has a checkbox for which course I want to TA. I figure my chances are best with the least popular course. So, would you be willing to tell me which course the TAs tend to *not* want?"

"I guess that's no secret. It's statistics. Sometimes that one goes begging. Everybody hates statistics."

"You mean that? I love statistics! Really, that's my first choice."

She takes a red pen and draws a big circle around the section of the application where I had already checked statistics.

"No promises, but I'd say your chances just went way up. Now go find a home for those typewriters and let me get back to work."

I go back to the Y, where Betty seems more cheerful than she was yesterday. Adela is there, so I hope she's given Betty some encouraging news. I tell them both that I've applied for a TA job. The announcement is met with silent stares. Finally, Adela comes around.

"That's great, Noelle. I think you just caught us off guard. We prefer to forget that you're just a summer hire here."

"Are you sure you'll get it? Aren't those pretty competitive?" Betty is concerned about my chances as well as her own.

"I don't really know, but I'm hopeful. I should know in two or three weeks. Classes start August 26."

"Well, if it doesn't work out, maybe we'll need you part time here. I don't suppose you want to keep doing the brides thing?"

"I think I could do the bride-sitting; it's pretty entertaining."

Walking down Wingate with a load of green beans and tomatoes from the farmers' market, I see a young woman sitting on the stoop of my building and open my mouth to shout Ruth's name. But it's not Ruth, it's my sister Lulu.

"Hey, you're early!" I put everything down to hug her and then inspect her face to see if the change of arrival is a good or bad thing. She's beaming, so I give her another hug and turn to open the door. That's when I see that she's been leaning against a huge suitcase, which is leaning against a large cardboard box with an enormous spider plant on top, wreathed in macramé. A stab of worry goes through my chest but I force myself to be calm.

"So, Lulu. What's all this? You planning to move in or something?" *Keep it light*, I tell myself.

"You wish, Nobi," she says, using the name she called me as a baby. "You would *love* to have your baby sister right here! But no, I just brought you some more stuff from Granny's."

I'm ashamed of the relief I feel. I love my sister but at the moment I love living alone just a little bit more.

We haul everything up to the third floor and she explains that she wanted to see the campus on a school day, so she traded days with another cashier and came a little early. I tell her that's great but unless she brought a bed in that suitcase she's going to be sleeping on the hard floor. I tell her some of the story of the missing furniture but make it sound like the former tenant just came and picked it up. She's not really interested and doesn't mind the floor, so I stop worrying and start cooking. I say a silent thank-you to my table and chairs for returning themselves to me.

Over dinner, she tells me that Granny is about the same, that her boyfriend is kaput, and that she has big news. I refuse to guess, so she announces that she's going back to college.

"I like the bank, but I look around and everyone who stands at the counters doesn't have a four-year degree and everyone sitting at a desk does have one, so I figure I need one if I'm going to make some real money. I don't want to stand there counting change for the rest of my life."

This is great news, if a little surprising, since Lulu wasn't such a great student in high school. Good enough, but not all that interested. It seems that the reality of the workplace has opened her eyes.

"So, where are you thinking of going?"

"Here, of course!" She watches my face. I keep it steady.

"Nah, I know WashU is out of my reach. I should have worked harder in high school."

I wonder about the University College night school, but I can see she's got her own plan so I don't bring it up.

"State school is good enough for me. I just wanted to walk around campus and pretend I was going to school with you again. Just for a day or so." She smiles a little wistfully, but she's clearly thought this through, so I encourage her, like the good RA and big sister that I hope I am.

"Have you thought about a major?"

"Business, of course. I like banking, I just don't like the idea of being a bank clerk forever."

"In that case, can you go at night and get the bank to pay for it? Of course, that will take longer."

We do the math, and best case it would take four years of very hard work, assuming that all her community college classes would transfer.

"Of course, you'll be working full time and making money all that time."

It seems like a long time to her, and I can't argue that four years isn't a long time when you've just turned twenty. She looks wistful again.

"Why don't you apply to a couple of schools, go for scholarships? Try some private schools, they have more money than the state schools."

She cheers up and we go out for a walk in the fading light. She's enchanted by Delmar and the fact that I live so close to so much activity. She's especially entranced by Blueberry Hill, and I promise her that we'll have lunch there on Saturday. She can try toasted ravioli, a Saint Louis specialty.

CHAPTER 27

We get to the Y a little later than usual on Friday morning, and I introduce Lulu and send her out to explore campus. I ask Betty if I can borrow a yoga mat for Lulu to sleep on and she tells me to take two, since we have more than we need during the summer.

"In fact, just keep them until we need them in September. Less to store around here."

Arlo stops by with the sheets and says he's ready to have them sewn together. It's now four sheets and I accuse him of being four sheets to the wind. I don't think to ask him for the written permission to hang the giant artwork until he's left.

Lulu doesn't show up at lunchtime, so I eat my share of the sandwiches we brought and put the rest in the refrigerator. She finally appears at three-fifteen looking flushed and full of news.

"I went to the admissions office," she announces breathlessly, "and I got an application and a financial aid form. And then I went to the B-school." *Ooh*, I think—she's already picked up the lingo.

"And they said sure, I can apply as a junior, but they asked me a lot of questions and they didn't seem all that excited about my background. I guess my SATs aren't quite what they expected." I wonder why she's so excited when the news was less than encouraging. "But! They told me that Fontbonne might be a better fit. I can't believe it's right next door. It's practically part of WashU!"

I haven't even heard of Fontbonne, so I'm pretty sure it's not almost WashU, but I don't say that.

"So that's where I've been." She says that with some finality. Betty and I are waiting expectantly. "Hey, didn't you bring some sandwiches?"

I tell her where to find them and Betty and I roll our eyes at each other. We both know there is more to the story. The sandwich break is probably as much to build drama as to slake her hunger. She comes back with her mouth full, so hunger must be at least one driver.

"They have an amazing BA program, and I can get a BS in two years if I get in, which they pretty much promised I will."

"BA or BS?"

"BS in BA—Business Administration." Ah. She's really into the jargon.

"So can you help me with the forms?" She looks around. "Maybe I could use a typewriter? Oh, and they said I don't even have to do a parents' confidential statement since I'm over twenty." Seven days over, but that's good enough. I wonder if she remembers the trouble I had getting mine done. That was one of the years our dad was missing.

"We'll do that at home tonight," I tell her. She frowns, questioning. "I got a new typewriter; it's a long story."

Lulu talks about Fontbonne all the way home. I make her carry the yoga mats thinking that will slow her down a little, but it doesn't. When we get upstairs, she wants to start on the forms right away. I'm hungry and tell her it can wait until after we eat. I can see that she's anxious to get going, so I give her a notebook and a pen and tell her to read through the application and start making notes. Or she can start writing the essay if she wants.

"Think of it as homework—it's your very first assignment at Fontbonne and you want to get an A, don't you?"

She sits down and is perfectly quiet while I make salad and macaroni and cheese. By the time the food is on the table, she's got pages of notes and the beginnings of an essay. I am impressed with my baby sister.

When we are finished eating, she discovers that she's exhausted, so she lounges on the yoga mats while I go through the things she brought me from Granny's. There are knick-knacks wrapped in scarves, dishes wrapped in clothing, three vases wrapped in kitchen towels, and other not-especially-useful bits and pieces. I suspect these are treasures she couldn't bear to get rid of but didn't really want to keep either. When I get to the loopy potholders we had made when we were five and seven years old, I know I'm right.

"Thanks, Kiddo," I tell her. "Great stuff."

"Are you all the way to the bottom?"

I look again and find a flat paper bag from a store in the mall that I know she frequents. Inside is a dark teal version of the raspberry dress.

"Oh Lulu, you shouldn't have done this. But I looooove it."

"End-of-season sale." She is glowing. I hold up the dress, twirl around, and lean over to give Lulu a hug.

"Now, about this spider plant."

"Mom made me bring that," she says. "She read somewhere that they clean the air and improve your health. She says it will be happiest in the bathroom. Or maybe she said the kitchen."

The plant is way too big for my bathroom. I stand on a chair and hang it from a hanger in the kitchen where some former tenant must have hung a spider plant her mother forced on her. Somehow I don't think David Black had a spider plant. It takes up too much room in the kitchen, but it can stay there for now. I'll move it to the living room later. I sigh thinking that it would actually look nice with my missing bamboo couch.

CHAPTER 28

On Saturday morning I suggest a trip to the Arch, but Lulu has new ideas about her essay, and we spend most of the day on her application and financial aid forms, with a break for burgers at Blueberry Hill. I tell her we'll celebrate her twenty-first birthday here. She can stay with me from then until school starts at Fontbonne.

"Oh no," she says. "I'll already be here. I'm going to apply to start in January."

I'm not sure if "here" means Saint Louis or my apartment, but I decide to worry about that later. Maybe the scholarship will cover the dorm. If she gets in, which I realize we are both counting on and maybe counting too much.

"Kiddo, I hope this works out. But you're not in yet. You have to get transcripts and your SATs, maybe the ACT if that's what they want."

Lulu's face clouds over. "I know that. I know it perfectly well. But just let me have this hope, can't you? Can't we be happy just for today?" She starts to sob, way more than the situation calls for. I reach out and she grabs me. "Granny is dying."

I hug her and we both cry for a while, and then we talk about Granny and how she really is and how the doctor told Mom last Sunday that there isn't much hope. She's been having small strokes that take away more and more, and she hasn't opened her eyes since Sunday. Lulu just hadn't been able to tell me.

Today's wedding is at two, and I couldn't find anyone else to take over when I found out Lulu was coming, so we dry our tears and both head to campus after lunch. She takes her paperwork, although I encourage her to let it go for a few more hours. We calm down on the walkway and are able to laugh at the scene we must have made in Blueberry Hill. I tell her that I'm sure crazier things have happened there.

As we pass the Women's Exchange and start up the pedestrian overpass at the edge of campus, we both notice that the shop is open and has furniture on the sidewalk. A bright orange "Back-to-School" banner is strung across the front of the building. There on the sidewalk is a wooden-framed couch, shaped like my missing one but not bamboo. We go down and take a closer look. The cushions are missing, and the clerk doesn't know if they even have them, but she says we can have the frame for five dollars. I tell her we'll take it and we'll be back in a few hours. She insists that we pay now before she'll put a sold sign on it, so I hand over the cash.

The wedding party is late and a little flustered, and Lulu forgets her application and helps them as if that were what she did for a living. She's better at this than I could ever be. If I'm honest with myself, she's just better all around with strangers. She sorts out shoes when one girl's are too tight and another's are too loose by the simple means of switching them. She adjusts hairpins and even redoes one bridesmaid's hair entirely, drawing the loose shaggy curls into a neat little French braid that leaves the girl speechless with gratitude.

When the door closes behind the bridal party, she turns to me with a dark look. "Don't you ever even think about cutting your hair in that Farrah Fawcett look. You'll be just like that poor kid—looking ridiculous. I'll have to drive over here and braid it for you." She looks at me critically. "Let's just try something."

She fiddles with my hair for a while and then teaches me to French braid it. She makes me practice until my scalp is sore and my shoulders are stiff, and when I look in the mirror I am thrilled. Goodbye '60s, hello future. And no shaggy Farrah look, either.

The bride comes back herself this time and takes a minute to compliment me on my hair. And then she hands Lulu a tip and sends her minions to gather up their belongings.

We stroll home and Lulu talks about the bridal consultant business she will create when she gets her business degree. When we cross the overpass, we realize that we've now got to struggle home with the couch, a couch we won't even be able to use when we get home since it doesn't have cushions, just the webbing the cushions used to rest on. We discuss getting one of the cars, but we can see that the best we could do would be tying it to the roof, where it would probably slip off, most likely onto the hood, blocking the driver's view. So, we struggle down the walkway, trying various positions including resting the webbing on our shoulders with our heads sticking through. I picture a big cartoon but then think maybe this isn't something I want to remember.

Once we've wrangled the sofa up the stairs, Lulu puts the yoga mats on it. They don't fit at all, too short for the long couch and too wide for the low back, but we sit there anyway and cry a little more about Granny before we finish the leftover macaroni. We go to bed early although I lie awake for a long time and I suspect Lulu does too.

CHAPTER 29

The phone rings way too early on Sunday morning for it to be anything but bad news. Mom is strangely calm and tells us that Granny died quietly in the night and that she'll wait until we get there to make funeral plans. I call Betty to let her know that I'll be away for a few days and then we pack to leave. We don't want to be apart, so we take Lulu's car. I can take the Greyhound home. I move Granny's car to the lot behind the apartment building to make sure it's out of the way of street sweeping.

We don't talk very much for the first hour, but then we start telling Granny stories and are almost cheerful by the time we get home. Mom is there, along with flowers and food the neighbors have already brought in. *Thank goodness for traditions*, I think.

Funeral planning is emotionally hard but technically easy once we've chosen a funeral home. We meet with a nun from the parish who talks us through readings and hymns. Mom tells us about a friend whose husband died. The family had no church affiliation and had to figure it all out on their own—where to have it, what to say, how to let people know. *Thank goodness for the rituals we grew up with*, I think.

The rosary is on Monday and the funeral on Tuesday, and then we are alone in the house with even more flowers and food. With no outsiders to put on a front for, we let ourselves go and wail and complain and laugh and finally talk, just a little, about the future.

Mom is adamant that I leave for Saint Louis as soon as possible, at least by Thursday. She seems to think that she is imposing and that I have important work to be doing. She is sure that she can handle everything and anyway Lulu is grown up and works in a bank and can take care of all the financial parts. I finally agree to leave on Friday morning. We make multiple trips to Granny's house. Now that there is no pretense of her ever needing anything in the house, we make some headway, setting aside underwear and pots and pans and garden tools for St. Vincent de Paul. But after a while, we reach a sort of limit beyond which we can't make decisions any more about this lamp or that ceramic cardinal or her big wooden radio. We agree to let it go until one or all of us can face it. I want the bed, but I couldn't take it even if I had my car, so I set aside some smaller furniture and books and trinkets to get later.

On Thursday afternoon we take a tentative look at Granny's clothes. Mom and I demur, but Lulu forges ahead and works through the dresses and skirts and blouses, making piles on the bed. She gives me a stern look and I know that I'm going to find one of these piles in my possession sooner or later. I hear her typing in the night, and in the morning there is a large suitcase, one of Granny's, waiting by the door. An envelope with my name on it is taped to the handle and I put it in my pocket to read later. Lulu drives me to the Greyhound station and hugs me goodbye with tears in her eyes. I realize that none of us has mentioned Fontbonne since Saturday night.

On the Delmar bus to U City, I look around as if Lamont might be riding again today. He's not, of course. It's much later in the day than that first trip, and there are no boom boxes playing "Summer in the City." I look out the window and watch the now-familiar sights go by. At my apartment, Granny's car is just as I left it, and I take the week's mail and climb the stairs with the suitcase. I feel like I'm always schlepping something up these stairs. Schlepping is a perfect word for it, I think, a word I'd never heard before I set foot on the WashU campus. Now I hear it almost every day. The yoga mats are still on the couch frame, looking ridiculous. I stack them on the floor and sleep there.

CHAPTER 30

I sleep through the Angelus bells on Saturday and wake in mid-morning, in a panic that I'm late for work. I realize that it's Saturday and I call Betty to assure her that I'm back and available for today's two weddings, much to her relief. She says the right post-funeral things, focusing on me and withholding any thoughts she has on Granny being in a better place, for which I am grateful. Church teachings aside, the cold, damp earth is not a better place for my Granny than her own little house, and I don't want to hear anything different. I can be childish about it if I keep it to myself.

The suitcase is mocking me, so I heave it onto the couch webbing. Before I open it, though, I look for the envelope with Lulu's note. She took pains over it, I can tell. She says that the clothes she's packed are simple and classic and I should just put them in the back of the closet until a day comes when I need something different, and then I can find it. She also suggests that since I have Granny's sewing machine, I can just cut the top off any dresses that are too old-ladyish and make the rest into a skirt. She's also slipped in what she calls accessories—bracelets and earrings and necklaces. She says that we won't wear them now but we might later and they'll wait for us without taking up much space. I look through them, trying to see them with Lulu's eyes, and once in a while I think I might be getting a glimpse of what she means.

I'm sorry I agreed to take the weddings, but I've had a whole week with no pay, so I tell myself to be grateful. Feeling perverse, I pull out a plain black dress that I assume Granny saved for funerals. Perfect, I'm in a black mood. I put it on, and it's shorter on me than it would be on her. It looks almost okay. I put the black ribbon on my hat, slip my feet into my Dr. Scholl's sandals, and head for campus.

I'm not paying attention to the weather, and it starts to rain when I'm still on the walkway. Too close to campus to turn back for a jacket or umbrella. I rush to the Y, unlock the door, and inspect myself in the long brides' mirror. The hat gets a shake and some attention with paper towels and looks okay again. My hair is a mess; the straw hat didn't keep the rain off. The dress should be a wreck, but it's polyester and looks pretty much like it did when I put it on. Feels icky, but looks okay. I comb out my hair, do my best to duplicate the French braid Lulu taught me, and start getting ready for the first of today's brides.

Neither of today's brides leave tips, but that suits my dark mood. It occurs to me that if I had tried to be a little more cheerful they might have been more forthcoming, but I've learned not to expect them every time and I know there isn't really any correlation between my behavior and theirs. The first wedding is uneventful.

The second one is a nightmare, with the mother and the mother-in-law-to-be jockeying for position. There is discussion, in loud voices, about changing the order of appearance of the bridesmaids. The bride points out that her sister is maid of honor, and the others are in order by height, as are the groomsmen. I am grateful on their behalf, having once been paired with a groomsman six inches shorter than myself. But the mother-in-law is arguing for seniority, which I finally work out means how long the bridesmaid has known the bride. This, I assume, puts her daughter at the bottom of the pack, so to speak, which means that she is farthest from the bride but first down the aisle. I am pleased to see that neither the bride nor the soon-to-be sister-in-law pay any attention at all to this argument. At a quarter to wedding time, I shoo out both mothers, telling them it's surely time for them to be escorted to their seats. I'm expecting calm to reign, when out of a corner rises up a stepmother, taking me to task for not including her in the mother exit. I apologize and apologize again and try to start her up the steps, but she seems to be unable to berate me while walking and holds tight at the bottom of the stairs. Just as I'm about to say something I'm likely to regret, the door opens and a groomsman sticks his head in, asking for Mrs. Whoeversheis. The sight of the handsome young face gracing a black tuxedo changes her mood in an instant. She holds out a hand to him and he takes her off with a flourish and a whisper in her ear. She doesn't even pause and turn back to stick her tongue out, which I am half expecting.

I take a moment to breathe and then turn to the younger generation. They are nowhere in sight, but I can hear them in the workroom with the door closed. They sound cheerful, so I leave them alone. They get themselves out on time and up the stairs with no squabbling about order. The bride tells me that they've left a little sip of something for me near the sink. I go into the workroom and find a tumbler with a few ounces of champagne. The bottle is nowhere to be found, and all the glasses except mine have been washed, dried, and put away. There is a little dish of mints next to the glass of champagne. I enjoy every drop, plus the mints, and wish them all happiness. I don't even think to be angry about their breaking the no-alcohol rule. They deserved it, all of them, and so did I.

On Sunday I let myself be crabby and lazy. I drive my car across the street to All Saints, just to make sure it starts. After Mass, I drive it to the Schnucks in Clayton, where the name of the store no longer makes me snicker. The rest of the day, I sleep and read the paper, and snack on the groceries I brought home but can't bring myself to make into some kind of real meal.

CHAPTER 31

The Y is busy from start to finish on Monday. Jackie and Dots are both back at their jobs and have a lot of catching up to do with each other and with Betty, about Ray and their personal lives and the student programs that are about to begin. I feel a little left out but also relieved that I don't have to talk about Granny's funeral and the little house that will soon be sold and gone. I spend all morning typing correspondence that has accumulated while I was away. I think that if I stay at it all day and work a little late I can finish all of it, or almost all.

After lunch, Betty says we are having a staff meeting and I need to be part of it. The main topic is Campus Y participation at freshman orientation, which happens all over the main campus. The Y has a pretty standard formula, but the three regular staff members want to see something a little special this year. Without the big personality of Ray, they say, we need to give students another reason to take a look. We need, of course, a Big Draw. And we've got that. In my absence, Betty has made sure that Arlo really does have all the permissions he needs. And I promise to do the sewing tonight so that Arlo still has a week to do the artwork, which we all know he will do in a single session, no matter how long that session might run. What we don't quite know is what the Big Draw is, once a student sees the sign, is impressed by it, and throws open our door to see what the hoopla is all about.

Next topic is food. Always food for students. Music, ditto, and it doesn't even matter what it is. But everyone will have food and music. What else do we have? We brainstorm about the Big Draw theme and how to tie that to the Y programs. "Draw a Breath" for yoga, or maybe "Withdraw for an Hour." For Kinloch and other children's programs, "Draw a Better Future" or "Draw Their Tomorrow." We become engrossed and forget about the missing Ray and, in my case, my more recent grief.

After two hours, though, we have exhausted the theme and ourselves, and we call a halt. We have plenty to work with, and Jackie can take over the implementation. I experience a tiny sense of loss that I won't be involved. On freshman orientation day, I'll be engrossed in grad school orientation.

I remember the typewriters gathering dust in Economics and walk over to the dorm area on the South Forty. Going through the underpass, I see that Ray's memorial is still there, with a few RIPs and other notes to Ray scrawled near and on it, but newer messages are encroaching. Soon it will disappear. Everyone at the housing office is enthusiastically welcoming incoming freshmen and the rest of the student body and seeking participation in yearbook, newspaper, and all the other areas of campus life that run on student energy. The director of housing has left for the day, but I find a head RA who is willing to listen to my idea. He's a little skeptical.

"Most kids show up with a typewriter," he states confidently.

"Even the full-scholarship ones?"

"No one ever came to me when I was an RA and said they didn't have a typewriter."

I think about that. I would never have gone to the RA on my freshman floor and pleaded poverty. I wanted to succeed, but I was desperate to fit in, too. I don't want to say that to him and I don't think he would buy it anyway, so I change tactics.

"Well, think about it. Maybe just ask the RAs if they could casually take a look, see if someone might need one. It doesn't need to be a big deal at all, they can just spread the word that there are some extra ones if anyone forgot theirs."

He agrees to consider it, but I don't think he will, so I push just a little more.

"If you want, I can talk to the RAs. You're probably having a kickoff meeting?"

He agrees to that, probably just to get rid of me. He doesn't tell me when and where, but I can see the meeting posted on a bulletin board, so I just tell him I'll see him at the meeting and leave him to wonder how I know, if he thinks about it at all once I'm out the door.

My last week at the Y is a rush of work and emotion, and I am both sad and relieved when Friday arrives and I say a sort-of goodbye. We go out to lunch at The Rat, which I now know is the Rathskeller, and I leave with tears and a Campus Y T-shirt, promising that I will show up for yoga, starting in two weeks. I walk home and find a letter in my mailbox letting me know that I was selected to be a TA and will be TA-ing freshman statistics.

At home, I get out Granny's mixer and baking sheets and make cookies to celebrate. I eat too many of them and blame it on Granny, for dying and leaving me bereft and in possession of cookie-baking gear.

CHAPTER 32

Saturday morning I'm awakened by loud voices and doors slamming. I look outside and see that someone is moving out of my building. I go outside to see if I can help, but whichever one is the outgoing tenant seems to have rallied enough friends to carry everything down in one trip.

"Just the boxes, right?" someone calls from a second-story window.

"Yeah, no room for the furniture and I don't need it in LA anyway. Marzello can sell it to the next tenant. Oh hi!" He's just noticed me standing on the stoop. He introduces himself as David Black in 2B.

"You live here too? Sorry we never met, and now I'm moving out. Actually, I hardly lived here. My dad rented the place for me and bought all this new furniture when I got accepted at WashU Law. But then I got a gig in Chicago and spent the summer there. Now I've got a gig in LA, so I'm driving to the coast pronto!" He's in high spirits and talking a mile a minute. Now he pauses.

"You don't need any furniture, do you? It's a shame to let that rat Marzello have it all, but I don't have time to sell it."

I am trying to process that this is David Black who may or may not have known Ruth last spring break and who has a father who buys him an apartment full of furniture and who blows off law school for a gig. I can't imagine what sort of gig would make me give up law school at the last minute.

He only sees that I'm pondering his last paragraph.

"Well, Joey's still up there, so if you want anything, just take it. Better do it today, though. Who knows when Marzello will be over here raising hell about my rent."

And with that, he is gone. My brain is trying to rearrange history. David Black was not the last tenant in 3D, apparently. It's unlikely that he was Ruth's Dave Brown if he only moved here for the summer. But he did just offer me free furniture, which I can be pretty sure is free of crab lice. I run upstairs, then run back to ask if he had a cat, but he's gone and so are his buddies. So I go to 2B, where Joey is sweeping the floor. I marvel at his furniture, which looks brand-new and is nicer than anything my family ever had. Clearly, Mrs. Marzello will be able to sell this for more than one month's rent.

Joey helps me slide the mattress off the box springs and we push and pull it up to 3D. We go back for the box springs. We can't get the bed frame out of the room and can't figure out how to take it apart, so I thank him and go home. I'm sure the bed is lice-free, but I spray it thoroughly anyway.

I eat cookies for breakfast while I ponder the twisted story of Dave and David and cringe at the assumptions I've made.

By Sunday, I'm tired of cookies but still feeling down, so I tap on Marianne's door to ask if she wants to get together and catch up. I tell her there might be a few cookies upstairs.

"I was just running out for bagels," she says. "I'll be up in fifteen minutes, or twenty if there's a line."

She knocks on my door thirty minutes later with a mug of coffee in each hand and a brown paper bag under one arm.

"I remembered you don't drink coffee, so I took time to make some," she says with a grin. "Here." She hands me a mug. We slather butter on the bagels and Marianne eats hers while examining my latest Big Art.

"You should hang these in the window," she says. "Block some of that light on hot days, and I'll bet those sycamores out there will make some interesting shadows." The sun has moved far enough by now that I don't have as much shade as I did in June and July, and the apartment can get even hotter than it did during the July heat wave.

"Hey, you finally got a bed, but you still have that wreck of a couch. And what are you going to do about a desk? And bookshelves? You know classes start in four days, don't you?"

I do know, but I have put off dealing with it day after day.

"Come on," she says, licking the last of the butter off her fingers. "Kmart opens in fifteen minutes. Let's figure something out."

We take her car since it's a VW Squareback with a roof rack and we don't know what we'll figure out. When we get there, the end-of-summer sale is in full swing. We aren't interested in beach wear or lawn chairs, but when I spy a wooden picnic table for $8.99, I see possibilities.

"What do you think? I see a desk."

She ponders, sits on it, bounces up and down. "Well, it's big enough to spread out a lot of paper, and it's sturdy. I think it's a winner. You can't sit on those picnic benches, though."

"They can go on the wall under the window. Or I'll stack them up and call them bookshelves. And it's $8.99 for God's sake."

We find a clerk who locates one still in the box and helps us get it through checkout and into the back of the Squareback. It hangs out the back, but it's not raining and we don't think it will fall out. We start back toward U City, going south on Kingshighway. We pass through a wave of barbecue smoke and discuss stopping for lunch but decide to get the precarious cargo home. And then the car stops, right in the middle of the southbound side of Kingshighway. We are many blocks north of Delmar.

"Damn." Marianne turns the key. Nothing, not a whimper. "Please please please." She tries again. Still nothing. Cars are swerving around us, some of them honking. Marianne flicks the turn signal. Nothing happens.

"This is not safe," I say. "We could get rear-ended. We could get smashed just getting out of the doors." Other things could happen too but we don't say them.

A car pulls up behind ours and stops. Two large Black men get out, and one comes up on each side of the Squareback. We lock the doors, roll up the windows.

"Miss?" One of the men has bent down and his face fills the window next to Marianne. She is frozen.

"Miss, do you need help? Do you want us to push you over to the curb?"

Marianne unfreezes.

"Yes! Yes, that would be great." She reaches for the door handle.

"Miss, stay put. You need to steer. Put it in neutral and then get ready to brake when we get to the curb."

When we are parked, the face comes back. "What happened, did it just stop?"

Marianne nods.

"Does it do anything at all when you turn the key?"

Marianne clears her throat and looks out the window. Her tongue comes unglued.

"No, it's so strange. It just stopped and now it's like there's no battery or something. Thank goodness you came along. Anyone could have hit us."

"Well, if you'll pop the hood I can take a look."

Fear has melted away and we both get out and look under the hood, all four of us.

"I'm no mechanic, but I think that wire came loose from the battery," says one of the guys.

The other one reaches over and reattaches the wire to the battery, then rubs his hands together to dislodge the grease. "Try it now."

The car starts and we all smile and shake hands. Marianne tries to pay them, but they refuse. "Just do someone else a favor sometime."

They drive off waving and we get back in the Squareback.

"We are so disgusting sometimes," Marianne says, and we drive home in silence.

The box is too heavy to get up the stairs so we open it and take the pieces up one at a time and Marianne holds the parts while I bolt them together. By the time we are finished our embarrassment has dissipated. We put the picnic table under a north window and formally put the typewriter on it and declare it to be a desk.

"Those benches make crappy bookcases," Marianne informs me. "But I guess they'll do. And you still need a desk chair."

We have another round of bagels and Marianne apologizes for not being around when I got back from the funeral.

"I should have been here to sit shiva with you."

I ask her what she's talking about and she tells me about the Jewish custom of sitting with the family for seven days after a death.

"I didn't know you were Jewish."

"I'm not, I found out about it at WashU. Everyone's Jewish here."

This is a surprise to me, but she explains that back when the Ivy League schools had quotas limiting the number of Jewish students allowed to enroll, many New York families sent their kids to WashU, which did not have quotas. The quotas at the Ivys were lifted in the 1960s, but by then a lot of families had strong connections to WashU, so there are still a lot of Jewish kids from New York in the undergraduate population.

"You learn a lot of interesting things," she sums it up.

"Well, I guess we had Catholic shiva," I tell her. "My mom's house was still full of pot roast and angel food cakes and Jell-O salads when I left."

CHAPTER 33

The RA meeting is on Monday afternoon, and so is orientation for new TAs in the Economics department. I can't miss the TA meeting, so I cross my fingers that we'll be finished before the RA meeting is over. I only need to get there at the last minute, although I'm not sure when that will be. I find the room for the TA meeting and make sure I'm there in plenty of time. I wear the hat and the French braids and the new teal dress. We all arrive almost at once, and no one is there to greet us. We give each other the tightlipped smiles and nods typical of strangers meeting in awkward situations, and it occurs to me that Economics attracts introverts. I try to make conversation with the person closest to me, but it peters out and I give it up and wait.

Someone with a clipboard arrives and checks off our names. He doesn't introduce himself and he doesn't have us introduce ourselves. He gives us a handout listing all our names next to the classes we will each TA. Two of the TAs object to their assignments, and he tells them that we can trade with each other if we want to. No one says anything and we move on to the second handout, which is a list of our responsibilities as TAs. Clipboard

Guy tells us we can read it later; he clearly does not want to be here. One of the new TAs scans through the document and asks questions about office hours. He wants to hold them in his off-campus apartment. I expect the Clipboard Guy to shrug off the question, but he doesn't have the chance. One of the new TAs, the only other woman in the room, tells him no, he can't do that. He asks her where it says that, and they get into a debate about propriety and ease of access. Eventually one of the other men speaks up and tells the first guy to get real, he can't use his TA position to get girls. The other men laugh and I look at the woman and roll my eyes. She grimaces.

Clipboard Guy asks if there are any more questions, and no one speaks. There is a general movement toward the door, and I bump into the woman who had objected to the TA holding office hours in his apartment. She is seething.

"Can you believe that guy?" she says.

"No!" I say. "Well, yes. I can. I just can't believe that guy with the clipboard didn't say anything. Who is he, anyway?"

"Beats me. But what really frosts me is that the jerk argued with me when I called him on it. And then when Mr. Shirt and Tie finally speaks up everyone just laughs."

We walk in silence out of the building.

"Hey, I'm Lisa. You doing anything? We could get an ice cream or something."

I tell her I'm trying to get to a meeting at the housing office and find myself explaining about the typewriters.

"Are you kidding me?" she says. "The guy thinks every single freshman gets here with a typewriter? I was a freshman here and I didn't have a typewriter. I was lucky because my roommate had one and was really nice about me using it. I didn't get my own until I was a senior and that was just because someone left one in the trash and I took it out and cleaned the keys and got it to work."

I stare at her.

"You want to come along? Your pitch is way better than mine."

"Sure, and then we can get ice cream at Fat Al's. You been to Fat Al's? It's the best. Might not be open yet, though."

I stand back and let Lisa talk about freshmen and typewriters and the reticence of "full ride" students. "They're trying to pass for regular students," she says emphatically, "and it's your job to support them. So just take a look, make sure the number of typewriters on your floors is the same as the number of students. If there's a gap, we're here to fill it."

Now I'm worried that we'll run out of typewriters and I'll be like Joe, buying them on street corners. And I don't think Mallinckrodt is going to pony up typewriters for WashU students. Or maybe they will. I'm pretty sure I saw a building named Mallinckrodt somewhere on campus.

Fat Albert's is student run and won't be open for a few more days. So we go to Baskin-Robbins, which is just barely off campus. I tell her how impressed I am with her speech to the RAs.

"If you want something, you just have to say it straight out. Even if what you want is for them to take something, not give you something."

We make a pact to keep an eye on the creepy TA and say goodbye. I walk along the north edge of Forest Park Parkway along overgrown railroad tracks that stop abruptly at the western end of campus. The Women's Exchange is still having its back-to-school sale, so I stop in and ask about desk chairs. They have a few solid wooden armchairs for five dollars and I buy one and, once again, find myself struggling down the walkway toward the Loop with more than I can carry.

CHAPTER 34

Graduate orientation starts at ten on Tuesday morning, and I'm as ready as I can be. It's murderously hot, so I'm in shorts and the nicest T-shirt I own, one with cap sleeves and no writing. There is an hour-long session for all first-year grad students in the school of Arts and Sciences, and it's a predictable series of talks on ethics and health insurance and where to cash checks. I look around the room and see a lot of shorts and tees, but not as many as last year.

We split up then and go to our departments, where we are met by the same secretary who gave me the typewriter. She's busy with name tags and handouts and doesn't recognize me right away. Eventually she comes up to me and reads my name tag and asks me about the typewriters. I tell her about the speech to the RAs and how Lisa took up the cause for scholarship students and that we'll either get rid of none of them or all of them. She tells me they call that a success catastrophe and not to worry, she's sure there are old manual typewriters stashed all over campus.

"Where's your hat today?" she asks as she turns away. "That hat is *you*!"

Great, I'm going to have to wear a straw hat for two years, summer and winter. I picture it piled high with snow. I see myself at graduation, mortarboard perched atop bedraggled shreds that are barely recognizable as my eighty-eight-cent hat. I'm amused, though, and have my first twinge of belonging in the Econ department.

The department chair arrives and welcomes us and asks us to introduce ourselves. Besides Lisa and myself, we have two Steves, three Fredricks, a Dan, a Don, and three Roberts, although one goes by Rob and one by Bob. One of the Steves says we can call him Stephen. One of the Freds, seeing where this is going, calls dibs on Fred and another one quickly claims Rick. The third one laughs good-naturedly and says we can call him anything except Fritz. Don is the creepy TA who wants to hold office hours in his apartment. He seems more normal today, everyone does, probably thanks to the welcoming secretary, the warmth of the department chair, and the food piled on a table for us.

The department chair tells us that first semester we have three required classes that we all take, plus one elective. The elective must be chosen from a set of six or so, designed to give us direction.

"You're not just here because you like math and money," he says. "And I hope you're not here because you wanted to loaf for two more years and you liked that one Econ class you took senior year. If that's you, get out now."

He laughs with us, but then he looks over his reading glasses and no one moves. He looks a little longer, until everyone but him is uncomfortable.

"Okay then, we're clear on that. You need a direction, a way to apply every single thing you learn here to the rest of the world. You can create a specialty if you want, but see me this week if you think you're one of those." He sounds like he is open to innovation, but it better be solid.

Most of the elective classes are co-listed with another department, which makes sense once I think it through. Choices include Economics of Medicine, Political Economics, Economics of Nation-Building, History of Economics, Agricultural Economics, and Fear and Greed in Saint Louis. The last one doesn't even have the word Economics in the title, but I keep coming back to it, possibly because I've just read *Fear and Loathing on the Campaign Trail*, which I found to be both terrifying and hilarious. I read and reread all six course descriptions. Fear and Greed claims to be "a case study of the economic trends and policies that brought about the current racial stratification of Saint Louis, with comparisons to other US cities and contrasts to cities in Europe and elsewhere." I can't get interested in agriculture (cassava in Indonesia?) or medicine (pricing of care and drugs) or history (starting with arbitrage in Dutch futures markets in the 1600s). I'm afraid I am, or was, one of those people who chose Economics because I liked undergrad math but not math theory and found economics to be an interesting type of applied mathematics. I think about all the times I've heard the phrase "North of Delmar" in the last few months and sign up for the elective on fear and greed.

CHAPTER 35

Wednesday is taken up by course selection, which for new students involves standing in various lines for hours in the Women's Building gym. At least space is reserved for us in our courses and none of us end up in tears, as some freshmen do.

Two of my core classes meet on Thursday, and I enjoy the first lecture in the morning class. This class will require one extensive term paper. I know I'll worry about it all semester because although I like writing, I hate not knowing if I'm right on or completely off until I get my grade. The subject matter is interesting, though, and it's Day One, so I resolve not to obsess about it. My eleven colleagues seem interested, and some of them stay behind after the morning class and walk over to Holmes Lounge for coffee. I'm in line behind one of the Freds, who asks for iced coffee. It's a hot day and iced anything sounds good. When I get my glass, Fred is at the end of the counter adding milk and sugar.

"Nirvana," he says, looking up and taking a sip. He has a great smile.

I take a sip of mine and wrinkle my nose. I remember that I'm not a coffee drinker; cold it's even worse.

"Don't drink that stuff straight! Here, let me." He takes my glass and adds a generous pour of milk and almost as much sugar. He gives it a stir, takes a sip, and hands it back to me.

"Try it now."

I can't believe the transformation. "It's like drinking ice cream. I've never had iced coffee before. I've never even heard of drinking coffee cold."

"I could guess. And I'm Tom, not Fred."

I look around and see my classmates across the room, Fred among them. He looks a lot like Tom, but without Tom's friendly smile.

"Sorry," I say. "First day confusion. But thanks anyway. Oh, I'm Novelle. I'm . . . um . . ." I glance at my classmates, who are sitting and talking now.

"You'll get the hang of it, Novelle," Tom says and heads out the door toward the quad.

I catch up with my classmates, a little flustered, although they don't know me well enough to notice. Lisa asks how the typewriter giveaway is going and explains it to the others. They murmur things like "nice of you" and go back to discussing price supports. I tell Lisa that I need to check back at the housing office and she offers to walk over with me. As we leave, we hear someone say "do-gooders" behind us. I look back to see who said it, but no one is even looking at us.

"At least it wasn't that creep Don," Lisa mutters. "But it means we've got another clueless dimwit to educate."

The secretary in the housing office is glad to see us.

"The RAs keep coming in here and asking where the free typewriters are. I had no idea what they were talking about. They said someone in a hat talked to them last week about typewriters for kids who needed them. That must be you."

I glance at Lisa, who is the one who did all the talking. She is stone faced and silent. I turn back to the secretary and ask how many they need, and she says eleven so far but there will probably be more. She offers to pick them up with the housing office van—by which, she says, she means that she will send some hulking guys. She knows that old manuals will be heavy. I give her the name of the secretary in Econ and she thanks both of us. We walk back toward the main campus. Lisa is still silent.

"You okay?" I ask. "Pretty unobservant of them to confuse us like that."

I expect a wisecrack, but instead Lisa says, "Nothing new there." She grabs my hat and perches it on top of her short, curly hair, where it looks utterly ridiculous. "I just need me a hat!" she says, and she sprints ahead and tosses it back to me like a Frisbee. I catch it and throw it back, and we work our way back to the Econ department, me chattering about how glad I am that the typewriter project worked out and the two secretaries can take it from there and I can let it go.

The afternoon class is less entertaining but more mathematical and I'm glad to see that it will be mostly problem sets, which I relish. I like knowing there is one answer and working through the problem until I find it. When we leave class at four, Lisa comes up to me again.

"You know those typewriters," she says. "Do you think I could get one?"

"I don't see why not. Just ask the secretary—I'm sure the housing people haven't gotten over here to pick them up yet."

That doesn't seem to be the answer she wanted and she's quiet, apparently looking for another way to ask.

"If you want something, you gotta say it," I say, quoting her own words.

That gets me a sharp look and Lisa stops walking and looks like she might turn away.

"Sorry, but really, just tell me," I say. "Maybe I'm a clueless nitwit, but I can learn. It's just a typewriter we're talking about, and a used one at that."

"It's for my brother. I thought we could share, but it's not going to work. I'm going to need it a lot, and he's just sixteen so he'll use any excuse to avoid doing his homework."

"You live at home?"

"Christ, yes. I'm still passing, okay? Oh, I'm Black, I'm not passing as white. I'm just trying to pass as a regular grad student like you. So, yes, I live at home instead of spending my stipend on rent. And yes, home is north of Delmar, and I take the bus. All I want is a typewriter, and here I am giving them away to everyone but my own self." She stamps her foot, just barely. "I'm sorry."

"Well, don't be sorry, I am a nitwit. And I just remembered that I took the first free typewriter over to the Y to give to—well, it doesn't matter, but it's still there and it's yours. Let's go get it right now."

I picture us lugging it across campus and then Lisa sitting on the bus with it in her lap as though she were an itinerant writer or worse.

"No, wait. Let's go get my car instead. We'll come back and pick it up and I'll drive you home."

I expect her to object and I'm relieved when she doesn't. I have a flash of understanding about Betty telling me to just accept things she's offered me.

My car keys are upstairs, and Lisa goes up with me to get them. She looks around at my pathetic couch and paper curtains and rugless floor. "Wow, classic typewriter," she says, focusing on that instead of my sorry excuse for a home.

"Yeah," I say. "That's where this whole thing started. You won't believe it, if I ever get up the energy to tell you the whole story."

Finding a parking spot near the Y, picking up the typewriter, and getting it back to the car takes a while, since a student cabinet meeting is going on and Dots insists on introducing me all around. Once we're on the way, traffic is heavy as we inch up Skinker and onto Lindell toward Kingshighway.

"Left here," Lisa says, and I slow to turn.

"Not Kingshighway? Is this a shortcut?"

"Turn right."

I turn and we are on a street of beautiful three-story apartment buildings, brick with ornate white plaster trim, set back from the street farther than in my more mundane neighborhood.

"Next block, you can see it now. It's the third one on the right."

"Why are we stopping here?"

"I live here. Come on."

"But you said you live north of Delmar. This is so not north of Delmar."

"Oh, it's north of Delmar. Just look at it. Look hard."

I look and it's still a street of beautiful buildings, and I say so.

"Really look. Okay, here's a hint. What's *not* here?"

"Well, cars, but there must be garages in the alley."

"Huh. What else? You see any curtains, any lights on? You see any *people* here?"

There are lights and curtains in all the units in her building, and in one or two others.

Everything else is dark. I look closer, now that I know what I'm seeing, and there are broken windows and boarded-up front doors.

"Okay, I get it. It's *like* north of Delmar, but why? It's right by Lindell, next to Forest Park, almost in the West End. It should be . . . not like this." I look around again. "What's going on?"

"Let's get this typewriter upstairs. Lock your car. Wait, move it up a little so it's not under a streetlight."

We go upstairs, Lisa doing the lugging this time, and I meet her family and end up staying for dinner. Lisa's parents ask me the usual questions about where I'm from, where I did undergrad, and what I want to do when I graduate. They just nod when I say I'm not sure. I admire the apartment, which is larger and nicer than my mom's house, and ask Lisa's brother Jeremy about school, which is normally the wrong thing to ask a kid, but everyone does. He is precocious and launches into a detailed description of his classes, which may or may not be intended to make sure I never ask that question again. He's cheerful about it, though, and actually seems to love school. His parents make him stop after a while and he goes off to inspect the new typewriter. After he's gone, I feel comfortable enough to ask about the neighborhood. They have a lot of ideas about what might be happening, but they don't really know. They assume that the city, or a developer, is planning to tear it all down and build something, they just can't figure out what. They are pretty sure that their building is still occupied because the owner lives in it and doesn't want to move after forty years.

"She's white, of course. The neighborhood was always integrated, at least enough that the city made a big deal about the integrated DeBaliviere neighborhood. But lately, it's only integrated if you count the couple of blocks closest to Skinker, where students live. It's funny, people used to say 'DeBaliviere' with a sort of French accent, or what we thought was French, like it was this grand place. Now everyone says 'Debolliver' with a sort of shudder, like 'Diabolical' or something."

Lisa and I take the dishes to the kitchen and do the washing up. She closes the kitchen door and tells me she intends to find out what is going on.

"I think it's a plot to get the Black people back on the other side of Delmar. I just don't know how they are doing it. I can imagine why, but I can't see how it's going to play out."

"And you're whispering because you don't want your parents to know?"

"Mom says, 'You'll get your head bashed,' and I say, 'I get bashed every day one way or another,' and she says, 'I've got too much invested in you and I don't want to have to start over.' It's almost a routine we do. Mom knows."

I tell her it's been a long day and I need to go. We walk back through the living room, where her mother is looking out at the street.

"Everything okay out there?"

"Yes, just enjoying a little bit of breeze."

But the way she is turned, I get the impression that she's making sure my car is okay. Lisa and her dad walk me to the car, very casually, and I get in and wave at her mom in the window. Lisa and her dad are still watching me when I turn the corner toward Lindell and home.

CHAPTER 36

My Fear and Greed class meets on Friday morning and I'm the only Econ grad student in the class as far as I can see, although it's hard to tell. There are at least fifty students in the room. I expected Lisa to be there, given her interest in Saint Louis and the change going on in her neighborhood, but I don't see her.

Professor Stone shows up just a little late. He's tall and lanky and thirty-five-ish and strolls in with a dog as long-legged and casual as he is. He shuffles papers, lifts his face, waits for silence, and begins his first lecture.

"Del Mar!" he roars. "Who can tell me what Delmar means? Anyone?"

It's obviously a trick question if not a rhetorical one, so no one bites. He expects this, and he waits. And waits, until finally someone can't take the silence.

"Of the sea?" a soft voice finally says.

"Correct!" he roars again. "And what happened to the sea? What happened to. The. Sea?"

He doesn't want an answer this time; he pauses only for a second and then roars again:

"It parted."

He lets that sink in. I get it, and maybe most of the students have been in Saint Louis long enough to get it.

"It parted, and then some people raced to safety and some people drowned. And then what happened? The sea returned to its natural state."

Some students are scribbling frantically, and I imagine them to be reporters racing to file a story on a great leader's speech declaring victory or defeat. I sit back and watch. I'm impressed, but he's just being a showman at the moment. I'll know soon if he really has something to say. There's still time to switch classes if he's all about himself.

At the end of the hour, I am convinced, or nearly so. I'm too cynical to be one of those who surged to the front of the room with questions, either legitimate or designed to impress. But I'm convinced enough that he has a solid syllabus, so I go to the bookstore and buy one of the three required books. Dr. Stone didn't write this one, which I consider a good sign. The other two books are available at a bookstore in the Loop—on Delmar, in fact; he made a comment in class about supporting the local economy. I suspect he's also making sure all his students leave campus once in a while. I walk back to the Loop and buy the two books, stop at the apartment for lunch, and head back to campus.

I catch up with Lisa after our afternoon class and ask her which specialty she signed up for.

"I kind of thought you might be taking the Fear and Greed option."

"Nope, I see enough of both of those things. I'm doing political economics. I want to get something done!" She tells me that a few of her high school friends went to UMSL—she looks at me to make sure I know that means University of Missouri at Saint Louis, which I do because I figure it out on the fly—and she would hang out with them and some of their classmates, and they all wanted to change the world. "They were studying social work and criminology and education, things like that. And I would think, okay, that's cool, you can change the world that way. But that is too small for me, too slow for me. I want to figure it out and change things."

At that point I'm convinced that she could change anything, but then her chin and her voice drop.

"I still don't know how, though. They are all teaching and social working and whatever, and I'm still in school and I don't really know how to do squat. I don't even know what squat is."

I think about my important bride-sitting job and giggle.

"You think you don't know squat?" I say. "Let me tell you about me! I babysit brides on Saturday night! How's that for bringing about world peace?"

"Hey, it's WILD tonight! Let's go WILD and save the world tomorrow." So, we follow the crowds to the quad for the twice-a-year Walk-in-Lay-Down Theater where everyone eats hot dogs and drinks semi-legal beer and watches movies. We run into Marianne and I introduce her to Lisa.

"Novelle has just the right sofa for WILD," Marianne tells Lisa. "She should have brought it and left it here. Or traded with some drunken frat rat for a real sofa. Hey, let's pick one and kick the drunks off and take it home."

I give her a shove and we find some guys with a keg who are not too drunk to give us a beer but are way too drunk to insist on quid pro quo. After the first movie, we leave WILD to the undergrads and go home. It's been a long but educational week.

CHAPTER 37

With school in session, it seems like it should be Labor Day weekend, but it's not. It's still August and it's sultry. I spend the morning in the cool, quiet Y, reading *Streetcar Suburbs*, which Dr. Stone wants us to have finished by the next Friday's class. I get so engrossed that when the bridal party for the eleven o'clock wedding knocks on the door, I'm startled. The bride has been up since five getting hair and makeup and dress just right. The bridal party clearly wanted an evening wedding but were overruled by one of the mothers, who doesn't like to be out late. The bride is doing her best to appease her bridesmaids, who feel ridiculous wearing formal dresses before noon. I get out the Y's new tape player and play Pachelbel's "Canon," which seems to calm them down and they hum their way up and out.

I go back to the book, which I've nearly finished, and realize that it's not about fear or greed and not all that much about economics. I think about that for a while and decide it's a good sign, a sign that Dr. Stone is not the strident radical his dramatic opening hinted at. I finish before the wedding is over and discover that eventually the author does conclude that America's capitalistic economic system resulted in the socioeconomic segregation and class warfare of the twentieth century.

I have a couple of hours between weddings, and I go out into the sunlight and stroll through the quad. The maintenance crews have already cleared away the WILD remains and are repairing the grass. I'm glad I have a job inside, out of the heat. I go back underground and make a few notes about streetcar suburbs and then read through the first few chapters of the statistics class I'm TA-ing, in case anyone already needs help when I have my first office hours session on Monday.

The evening wedding is small, just the bride and her maid of honor. They seem older than the usual bridal party and are utterly calm and cheerful, with the most elegant dresses and hair I've ever seen. The bride's uncle comes to claim them and takes away their dress bags and shoe boxes. They tell me not to wait and leave a completely undeserved tip.

I am as thrilled by the free hour as by the tip, and I lock up and walk home. When I leave campus on the pedestrian bridge, I look down and realize that the abandoned railroad track below was almost certainly laid for a streetcar. "Duh," I say to myself. "The Loop is a streetcar turnaround. I live in a streetcar suburb."

The steamy weather has threatened all day to turn into a thunderstorm, which breaks as I'm starting down Wingate. I run the last block and arrive at my stoop panting for breath and wiping rain out of my eyes. A dirty sweater is lying crumpled on the step and I nudge it with my foot as I fit the key in the lock. I hear a noise and look down. Two eyes look back out of a matted cat face. The face is that of a stranger, but the next meow I recognize. DB is back.

I scoop him up and almost wish I hadn't. He's sticky and smelly and possibly harboring fleas. But I take him upstairs and shrug out of my backpack. I can't think what to do next, so I put him in the bathtub and run warm water in the lavatory. One of the very few things I know about cats is that they hate baths and water in general, so I close the door before I lift him into the sink. He seems to weigh almost nothing at all. He squirms but doesn't bite or scratch. Once he is thoroughly wet, he doesn't even squirm. I get him as clean as I can, dribbling water on his face and cleaning his ears with cotton. I change the water three times before it stays clear when I rinse him, and I lift him out and rub him dry. I set him on the bamboo chair, wrapped in a towel, while I rinse out the tub and lavatory, and when I return to pick him up he meets me at the bathroom door, looking up and meowing.

"Well look who's back," I say, and open a can of tuna.

He sleeps for a long time on the bamboo chair, so I sit at my desk and look out the window and write a letter to my mother. When he wakes up, I feed him again, and when I leave to mail the letter, he follows me out and disappears around the corner of the building.

CHAPTER 38

Monday and Tuesday pass smoothly and no undergrads appear for help with statistics, so I've earned my first week's pay for little effort beyond reading a few chapters of the textbook. On Wednesday morning I drop by the Y to pick up the weekend's bride list. As I leave, I'm met with an outrush of students heading for Graham Chapel, and they carry me along, talking loudly about this year's first speaker, Angela Davis. It's a short walk, but I hear a lot about Angela Davis and the speaker series. Older students are explaining to younger ones that no classes are scheduled on Wednesday at eleven so that all students are free to attend. I had read about Angela Davis in the previous day's *Student Life*, but I hadn't grasped that we would be getting a speaker every single week for the entire school year.

It's only ten-fifteen, but we are almost the last people to get seats. We are squeezed together and everyone is talking. Students behind us are debating whether or not the white kids should leave and let more Black kids in.

"She's an icon, they need to be inside, in here, in the same room with Angela Davis!" one young Black man is insisting.

I'm ready to get up and let someone have my seat, but I'm wedged in and even if I got out of the pew it's unlikely I could get back to the door.

The debate goes on.

"Don't you want us to get some enlightenment too?"

"You can raise your consciousness out in the grass next to the loudspeakers!"

At eleven exactly, the chancellor appears and silence reigns. Ms. Davis is introduced to raucous cheering that goes on for several minutes. She is armed with facts and humor and when she finally leaves the dais, I am ready to quit school and nominate her for president. That lasts until I'm outside, but her words ring in my ears the rest of the day. It feels like a kick-start to something that I hope I'll figure out in my semester of Fear and Greed.

On Thursday I make sure I get to the Y before it closes. Betty is feeling guilty that I've given up so many Saturdays to bride-sitting, but I remind her that she's paying me, and now that classes have started it's enforced study time. As I'm leaving, she points to a pile of what looks like laundry. It's Arlo's bedsheet banner.

"Will you take that thing home?" she asks. "If it lies around here it will end up in the storeroom where no one will ever think about it again and we'll just throw it away in five or ten years."

I pick up a corner. Pale blue sheets striped with black poster paint and now with cobwebs and most likely bird poop.

"You've got a sewing machine; I'm sure you can do something with them. Maybe the paint will wash out. Or you can just use the unpainted parts. There's a lot—four sheets, right?"

I wrinkle my nose.

"Okay, then just toss them in a dumpster for me, would you?"

I stuff them in a box and start across campus, thinking I'll find a dumpster near the end of the walkway. But I'm thinking about Angela Davis and miss any dumpsters I might have passed. I can still put them in the dumpster at home, but now it seems a waste to throw them out. I can see a corner of the hand drawing and that reminds me of my paper Big Art "curtains" that Marianne makes a new joke about every time she sees them. They are looking pretty ratty and they now make the room dark unless the sun is shining directly on them.

I stop at the Laundromat and shove the sheets in an extra-capacity machine. I don't have detergent and look around for the machine that sells small boxes for high prices. Instead, I see Tom from Holmes Lounge, the Tom who told me about iced coffee.

"Hello," I say to get his attention. "You're Tom, right?" I give him a big smile.

"Oh, hi, um . . . Noelle?"

"Close. It's Novelle, but I answer to Noelle too. People see Novelle and think Noelle." Why am I babbling?

"Come here often? I guess that sounds like a bad pickup line."

"It does, and I guess the answer is not often enough. I forgot my detergent. I don't suppose I could borrow a cup of . . ." I peek into the laundry bag at his feet. "Rinso? That sounds like a pickup line too, so we're even."

I put the Rinso in my machine and get it started on the super cycle. Maybe a lot of the poster paint will wash out and just leave an arty effect.

"Thanks," I tell Tom. "See you around—I've got to zip over to the hardware store."

I go looking for a cheap and easy way to hang the sheets over my large windows so that they'll look enough like curtains that I won't get smart remarks from Marianne. Real curtain rods are more expensive than the sheets deserve and more than I've got with me. The same man who sold me the shower hardware back in June is at the counter and eventually tracks me down. I don't want to say "I'm looking for a very cheap way to string up old sheets to make crappy curtains," but there's really no other way to put it, so I say that, leaving out the adjectives. He comes up with L brackets and wire cable.

"You could use nylon cord instead. It would be a little cheaper. But if the window is more than about thirty inches wide, the cord is going to sag. Even the wire will sag if the span is too long. You'll have to really pull it tight."

I picture the pairs of double windows and decide that each pair is probably sixty inches.

"I could put a hook or something in the middle, right? Like a plant hanger?"

He agrees and I buy it all and rush back to the Laundromat. If you're not there when the washer shuts off, the laundry is likely to be on the floor when you do get there. I know I'm cutting it close.

But the washer is still in the spin cycle. Tom is folding shirts and comes over.

"Did you get what you needed? Central Hardware on Kingshighway is a lot bigger."

"I just needed simple stuff. They had everything."

The washer shuts off and I look around for a dryer. The place is full and the dryers are all in use.

"You can have this one," Tom says. He's taking a load of towels out and stuffing them in his laundry bag.

I ignore the glares of two girls who were obviously hoping for that dryer. Laundromat etiquette is pretty clear and I should give way to them, but I'm flustered and pretend I don't see them. I put two dimes in the dryer and start it. Twenty minutes won't get the sheets completely dry, but it will relieve me of one-third of my guilt.

I look up and see the glares and give them a guilty smile. I also see that Tom has taken his towels out of his laundry bag and piled them on a table, where he is now taking his time, folding them very carefully. He looks up.

"That's a lot of sheets," he says with a curious smile.

I give in and explain that they were passed on to me from a banner project and I'm hoping to use them for curtains, if enough paint washes out and if the hardware plan works out. He perks up at this.

"I could help with the screws. I've got a drill in my trunk. And a screwdriver."

I look at him carefully to see if there is any double entendre in the double reference to screws. I'm not 100 percent sure, but I decide to take a chance. I give him my address and he goes to retrieve his car.

He's already there when I arrive, regretting that I've invited someone I don't know at all into my apartment. But while I'm getting my mail, Marianne comes in behind us, filling the tiny lobby to capacity. I introduce Marianne and Tom, explaining that he's going to help me put up new curtains, and giving Marianne a wide-eyed look that I hope she interprets as an indication that she should come along too.

"This I've got to see!" Marianne says almost too enthusiastically. "I've been on her about her crappy paper curtains forever." She must realize that she's overdoing it. "Not that my apartment is exactly a showpiece."

Tom looks a little disappointed, but then seems to change his mind and makes a joke about string theory, which gets him blank looks from both of us. He has to explain what string theory is, and by the time we get to the third floor, Marianne and

I understand that it's a physics concept and might have something to do with the fifth dimension. It's clear that the fifth dimension he's describing is not the rock group.

Inside, I rip down the Big Art and we get to work installing the brackets and stretching the wire. Tom says he thought we were using string, not wire, and he had a theory about that.

"String theory," Marianne and I groan in unison.

"Physics humor," Tom says. "You gotta take it where you can find it."

The plant hook goes up to support the middle, which Tom says is unnecessary. I tell him it's really so I can get my grandmother's grandmother of all spider plants out of my kitchen, and he lets it go.

As he's packing up his tools, he casually asks if anyone wants to go out for something to eat. It's all-you-can-eat night at the Pasta House. Marianne and I look at each other, shrug, and agree that pasta sounds good.

We settle into our seats, decline the waitress's offer of wine, and order our first courses: spaghetti for Tom, lasagna for Marianne, and rigatoni for me. We trade stories about our first week of grad school and drink iced tea. Tom twirls a strand of spaghetti on his fork and says "anyone for spaghetti theory?" with a twinkle in his eye. This time we are ready for him and we laugh.

When the waitress comes back for our plates, Tom asks for toasted ravioli and the waitress looks at Marianne and me.

"All-you-can-eat night," Tom says. "Live it up."

We order toasted ravioli too, although I at least am pretty full of rigatoni. I'm glad when the plates arrive and there are only two raviolis on each. Tom eats his and asks for another order while

Marianne and I eat ours more slowly. I turn my head and fake an anxious look into the kitchen.

"I hope the supply exceeds the demand," I say, and get a look from the others that probably matches the look Tom got when he told the string theory joke. "Okay, Econ humor is pretty bad too."

Tom orders a third plate of ravioli and looks at us expectantly. Marianne says, "What the heck," and has one more, but when the waitress returns yet again, Marianne raises a hand and says, "No more," in a firm voice.

The waitress doesn't look at Tom; she just says she'll bring the bill. Tom insists on paying since, he says, he ate enough for three. Marianne and I leave the tip, and a generous one because, as Marianne says looking meaningfully at Tom, we may want to come here again.

Tom drops us at the curb and we walk into our building. When the door is closed behind us, I look at Marianne.

"What did you think?"

"I like to see a guy enjoy his food," she answers, and we giggle like teenagers and go our separate ways. Upstairs, I decide I like the curtains. The shadows thrown by the streetlight make interesting patterns and disguise the faint wash of poster paint still visible. I rehang the spider plant and think I could root a few of the babies and hang more pots if I decide to disguise the curtains a little more. I look at the pathetic sofa and sigh. I've folded all my extra blankets to make what looks like a seat cushion but doesn't feel like one. I remember David Black's down comforter and add it. Much more comfortable, but a long way from my old bamboo couch. I tell myself that if I get tips this weekend I'll go to Kmart and see if I can find cushions or at least foam that I can cover somehow and make cushions.

CHAPTER 39

At the second Fear and Greed class, Dr. Stone arrives a minute or two late again, and again with the dog, who lies down and goes to sleep. He pauses as though for dramatic effect, then lights up a cigar. He's standing under a NO SMOKING sign, and I groan. This is the newest building on campus, and the ugliest, but with the upside that it's one of the few buildings where smoking is not allowed in any of the classrooms. He takes a long draw and sends out a chain of smoke rings. Finally, he looks around at us.

"Anyone mind if I smoke?" He actually looks back at the sign and then raises his eyebrows in a question.

I raise my hand. I hate cigar smoke and hate going home with hair and clothes reeking.

"You can leave then." He says it as a joke and it gets a laugh. I slowly put away my notebook and pen, get out of my seat, shrug into my backpack, and walk toward the door.

"Wait, don't go, I'll put it out." He says it mildly, almost like he doesn't mean it, and I watch while he does put it out completely, no lingering wisp of smoke. I look him in the face, smile just a little, and take a seat in the very back of the room. I hope I haven't just guaranteed myself a C. I also hope we don't have to go through this routine again next week.

"Who did the reading?" is today's opening. Most hands go up. He canceled our Monday class, so we've had a week to read *Streetcar Suburbs.*

"All of it?" A few hands go down.

"Who didn't read it?" He says this very casually, and then adds quietly but still watching us, "You're the ones who should leave." No one leaves and I feel just a little better about smarting off earlier.

He then launches into his lecture, which never mentions the book, or Boston, which is where it takes place, or Delmar. Fear, greed, and economics are also missing. At the end, he resumes his opening posture.

"Who here lives in a streetcar suburb?"

No one raises a hand, and I'm not sure if it's a rhetorical question or not. If I'd been in the front row I would probably not have raised my hand either, afraid of . . . something. But I'm in the back, so I raise my left palm, elbow on the desk as if this is too obvious to bother with, and keep my eyes focused on writing in my notebook as if I had better things to do than answer stupid questions.

"I checked, and as far as I can tell only four of you should have your hands down. The rest of you, not including Ms. Hat in the back, should read the book again or drop the class. Now that you know where you live, and after you've read the book, think about fear and greed and economics. We'll discuss that next time. Class dismissed."

I slip out the door, both embarrassed and pleased. And a little nervous about the assignment. I like economics because the assignments involve getting to the right answer, not thinking about something vague and then worse, talking about it with forty other people. Assuming forty people are still in the class next week.

Friday afternoon is our third Quantitative Methods in Economics class, which all twelve of us are taking. It's a two-semester course taught by the adviser for all first-year Econ grad students. His name is Dr. Beagle and he is about ten years older than most of us. He tells us to call him Jim. Since he is our adviser, he tells us, he plans to use the first fifteen to twenty minutes of the ninety-minute Friday class making sure we are all getting on well in our classes. He also tells us that we are each to meet with him for an hour twice a month, one-on-one. To me, this sounds supportive.

To Lisa, it sounds fishy, she tells me as we leave class. "What's all that one-on-one about? Can't he just hold office hours and we'll see him if we need him, like everyone else does? I mean, we're grad students, not eighteen-year-old freshmen."

Put that way, I see her point. But we can't come up with any reason he would do it other than to make sure we have help if we need it.

"If it were just you and me, then I could think of something, but it's ten guys too. And anyway, twelve is too many for a married guy." She had noticed what I hadn't looked for, a wedding ring.

It's Labor Day weekend, and it's still as hot as July. The weather forecast is for high afternoon temperatures but chilly mornings, and I remind myself again to do something about replacing my bell-bottom jeans with something less obviously dated.

I spend Saturday morning on a trip to Kmart looking for couch cushions or something that can be made into couch cushions. They sell foam blocks in standard sizes and I buy two that fit my couch precisely and thank manufacturing economies of scale for standard sizing. I walk through the fabric department and, since it's Labor Day weekend, find a sale on pretty much anything with a flower on it or in summer colors. I pick a blue-and-lime striped canvas-like fabric that I am almost certain won't clash with the bamboo chair or the blue curtains. I take it home, wrap the fabric around the foam, and put it on the sofa and sigh with relief. I'm almost there—my home will soon be almost normal again.

After the evening wedding, I look carefully at how the chair cushions are made, lay the new fabric out on the floor, and get started. I misjudge how clingy the foam is and how little it wants to slip into its new casings. I should have left the long edges open instead of the short ends. I go downstairs to see if Marianne can provide two more hands. Tom opens the door.

"Oh," I say. "Tom."

"Novelle! We've been talking about you."

I realize that the discomfort I'm feeling is a smidgeon of jealousy and just as quickly know it's misplaced.

"That's great," I say. "Were you talking about how I need four extra hands for about five minutes?"

"We were," Tom says, and they grab the bottle of wine they were drinking, and we all go upstairs.

The foam blocks realize they have met their match and succumb to the indignity of the new covers. Just to show them who's boss, we then sit on them and drink wine, and I tell Tom the long version of the curtain story. His face has the look of someone who had a close call and escaped unscathed, but he does say that he was thinking about curtains for his apartment.

I tell him that I'll make them for twenty-five dollars or rent him the sewing machine for ten dollars, delivery not included. We finish the wine and they say goodnight and leave.

I go to bed alone but feeling good about the couch cushions. The jealousy was a momentary thing, I tell myself. I do envy Marianne for having someone, though. Or maybe I just hope there's someone out there for me.

Sunday morning, I wake up shivering and close all the windows, then go through my closet. My choices for less-sweltering weather are limited now that I've banished my bell-bottoms. My old denim skirt is too short now, but I wear it with my dark blue yoga tights and decide it will do. Molly's is closed until Tuesday, when I promise myself I really will see if she has anything left from last year's student wardrobe castoffs. I look through my old jeans again and pull out a pair with no patchwork or embroidery. I rip open the side seams from the knees to the hems and resew them without the flare. They are too tight to be fashionable, but at least they aren't bell-bottoms.

The day warms up and I study with the windows open. I can smell the change of season in the fragrance of drying sycamore leaves still swaying outside. But it's chilly again by four o'clock and I look in my closet again. David Black's flannel shirts are still there, folded on a high shelf. I take one down and put it on, expecting a loose shirt I can wrap around me. Instead, it fits like a blouse. I look at the buttons, take the shirt off, and check the tag. It's a woman's shirt. David Black's a cross-dresser? Or did these shirts belong to a girlfriend? Then I remember that David Black never lived in 3D and the only thing in the apartment that really did belong to him is the bed that he passed on to me when he left 2B. And possibly the cat, who has stopped by only once since his messy return a week ago. Maybe my change of schedule doesn't suit his.

Monday morning the radio says it's forty-five degrees, and I stay in bed reading *The Power Broker* until the brilliant sunshine entices me outside. It's dry and cool and invigorating after months of heat and humidity. I wish I had a bike—the weather makes me want to ride through Forest Park. Instead, I drive, park at the first space I come to, and walk to the zoo. It's jammed with people, but I have no agenda and wander around until I'm tired and make my way home to grade my first problem set from the statistics class I am TA-ing. I read one more chapter of *The Power Broker* before falling asleep—it's a long book and I want to get a head start before Dr. Stone gets to it.

CHAPTER 40

I run into Marianne between classes on Tuesday. "So, you and Tom! How did you run into him again? Isn't Physics all the way down in Crow Hall?" She caws a few times and while I'm rolling my eyes she says she saw him in Graham Chapel at the Wednesday Assembly Series the week after we had dinner at the Pasta House.

"He was there? He didn't even go hear Angela Davis!"

"Yes, and you went on and on about that at dinner: Angela said this and Angela said that. He did ask who was up next and I told him Vincent Canby. I'm pretty sure he'd never heard of Vincent Canby, but there he was in the very last row where he could see everyone as they came in."

"And there you were!"

"And there I was, pretending not to look for him." She laughs. "At least he read up on Vincent Canby before he got there. Probably just the *Student Life* article, but he was trying. He really liked Vincent Canby too."

I'm in a hurry to get to Molly's before my afternoon class and Marianne decides to tag along. While Molly helps me sort through potential pants, Marianne tries on hats.

"That hat of yours is starting to look like you borrowed it from a scarecrow," she says, admiring herself in what she claims is a Greek fisherman's cap. "You can wear it until Halloween and then it's going in the dumpster."

She's right, except that it should probably go in the dumpster now.

"Oooooo, now this is a hat!"

Molly and I turn to look, and Marianne is lifting a dark-red velvet hat with a wide brim from a leather hatbox. She puts it on my head and spins me around.

"Whoo-eee. That is it."

She's right, this is the hat, but the fifty-dollar price tag is way out of my range.

I twirl around and declare it to be just a tad small and completely impractical for rainy Saint Louis.

"It will look great with a dusting of snow," I say. "For about two and a half minutes."

We go back to pants and turtlenecks and come up with a couple of each. I try them on and look in the mirror. I thank Molly for saving me again from fashion faux pas.

"Thank those girls who got all the latest things for Christmas last year and were done with it by June," she says. "I've just been holding onto it until the weather turned cold again."

"Hanukkah," says Marianne, who is now wearing a balaclava in red and green, obviously homemade. "Need one of these?"

We ignore her.

"You're going to have to go back to Clayton for shoes, though," Molly says. "Those Keds aren't going to get you through. Or go downtown. Stix, Famous-Barr, Baker Shoes. Lots to choose from."

I lock my knees, look at my feet. She's right. I've spent four years in a small college with tunnels between all the buildings and no need to go outside if the weather was bad. I vaguely remember a pair of brown suede desert boots in high school. Maybe there's some sort of updated style.

Wednesday I have yoga and arrive at the Y early to catch up with Betty. She's in the cleaned-up storage room with Dots and Jackie. They've decided to convert it to a quiet lounge.

"Look at this stuff!" Jackie holds up pieces of leather that a board member has dropped off, impressed by the Big Art and Big Draw programs. "We're thinking of making beanbag chairs with this."

They talk me into bringing in my sewing machine to piece them together, swearing to do all the work themselves.

Thursday is the last farmers' market of the year. I stock up on apples and tomatoes and get into a conversation with a guy who lives in a big apartment on Leland in a sort of co-op. Craig is in charge of buying food and invites me to join them for dinner. The apartment is only a block from mine, so I go along and help cook rice and vegetables and a huge apple pie. The talk at dinner is about eating plant foods instead of animal foods. Most of them still eat eggs and milk; they even make their own yogurt. But at their communal meals, they only eat plants. I look at my plate and realize that I haven't missed anything, but then my eating habits are not exactly habits, and I probably eat lots of meals with no animal anything. They are all friendly in a casual way and lend me a copy of *Diet for a Small Planet*. Craig walks me home and tells me to drop in for dinner any time, there is always room for whoever shows up. I like the idea of having more friends in the neighborhood and promise I'll be back.

The whole neighborhood seems livelier now that school is in session. Or maybe it's the cooler weather too. Children are playing on the swings and slides across the street from my building, and some elderly people are sitting on the benches. Maybe some of them are Russian immigrants.

Friday morning the radio announces that it's forty-four degrees, a record for Saint Louis on this date. It's warmer by the time I leave for school and I'm fine with a sweater, but I take time to send my mom a note to mail the box of blankets and sweaters and my winter coat. I drive to Clayton in the evening and buy what Molly would call real shoes.

I'm now set for cold weather, so the temperatures go back to the eighties and nineties and rain leaves town, apparently for good. I don't even open the box Mom sends until it occurs to me that she might have been a normal mom and sent cookies. She didn't.

CHAPTER 41

In October, at my third one-on-one with Dr. Beagle, he hits on me. He's always been a bit too friendly for an adviser, but it's always been in a boy-from-school sort of way. This time, however, he tells me that I remind him of a deer and asks what kind of animal he reminds me of. *Beagle*, I think, and then nothing else will come to mind and I realize that this isn't an adviser's question, it's a come-on. It's all very light and easy, but there he is, leaning back in his chair and smiling at me, waiting for an answer.

I smile back. I reject the impulse to get up and walk out. I could risk it with the cigar incident in Dr. Stone's class, but that wasn't exactly personal and it was in front of a large group, and Dr. Stone only controls one grade. He's not my adviser. He won't be controlling my thesis next year. I decide to laugh it off: "A beagle, of course." I'm sure he's heard that since kindergarten, but he's the one who brought it up. I tell him I need to leave a little early today.

I head off campus in case he's watching, but when I get to Delmar I remember that this is the day the Y is making beanbag chairs and I have promised to help. I walk back to campus on

Wingate and wonder if he lives in one of these houses. I decide it's unlikely, he seems too young, but I hurry on anyway and run across Forest Park Parkway instead of taking the overpass. I wonder who I think I'm fooling and why I'm bothering.

I forget about it at the Y, where enthusiasm for beanbag chairs is high and enthusiasm for actual sewing is low. I take over, which I knew would be the case anyway, and we finish three and decide that is enough. No one has any ideas for using the rest of the leather, so I fill a bag with as much as I can carry. Betty gives me a lift home with the sewing machine and I feel safe in her presence and in her car.

I stew about Dr. Beagle for another day or two and gradually forget about it. We've started discussing *Power Broker* in my Fear and Greed class. This one is about New York and I'm beginning to understand Dr. Stone's method. We're reading about Boston and New York, but he now starts every class with an article from the *St. Louis Post-Dispatch* or the *Globe-Democrat*. We are encouraged to draw our own conclusions in short weekly essays.

The hot days and cool nights continue into the second week of October, when the temperature suddenly drops into the thirties one night. The next morning, I finally dig through the box my mom sent, looking for the wool pea coat that I've had since senior year of high school. I lift it out and find that the moths have spent the summer feasting on it. I shake out my sweaters, which are mostly not wool, and put on two of them. This won't work. I try a sweater-and-flannel-shirt combination over my turtleneck but I feel like a sausage and the shirt won't button. And then I remember David Black's coat, still on the top closet shelf. I remember it as nylon, or maybe smooth cotton, surely nothing moths would enjoy. I have an odd premonition that it won't be on the shelf, but it is. I try it on and zip it up.

It's roomy, too roomy to have belonged to the same person who wore the flannel shirts. But David Black and his mysterious ways have ceased to worry me, and I shoulder my backpack and leave. Locking the door, I wonder if anyone will recognize the coat and ask me about David, or not David, but whoever was wearing this coat last year. I run into no one in my own building, and by the time I reach the walkway I realize that half the world is wearing navy blue nylon and no one is going to look twice at mine.

My next one-on-one with Dr. Beagle is businesslike. I've prepared a list of questions and rocket through them in twenty minutes. I tell him it looks like we are finished, so I'll spend the rest of the time in the library. I've practiced this line, having tried several and reached the conclusion that can't be open-ended and can't end in a question. I even debate telling him I'll be in the library, so I add that I need to catch up on newspapers for another class, which I don't name. The newspapers are the most public section of the main floor. He answers by blowing me a kiss, and I leave quickly. I go to the University City library and read the papers there, in case he calls me on it next time.

It's dark when I leave and I'm a little creeped out. Between articles I'm stewing about both incidents. I am letting him see that I'm uncomfortable, which I know instinctively isn't good. He must know that I am thinking about him, even if I'm not attracted to him. Maybe that's all he wants.

CHAPTER 42

In my other classes, I become more confident and start participating in discussions. By now, everyone in the group, with the occasional exception of Don, has settled down and stopped posturing and talking about "in my undergrad . . ." and we help each other out more than we compete. We have even talked to the department chair about ending the practice of grading on the curve for our group. "We're not the marketplace. We'll learn more if we support each other than if we are encouraged to mislead and backstab."

He is not convinced that grading on the curve creates competition, but we roll our eyes in unison and tell him to get real and he tells us he will allow it for a semester, as an experiment. We wonder who is designing the experiment and decide that he will probably assign that task to Student T, but we keep that joke to ourselves. We certainly don't share it outside the Economics department because even the dweebiest of us knows that it's a lame joke that's not even all that funny for statisticians, whom we consider to be even more boring than economists.

- - -

One night I drop in at the co-op apartment on Leland and arrive in the middle of a loud discussion. I unpack the salad I've brought and try to figure out what everyone is so passionate about.

"Okay, so how many Black people are sitting at this table? Any of you Black?" Obviously, no one is Black; the speaker is posturing. "James, what's that look about?"

"My gran was Black. Well, half. Or quarter I guess it was."

"So that makes you like sixteenth?"

"I guess. My mom never said anything about it."

The previous discussion stops; everyone is interested in James's Black gran.

"What was that like? Having a Black grandmother?"

"Don't know really, I never met her."

"My grandma died before I was born too."

"Oh, she didn't die, I don't think. I don't know I guess."

I'm still standing there holding a bowl of lettuce and whatever else was in my refrigerator. I can't imagine not knowing if Granny were dead or alive. Then I remember that I have another grandmother somewhere. I never met her either. Someone takes the bowl, puts it on the table.

The original speaker resumes his topic.

"See, that's what's wrong here. Joe never even met his grandmother who was partly Black. He never ate a meal with her. And we have never had a meal here with anyone who wasn't white."

A small voice: "Jews are white, huh?"

No one replies to that.

"We are all so like standin' with the brothers and anti-discrimination and yet no Black person has ever had a meal at this table. We've had what? Hundreds of people, like Novelle there, she just appears and we invite her to dinner. But never a Black person."

This isn't what I came here for, but I'm spellbound.

"And you know what else? We can't even fix it. Because now that we know this, what are we going to do? Go out looking for a Black person to invite to dinner and bring him here and . . . and what? Say hurrah for us? God, we can't do it now. God. We are the face of racism."

I suspect that more than one person here has had a toke or two, but that only means he's more verbose than usual, not that his thinking is skewed. He's right. He's so right.

Bowls are passed and the conversation moves on and everyone eats as though we were normal, liberal, change-the-world people. But we're not. Or worse, we are.

CHAPTER 43

On November 1, I find myself walking toward Delmar with a woman whose face is familiar and I ask if she lives in the neighborhood, making small talk.

“Oh no, I own the card shop on Delmar, the one that’s closing. I go to early Mass at All Saints and then go to the shop to catch up on the bookkeeping.”

I try to remember the card shop and finally picture a tiny slice of storefront down toward Skinker. I’ve been in once or twice.

“I’m so sorry you’re closing. I like your little shop.”

“Well, I’m not getting so much business anymore. I finally figured out that when the new bookstore opened at WashU a few years ago they started carrying cards and the students stopped walking all the way over here. Not that they were my main clients, but they made the difference. And then Paul’s Books started carrying a few cards—the moms are all in there buying books for their kids. Don’t get me wrong, I was thrilled when Paul moved in. That really perked up the whole Loop, and of course that wouldn’t have happened without Blueberry Hill. I think that went in in 1972. But all that, plus the little influx of Russian Jews right around the shop, well, I just don't know what to sell to them. I don't even know if they send cards to each other."

I make sympathetic noises, thinking to myself that this is supply and demand, simple economics. It seems less simple now.

"But I'll survive. I still have the Laundromat and people will always need clean clothes, right?"

I think about my secret wish to have a washer and dryer in the basement of the apartment building. That could wreak havoc on the demand side of the Laundromat business. So, I say, "What would happen if more landlords put washers and dryers in the basements of all these buildings someday?"

She doesn't seem worried, just thoughtful. "Well, that's a lot of machines to take care of. Maybe I'd go into the maintenance business." She smiles at me, triumphant. "In fact, maybe I'll get in ahead of them. What's your landlord's name—maybe I'll talk to him about that."

I tell her that my landlord is a landlady and that I'll stop in with the number in a day or two. She tells me her name—Mrs. Como—and we say goodbye. As I walk on toward campus I think about resilience in the extremely local economy. I also think about Mrs. Marzello and wonder if that's the best place to pilot a new business.

I don't know how long the card shop will be open, so I take Mrs. Marzello's phone number around the next day. I start to buy a Thanksgiving card for Granny, and then remember that Granny is unreachable now. I buy one anyway to send to Mom and Lulu. Mrs. Como looks at the slip of paper I've handed her. She hands it back. "Marzello, now. I don't really want to get in with that bunch." She presses her lips together and I'm pretty sure I'm not going to find out anything else. I pay for the card and leave.

"Bye," Mrs. Como says, voice soft and friendly now. "Let me know if you think of someone else."

I wonder about that and decide that the only way to find out is to ask. So, I make a salad that night and knock on the door at Craig's apartment on Leland. Craig isn't there, but no one thinks anything about that and we all sit down to eat. I tell them about the card shop closing and get a few sympathetic murmurs. I can't figure out how to get where I want by going in that direction, so I wait a bit and ask if their landlord happens to be named Marzello. That starts an animated discussion, more like shouting, with everyone trying to tell me horror stories at once. When it finally calms down, I sort out that several of them have lived in my building or its twin and have endured cold, water leaks, and general ineptitude at her hands.

"I take it she doesn't own this building?"

"Are you crazy?" is the gist of the many responses I get.

So, I tell them about Mrs. Como and her idea about laundries in buildings. They look at each other and then confide in me that their landlord lives in Florida and that they have stealthily replaced the lock on the door to their basement and installed their own washer and dryer, which they promptly say I can use any time I like. With a little prodding I get the names and numbers of two other nearby landlords who are not as inept as mine nor as absent as theirs. I take them home along with my new laundry room key and present the names to Mrs. Como on the next afternoon, which turns out to be her last day at the store.

The next time I'm at Leland, there is a heated debate going on about the presidential election. That the post-Nixon, unelected Republican Ford should have any chance at re-election shocks me. I voice this opinion and am smacked down with the poll numbers, which have shifted dramatically after the first debate. I also learn that as Missouri goes, so goes the nation: So far, the candidate that wins in Missouri has always been the next president. They entreat me to change my voter registration to Missouri, since the deadline is looming. We all know that it's coincidental, not causal, but their passion is one of the things that endear me to this motley group, so I promise.

A few days later I get a letter from Mom saying that she and Lulu are driving to Saint Louis for Thanksgiving; it's too sad to celebrate at home without Granny. I panic about cooking a holiday dinner, that the responsibility has somehow skipped a generation, leaving me completely unprepared. But they arrive on Tuesday night, and they do the grocery shopping on Wednesday while I am at school, producing a new worry that they will bring home either TV dinners or a frozen turkey that won't fit in my oven and won't thaw in time anyway. They do neither of those things, and although the roasted chicken and mashed potatoes aren't as good as Granny's, that is mostly because we miss her.

Lulu goes to Fontbonne Wednesday afternoon and comes back upset because she can't start at Fontbonne in January. Her admittance has been delayed until fall so that she'll be in sync with the core business courses. And since her scholarship is only for two years, she can't risk missing required classes. I tell her it will be much better to start with a bang in the fall instead of a whimper in January, but I don't think she believes me. She certainly doesn't want to believe me.

They leave early Saturday and I send them off with a promise to be home for Christmas. We all know that it would be too sad to have Christmas anywhere else.

I spend the rest of the weekend reading *The Urban Prospect*, which is the final book for Fear and Greed. Lewis Mumford's essays do and don't have any relevance to the course. "The segregation of the spiritual life from the practical life is a curse that falls impartially upon both sides of our existence," is one of the lines I encounter that weekend. As a writer, Mumford really got around.

CHAPTER 44

December starts out very cold and I notice that the apartment seems chilly most days. I put on more sweaters and work at the kitchen table, which is away from all the leaky windows. I run into Marianne one morning and ask if her apartment is cold too. She says that it is and that it seems colder than last year. She doesn't know which unit has the thermostat, so we agree to find out that evening.

When I get home, I call the number for the Marzellos, but no one answers. I hope old Mrs. Marzello is all right. I wait an hour and try again, and still no answer. At seven-thirty, Marianne and I set out to knock on every door in the building. This is a little weird and a little exciting, since I've never met anyone but Marianne, even after six months of residence. The other three units on Marianne's floor are grad students, and they are cold and don't have the thermostat. On the second floor we find one unit with Russian immigrants who don't speak much English, but with enough sign language it becomes clear that they are cold too, and unhappy about it. We get far enough inside to see that several people live in the unit and that there is no thermostat unless it's in the bedroom or bathroom, which seems unlikely. Two more units on that floor have grad students and no thermostat, although the one in 2D wants to know why I bang on my pipes every morning. I tell him I don't, that I thought that was him. Neither of us believes the other. On my floor, only one knock is answered, and he doesn't have the thermostat either.

"I don't think it's on the third floor," Marianne says. "It should be in the middle, shouldn't it? So where is it?" I don't have an answer, but I tell her I'll try the other two units on my floor later and that I'll call the Marzello number again too.

After several days of trying, we give it up. One door on my floor is never answered, although I've seen lights on, and the other person only shouts through the door that he's studying. No one ever answers at the Marzello number.

During reading week, I stay at the library until it closes at midnight, run home to get warm, and jump into bed. Sometimes the radiators feel slightly warm in the evening but otherwise they are stone cold. In the mornings I take a hot shower and leave. I'm not happy about spending money eating meals on campus, and on Saturday I spend the morning at home cooking, which warms the kitchen a little. On Saturday afternoon I go to the Y early to wait for the bridal party, curious about who would get married right before Christmas. I soon find out—she's pregnant. But she seems happy and her bridesmaids treat her with a tenderness I haven't seen in any of the other weddings.

Sunday morning I go to Mass and stay in the church until the library opens, then rush to campus to finish my last paper, which I type at the Y. My fingers are too numb to type at home.

At my last meeting for the semester with Dr. Beagle, he tells me that I've done very well and that he hopes the grades on my exams are in keeping with my homework and participation grades. I don't like the look in his eye when he says this.

"I didn't have any trouble with the exams," I say, hoping he'll tell me if something is wrong. I decide to push a little rather than worry all through the semester break. "Is there something I need to know?"

He doesn't answer directly. "I thought we could celebrate a little." He moves closer to me. "It's a cold day out there. We could do something to warm it up."

"Good idea," I say without thinking, but moving toward the door. "Let's get coffee at Holmes Lounge." By now I've got the door open and I'm in the hall. He follows.

We walk across campus with me hugging my backpack to my chest with both arms and moving quickly. As we round the library and head for the door of Holmes Lounge, we can see that it's busy, with a steady flow in and out. Dr. Beagle stops.

"I just remembered that I have to be in Clayton at four o'clock. Three o'clock, I mean. See you in January." And he is gone.

I am shaken and then I am angry. I don't know how grading works. I've always assumed that the professor assigns a grade and that's it. But he implied that there was more to it, that he had some say. I know I will stew about this all through Christmas and New Year's, so I decide to do something about it. I retrace my steps to the Economics department. My old friend from the typewriter project is at her desk and we chat a little about that. All the old typewriters are gone, and she seems to have a new best friend in the housing office. Finally, I get to the point.

"Are any of the final grades posted yet?"

"All of them except Dr. Beagle's. His are late for some reason. I've been leaving messages. Go ahead and check—they are in the hall out there. Just look them up by your social security number."

One A and two A-minuses. All I could want. I go back to thank the secretary.

"One more thing, though. Those are the exam grades, or the final grades for the whole course?"

"Just the exams are posted, but I can tell you your grades in the class if the professor has handed them in. And everyone has except Dr. Beagle. Everyone else is as anxious as the students to get out of here."

She looks them up in various notebooks, writes them on a slip of paper, and hands them over. Two As and one A-minus.

"Thanks, this is a relief," I tell her.

"Why, was there any doubt? You know you are doing well, don't you?"

"Never mind, it's just something Dr. Beagle said."

"Oh, what was that?" Her voice has taken on an edge and I don't know what is behind it.

"Nothing really, I was just worried I guess. End-of-semester stress or something." And I tell her to have a great holiday and turn to leave. I'm not going to worry about my fourth grade. I'm just not.

The secretary calls me back.

"One more thing, Novelle. Don left the program last week and didn't turn the grades in for the course he is, or was, TA-ing. The chairman asked me to see if you could do half of them—I'll get someone else to do the rest. It's only micro 101, mostly multiple choice with a few short-answer questions."

"I was supposed to leave tonight . . ."

"Oh, it's okay—as long as you have them in by the thirtieth. We explained to the students already. And of course we'll pay you extra."

I don't see any way to say no, so I say yes and add grading papers to the list of things I'm not going to worry about today.

I go home and pack, try Mrs. Marzello one last time, and then throw my duffel in the car and leave for Christmas at home. It's after five and quite dark, but I see a shadow that might be a cat cross in front of my headlights. I stop the car and look, but whatever it was, it's gone.

CHAPTER 45

At Mom's, we all talk at once. I've put the worry about Dr. Beagle and my last final grade aside. Lulu is over her disappointment and talking endlessly about starting at Fontbonne in the fall. She's thinking of moving to Saint Louis in June and staying with me while, she hopes, getting a job at Commerce Bank on Delmar. I don't say no, but I tell her she'll probably make more money where she is because she'll probably have to start at the bottom at a new bank.

Mom has typed through reams of paper and signed up with Manpower. "Manpower sounds like ditch diggers, but I'm just too old to call myself a Kelly Girl." She's been working in the office at a department store during the Christmas rush, and that will continue until New Year's. In January, she's hoping for something more interesting.

"But meanwhile," she tells us, "I get a 25 percent discount at the department store, so I've been trying on clothes for the kind of job I'm going to get in January. I'm pretty sure the suit I have my eye on will be on sale after Christmas. Thirty percent off, plus my discount! Now that's a Christmas present!"

I'm happy to be here, even with Granny gone. Granny's ancient Christmas ornaments have been added to our haphazard and homemade ones, making an odd but festive display.

Since we are all saving up for our future lives, we've decided not to exchange gifts. We all cheat a little. My favorite is a 1940s felt hat of Granny's in a black-and-pink hatbox that Lulu found in Granny's attic and wrapped up for me. It's in beautiful condition and even has a jeweled hat pin. I wear it to church on Christmas morning even though I can't picture wearing it on campus.

Mom wants to cut my hair as her Christmas present to me and we discuss it on and off for hours. Mom argues for the popular layered look. Lulu wants to make sure I can still do the French braids. Mom points out that the long, straight look is now frumpy. Finally, I agree to a trim. Mom sighs and gets out her scissors.

"Just as well. If I give you a stylish cut you'll just let it grow out and it will look worse than it does now."

She's right, I'll never spend the money to keep the look going. I'll blame it on the cost but really, I just don't like the idea of going to a salon and having to make small talk and let someone touch my head for an hour and then make noises indicating that I'm thrilled with the result.

I put on a cape and tell her to go ahead, with Lulu standing by to make sure Mom doesn't cut layers à la Farrah Fawcett. "No wings," I tell her as firmly as I can.

She cuts it just above my shoulders, with just a bit of a layer, about an inch shorter all around. No bangs. I make it swirl around my shoulders and give her a hug. The last vestige of hippy Novelle is gone.

I have to return to Saint Louis on December 26 to finish grading Don's exams. I am also on duty for a Christmas-themed wedding on December 30.

CHAPTER 46

When I drive down Wingate about 11:15 p.m., yellow lights are blinking in front of my building. I park and approach on foot. Three or four men are working in the front yard with shovels, and the walkway to the door is blocked with sawhorses.

"You can't go in there," is my welcome home. I don't recognize the speaker, who is large and holding a work light over a trench in the ground, which is next to the building. It's very cold but I get a whiff of sewage. I look up and see that all the windows in both buildings are dark.

"I live here," I tell him, although I can already see that it doesn't matter what I tell him.

"You'll have to stay somewhere else. Go stay with a friend or something." His voice is not the least bit friendly or sympathetic.

I don't know anyone who is in town on the day after Christmas, except maybe Lisa or Betty, but I'm not calling their houses at this late hour. If I can get past this guy, I'll get through the rest of the night no matter how cold it is.

"Okay," I tell him. "But I need to go in and call someone."

"You can't go in." He aims a flashlight at the door and I see that it's been padlocked. I walk over and read the lockout notice from the U City Health Department.

"What happened?"

"You can't stay here," he repeats, louder and angry now. I look at the diggers and the trench and realize that they've all been out here in the cold and the dark, probably for hours. I'm not helping anything and it's only getting later and colder. Maybe someplace is open on Delmar where I can hang out for another hour and then sleep in my car until the library opens in the morning. The idea of trying to sleep in the car with no blankets is chilling in more ways than one.

I walk back to the car, looking around at all the other buildings that have lights here and there and envying every single person who happened to rent an apartment in any building other than mine. Through the bare trees I can see the co-op apartment on Leland. It looks like the kitchen light is on. I cross the street and walk up the steps into the park and around to the front of the building. Definitely lights on up there.

I knock tentatively at the door, and it's opened immediately. Two guys I barely know are there drinking beers. They are thrilled to see me, but only because they've just finished a project and want to show it off to someone. They take me into the kitchen and—ta-da!—show me the doorway they've made between their kitchen and the one in the adjoining apartment.

"We finally got a chance to rent that apartment and make the co-op bigger, so we decided to chip through the brick while everyone was away for Christmas!"

"Cool!" I say, because that is expected and because it's warm in here and I'm happy to be inside. But I'm a worrier, so I say tentatively, "It's safe, right? I mean, that's a structural wall, isn't it?" I don't want to find a safe haven only to have it collapse in the night.

"Oh sure, look." Andre points out the thick wooden frame inserted in the gap. "Rick looked up the code and did the math. He's an architecture student."

Rick is the other guy, and he's looking very cheerful. "Actually, I had a structures guy look at the design."

I'm also worried that they didn't clear this project with the landlord, but he's warm in Florida and not likely to appear any time soon, so I let it go.

I have a beer to celebrate, even though a cold drink is the last thing I want. The first thing I want is a place to sleep. But I join in their talk about the expanded co-op, and they don't ask why I've shown up so close to midnight on the day after Christmas. Finally, I switch the topic to myself.

"Hey, I don't know if you guys saw what's going on over on Wingate. Apparently the Health Department locked my building and there are some guys digging up the sewer, or something. Smells like sewer anyway. They won't let me into my apartment."

They look puzzled and finally Rick says, "I thought you lived here."

I laugh because I'm giddy and Rick laughs because he doesn't even know who lives in his own co-op. Andre catches on quickly and asks if I need a place to sleep.

"If you wouldn't mind. I'll be happy on the sofa, or the floor, or anywhere really."

"Stay as long as you want; no one is staying in the hole at the moment."

The hole is a tiny room whose one small window is into an air shaft. When no one is sleeping there, it tends to fill up with other people's excess, along with six-packs and bags of rice and beans. They clear a path to the twin mattress and find a sleeping bag, and I zip myself in and fall asleep.

The hole is very dark and quiet, and I sleep late. When my eyes open, they are looking into green eyes in a black face. Cat eyes.

"DB?" I get a meow and a rub on the chin, and then he hops down and walks out the door, looking back over his shoulder. I follow him to the kitchen.

Andre and Rick are more subdued this morning and momentarily surprised to see me. Andre puts a mug of coffee in front of me and Rick pushes a brown bag toward me, which turns out to contain fresh bagels. They ask about my predicament and work up a little outrage on my behalf. We review everything we know about the situation, which is that it was cold in there before I left and now the door is padlocked, apparently by the Health Department, although Andre waggles his eyebrows and says it might be some sort of power play to get us all out of the building. None of us can figure out a reason, but as the caffeine kicks in, we make up a few stories about Russian spies and the Saint Louis Mafia. We talk about organizing the tenants until I point out that we have no idea where they have all gone.

By eight-thirty, we've exhausted the topic and they are anxious to get back to their project, which requires hauling bricks downstairs and cleaning up the debris and plaster dust that cover every surface except the fresh bag of bagels. I offer to help, saying it seems like the least I can do.

"It's our mess, we'll clean it up. You've got enough trouble," Andre says. "You must be back in town so early because you've got something urgent to do. Unless your family is like mine, that is."

I tell them about the finals that need to be corrected by Thursday and they tell me to get on with it.

"Better you than me," Rick says. "I'd rather bust rocks than grade Econ finals."

"Okay, I'll cook dinner if the kitchen is clean enough by then."

I spend the rest of the day grading the exams, which I find is just hard enough to be engrossing. Rick and Andre start hauling the bricks, which are in the other kitchen. There are a surprising number of them. I had no idea how thick the wall was and I worry a little more about their knocking a doorway in it.

At noon, I take a break and check on my building. No one is around, but the trench is now at least six feet long and four feet deep. I read the notice on the door, which says we are locked out for unsafe conditions, not specifying what the conditions might be. I return to my grading. Andre and Rick have gotten distracted by ideas about reusing the brick and they don't get any cleaning done. At five o'clock I knock off and help sweep up and then wash down every surface in the kitchen on our side, plus the hallway where we've all tracked the mess. We hang a sheet in the doorway to keep the rest of the dust on the other side.

When we're finished, we are all tired and no more is said about me cooking dinner. We go out to Blueberry Hill instead. Over burgers, we talk about the expanded co-op, and they ask if I'd like to move in. I tell them I have a lease through May and it might not be wise to try to break a contract with an unpredictable and frequently intoxicated woman, although unsafe conditions might be grounds. I decide to be completely honest and add that I am really enjoying living alone. They nod and say they understand, but I can see that they don't. Some people need more companionship than I do. They tell me I can stay in the hole as long as I like and maybe I'll change my mind. Maybe I will, but I don't think so.

We change topics and I ask about the cat.

"Cat? Sometimes there's a cat around. I don't know if it belongs to anyone. I haven't been feeding it." Andre turns to Rick. "Have you been feeding any cats?"

"You remember the black cat—Margie brought it home maybe two months ago. She saw it outside and was afraid someone would see it and use it for some creepy Halloween thing. She was going to keep it inside until after Halloween. I don't know if she did, though. There's a bag of cat food in the hole. Maybe it feeds itself."

Tuesday morning I work on exams for an hour and then check on my apartment. There are several men there, and one woman who has a clipboard and a flashlight, which she is shining in the trench. They are talking about connections and depths and cracked iron, and no one seems happy, so I go back to the warm apartment on Leland and continue grading.

Rick and Andre are not around, and I make myself an almond butter sandwich for lunch and think I could get used to almond butter. I call my landlord and the phone rings and rings. At two, I go to city hall to see what is going on, and they tell me the Health Department is county so I'll have to go to Clayton. I resign myself to another night in the hole, which I'm rather enjoying although I would like to get into my apartment for clean clothes. I resolve to finish the grading as soon as possible so I'll have time to go to Clayton on Wednesday.

Wednesday morning I finish the grading, fill in the grade chart, and drop the whole packet at the Econ department. At my apartment building, the trench has been filled in, but the door is still padlocked. I drive into Clayton, where the county government center is much bigger than U City's city hall. I wander around getting more and more frustrated. Eventually I find the Health Department and wait in line to talk to someone, who sends me to someone else. She looks up the address and looks at me over her reading glasses.

"Marzello?"

"Me, no, that's the landlord, I'm just a tenant."

"Lucky you," she says under her breath, and then tells me that the county has signed off and U City has to issue occupancy permits. "Good luck," she whispers as I stomp out.

I'm up early on Thursday, so I check again and the lock is still in place although the notice is gone. The church bell is ringing for morning Mass, and I cross the street and go inside. I could use a few minutes of calm, and a little prayer seems like the only thing likely to hurry my housing situation along.

When I check back afterward, the padlock is gone, and I go inside and get my mail, then run upstairs. It's frigid inside. If anything, it's colder in here than it was outside. Everything is fine in my apartment except the temperature. The radiator is like ice. Anger rises and I whip out the phone book and call the city.

"I'm standing in a freaking igloo," I shout into the phone. "I've been locked out for days and now I finally get in and it's freezing. How did you sign off on the occupancy permits if the place has no heat in freaking December?"

"Is this the twelve-unit on Wingate? Sometimes it takes a few hours for steam boilers to get going after they have been shut off for a while." Her voice is calming, and although I don't feel like calming down, I do grasp at this shred of hope.

"Turn on all the faucets, make sure the water is running," she goes on, probably thinking that doing something will let me get myself under control. "Leave them on for a minute, make sure the water all goes down. The inspector should have checked the traps to make sure they aren't frozen, but it can't hurt to make sure. They had the water off for several days after the sewer pipe burst."

"Okay," I say, and turn on all the faucets full blast. "They seem to be working all right."

"Check underneath wherever you can for drips, just in case there was ice and it did some damage. They were supposed to be running a heater in each apartment."

I don't find any leaks, and I'm calmer now, but it's still cold and I'm not as confident as she is that the boiler is just coming up to speed.

"I don't see any problems," I tell her, "but it was freezing in here all during December. Some days the radiators were cold and some days they were just barely warm. Don't they have to keep it warmer than that in here?"

"Of course they do. Who is the landlord? Oh, I see. It's Marzello, isn't it?"

I confirm that it is and her tone changes.

"I'm going to make some calls now, and if you aren't warm—and I mean really warm—by tonight, you call me back. We're open until five-thirty so call by five-fifteen."

That sounds promising, so I don't go back to Leland just yet. I take a look around my apartment. It's not only cold, it's dreary. The sky is heavy with clouds outside, the curtains hang limp, and everything looks like a bad movie set. There is no sign that it was ever Christmas. What happened to the apartment I loved? I turn on some lights, look through the cupboards, and make soup with lentils and all the vegetables in the refrigerator that I can salvage.

I pull a chair up next to the stove and write a few letters. The one to my mother is not exactly fictitious but doesn't contain the whole truth either. The line between fiction and fact is thin, and this takes concentration. Only when I've signed the letter and gotten up to find a stamp and an envelope do I realize that the ticking noise I've been hearing isn't a branch tapping a window, it's the radiators coming to life. I can feel just a little warmth in each one. The apartment is still cold, though, so I pack up the soup and take it to Leland. It will take a few hours to conquer the chill, but I'm hopeful that I'll be able to move back in by bedtime.

CHAPTER 47

After New Year's Day, I still have a few weeks before classes start. I have lunch with Betty, and she tells me that the search committee for the new director of the Y has narrowed the list of candidates to three and that interviews are the following week. I tell her that I'd forgotten all about serving on the committee, that the Y seems to be humming along just fine with her in charge. I don't really know if it is or not, since I'm only in for weddings and yoga, but it feels true. She shrugs and gives me the dates and times for the committee meetings.

The two men are interviewed on Tuesday, one in the morning and one in the afternoon. The committee goes to the faculty club for lunch and I'm glad I've dressed up. I'm even wearing Granny's hat, although I've turned the brim down and pulled it down low. I hope it looks funky and not ridiculous with a black turtleneck and denim skirt.

After the second interview, we agree not to discuss the two candidates until the third one, who is Betty, is interviewed on Thursday morning. We'll then have lunch at the faculty club again and try to reach a decision. I gather up my notes and leave, being very obvious about not sticking around to talk to Betty, in case they are concerned that I worked for her last summer.

Back in my apartment, which looks much nicer when it's warm inside, I revel in my free evening with no homework and no meetings. I get out the scraps of leather left over from making the beanbags at the Y and consider what I can do with them.

A tote bag would be great for occasions when my green canvas backpack is not appropriate. I choose colors and draw sketches and cut squares and strips. On Wednesday I get out the sewing machine and piece squares together, try a few different handle configurations, and add a flap to keep out rain and snow. I've decided to scrap the canvas backpack altogether. I've been using it, after all, since high school.

Thursday morning we interview Betty. The format and questions are the same as before, since we are working from a written agenda. As Betty is standing up to leave at the end, though, one of the board members asks her if she'll stay on if she doesn't get the job. I look around, expecting someone to say something, but they all look at Betty. She looks up, a little puzzled, and says, "We'll have to see." And then she smiles and continues out the door, closing it behind her. Two of the committee members start whispering to each other and another interrupts and moves us toward the door.

"I thought Adela was on the committee," I say as we walk into the faculty club. I've just remembered that Betty told me that months ago.

"She had to go out of town," the committee chairman responds.

"She always goes away the first two weeks of January," says another member, and the chairman gives him a sharp look, which he misses.

Once our faculty club salads are served, we go through the candidates' questions and answers one by one. It's pretty clear that the first candidate is not anyone's favorite. The second is a stronger candidate. He has been a youth minister for several years and would like to move to a campus setting, he told us. He used the word "ecumenical" a lot and always called the Y the "Young Men's Christian Association," which irritated me given that non-Christian students and young women outnumber the young Christian men involved in Y programs. We've even got a poster that says campUSY, a play on United Synagogue Youth that amuses everyone once they figure it out. I'm looking through his resume and see no reference to working with anyone over high school age. I decide to speak up.

"I'm not sure about this guy," I say. "He hasn't worked with college-age students at all. He also seems pretty fixated on the C in YMCA and unaware of the W in YWCA. It's not like anyone prays here."

"Maybe that should change." I look to see who is speaking and it's the only other woman at the table. I don't know her, but she's wearing a YWCA pin on the lapel of her jacket. Did someone mention a delegate from the metro YW sitting on the committee? Maybe that's her.

No one responds to the suggestion about praying, but ardor for Candidate 2 seems to be flagging. They go back to Candidate 1, whose background is in Boy Scouts. After the comments about college-age students, though, no one can find much to say in his favor beyond his excellent references from parents of Scouts.

The chairman suggests they consider one of the highly ranked candidates who didn't make the top three.

"We didn't talk about Betty," pipes up the YW rep.

"Oh, of course." The chairman gets out the list of interview questions and asks for comments.

"Well, I guess we have to say she has the right experience." That gets chuckles.

"Good references." Murmurs of agreement.

"Talked a lot about programs she would initiate."

"It sounds like she's a good fit then," I say, wondering why I'm saying this instead of one of them.

"But we really need a man in this job right now," the chairman says directly to me. No one objects.

"Why is that?"

"We need a strong leader to pick up where Ray left off—it's not like we can transition. If Ray were retiring maybe we would consider something else."

Some of the others find their voices and agree that a woman would definitely be possible, just not right now.

I'm shocked by this statement and aware of myself as the person at the table with the least power, if I have any at all. But I also have nothing to lose and I'm feeling a little feisty.

"If you won't even consider a woman, why did you interview her?" I ask, trying to keep the sarcasm out of my voice.

I instantly think of several possible responses to that, things like respecting her contributions over the last six months. But I don't get them. I don't get anything. After a minute or so of paper shuffling and speaking to the waiter, the chairman calls for a vote and Betty is the new director. It doesn't feel like a victory, though. No one makes eye contact or comes up with anything to say to me, even about the weather or my Christmas holidays. I gather up my folder and my new tote bag and leave alone, feeling worse than if Betty had not been chosen. At least then I would have been pumped up on righteous indignation. I force myself to think about something else and spend the rest of the walk home designing a leather hat in my imagination.

I wait a few days and then stop in at the Y to see if Betty has been told. I wear the leather hat and use it as an excuse. I'm going to walk in and watch her face to see if she knows she's the new director and to see if the hat is a joke or a hit. If she doesn't seem to know about the job, we'll talk about the hat, and I'll check on future weddings, and then I'll leave.

"Love the hat—where did you get that?"

"Thanks, you really like it?" I twirl. "You wouldn't just say that?"

"Of course not. I wouldn't lie to the girl who *got me the director job!*" and she hugs me, and we do a fairly grown-up version of jumping up and down and squealing like teenagers.

"It wasn't me, it was you," I finally remember to say.

"I'm not so sure," she says, a bit darkly. I decide not to pursue that and we talk about rearranging Ray's office, now that it's officially Betty's office.

CHAPTER 48

Classes resume, and the second semester of Advanced Micro and Advanced Macro are grueling, covering a lot of theory that I struggle to master. Advanced Statistics provides relief in the form of problem sets. For my fourth class, I choose Quantitative Economics because it's a computer class and I want to be prepared if I need to do statistical analysis for my thesis.

The second week of class, Don shows up, with no explanation for leaving before grading exams last December and arriving late. He's a little subdued but still slightly creepy and I don't make any effort to talk to him.

Lisa and I start studying together in the evenings, usually at my place where there are no interesting family conversations to distract us. Sometimes Marianne joins us for the company, but she's spending more and more time with Tom. We invite the Fred who inevitably became Fritz too, because he's the funniest of the guys and seems like the least likely to complicate things by hitting on us or telling frat-boy jokes.

There are no weddings in January or February, and the weather is cold week after week, so my world contracts to

Wingate, Olin Library, and the Econ department, with side trips to the law school and grocery store. When the laundry piles up, I make a casserole or a salad and show up at the co-op on Leland, where I feel like I've entered the real world, or at least a different and more interesting world.

One-on-one meetings with our shared adviser resume the first week of February, and by the second meeting Dr. Beagle has resumed hitting on me. He's more direct now about wanting to sleep with me.

"I think it's a good idea because my wife's name is Noelle and if I mix up the names, you know, when we're doing it, she won't notice."

I treat it like a great joke in spite of feeling like a mouse trapped by a cat. He did, in the end, give me a B+ for the first semester, but the stakes are higher this semester. Thesis topics are due the last day of classes in May and he has to approve them. And he keeps all his suggestions light enough that I can almost convince myself that they are the jokes I pretend they are.

On the first Sunday in March, I'm idly skimming the parish bulletin after Mass at All Saints and see a funeral notice for a Mrs. Marzello and I feel a little punch of grief for the old woman who was kind to me on the phone, even if not always as effective as we both wanted. Curious to see if she looks like she does in my imagination, I go to the rosary. Driving to the funeral home, I get cold feet, wondering how I'll explain myself if there is a reception line at the casket.

I needn't have worried. The place is packed and I have to park blocks away and walk. I work my way in, smile as sadly as I can at anyone who looks at me, and sidle up to the casket. Just before I get there, it occurs to me that this funeral might not be for the old lady, it could be for the daughter-in-law; she's drunk herself to death. *Well,* I tell myself, *if that's the case no one will recognize me.*

It is the old lady after all, unless the daughter-in-law has drunk enough to look like she's ninety years old. Her face is sweet and kind-looking, even after embalming, and I'm glad I've come. Someone murmurs at my elbow, but the room is full of conversation and I can't make it out, so I just smile and nod and turn away. I stay for the rosary, which has a calming effect on me, and slip out during the blessing at the end to make sure no one asks how I am connected. At least now I know why she stopped answering the phone.

Spring break looms in late March, and I have two things I want to accomplish: a thesis topic and a start on my summer job search. I tell Lisa and Fritz this during a break in an evening study session, and they both laugh. Lisa and her UMSL pals are going to New Orleans, and Fritz is going to meet his brother at Padre Island. I know people do these things, but they've never seemed like things I would do. They both press me to join them and for once I am almost tempted, but it only lasts a moment, and I go back to the thesis topic.

"I'm serious, I want to have a topic ready early. What if Dr. Beagle doesn't approve it? I need time to work out an alternative. If we wait until the end of May and he doesn't approve, then what?"

"Ah, Novelle," Lisa says. "The Beagle will approve anything you give him."

It instantly becomes clear that everyone has seen him hitting on me and they must think I'm having an affair. I feel my face get hot.

"Why do you say that?" I say slowly, preparing to defend myself.

"Because he's a horny toad and he'll do anything if he thinks he might get a piece of you in return."

"Me?" Still preparing my defense, although maybe I had this all backward.

"You, me, Fritz here, the guy who picks up litter in the quad. The Beagle doesn't care."

She is waving her arms and rolling her eyes. She leans over and presses her face against Fritz's. "Oooo, Fritzy, you are so, so frangible."

Fritz coos back, "I could just take your backwardation and monopolize it. Your tangibles make me swoon."

"I looooove your J-curve!"

"Your derivatives are driving my volatility."

We are all laughing now, me mostly with relief.

"Thanks, I needed that," I say when we've stopped laughing.

"You really didn't know? You thought it was just you?"

I'm embarrassed at my naiveté but I nod. "I guess so." I send out a big puff of air. "I am such an idiot."

"Now that we're done laughing about it, it really is a problem," Fritz says. "We won't actually know if our topics are crap or not."

We make a pact to ruthlessly criticize each other's topics to make up for our unreliable adviser.

CHAPTER 49

On the Monday of spring break, I have so much laundry I take it to the Laundromat and notice that the former card shop next door has a new sign on the window, Maintenance Services. Once my laundry is in the washers, I open the door and find Mrs. Como.

"Hi, Mrs. Como, remember me? Novelle? We talked one morning last fall. It looks like you've got a new business going on here."

She tells me about her efforts to put mini-laundries in apartments in the Loop.

"I'm working through the zoning issues and so on. It's taking a while, but I'll get there. I've got a couple of buildings lined up. I figure I can mop the stairs and do a few other things too. I'll bet no one ever mops your stairs, huh?"

I tell her no and feel like I should have mopped them myself by now. She tells me her new business venture was all my idea and I tell her it was not and she says when she gets the contract at my building she'll give me free tokens. I tell her I hope she does get the contract and then she remembers where I live.

"Oh wait, you're Marzello, aren't you?" and she gives me tokens to the Laundromat, which I take because it leaves us both feeling good, even if I did nothing at all to earn them.

I move my laundry to dryers and sit down and write in my notebook under Thesis Topic: "Scaled-down: how small economic systems live and die and are reborn" and add a note: "based on the Delmar Loop." I doodle a little and try some alternatives: micro and macroeconomics on a micro scale. I move to the typewriter and start writing a narrative description. It will take many pages and multiple drafts to get to my final two-page proposal, but I'm on the way.

The days are as long as the nights now and I want to spend time outside again. Tuesday morning I even go to the zoo. I walk around in the morning chill, seeing almost no people but a lot of animals. I feel like they are watching me this time, instead of the other way around.

The day turns drizzly and I go home and work on my resume and try to imagine where I might send it. I want to stay in Saint Louis to avoid the cost and the hassle of sublets and moving for just a few months. Early the next morning, I head to Olin library and ask the reference desk for help. Where might a fledgling economist get a job in the Saint Louis area for three months, a job preferably on a bus line and not requiring an expensive new wardrobe? I don't quite describe it to the librarian that way.

He is an undergrad who had probably pictured himself spending this week in Fort Lauderdale, but he does try. I look through a few periodicals and read up on the Saint Louis branch of the Federal Reserve Bank, which seems like the best possible place for an econ student to work. I stop in at the Econ department to see if they help with job placement and they send me to the university placement office, which of course is where I should have started.

There are no summer job listings for any type of professional job, just house sitting and childcare. They do have a robust list of full-time jobs, and I page through those looking for employers if not jobs. I can write letters and send resumes and see if anything turns up.

After a week of mostly my own company and cooking, I go in search of company and food. Marianne is lonely—Tom has gone to his mother's for spring break—and we decide to go to Ted Drewes, an ice cream place everyone raves about. We drive down Grand, the part of town known as South Saint Louis, capital S. We've heard about it but neither of us has ever been here. No Black faces here, no boarded-up buildings, no litter. We see the sign for Ted Drewes and discover that we've been foolish—it's not a diner, it's literally an ice cream stand, and no ice cream stand is open in March.

We check the map, plot a course home, and pull back into the street.

Thump-thump. Thump-thump. Oh no, that has to be a flat tire. I pull forward to position us under a streetlight, and we get out and open the trunk. I know I have a jack, and a wrench, and a spare tire, although I haven't checked the spare since I left home with the car last summer. I mentally kick myself for that and get to work assembling the jack. It takes us a few tries to even start jacking up the car, and lots of vehicles pass us, too close for comfort. I wish I'd found a safer place to do this. We finally get the lug nuts off and the new tire on after dropping it on my fingers a couple of times. A few cars honk at us as if we're in their way. When we are pretty confident that the lug nuts are tight enough, we heave the old tire in the trunk along with the jack and wrench and wipe our hands as well as we can on the towel Granny left with the spare. I laugh a little at the thought of Granny changing a tire.

We get back in and start off slowly. Marianne sighs deeply. "We should have had this flat tire on North Kingshighway," she says, and I remember the battery problem and have to agree.

CHAPTER 50

Classes resume with a vengeance, it seems, and the undergrads who come to my office hours seem more anxious than the ones I helped in the fall. I wonder if the professor is doing something different, but after asking a few discreet questions I decide it's all within the normal variation of groups of people I've known elsewhere. Every year in the dorms the freshmen had an entirely different group personality, it seemed. I give these students as much time as I can and encourage them to chill out occasionally.

Our study group expands to include Steve, and we are more focused and more determined to get grades that will prove that the grading curve is detrimental to learning. At our first meeting, during a break, I tell the others the story of the flat tire and how after all that when we finally got to Ted Drewes, it was closed. Lisa snorts.

"That's what you get for going to Ted Drewes. Next time go to Crown Candy." She looks around at our blank faces. "Not one of you knows about Crown Candy?" She shakes her curls dramatically, profound sadness on her face. "Okay, if I get an A on my Macro midterm, I'll take you all there for malts. You'll see."

A malt isn't much of an incentive, but we all pretend it is, just for comic relief. We drill ourselves on the Advanced Macro II material until I start to worry about my other grades. We all get perfect or near-perfect scores, which are all As without the curve to drive down the two exams with a single error.

We're at my apartment when we compare grades, and Lisa gives a whoop.

"Road trip, boys and girls—we're going to Crown Candy!"

Steve offers to drive, and we get in his car. "Where to?"

"You can go up to Natural Bridge and take it all the way in." Steve puts the car in gear.

"Or go down Delmar to Kingshighway or maybe Grand and go north from there." Steve puts the car in park.

"Where is this place exactly?"

"Just off of I-70 really, a few blocks."

"North of downtown?" He says "north" like it's a foreign language.

I can see where this is going, and of course Lisa probably knew from the instant she said "go north." I leap in as if I go there all the time. "Yes, north of downtown, a little. Let's go. I want that free milkshake. If you can drink five of them in thirty minutes, they are free and your name goes on a plaque." I heard that from Betty but I pretend I've seen it done.

Steve struggles with himself, but he puts the car back in gear and goes north on Skinker, I suppose to stay out of the city proper as long as possible. It doesn't take long to get there, but Steve keeps insisting there is nothing up here. Lisa tells him where to park, and he looks around as he locks the car, but he knows he can't back out now. It's a rainy night but there is still a crowd. Most of them are at the candy case, though, laughing at the chocolate pigs and other shapes. We crowd into a booth and order banana malteds all around.

When we leave, even Steve is talking about a return trip. "There are so many white people here," he says. It's too dark to see, but I'm pretty sure Lisa rolls her eyes with enough vigor to cause eye damage. Then I see her put her arm through Steve's and give him a big smile. "We're going to work on your education, mister."

In early April, I tell Fritz and Lisa and Steve my thesis idea and they are enthusiastic and talk through it with me. Lisa is still thinking about hers, and Fritz has an idea about federal regulation of savings and loans. He has complete confidence in his outline, and I for one am grateful because I find that area of economics beyond boring.

At my next one-on-one with the Beagle, I take control of the conversation and tell him about my thesis topic. He is more enthusiastic than expected and I remember what Lisa and Fritz said about him accepting anything. I bite my lip to keep from laughing at the memory of J-curve and ask him if maybe the Loop is too small for a study. He mistakes my contorted face for something other than what it is and says that we should discuss sample size over a screwdriver at a place he knows in the West End. I tell him maybe another time and get out before I lose control and tell him where to put his screwdriver.

I've had no responses to any of my letters about summer jobs and am starting to worry. Classes end in less than four weeks and Betty has been asking if I want my summer job back. I put her off, feeling bad about that, but she is understanding and says there is no rush.

"Look what happened last summer," she tells me. "You just walked in and that was that. I'm a magnet for good staff."

"Yep, you'll hire anyone with a hat on her head and panic in her face."

"You didn't have the hat the first day and that was good sense in your face."

I tell her that she was a lifesaver and ask if she would take a look at my resume. "It's like there is something poison in there that's putting people off. Maybe you can find it."

I hand it over and she takes her time reading through the two pages. She turns back to the first page and starts over, which must mean she's struggling to find something to say, good or bad. I drift away and stare at the Big Art the spring class has hung in the hallway. Finally, she calls me back.

"You know Mike Goya on the board, don't you?"

"He was on the search committee, but that's all. I've never really talked to him." And I'm not sure what he thinks of me after that last committee meeting, but I don't say that. Betty will never hear the details of that meeting from me.

"He works for the city. Why don't you call him? Don't ask for a job, just ask his opinion. See if he can give you some people to call. No pressure on him that way, harder for him to say sorry but no."

I don't want to call people, I want to send a letter and wait for them to call me, but time is getting short, so I agree. She gives me the number and tells me to go back in Jackie's office and call now. She knows me too well.

The thought of getting it over with and not stewing over what to say is enough to make me obey. I think through my introduction and dial. Mike is on the phone, his secretary says, but I say I'll wait for him.

"Novelle, great to hear from you." I'm startled. I was all prepared to remind him of who I am and how he knows me. "What can I do for you?"

I get as far as telling him that I'm finishing my first year of graduate economics.

"And you are looking for a summer job, I'll bet," he finishes for me. He laughs and I wonder if Betty called him while I was walking back to Jackie's office and practicing my introduction. I admit that I am looking for leads.

"I was at a transportation advisory committee meeting last week at East-West Gateway—do you know about the EWGCC? They're the COG and the MPO for the SMSA."

"Oh, right," I mumble, scribbling down the letters so I can look them up later. "I hadn't thought about applying there." *Because I didn't know it existed.*

"Not normally a place for an economist, but at that meeting last week, they were talking about light rail for the area. I think it's a real long shot, except that we do have that one reach of rail corridor out to campus that has been protected all these years. Anyway, Bi-State is funding an economic impact study, just as a tentative first look into it." I add Bi-State to my research list.

"But the decision was made that East-West Gateway would do the study. I'd be amazed if they had anyone with any economics background on staff, so they are probably looking for someone."

He pauses, and I make interested noises.

"Or maybe they aren't, but that doesn't mean they don't need someone. You should call and make a case for hiring you."

"I could write up a proposal and send that to them."

"No, that's too easy to ignore if they haven't figured out that they need an economist yet. Call and tell them you talked to me and that you'd like to talk to them about the study. That way you can change course depending on what they say. You're not locked into whatever you put in your proposal. Also tell them that you're ready to start on May whatever, as soon as your last class is over. And that you want to work full time all summer but that's all. That way if they are concerned about hiring an economist that they won't need when this project is over, they have an out."

I get a name and number and he tells me to call right now, today. I wonder again what Betty might have told him about me. But I do call and talk to Lee Sherman, who is interested but too busy to talk, so we set up an appointment for the following Monday. I'm relieved that he calls it an appointment and not an interview, then worried that if it's not an interview it might just be about the project and not about a job. I push that aside and put a thank-you note and resume in the mail to him, and then I go to the library to look up all the initialisms and read whatever I can about EWGCC.

A letter from Lulu is in my box that night and I read it on the way up the stairs. She's all signed up to start Fontbonne in the fall and wants to come live with me and work at Commerce Bank for the summer until she moves into the dorms in the fall. I sit down and write her a letter back, telling her that she's better off staying where she is. It will look better on her resume, I explain, if she doesn't job hop too much.

Even I am not convinced by the letter. I know the real reason is that I love my apartment and my hours of solitude. If I'm working at a busy office with people I don't know on a subject I don't know a lot about, I won't want to come home to my sister's chatter every night. I look for a stamp, determined to mail the letter as soon as possible so she doesn't start making plans and packing.

I can't find a stamp, so it will have to wait until tomorrow. Throughout the evening's study session, though, I keep seeing her excited face. She's already had to wait for fall semester instead of starting last January. Do I really want to crush this plan too? Before I go to bed, I write another letter, this time telling her that early June would be a good time to arrive. At least I'll have a week or two to get used to a new job, assuming I get one. I look for stamps again and find one in my wallet and I go out and mail the letter before I change my mind again.

On Monday I take the bus downtown. EWGCC is in the Pierce Building on Fourth Street, about as close to the Arch as it can get, and the Delmar bus takes me practically to the door. Lee is wearing a suit and I'm glad I wore my funeral outfit. We talk for a while and then join what he calls a team meeting in a conference room. I'm introduced to Dale, Patricia, Jerry, and Mike. I'm glad there is at least one other woman on the team. She tells me to call her Pat.

"She passed scrutiny then?" Dale asks.

Lee laughs. "You tell me."

They explain the economic study and I forget that I'm nervous. The study has only the barest outline so far, and we talk about how we would structure it. I'm able to remember that a COG is a council of governments and an MPO is a metropolitan planning organization and that EWGCC fills both roles for the standard metropolitan statistical area that is known as metro Saint Louis. I also learn that East-West Gateway is the one thing that is never called by its initials. I talk about various ways to do cost-benefit analysis and about social costs and benefits, and about stakeholders, which they already know a lot about. Ninety minutes fly by and Lee calls a halt. We walk back to his office and he thanks me for my input and tells me he'll be in touch in a few days.

I walk around the Famous-Barr store and discover the bargain basement and mezzanine. I try on a few things, but leave empty handed. Time enough if I get the job.

— — —

On May 3, I finalize my two-page proposal and hand it to the Beagle. I give a copy to the department secretary, and she tells me to give it to Dr. Beagle.

"I gave him a copy earlier," I tell her. "I just want to make sure there's one on file."

She looks at me closely, then gets out her RECEIVED stamp, sets today's date, and stamps it.

"Don't worry about it. I'll put a copy in your permanent file right now."

CHAPTER 51

Wedding season seems to begin the first week of May, and I stop at the Y to pick up the weekend's contract. Betty is on the phone and hands me a phone message slip. Lee Sherman has called. I close my eyes, take a deep breath, and dial.

As soon as he takes the call from his secretary, I know I have the job. We discuss only the start date and salary, and he tells me to check in with Jimmy in Human Resources as soon as I arrive. There will be paperwork, he says grimly. I'm happy to fill in any number of forms to have a job like this, but I thank him formally and start worrying about my workplace wardrobe. Lulu calls that night after the rates drop and begs to come earlier than June 1. I ask why the rush and she hedges. She swears that she is not in trouble, and I want to believe her. I talk to Mom for a few minutes, and detect no concern in her voice, so I assume it's just Lulu being excited about the adventure of moving. And I'm in a great mood about the job, so I agree and tell her to come as soon as she likes.

In our weekly group meetings, I keep a close eye on Don for signs that he might bolt again and leave his exams for the rest of us to grade. I haven't left time between my own finals and my start date at East-West Gateway for any emergencies. But I'm the only TA who is spending the summer in Saint Louis, so I'll be the obvious choice if he does skip out.

On Saturday morning I trek over to the Y to type a term paper on the electric typewriter, which I have decided will save me at least thirty minutes, and I will already be there when the bridal party arrives. A few minutes later, I hear pounding on the door and look up, startled. It seems way too early—the wedding isn't until four o'clock. The clock says two-thirty and so does my watch. Maybe I got the time wrong. I run to the door and sweep it open with a smile ready to welcome the bride.

Instead, I see Lulu. She hugs me and says she took me at my word and came as soon as she liked. When no one answered the door at my apartment, she assumed I'd be on bride duty. I offer her my apartment key, but she says she'd rather wait, so I tell her she can handle the bride today while I work on my paper. She seems a little surprised that I'm so intent on working on a Saturday afternoon, but I remind her that this is what's in her future at Fontbonne and go back to the typewriter.

By the time the wedding is over and Lulu has picked up after them, I've finished my paper and am ready to leave. We walk slowly across campus, Lulu describing the bride and her entourage.

"Has anyone ever called off the wedding after they got here?" she asks.

"Not when I was there, why? Did something happen today?"

"Mmm, no. Just a feeling I had. I'm not sure she wanted to go through with it."

"But she did?"

"Yes."

We walk on, and then Lulu says, "She had these bruises. Like someone had squeezed her upper arms really hard, you know? Dug in their fingernails. The sleeves covered them, but just barely."

I don't know what to say to that and neither does Lulu, so I ask her about her plans, trying to sound casual but hoping to hear that she's going to talk to the bank on Monday morning. Or that she's already sent them a resume or talked to them on the phone.

"I thought maybe I could take your old job at the Y." I was not expecting that, and I tell her that it doesn't pay much more than minimum wage and I don't even know if it's open. Betty may have filled it by now.

"What about working at Commerce Bank, like you said before?"

She turns to me and I look at her and see tears.

"I'm not working in a bank ever again."

Gradually I get it out of her, the touching, the hinting, and eventually getting pressed up against the wall in the basement.

"Did he . . . ?" I think about her comment about the bruised bride.

"No, no, I kicked him and ran upstairs. I never went anywhere in the building after that unless one of the girls went with me. That's when I found out he's done it to a lot of girls. That's why I got the job so fast. Someone is always leaving, there is always an opening."

"Didn't you tell anyone?"

"Like who? I talked to the other girls, and everyone just says, 'Oh, that's how he is.' But I'm not putting up with it. He hurt me." She sucks in her lower lip and I see that it's red and swollen.

"Okay, no banks. And we'll see about the Y. But why don't you go over to Fontbonne on Monday and see if there is anything there for the summer? You might as well learn how that campus works instead of this one. It's a longer walk, but you could probably drive, assuming they have free parking. Parking here is impossible."

The conversation moves on to easier topics and Lulu regains her normal animation, and she seems fine by bedtime. But I notice that she spins the couch around to face the window. Maybe she's putting the back of the sofa between her and the door and maybe she just likes looking out the window.

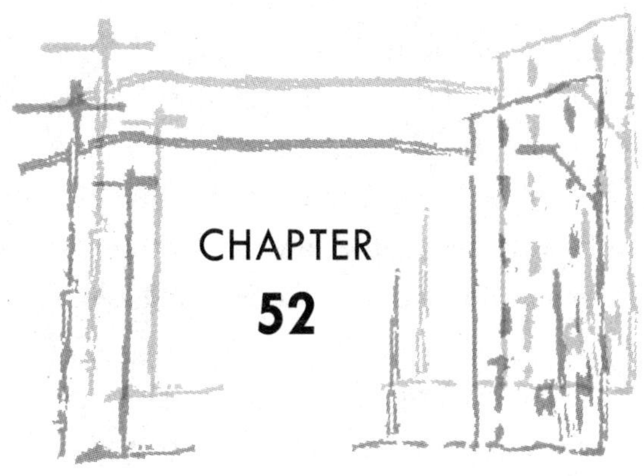

CHAPTER 52

I mostly study in the library through reading week and finals, which keeps me from having to be rude to Lulu, who wants to talk to me about her summer job. She's working in the Fontbonne housing office, where she is helping match incoming freshman roommates. Lisa and Fritz and I move our study sessions to Fritz's apartment for the last two weeks. We all decide to skip our last one-on-one meetings with the Beagle, although I at least call and leave a message telling him I'm up against a deadline and he can leave a message with the secretary if there is anything I need to know.

On the last day of finals, Lulu and I have a celebratory dinner at Blueberry Hill with Fritz and Lisa and a few other classmates, and Lulu and I walk slowly home through the warm evening. It suddenly feels like summer in every possible way. We stay up late and Lulu tells me about the bank again, and when she's let it all out she moves on and tells me about her new co-workers and how roommate matching is done. I know all about that from my own RA experience, but I don't tell her that, I just let her talk as long as she wants. She's still sleeping with the couch facing the windows, and I finally ask her why, and she tells me that she just felt safer in the beginning but now she likes looking at the trees and the stars and the moon when it's out. I tell her to wait until we have a thunderstorm and then we'll see how she likes it. After that, we tell stories about the storms of our childhood until we both fall asleep.

I spend the next two days grading freshman finals and then have the weekend free before my first day at East-West Gateway. I tell Lulu she has to help me find office-suitable clothes and her face lights up.

We start at Molly's, which does not make her happy.

"That's icky, wearing other people's old clothes."

"They can be washed, and they are cheap. Let's just look, okay? Then we can go downtown. Please, baby sister? Pretty please?"

She smacks me on the shoulder and says okay, but if it's smelly in there she's waiting in the car. I say she can't because we are walking, which for some reason cheers her up.

"Oh, it's on Delmar?"

"Close enough."

We walk in and look around for Molly and find her at the back door dealing with bags and boxes just dropped off by the WashU housing office. Lulu wrinkles her nose. I look down my own nose at her and put on a nanny face that says "mind your manners."

"Novelle! Long time! How are you?" Molly slides her eyes to Lulu and catches her expression. "Novelle, can you just take these boxes and put them in the women's clothing area? I'll be there in a minute."

I pick up two boxes and shift my eyes from Lulu to another box and back again, still with the nanny look. She gingerly picks up the box, holds it away from her body, and follows me to the front of the store. She drops the box, and then she leans down and picks up a sweater lying on the top. It's got an L.L.Bean label and is made of fine cotton knit. It has cap sleeves.

"You could wear this."

That's all it takes. Within minutes she's sorted all the women's clothes into piles for the store, piles for me, and piles for herself. Molly shows up and raises her eyebrows all the way up to her hairline.

"What's going on here?"

"Um, this is my sister Lulu and she's either your best customer or your newest helper." I give Lulu a stern look and she hops up off the floor.

"You have the coolest store!" she says, reaching out to shake Molly's hand. I leave them to chatter about the new arrivals while I try on the things Lulu picked out for me. By the time I've finished and have a pile ready for Molly to price for me, they are in deep discussion about brands and fabrics and I don't know what all. I have to clap my hands to get their attention.

"Lulu, let's go," I say with a malicious grin. "Aren't we going to Famous-Barr?"

Molly and Lulu look at me with no comprehension in their faces and turn back to continue their conversation. Eventually I shake them apart and we agree to spend the rest of the day helping sort and price the clothes (Lulu) and household goods (me) in exchange for twenty-five dollars' worth of clothing—plus she'll throw in BBQ for lunch. Famous-Barr is forgotten, and Lulu doesn't even complain about carrying boxes all the way down Delmar. When we get to Wingate, however, I tell her we were going on another block to Leland. I let myself into the basement laundry and start washing the new clothes, then take Lulu upstairs to introduce her to whoever might be there.

Craig has long since moved to New York, but Andre and Rick are there and so is DB the cat. We pitch in and help cook supper and they tell us about their new food co-op. They are running it in the kitchen of the adjoining apartment for now, but they have big plans to rent a storefront in the Loop. I sign up on the spot and am assigned leafletting duty. I turn that over to Lulu and tell her it's a good excuse for going into every storefront on Delmar. She realizes that no one expects her to stand on a corner handing out leaflets to passersby and agrees to help.

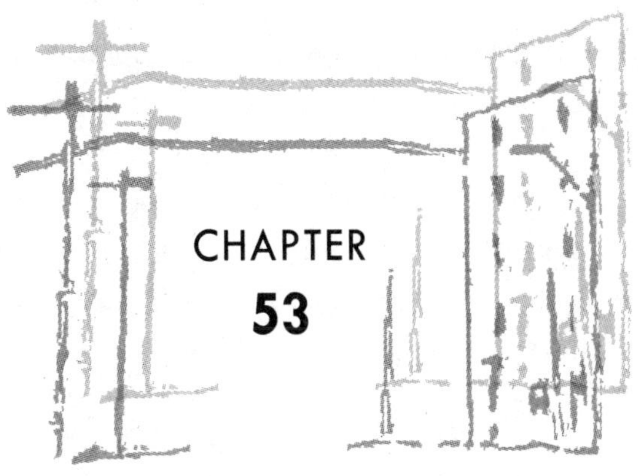

CHAPTER 53

Monday morning I'm up early for my first day at work. I debate about taking my lunch, not knowing what the others will be doing, and opt for tucking a peanut butter sandwich into the bottom of my leather tote. The tote doesn't look very professional, but it's all I've got. I pull on pantyhose for the first time since Granny's funeral and declare myself ready. Lulu oozes out of bed and DB meows.

"When did he get here?" Lulu shrugs and asks about coffee. I tell her she's on her own there and leave for the bus stop.

The first day is full of forms and a scramble to find me a desk, followed by an office tour and introductions. People seem less friendly than they were during my interview, which puzzles and worries me. Just before lunchtime I overhear a tense hallway conversation between Lee Sherman and one of my cubicle-mates. It ends with "she's a Planner I, just like you," and five minutes later I've got an invitation to join a few others for lunch.

A lot of the afternoon is devoted to finalizing the plan for the economic study, and I'm impressed with the progress the non-economists have made. I learn a little about the others, most of whom are very close to my age and are University of Illinois graduates.

When I get off the bus at Wingate that evening, I'm hot and tired and my head is full of names and numbers and concepts. I'm looking forward to the peace and quiet of my apartment and my view of thc trees and sky. Instead, I find Lulu, looking fresh and cool in cutoffs and a T-shirt, sitting on the sofa with DB watching *Wheel of Fortune* on TV. I don't have a TV.

"Hey, Sis, guess what? We got a television!"

"I see that. What's the skinny?"

"Some kid left it in her dorm room. I sent her a letter last week and she wrote back and said I could have it, so here it is. I'm going to keep an eye out at the end of summer session. Maybe someone will leave a color TV." She turns back to the show and I sigh. I loved my first day of work, but I want to sit in a dark quiet place, alone, for a few hours. I think longingly of the hole on Leland, but that's out. It's too close to a large table full of people, all talking.

"Mac and cheese again?"

"Sure, I could eat that every day."

"Maybe you could make it sometimes then."

The TV goes silent and so does my sister. I bang pans around and feel sorry for myself and angry at my unwanted roommate, who never does anything around here, nothing at all, and how can she expect me to cook dinner for her every single night. She probably expects me to do her laundry too and all the cleaning and taking out the trash.

"Novelle?"

"What?"

"Are you mad?"

I don't say anything because I know I'm being unreasonable, and I don't have the energy to have an adult conversation.

"Maybe a little. Really, I'm just tired. Today was a lot to take in."

"Well, get out of here and go put on something cooler." She takes the pan out of my hand and puts it on the stove. "Sorry, I was excited about having a TV, I guess. I thought you'd like it."

"It's just a bit . . . too much noise right at the moment."

Lulu finishes cooking while I shower and change, and we talk about our days and then watch *The Mary Tyler Moore Show*. "I want to be like her," Lulu says. "You can be Rhoda."

"If I'm Rhoda, you're Brenda," I remind her. No one wants to be Rhoda's sister Brenda.

By the third week of my new job, I've already worn everything suitable at least twice, not counting switching around the skirts and tops. I'm whining about it while Lulu is brushing her hair one morning.

"Try my bank clothes, I don't need them." She's dressed and ready to leave in her usual cutoffs and T-shirt. I blink a few times. This is worth a little TV noise. Her heels are higher than I like, but she even has one pair of shoes I can wear.

At the office that day, the entire transportation team meets, and I am asked to give an update on the economic study. By now I've become the de facto head of the team. I wasn't expecting to stand up in front of everyone and am momentarily frozen. But I have no choice, so I stand up, walk to the head of the table, and face the room. I open my mouth, and words come out. After a minute or two, I discover that I'm enjoying talking and people are actually listening. When I finish, they applaud. I sit down feeling like a different, more grown-up person. I can do public speaking after all. The fact that every speaker after me is applauded doesn't detract from my euphoria in the least.

Later in the meeting, the traffic study team leader gives an update and says that it's time for the summer speed-and-delays and occupancy counts. Normally I write down unfamiliar terms so I can ask about them later, but today I'm mostly thinking about my cool self.

"Novelle, are you in? We need everyone's help on these."

Everyone is looking at me and I've now got my eyes wide open, wondering what's going on and if no is even a possibility. The room is quiet.

"Don't make her do speed-and-delays; you West County people can do those," Dale says. "She can do occupancy counts with me." Dale turns to me. "I'll pick you up at six-fifteen tomorrow."

"The morning six-fifteen?"

"Yep, we'll be counting from six-thirty until nine-thirty. The good news is, we dress down."

Dale fills me in on occupancy counts, which involve hanging out on a freeway overpass counting how many people are in each car passing under us. We each count two inbound lanes, using special clipboards with counters on them and total each thirty-minute segment. It's a long-term study to monitor the effectiveness of the carpool matching program. I had no idea. I don't ask about speed-and-delays. It was clear that it would involve driving to the far reaches of the metro area at some ungodly hour. It was also clear that there is a divide between city-dwellers and county-dwellers. I am guessing that being in an old neighborhood five blocks into the county puts me in both camps, although it could be that I'm in neither.

The next day after the counting is complete, Dale and I not only parade around in casual clothes, we also leave ostentatiously early, bragging about being on the job at six-thirty. I decide I like going to work early and start taking advantage of the agency's flex-time pilot, which allows us to start any time between six-thirty and nine-thirty, leaving nine hours later. The pilot is supposed to encourage the big employers downtown, like Pet Milk and Boatmen's Bank, to do the same thing. The point is to spread out rush hour and ease traffic jams—and therefore reduce air pollution. I had no idea about this either.

By mid-summer, I'm an old hand at East-West Gateway and am part of a group that regularly goes out for drinks on Friday night. We never go anyplace downtown, though. There is usually a loud friendly argument and then we end up on the Hill in South Saint Louis or in the Central West End, or in the Loop. The Black employees are always busy when we go to the Hill and sometimes even the West End. I finally ask Sue about it one morning when we are alone in a conference room checking data.

"Have you ever been downtown after six? There's nothing open. No one lives within a mile of here except those old people in Mansion House. They do have a great view, though."

"The Hill isn't that far out; why doesn't Denise ever go with us there?"

Sue just looks at me and goes back to the data. I think about it for a while and realize that the Hill must not be considered safe for a young Black woman. Or maybe it's just too far from her home, and like me, she takes the bus. But someone always gives me a ride home. Maybe that's the problem. No one minds driving to the Loop at night.

Later in the summer, the agency sponsors a public participation meeting related to a proposed bus fare hike and we're all asked to assist. The evening meeting consists of a panel of managers from Bi-State Transit listening as rider after rider gets up and tells us that they can't afford a fare increase. The head of

Bi-State tells them that twenty-five cents is cheaper than any other bus ride in the United States. I find the meeting boring and useless, and the next time we're assigned to work at one, I try to get out of it. But Judy, who is in charge of this second one, takes me aside and lectures me about the value of public input and how to do it properly.

"We're running it this time, and it's a complicated topic about redevelopment in a North Saint Louis neighborhood. You need to be there." I don't know if she needs me or she thinks I'll learn something.

This time, the East-West Gateway staffers are table captains for strategy sessions with local residents and business owners, and we are all excited about it. We have a lot of background information, and we've rehearsed questions and answers and even ways to calm an angry situation. On the night, we are supposed to assemble in the parking lot at Laclede Elementary, and we arrive in various cars. The police have a barricade around the building. We wait for an hour and are told that there was a bomb threat. We wait another hour and are told to go home. We go to a bar instead, most of us. Tom's Bar and Grill in the West End. Judy doesn't join us.

Nothing is said at work the next day about rescheduling, and nothing is said the day after or the day after that. By the next week, we've stopped talking about it.

We keep working on the economic analysis, which involves trips to various libraries and discussions with the transportation departments of Saint Louis, all five counties in the metro area, and the larger cities in those counties. Calls are placed to other large US cities that have new transit systems, like the brand-new Washington Metro, and others that are considering them. We talk to business groups, the Chamber of Commerce, and even the League of Women Voters. The engineers talk to manufacturers of track and train cars. I leave most of the talking to the others and spend my time crunching the numbers we get and writing the text around them. We send the outline, then the first draft, then the working draft, then the quarterfinal, semi-final, and final drafts to our own transportation board. Okay, maybe not that many drafts, but it seems like it.

We confer with Bi-State Transit. We calculate and argue and recalculate and rewrite until we are all thoroughly sick of light rail and time frames and financial viability. We wish with all our hearts that more of the streetcar track system had been on its own right-of-way instead of on the streets. We have just the one enticing, fourteen-mile stretch. We don't even care about the track; what we want is the right-of-way that eliminates the cost of land to buy new right-of-way. We are too young or too new in town to remember when the streetcars ran in Saint Louis, but that stretch, so visible in the east-west corridor between Forest Park and Delmar, running all the way to WashU, haunts us. We lose a little of our academic perspective. We want to use that bit of right-of-way. We want to jumpstart light-rail in Saint Louis.

We pull back and argue against our biases, and still those fourteen miles stare us in the face. We look for possible station locations, the big draws besides downtown, the airport, Barnes Hospital, and WashU at the end of the streetcar line, where the tracks shine in the sun and mock us for abandoning them.

As August draws to a close, we put it aside for one afternoon and ride the tram to the top of the Arch, which I've looked at every day from the office windows. We lean and stare out the windows at the top, looking east into Illinois and west over downtown and out toward the Loop, and straight down into the grass below us. Maybe it loosens our perspective, just a little.

I take the Lindell bus home that evening, and a little way past the Central West End and the Barnes Hospital complex, I get off early and walk through Lisa's neighborhood of empty apartment buildings, west to WashU. I think I have an inkling now about what's going on in DeBaliviere.

CHAPTER 54

All summer, I've tried to work on the thesis that was approved in May. I want to get ahead of it so I'm not in a panic all fall. But every time I sit down to work on it, my mind goes back to the economic feasibility of light rail, and I work on that instead.

I've also tried all summer to take trips with Lulu to explore the new state we've moved into. We manage a trip to Johnson's Shut-Ins in the Ozarks, but it is full of tourists and mosquitoes, and we give it up. We stay in Saint Louis and explore Forest Park and the Missouri Botanical Garden instead, and Lulu gradually spends more time with the people she's met at Fontbonne. When we crave ice cream, we go to Crown Candy or Ted Drewes; we love them both. Or we get chocolate sodas at the little ice cream shop in DeMun, just south of my campus and east of hers, officially in Clayton. We learn the subtle differences between living in the Loop, in the apartments between WashU and the Loop, and in the apartments sprinkled throughout DeMun. The faces, the cars, and the rents are slightly different. No one ever worries about being in DeMun at night.

The last week of August arrives, and Lulu moves into her dorm. She's in an upperclassmen suite and so excited she can hardly pack her suitcases. Her suite has a phone and she calls me several times wanting things she's forgotten. I tell her to make a list and come get them whenever she wants. She seems to feel like she's moved two hundred miles instead of two. I am glad to have my solitude back, but I miss her. It occurs to me that I never thought twice about what it meant to my mother and my sister when I went off to college.

At WashU, course selection is easy this year since we are returning students, and we only have two classes plus our theses to worry about. I sign up for Land Use Law. It's a law school class and I have to get permission from both Econ and Law, but that proves to be a formality. The law school is happy to have other students participate and in Econ I ask Dr. Stone to sign off. He just smiles like he knows something I don't and hands the signed form back to me. I'm in a hurry and don't discuss it.

The day between course selection and the first day of classes, there is a mandatory meeting for second-year Econ grad students. Everyone is there except Don. The rumor is that he enlisted in the Israeli army, but no one can substantiate it. The Economics chairman welcomes us back and doesn't mention Don. Instead, he tells us that Dr. Beagle is gone and will not be returning. His tone is grim and the single sentence ends with the kind of finality that closes the topic to questions. He goes on to tell us that the Econ faculty has reviewed all our thesis topics and assigned them to various faculty advisers.

My thesis is assigned to Dr. Stone, and I schedule a meeting with him. I'm happy to get him, sure he will like my topic, especially if I can tie in the streetcar somehow. Instead, he opens with "Drivel, Novelle. This is drivel." I am shocked and hurt and maybe even angry. I can't hide it and he sees it in my face. His voice softens. "Okay, not total drivel. In fact, if you had come here full of economic theory about the NASDAQ and municipal bonds and the impact of the Fed lowering the key interest rate a quarter of a percent, then I would cheer and say bravo, go for it."

"But then . . ."

"Because for that person it would be a stretch and it would inform everything *that person* knew and loved about the Fed and the market, and that person would spend the next semester drawing some remarkable conclusions. Can you see that?" I nod but I don't like this.

"But you, for you this is bread and butter. Write this up over Labor Day weekend and we'll get it published. Fine. But you didn't come here to write what you know, dressed up in some admittedly very interesting stuff you've figured out by living in the Loop."

I'm mortified and I don't even know if he's right or wrong. I'm too embarrassed and unsure of myself to protest, even though I think I should stand up for myself. I think he expects me to stand up for myself, maybe even wants me to.

"I'll think about that," I finally squeak out.

He looks at his watch.

"We've still got forty minutes, so sit there and think right now."

I turn a page in my notebook and try to think, but of course I can only think about what a disaster this is. I look up, wondering if I can ask to come back later.

Dr. Stone stands up and walks to the window, turns around. I recognize this—he is positioning himself to be profound, just as he did in class last year. I suddenly hate him for his poses and his theatrics. I close my notebook. He ignores the obvious sign that I'm leaving.

"Tell me, Novelle," he says in a conversational tone. "Does America have a national planning policy, or direction, or anything like that?"

"You know we don't," I say, and then do stick up for myself, rather sarcastically. "You don't need to ask me rhetorical questions."

"Fair enough, but one more: Where is all planning done?"

"It's all local. A little state, a little county, a little in the COGs like East-West Gateway. But mostly it's by city."

"Or even by neighborhood, where it's pretty unofficial."

"Right, like the Loop, as my thesis was going to explain." Again with the sarcasm, but he ignores that.

"So, what are the issues they are trying to cope with? I mean the core problems, not potholes and test scores and parking."

I take a deep breath and decide to go with it.

"Transportation, jobs, housing. Sprawl. Clean air and water."

"Yes, but what drives those things? What do those things drive? From an economics point of view."

Oh. "Greed. And fear."

His voice is soft now, and excited. "So go stand this thing on its head. Shake it, and let's see what falls out of its pockets."

I want to say, "What the hell do you mean, exactly? I'm literal. I don't know from pockets. And is the Loop in this thing or out of it?" But I don't. I think I might see what he sees, sort of. And I'm excited too.

On the way home, it dawns on me that I am free of the Beagle forever and that alone is worth starting over on my thesis. I'm a little concerned that Dr. Stone's enthusiasm will color his expectations and frustrate him if what I shake out is not what he already sees. But I can also agree that my original plan was too comfortable and that it would have been interesting but not challenging.

I want to talk about it, and I pound on Marianne's door before

I remember that she's moved in with Tom. I turn to run upstairs and call Lisa, but the door to 1A opens and a face peers out.

"Oh, I'm so sorry. I forgot that Marianne doesn't live here anymore." I don't want to introduce myself; I want to run upstairs. But I can't do that. I was too recently the new person living in this bizarre building that I thought was empty but wasn't.

"I'm Novelle, in 3D."

"Novelle in 3D? Of course you're in 3D—it's the only dimension available. Do you live in this building?" She stares at me, and I think that I should say no and back away slowly.

"Oh, I'm just kidding. I know you from dinners at the co-op on Leland. I'm Michelle. Michelle with a perm. You didn't recognize me, did you? Please tell me you didn't recognize me. Otherwise, I'm going to have to die of embarrassment."

The face of the Michelle I know from dinners at the Leland co-op reassembles itself under the wild curls.

"Of course. Michelle. I'm so sorry. Again. Can I just go outside and come in again?"

"No, you can't. I was just about to go ring every doorbell in this building until I found someone to help me carry my sofa inside. It's tied to the top of my car out back."

I forget about calling Lisa and follow Michelle back outside, happy that we only have to carry it to the first floor. There on top of her car is my bamboo couch. I feel a strong desire to sit down. I can't imagine telling her even part of the story of that couch. I help her untie the twine, slide it off, and carry first the frame and then the cushions inside. It's looking pretty good in spite of at least two moves. I decide to keep quiet and enjoy it here. I've got my own couch now, one that is indisputably mine. I look around, but no black cat slips into Michelle's apartment.

CHAPTER 55

Now that we have finished our core courses, we are all taking different classes and study group is less important, but we continue to meet and discuss our theses. We all have new advisers, and we've all had to rethink our original proposals to some degree. The Beagle, we discover, really did approve them all with no discussion.

One night Steve, whose main interest is the economics of health and medicine, is discussing the city-operated hospitals in Saint Louis and arguing that one would be enough, that it's too expensive to operate two. He is evaluating a proposal to close Homer G. Phillips, in north Saint Louis, and upgrade City Hospital in south Saint Louis.

"Do you know," he says, "that City Hospital isn't air-conditioned? Can you imagine recovering from surgery in the summer in Saint Louis in an un-air-conditioned hospital?"

"Homer G. has AC, they can just go there."

"But that's in north Saint Louis. You can't expect people living way down in Carondelet to drive all the way up to the Village just to get an air-conditioned room."

"It's the Ville, not Village, and why not? If you close Homer G, people all the way up Broadway will have to drive—or take a bus—all the way down to City Hospital to get any treatment at all, all year round—not just when it's hot outside." Lisa starts out calm, but her face is getting angry. She stands up. "And when they get there, is someone at City even going to let them in? And if they get in, are they going to wait and wait and wait and then die?"

Steve stands up too. "You mean because they're Black? That doesn't matter. It's a city hospital. Anyway, what about Homer G? What if I showed up there? Would they let me in?"

Lisa was building up steam, but that last sentence releases it all in a burst of laughter.

"Steve, they would. They might think you were an inspector of some sort, or maybe you were soft in the head, but they would let you in."

Steve says, "They'd let you in City Hospital too, I'm sure."

Lisa gets huffy again. "You want to bet on that? Let's try it. I'll go to City Hospital with a stomachache, and we'll see what happens. Then we'll take you up north and you go in with a stomachache and we'll see what happens. You on?"

I'm almost ready to do the test, but we need to get back to economics. "Why don't you call *Student Life* and get them to do a story on this? They can assign it to some freshman who has the brilliant idea of doing an exposé on how milk costs more at 7-Eleven than in a regular supermarket. Freshmen have time to sit around in emergency rooms. Let's call a truce here."

"Sorry," Steve says, and he does sound contrite. "It's just that the economics don't make sense for two public hospitals in a city the size of Saint Louis. All that overhead, and the WashU Med docs having to run all the way up." He stops.

The study session breaks up a few minutes later. No one is upset exactly. We sound just like we always do when we say goodnight. I lie in bed thinking. *Steve isn't a bigot, he really isn't. I might have said the same thing if he hadn't. Oh my God, I am a bigot.*

CHAPTER 56

By morning, I've convinced myself that I might have some bigot-like tendencies but I'm not exactly a bigot. I'm not George Wallace. I voted for George McGovern in 1972, after all. But I'm still not happy with myself. I really did buy Steve's argument for closing the north Saint Louis public hospital.

We don't meet for another week, and to my surprise the other three show up with copies of *Student Life*. My copy is still unopened in my tote bag. There is the story of three students, one Black and two white, going first to City Hospital and then to Homer G. Phillips, with the same complaint. The Black student had to wait quite a bit longer at City, and when they asked for ID and realized he was a WashU student, they checked him over and sent him to Barnes. The white boy with the same complaint at Homer G. Phillips was seen within fifteen minutes, kept for an hour in the ER until he said he felt better, and sent home with instructions to see his own doctor the next day. The story tried to make a big deal about the Black kid waiting longer and being sent to Barnes, but the story was as thin as the complaint about 7-Eleven charging more for milk.

"They all went together; that's not a real situation. And of course they'd send a student to Barnes, that's where the student health service is. And it's closer to campus. They must have seen through that guy."

"You can't compare the wait times either unless you know how busy it was in the ER. They didn't mention that."

Steve has been rethinking his assertions about public health care in Saint Louis and has been talking with Lisa all week.

"She knows people who work at both hospitals. She has all kinds of inside scoop." Lisa just smiles.

I walk the group out at ten-thirty and ask Lisa what's going on in her neighborhood.

"Is your landlady still holding out?"

"Yeah, she's solid. One more building on the next block is vacant, though."

"Do you still think you'll be able to buy your building? If the landlady changes her mind?"

"I don't know. We talk about it all the time."

"Your parents must make enough money to get a loan. I'm sure your family makes more than mine ever did." I think about my absent father and hair-cutting mother.

"Novelle, what is it you think about us? That my parents didn't save their money or something? That they wasted it on fancy cars or color TVs?"

"I didn't say that, I didn't even think that. I just wondered."

"Sometimes you are so thick."

"Okay, so explain it then." I'm getting a little angry being talked down to.

"Novelle, when your parents bought their house, did anyone help them? Their parents maybe?"

"Not a chance."

"They get a VA loan?"

"Probably. My dad was a veteran. Couldn't your dad? Or was he not in the war?" I'm trying to remember what, if anything, I know about Black men being drafted in World War II.

"He was. You really don't get this, do you, Novelle?"

I don't get it, and I wish I had never brought this up. And why does she keep saying my name like this?

"I guess I don't."

"The VA guarantees the loan, but they don't give you the loan. You have to get a loan from a bank. And if the bank doesn't want to give you a loan, they find an excuse not to. How the hell do you think the North-South split ever got started in Saint Louis? Someone—some group—decided that Black people could only get loans where that group wanted them to get loans. It's just that simple."

I stare at her. "I guess I should have known that, or figured it out."

Lisa shakes her head, goes back to casual mode. "Nah, it took me five years to get my dad to even tell me that, say it out loud. It's embarrassing. It shouldn't be, dammit, but it is."

I lie awake again that night, and in the morning I call my sister.

"Lulu, did you know anyone at your old bank who worked in loans, home loans especially?"

"Hmmm."

"Someone who didn't hit on you would be best."

"Well, there was one VP guy. He was older; he didn't hit on me."

I tell her what Lisa told me and ask if she would talk to someone, try to figure out if it was true. She thinks about it for a while and eventually agrees.

"I could say I have a friend who's Black—which is true, two girls in the suite next to mine are Black. And I could say a friend of mine might want a loan, which is pretty vague, right? And do they give loans to Black people. Is that it?"

"Yes. Wait, no, it's not. It has to be for a house in a white area. You'd need to give him an address or at least a neighborhood that's all white."

"Well, that's pretty much our whole town, right?"

I find I can't answer that. I've never thought about it.

The next week *Student Life* prints a letter to the editor chastising the reporter for drawing false conclusions. We don't get excited since we already agreed that the story was too weak. Freshmen, what do they know about scientific studies? We're focused on our thesis drafts at this point. Steve says he might write a rebuttal based on data he's been accumulating, but we tell him to let it go.

Another week goes by and Lulu calls to tell me that the bank VP assured her that the bank would give anyone a loan as long as they qualified, regardless of where the house was.

"Anyone at all, Missy, anyone at all. You just send them right to me." So, we don't know anything more than we did.

By the next week, no one has even read the latest *Student Life* by the time we get together. I get my copy out just before we break up for the night and page through to the letters to the editor. Nothing about the pseudo experiment with fake tummy-aches. I flip it closed and there it is on the front page: "Student Tells of Grandmother's Death at City Hospital." The story is an interview with a Black student whose family lives in U City. Her grandmother, who lived in the Ville, tripped and fell while shopping at the Famous-Barr store downtown. She broke a hip. The store manager, who was white, insisted that she be taken to City Hospital, which is much closer to downtown. "There was a lot of arguing," the student told the reporter. "By that time, she wasn't coherent any more like when she first fell, and the store manager was afraid she wouldn't make it to Homer

G. Phillips." They took her to City Hospital, and even though she was in an ambulance, they put her in a wheelchair and made her wait. She died in the wheelchair. The student went on to say that maybe the hospital was busy and maybe it didn't matter, maybe she would have died anyway. But she wanted people to know what happened. She doesn't try to say anything about race. She just tells her own story.

I struggle with my thesis, trying to turn it upside down and shake it. My notes are full of Mrs. Como's card shop and laundry business, Joe Edwards's bar, Paul's Books, even Mr. Lipschultz, the watchmaker. My worktable is covered with details of transit costs and benefits, both for the Loop and for the whole metro area. The vacant buildings in Lisa's neighborhood, so close to the Loop and the transit line relic, intrude on those thoughts. And the city hospitals won't return to their rightful, irrelevant place in my head.

I take it back to Dr. Stone. I tell him my research is flying off in new directions instead of coming into focus. He looks pleased.

"That's what you're here for, Novelle. Not to write a nice solid paper that no one will ever read. We want our master's students to leave this program with a broader vision, whether they end up at the Fed or city hall or teaching high school social studies. Don't try to make it too neat—it's messy out there."

This is a relief, but it's also a worry. I'm used to a plan and a schedule and the sure knowledge that I'll turn in a good product before the deadline. If I don't know where I'm going, will I ever get there?

"Okay," I say slowly. "So, it's all right if I end up with some questions."

"Of course. This isn't history or math or chemistry—although those people should end up with questions more often than they do."

"And it's okay to go into all this social studies—race and government and so on—in an economics thesis?"

"Again, yes. Saint Louis has an interesting history around race. They did the same thing most big cities did in terms of directing where Black people could live, and don't ever think it just happened the way it did. And the schools are not equal and city services are not equal. But we didn't have any race riots here in the '60s. Think about that—Kansas City, Chicago, Memphis, Louisville, Cincinnati—but not here. And I don't know why. Maybe we did some things better than those cities. But maybe that has also let us be complacent about dealing with racism here. Maybe that's why the city school system is in trouble. Maybe that's why this hospital question is about to boil over. Behind it all, or maybe beneath it all, is economics. So, when you keep thinking about the economics of transit and medical care and where people live, maybe you'll help move things along in a peaceful, positive way."

My brain lights up.

"My case study is in the wrong spot, isn't it? I mean, the Loop is interesting from an economics point of view, really interesting, and it probably has lessons. But its gritty little neighbor isn't the place I should be looking at in 1977. DeBaliviere is where it's happening now."

"Where something is happening. Do you know what exactly?"

"I know that the business area is pretty much dead, which isn't surprising since most of the apartment buildings are vacant. But a few are fully occupied. I don't get it."

"So go downtown and look up the property records. It's all public. Find out who bought what for how much and when.

Find out if any building permits have been issued, or at least requested."

I can feel my face light up. I know my way around city hall now. I can picture numbers and charts and graphs.

"The permits could be tricky, since they might be for individual lots, but they might be for large tracts if someone is planning something big. So the addresses might not be what you think. Ask for help."

I'm antsy to get to city hall, but I calm down and plod through my class homework and then make endless notes about what I need to find out from the public records. I wangle an invitation to dinner at Lisa's because I want to ask her parents questions about the changes over time in DeBaliviere, but we laugh so much about other things that I don't get around to it. I talk to Lisa later and she promises to talk to her parents.

On the last Wednesday in October, I skip the Graham Chapel Assembly Series and take the bus downtown. I spend the entire day there and come home with a headache and a full notebook. After that, my thesis starts to write itself. It takes more trips downtown and a great deal of time in multiple libraries, and more interviewing than I ever thought I would do. I long for my East-West Gateway team who did so much legwork on the transit study.

In November, Lulu is excited about her first visit home since June, but I tell her I can't go there for Thanksgiving, I don't have the time; I'll go for a whole week at Christmas. The look on her face is like a slap on mine. She bites her lip and doesn't say anything; she just walks out of my apartment.

I take my first, very rough draft to Dr. Stone, who nods his head and tells me to keep going. He gives me advice about drawing in education and medicine without getting bogged down in those.

"Just the highlights, a few solid numbers, a clear indication of how they fit. Not the whole story."

I tell him I'm going to work through the Thanksgiving holiday and should be able to give him a true first draft by December 1. He asks why I'm not going home, and I tell him this is more important.

"No," he says, "it's not. There will always be one more thing to read, to check, to write. For your whole life, that will be true. Don't start cutting out the essentials now. Go see your mom, and don't take this with you. Trust me, you'll come back with a better perspective."

I call Lulu and ask her when she wants to leave for home.

CHAPTER 57

By the first week of December, the study group is only meeting for lunch in Holmes Lounge after the Assembly Series, which none of us is attending although we pretend we are always going to go to the next one. We don't talk much about each other's theses; we're all too caught up in our own work. We save up stories to tell to make each other laugh and forget our looming deadline.

The second week of December, Fritz announces that he's landed a job at the Fed in Saint Louis. He's going to go backpacking in January and start downtown on February 1. The rest of us look at him with mouths agape. How did he manage a job search and who goes backpacking in January? He laughs.

"It wasn't that hard. I interned there last summer, remember. Basically, I just asked for a job and sent in a resume."

We continue to stare.

"And I'm going backpacking with a friend who doesn't have to be back at school until January 16. We're only going for a week. I like snow camping."

We recover and congratulate Fritz and ask him all the right questions. But I leave knowing my whole outlook has changed. I have to find a job.

A "real" job has always been out there in my consciousness, but it always seemed far away. I'm pretty sure I can go back to East-West Gateway, although they might want to make me into a planner since they are always looking for those. And that would be okay; I like the work they are doing. But I am so immersed in my thesis that I can't envision shifting to auto emissions testing or septic system planning for the rural parts of the county.

I dig back into my thesis and put the job question away for another day.

The next morning, I'm working at my desk at home when school lets out for recess at All Saints across the street. I love the muted sound of a lot of kids running around playing, and I get up to watch them for a minute. And then I go to Olin and read everything I can find on Saint Louis schools: the public schools, the Catholic schools, the other non-public schools, and the new magnet schools. I write page after page of notes and leave only when the library closes at midnight. I'm a little creeped out walking home so late, and few other students are out. When I leave the walkway at the beginning of Melville, I walk down the middle of the street the last couple of blocks to Delmar. A police car drives up and stops, blocking my way.

"Miss, I need to see some ID."

I've only got my student ID with me, and he looks at it with his flashlight and then shines the flashlight in my face, which seems excessive since we're standing under a streetlight.

"Don't you have a driver's license?"

"Yes, but it's in my apartment. I didn't think I'd need it to walk to school." I'm being sarcastic, not a good idea, but I'm nervous.

He looks me up and down for another minute, talks into his radio, and finally tells me I can go.

"You shouldn't be out by yourself this late," is all he says by way of explanation.

I was only a little creeped out on the walkway, and usually I feel totally safe when I get close to Delmar. Tonight, I'm scared and run the rest of the way home.

In the bright sunshine of the next morning, I brush off the police encounter and start writing again. The public-school situation in the city is grim and is one factor driving flight, both Black and white, to the suburbs. The causes are unclear. Efforts to desegregate the schools started early, in the 1950s, and may have helped or hurt. I can't tell without a lot more study, so I don't speculate in my thesis. But it is clear that the large number of Catholic schools has helped keep both Black and white families in the city. A new public magnet school shows promise too. It's not clear that desegregation is all that important to families. They all want top-tier education, and they prefer to have it in their own neighborhood. If they don't have it in their own neighborhood, they would like to move to a neighborhood that does have it, something that is often impossible.

Medical care is similar in that everyone wants access, but since it's not required every day like school is, people are more willing to travel to get it. Willing, but not always able.

I tie this to the statistics and anecdotal evidence I have for the DeBaliviere neighborhood, and I finish my thesis with six appendices of data and a solid conclusion that DeBaliviere is being systematically stripped of its Black population to return it to its former white splendor. The corporate gentrification about to begin is different from gentrification in Soulard and other parts of Saint Louis, where abandoned houses are bought one at a time by owners who move in and rehabilitate the buildings for their own use. In DeBaliviere, it smacks of the sort of forced relocation that occurred in earlier slum clearing movements that forced hundreds of families into poorly designed and dangerous public housing, with no hope of the kind of home ownership that allows white families to build wealth. DeBaliviere is particularly ripe for this action because of its nearness to the suddenly hip Central West End on the east, the up-and-coming Loop on the northwest, the undevelopable Forest Park on the south, and the venerable and stable Washington University on the southwest. If light rail is ever built, it will without question have stations serving all those neighbors. It has private schools nearby, and a commercial district ready for a Loop-like rebirth. It has everything going for it. And it's driven by fear and greed: fear of the Black people who lived there so recently, and the greed of developers who wear the cloak of civic leadership and carry the promise of a safe and prosperous future for DeBaliviere.

It's not quite that simple, and I make that clear. But there is no getting around it. I have the numbers to prove it.

CHAPTER 58

I defend my thesis three days before the end of the semester. I am worried about the political implications of my conclusions, even though they are only exposed to the few people who attend. I'm not Woodward or Bernstein. But if the panel doesn't like it, I don't have a Plan B. I've got a few months' rent in the bank, but I don't have the will to start over.

On the day, my oral presentation goes well, thanks to my practice at East-West Gateway. Following the protocol on the card given to me the day before, I ask for questions. Unwritten protocol, I've been told, holds that my adviser asks the first question. Dr. Stone stands up to do this, which I assume is also protocol. It feels like ritual. And then the ritual is interrupted.

"That's not even economics, that's, well, poly sci or something," one of the panel members almost shouts. He teaches undergraduate macroeconomics, I think. "We can't accept this."

His words hit me like a blow to the chest. This was my great fear. Why did I let this happen, why didn't I stick to numbers and graphs? While I remind myself to breathe, everyone else looks at Dr. Stone, who is still standing. He lets a moment go by, until he is sure the speaker is finished.

"I believe this is where the master's candidate takes questions from the panel. Does anyone have a *question* for her?" He pauses for a beat or two, but no more than that. "No questions, that's a little unusual, but the data and graphics Novelle has provided do give us a very thorough background, and I'm sure everyone has read them carefully." He looks over his glasses at the panel.

"Now then, we can entertain a very few questions from the guests in the audience." He looks out at the dozen or so people attending. My study group is there; we have a pact that we will attend each other's defenses for moral support. I also recognize a few people who attend every open presentation on campus; according to rumor they are there for the cookies and coffee that will follow. The others I don't know, probably first-year grad students looking into their own futures.

The complaining professor waves his arm, but the professor seated next to him gently puts out a hand and lowers it. Everyone else is smiling and I see a few discreet nods. I know what this means from my own sleuthing last year.

Dr. Stone looks at the panel and asks for unanimous acceptance of my thesis. I know that if he wasn't confident, he would have taken the panel into another room to discuss the merits. About half are discussed and half pass without discussion. Last year, no one failed to pass. I'm nervous anyway. I look at my fingernails and wonder why they look so bad.

Then everyone is applauding and I look up and realize that I'm safe. My friends are congratulating me as if I were on *Queen for a Day*. "Damn," says Lisa. "I so wanted to stand up and ream that guy. I was ready for him." And I'm sure she was and I'm sure that Dr. Stone saw that she was and made sure she didn't get the chance, however much he might have enjoyed it.

The next day I attend Fritz's defense, which is much less dramatic. He's the last of our group and finals are over. We are all truly finished with our master's program. We had planned to meet one more time to celebrate, but between moves and travel and family events, we can't find a date, so we put it off until the New Year.

As soon as Lulu is finished with finals, we pack up her car and head east. She's got four weeks off between semesters. I'll come back sooner to get going on my job search, but I'm not going to think about it, I tell myself, until after January 1. As we leave Saint Louis, I make one last stop to drop off the final typed copies of my thesis. The Econ office is busy, and I don't stop to talk. Leaving the building for the last time, I pick up a copy of *Student Life* and jam it in my tote bag. I'll check on the drive to see if there is any last gasp of life in the city hospital story. I fall asleep and don't wake up until we're almost there.

Mom is happy to have her girls home but also eager to talk about her new job in a law firm. She started in the typing pool, and a month later the firm installed a Wang word processing system.

"The other typists hated it, and I was the new kid, so I had to learn it. Now all the young lawyers want me to type their drafts. It's so much easier for them when they have changes, and they always have changes. Of course, the thing goes down fairly often and then I just go back to the pool and catch up on the gossip. There is a lot of gossip at that place. Makes the hair salon look pretty tame."

Lulu had a good semester and has declared her business major. The girl who hated math in high school now finds debits and credits to be a breeze. She tells Mom all about the accounting system she would have set up for Mom's hair salon business if only she had known.

Granny's house has been sold and the rest of her things are in Mom's attic. We go through a few boxes, but it's cold up there and we use that as an excuse to put it off for later. Maybe by summer I'll have a job and a new apartment with more room.

One night when Lulu is out with friends, I ask Mom if she and our dad had a VA loan to buy the house.

"Of course, how else could we have bought a house? Everyone bought a house, as fast as they were built. If you hadn't been in the service, you got an FHA loan, those were easy to get too. VA was better, though. The interest was lower."

I ask if she ever knew any Black people who got any kind of loan to buy a house.

"No, I don't suppose I do. I don't know any Black people, not in that way."

Ten days fly by and I take the train back to Saint Louis. I think about staying on until Lulu goes back, but I'm getting anxious about my job search.

CHAPTER 59

My mailbox is full when I get back to the Loop, and I drop it all in my tote and take my luggage upstairs. The apartment is cool but not freezing and I lean on a barely warm radiator while I sort through the mail. Three are notes that have been slipped through the gap into the mailbox. Lisa's says "Cool City!" and Marianne's says "Bitchin'" and the third is a phone number with "Call me" and a name I don't recognize. The first two are obviously congratulations on graduating, and the third is probably a come-on that I can ignore. I leave the rest of the mail and call Lisa to see if we can get together to celebrate a little. I'm hoping for an invitation to dinner at her parents' house, where it will be warm and cheerful.

Her mother answers and I wish her a Happy New Year and ask how she's doing.

"We're fine, but you are the woman of the hour! We're so proud of you."

That sounds a little over the top given that their own daughter just got the same degree I did, but I thank her and tell her it's a relief that it's all over now and we can get on with job hunting.

"Over? Novelle, it's just getting started!"

"Yeah, that's why I'm back early. I'm worried about finding a job. The economy's not that good."

She doesn't respond to that.

"Hello, are you still there?"

"Oh, I'm here. Novelle, is there any chance you haven't heard anything about your thesis since you left town?"

Now I'm silent. I've forgotten her congratulations and am afraid that my thesis was rejected after all.

"I'll get Lisa for you." I can hear her laughing in the background and she calls Lisa to the phone.

Lisa gets on and asks if I read the last *Student Life* before I left. I get it now—something interesting has developed after the hospital experiment, obviously something amusing or dramatic in a good way. Maybe the *Post-Dispatch* picked it up and did some investigative reporting.

"I guess I didn't. It's probably still in my tote bag." I empty it on the couch and find the paper, smooth it out. The headline below the fold reads: "Econ Thesis Outs DeBaliviere Developer."

"Oh," I say into the phone. I skim through the story.

"It's not very accurate, but kind of cool to make the front page. I'll have to send a copy to my mom. I can't believe I didn't see this—she would have been so psyched to see it."

"So, you really don't know? That it was in the *Post-Dispatch* four days later?"

"Oh no, the same story with the same errors? Like here where it says . . ."

"Shut up! No! They checked it out themselves. They actually got more information. But they gave you all kinds of credit!"

I don't know what to say to that, but Lisa is still talking anyway.

"Mom says can you come for dinner tonight. We got extra copies for you."

Of course I accept, and before I leave, I call Mrs. Marzello's number. I don't recognize the voice, and I don't ask for Mrs. Marzello or give him my own name. I just leave a terse message to tell her that the apartments on Wingate are too cold and the heat needs to be up to the legal requirement by five o'clock. "Is that understood?"

I get a "Yes ma'am" that almost makes me giggle, but I say, "Thank you. I trust that we will not need to call again." And hang up before he responds. *We?* I say to myself.

Dinner at Lisa's is lively and delicious, and we read the story several times, especially the part where I could not be reached for comment. We wonder if they tried or if that was a throw-away line. I flip back and look at the byline.

"I think this guy left a note in my mailbox. The name seems familiar. I guess I'll call him tomorrow."

The next morning, my first thought is "it's warm in here!" I am still excited about having my name in the paper, but I tell myself that it was in the Local section and probably just filler during a slow-news Christmas season. It's hardly going to help me get a job. I draft a new resume with my MA and thesis topic on it and leaf through the job ads in the Sunday paper. Nothing under Economist—no surprise there. Everyone is complaining about the economy, so "economist" is a bad word by association.

Around eleven, I get out the note that had been slipped into my mailbox. The name is the same as the reporter, and now I see the *Post-Dispatch* logo at the bottom of the sheet. I hesitate to call, though. The story has quotes from the developer about the benefits of the DeBaliviere project, and I'm not ready to face criticism and maybe say something stupid that will end up in the paper and ruin my chances of ever getting a job having anything to do with economics. The phone rings. I wonder if it's the reporter, but I can't not answer a ringing phone, so I do.

"Hello, this is Novelle."

"This is Richard from the *Post-Dispatch*. Sorry about leaving that note in your box, but I was hoping to catch you before you left for Christmas—or for good, now that you've graduated."

"Oh, well, you did. I mean I did. Leave, I mean. I just got back last night." God, I sound ridiculous, certainly not like someone who can weigh in on economic factors shaping the urban landscape. "I'm sorry I couldn't give you a quote for the story, but you got some good ones from my adviser about fear and greed—I couldn't have said it better anyway."

"Yeah, that worked out, but that's not why I'm calling now. I want to do a follow-up story. I read the references to the Loop in your thesis and wanted to see if there is a story there."

"You did what? How did you get a copy of my thesis?" *And are you going to pick it apart to my detriment?*

"I was at your defense. They might have thought I worked for *Student Life*—which I did, but years ago."

"But why would a *Post-Dispatch* reporter attend a master's defense? There are dozens of them."

"Oh, we got a call from a friend of yours who thought there might be something of interest to the community."

Had to be Lisa. I owe her one. Maybe. If this doesn't go haywire.

I tell him I'm writing a separate paper on the Loop and that I'll let him know when it's finished. I don't want him stealing my thunder, but I don't quite say that. He tells me he'll check back in a month or so and maybe we can meet at Blueberry Hill. I give him a vague okay, and we say goodbye.

A month isn't very long for me to get the paper written and submitted to an economics journal, much less get it published.

That could be a year away. But he seems interested in having an excuse for a business lunch at Blueberry Hill, so why not.

Glad to have a distraction, I get out my notes and return to my original thesis topic and outline a shorter and more anecdotal version. It won't go to one of the more academic economics journals, but I'm not interested in that right now anyway. I'm even thinking about sending it to an urban planning journal where it will be seen by a different audience, one more interested in how neighborhoods thrive and fail to thrive. I'll give it enough grounding in things like access to capital to give it credence on my CV.

As I'm musing about this, the phone rings again. This time, it's Steve from our study group and he wants to get together.

"Sure, when are you thinking? Is Fritz back in town? I saw Lisa last night."

"I was thinking tonight, just you and me."

"Oh, well, sure. Okay. Where should we meet?"

"I could pick you up, we could go to the Pasta House."

"It's not all-you-can-eat night there, is it?"

"I don't think so—are you really hungry or something?"

"No, not at all. It's just—well, it can get a little wild there."

After we hang up, I think this over and realize that it might be a date, and then I think that over. I'm not opposed to the idea, I guess. I just never thought about him that way.

Dinner is fun, and the Pasta House is pretty noisy even without the all-you-can-eat special. It's too loud for anything very date-like, so I relax and we talk about our respective family Christmases.

"You do anything for New Year's?" I ask, very casual.

"My folks do this open house for the neighbors. They started that years ago, one New Year's Eve when we had an ice storm, and the power was out, and everyone was asked to stay off the streets. My mother sent us kids around to invite all the neighbors to our house. Everyone brought whatever they had, and we had a great time. The adults had candles and the kids had flashlights. We could pretty much eat whatever we wanted, just sneak in and grab stuff. So, we've done that every year since. Early on we kept to the candle-and-flashlight tradition, but gradually we started having lights and then music, and now it's just a big noisy potluck open-house sort of thing. People stop by even if they're going somewhere else later."

Okay, so it's not clear if there's a girlfriend involved in that. I half hoped there was so I don't have to think about it.

"That sounds like fun," I say, and it does. "I never get around to catching up with neighbors or a lot of my high school friends when I'm home." I realize that all the high school friends I wrote to when I first went away to college seem a little remote now. Some are married, even. A few have kids.

Our toasted ravioli comes and I wonder aloud why this hasn't spread beyond Saint Louis. I love how they call it toasted even though it's fried. It does taste more toasty than deep-fried food usually does. We burn our tongues and gulp water and move on to local topics.

"So, the *Post-Dispatch* story about your thesis—congratulations!" He smiles like he means it. His thesis about savings and loans didn't have a local angle, plus he already has a job offer, so I guess my achievement is in a realm he can appreciate without envy.

"Yeah, it's kind of exciting. I'm not sure it's going to help me find a job, though. Not in Saint Louis anyway. There were some rather nasty letters to the editor in today's paper."

"Oh, I didn't think about that. Were they threatening?"

"Oh no, not that bad." At least not the ones I saw. Maybe there were worse ones the paper didn't print. "I knew it was controversial, that was the whole point, right? I owe Lisa for telling the paper about it."

"Lisa?"

"Well, I assume it was Lisa—it's her neighborhood after all, and she's the activist among us." I look at his face, which has fallen.

"It was you?"

I can see by his face that it was him, and I get up and give him a quick kiss, right there at the table.

"Well, I really do appreciate it. My moment of notoriety. Dinner's on me!"

We finish our pasta and argue about the check in a friendly way, and he ends up paying. We bundle up and go outside. He's antsy, and I don't know why. He's not trying to hold my hand or anything like that, but maybe he's too nervous. I'm half excited, half dreading whatever it is. I've really enjoyed dinner with him.

"Hey, Novelle. I want to ask you something."

Okay, here it comes. He's gotten my story in the paper and he's bought me dinner but I'm not ready to sleep with him, if that's what he's got in mind. I wish I had driven my own car. Not that I'm worried, other than that it might get awkward.

"Sure, what is it?"

"I'm just going to say it."

"Okay."

"Do you think Lisa would go out with me?"

"Oh!" Relief and jealousy in equal measures. "I don't know." I put on my thinking face while I recover. "It's worth asking, isn't it? She doesn't bite."

"Well, sometimes she sort of does bite."

Good, he missed both the relief and the jealousy. I smile at him and shake my head.

"But you like her in spite of that, so just ask. It's not like you'll have to face her in study group anymore." And then I think of something else. "I haven't heard, is she staying in Saint Louis? Did she find a job yet?"

"She said something about applying to the PhD program, but that was a while ago, so I don't know."

We get to Steve's car and he unlocks the door.

"Did you ever think about getting a PhD?" I ask. "I wonder why it never came up in study group or in the class sessions."

"Nah, I want to get to work. Enough of school. I really can't wait to have an office and everything. I want to *work*, you know?"

I'm not sure I do know; school has always seemed like work to me. But I can see that he belongs in an office, in a suit, with a briefcase. I'm not sure I'm cut out for that.

When he drops me off, he starts to say something like "hey, you wouldn't" but then he changes it to "I'll just walk you to the door, you know, in case any of those letter writers are hanging around."

"I'm fine, it's only a few yards," I tell him, but he gets out and walks me to the door anyway. He looks around, peers back toward the parking area. I open the outside door and thank him for dinner. He kisses me, very lightly, and goes back to his car. I hear him lock the door as soon as he gets in. I wonder about all those evenings he came to study group here. Was he always nervous about the neighborhood? The Loop?

I lie in bed that night and wonder about Steve and Lisa. I can't see it, Steve at the Fed and Lisa who knows where. I really can't see Steve parking his car in DeBaliviere after dark. But then, I remind myself, he did kind of come around about the city hospital. So, who knows.

CHAPTER 61

The next day the apartment is warm, and I get busy writing the Loop story. By the third paragraph it's lost its academic voice and has become intimate and anecdotal, with quotes from several business owners. The second page has a little data and a graph showing a decline in crime mirroring an increase in owner-run businesses. The turnaround period is too short to get solid population data, so I bundle up and walk to Delmar and sit on a bench and count people for two hours, categorizing them as well as I can by age and race. A waiter comes out of Blueberry Hill and asks me what I'm doing. She returns a little later and tells me that she's cleared a window table and I can work inside until the after-work crowd shows up.

I was ready to call it a day, but I can't say no after she went to all the trouble, so I go inside. The waitress comes over with a plate of fries—she says they were extra, but they seem to be right out of the fryer, and they are hot and delicious after my hours outside.

"Want a beer, or something hot? Coffee?"

"No thanks. Or . . . I don't suppose you have . . ." I almost say "cocoa" and stop myself in time. ". . . anything hot other than coffee?"

She thinks and then says: "What about an Irish coffee—I'll make it mostly cream and sugar with just a shot of coffee and a shot of whiskey." She turns and goes without waiting for an answer.

Joe Edwards delivers it and sits down across from me.

"You're the one who wrote the thesis on DeBaliviere, right?" he asks.

"Right, but now . . ."

He interrupts me: "It's a shame."

"My thesis?" *What the frick?*

"No, no, I mean the whole DeBaliviere thing. Should never have happened."

"Which part?" Surely he doesn't mean Black families shouldn't have been allowed to live there. "The developers buying up the properties?"

"Oh, that was inevitable, given the situation. I mean the whole thing. White ownership, Black tenants. Middle-class Black families were so eager for a good neighborhood, and the whole trend north was Black-then-blight, self-fulfilling because people just associate Black with blight. But DeBaliviere, that was okay for a while because the owners were all white and the apartments were so nice and overpriced. Black buyers couldn't get loans because it was south of Delmar, of course. Probably still can't."

"So . . . what happened?"

"The Loop happened."

"The Loop?"

"Once things started turning around here, I think someone got the idea that as long as there was a backstop to the west, they could flip DeBaliviere back to high end. They already had the Central West End up-and-coming on the east side of it."

"Back to high end *and* white."

"I don't think they can go that far; it will be a mix, like here. Smart move, I guess, but still a shame. Most likely they did a lot of little things to drive the prices down, create fear, you know. A few stolen cars, a few break-ins, buy the shops and board them up. Maybe they didn't even have to run their own motorcycles up and down the streets. Maybe when we got the biker gangs to stay away from here they went over there on their own. I don't know. I could be wrong about the whole thing."

"But you think it was all rigged?"

"That might be going too far. But it's possible, I guess."

"And they didn't have a guy like you to turn it around." Ick, I'm brown-nosing. But I do want him to keep talking. I also want to take notes, but I don't. I've completely forgotten about counting noses outside, though.

"Oh no, that wouldn't have worked there, not once the developer got going. I don't know if organic change would have worked there anyway. Any change needs a leader and capital. For better or worse, they've got that now. Remember that it's in the city and access to capital is different there. We still have the aura of 'County' even though it's just a few blocks west."

"Plus U City is a college town; I guess that helps." I try to sound like I know something too. Access to capital should have been my line.

"Not like most college towns. We've got a lot of older people, and immigrants. And all those grand houses between the campus and Delmar—those haven't been cut up into rooms for students, thank goodness. I like it this way, all a mix."

We sit in silence for a minute while I sip my Irish coffee and finish my fries, an odd but strangely satisfying combination. I decide to change the subject.

"I'm working on something lighter now, about the Loop. It

shouldn't generate any hate mail." I tell him about my original thesis topic and my rewriting it for a different audience.

A group comes in talking loudly and calling to Joe for beers. He smiles at me and gets up.

"Just don't make me out to be proprietor of a fern bar."

I go outside and count for another hour, noting a change to after-work traffic. And I realize I have the thing that will keep this from being just a fluff piece.

I write all evening and all the next day and finish "In the Loop" on Saturday. I know I should get someone to read it, but I'm too excited and I send it off to the *Journal of the American Institute of Planners*, feeling proud and sure of myself as I hand it over at the post office. I have a rare January wedding that afternoon and I hurry to campus early to make sure the steps are as ice-free and dry as possible. I'm still sweeping when the bride arrives, and for the first time it's someone I recognize.

"Were you in the Big Art class?" I ask her, and she tells me that's where she met her husband.

"I just graduated and we're both doing Peace Corps, so we had to slip in the wedding before we leave—that's the only way we can get an assignment together."

I start to ask about the Peace Corps, but her mother comes in and I realize this isn't the time. I do go over and slip into Graham Chapel, though, to see who she is marrying. I remember everyone who took that goofball class.

But I'm not expecting to see Arlo at the altar, in a tux, saying "I do" in a firm, clear, adult voice. I take a deep breath and let it out slowly. He's so attractive, so alive, and so not for me. But after they are all gone and I'm walking home, I do wonder about the Peace Corps. Would that be a fit for me? I divert to the public library and read up, take notes.

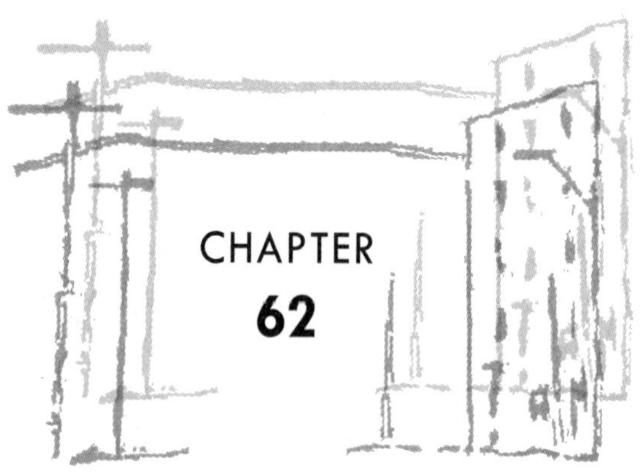

CHAPTER 62

By Monday, I am over the euphoria of my article and have decided that the American Institute of Planners will never publish it; I'm not even a member. Reading about the Peace Corps has left me feeling like I should be helping change the world. I need a local audience for "In the Loop," and a stronger case for neighborhood leadership and access to capital, which has become an earworm in my head.

I rewrite it, but this time I let it sit and go to campus to look for jobs in the January editions of all the professional journals I can get my hands on. I look through the Sunday job ads in the Chicago, Cincinnati, and Kansas City papers, and then look at the Memphis paper because surely winter is warmer in Tennessee than it is here. I make a lot of notes and go home and focus all my writing talent on tailored resumes and cover letters.

I am feeling a little depressed by Thursday afternoon and realize I need to get out and talk to people. I go grocery shopping and then make up a big pot of carrot curry and take it to Leland. There are a lot of people there; most Leland residents aren't undergrads who take off the whole semester break to ski or go to Hawaii. I am immediately immersed in multiple conversations and forget my own worries about job, publications, and unkind letters to the editor. Craig is there on a flying visit on his way to a new job in Chicago, working for a housing rights community organization. He invites me to spend a week or two volunteering once he gets settled. I start to tell him about my thesis but we are interrupted and move on to other topics.

By the following week, campus is more lively, gearing up for the new semester, the first semester since 1959 that I won't be in school. The idea shocks me, and I stop in to see if Dr. Stone is available.

"I'm thinking about the PhD program," I tell him. "Is it too late to apply for fall?"

He looks thoughtful, which I take as a sign that I'm not PhD material. "I'm sort of thinking about the Peace Corps too," I rush on. He raises his eyebrows, just a tiny bit. "And I've applied for several jobs, and I'm doing some writing for publication."

He looks at me for a few more moments. "Is that all? That's all you've done?"

I'm momentarily shocked until I realize he's kidding.

"Maybe I'm doing too much? Not focusing?"

"Oh no, that's not what I meant. It's hard to come down after such an intense semester that ended with all that publicity. You either crash or leap into more activity. Normal."

"Normal, that's good. But I do need to get moving. I should have lined up a job last fall."

"No, I don't think so. You're different, aren't you, after the *Post-Dispatch* article? You need to apply that experience to your decision on which way to go now."

"You sound like I have all kinds of options. I have no options—I'm looking for anything!"

That does not make him laugh. His face turns serious, almost angry.

"That's disappointing. I would say you do have options—Peace Corps is one option that you haven't even applied to. You've just asked about the PhD program, which is an option you have barely explored. And you've only put a few days into the job option, so you don't actually know if there are jobs out there for you or not. You may get a call tonight or have a letter waiting in your mailbox." His expression softens as my face gets red. "Tell me about what you are writing."

I tell him about the article I sent to the American Institute of Planners without saying they won't publish it. Then I tell him about "In the Loop" and my conversation with Joe Edwards.

"Sounds like you should call it 'Out of the Loop' and send it to *Saint Louis Today*. I'll read it if you like."

I have it with me, since I was planning to look up some information at Olin, so I give him my only draft, a little reluctantly. He tells me he'll make a copy and I can have the original back by the end of the day. He walks me out so he can drop it off for copying.

"I think you would make a good PhD candidate, Novelle," he says. "But maybe not this year. Go do something and then come back for a PhD." He grins at my worried face. "Go ahead and apply now, get it out of the way if you like. Then you can defer admission and not have to worry about it."

I thank him and tell him I'll be back for the paper. He says he'll leave it with the secretary and that meanwhile I should take a break and think about things without thinking about them so hard.

"Do something totally wacky," he says. "Tend bar. Feed the monkeys at the zoo. Be a tour guide at the Arch."

When I pick up my paper later, there is a note from Dr. Stone attached: "I like where this is going. Follow this trail and see where it goes. Leave your thesis alone. Everyone tries to publish their thesis and it's usually a failure."

The next Sunday, I find a job ad for a planner/analyst at the Saint Louis Land Reutilization Authority. It's a good fit if not a perfect one, but I know I'll be strong on the data analysis portions if not so much on working with community organizations. I tailor my resume, write a cover letter, and send it in. When I get back from the post office, I go back to the want ads and look at apartments for rent in the city, since residency is a condition of employment. I've said in my letter that I've been living in U City a few blocks outside the city limits while attending grad school and am actively looking for an apartment in the city. I circle a few ads to make that true.

The next day I call about several apartments and make appointments. I also arrange to look at one house for sale, not that I think I can buy something, but it's at least something wacky. The apartments are in the Shaw neighborhood, well into South Saint Louis. One doesn't have a shower, and one is nowhere near any shops. The one I like best is close to a library and bank, with a grocery and hardware store only a few blocks away. The bus stop is a block away. But as I walk around the neighborhood, I know I won't like it here after living in the Loop. The shops are strung out here and there along very busy streets. The Loop is like a little village center.

I stop at the zoo to ask about volunteering, without mentioning the feeding of monkeys. The most likely spot for me is in the gift shop or greeting people as they arrive. I get an application and read it as I walk back to my car. They want a one-year commitment. And of course that makes a lot of sense, but I don't feel like committing to anything for a year right now.

I go home and open the want ads again to see if there are any apartments available just east of Skinker near Delmar. They are either large and elegant, or one-room efficiencies with Murphy beds. I walk over, just to have a look, and realize that it is too far from the Loop; it won't be living in the Loop at all.

When I toss the Sunday paper, I keep the want ads. I need to look at more neighborhoods in Saint Louis. It's a big place. I get no calls about jobs, and my mailbox is empty. I go back to campus and get an application for the PhD program. On the way home, I stop at the Coalition for the Environment office on Delmar and talk to David Morris, the director and the only person in the office. He's more than happy to sign me up as a volunteer, and I spend a pleasant hour learning about their projects and stuffing envelopes. It's not feeding the monkeys, but it's something.

CHAPTER 63

The phone rings on February 1 and I squeeze my eyes shut and whisper, "Please be about a job."

"Hello, this is Novelle," I say in my professional voice.

"I'm calling from the city Personnel Department at the Saint Louis Land Reutilization Authority," I hear, and am suffused with happiness. A callback!

We make arrangements for an interview on Friday morning, and I hang up and dance around the apartment. I want to tell someone and am reaching for the phone when it rings again. This time it's Richard, the *Post-Dispatch* reporter, and I wish I hadn't answered this one. I've just sent my much-rewritten story to *Saint Louis Today* two days ago. I tell him that, figuring it might upset him but it will get me off the hook.

"I don't think I can tell you very much without repeating what's in that story. I did tell you I was doing that."

He is undeterred and I agree to meet him at Blueberry Hill at twelve-thirty on Friday, reminding myself that a business lunch was what he probably wants more than a story. If my interview at the LRA doesn't go well, the lunch will at least be a distraction.

I get one more call that day, from Michelle in Marianne's old apartment downstairs. She's planning what she calls a "hall party" on Friday night for the whole building. "I called you first," she said. "If you can make it, then I'll knock on the other doors. It's just stupid that we don't all know each other."

I think it's a great idea and tell her I'll be there and I'm good for whatever food she wants me to bring. We agree on cookies, and she's planning the kind of artichoke dip that goes in a hollowed-out loaf of bread. "If no one else comes, we'll still get together, just in my apartment."

I spend Thursday agonizing over appropriate interview clothes and making cookies for Friday. I don't worry about lunch with Richard at all.

On Friday I'm up early and find it's snowed overnight, at least three inches, and I've got to leave for the bus stop by seven-thirty to be in plenty of time for my interview. I run out and sweep the sidewalk as far as I can before I get dressed and leave for the bus. I can't believe I haven't done anything about something more professional than my homemade tote bag, but it's all I've got so I drop a notebook in and leave.

Traffic is slow and I am barely in time for the interview. The receptionist is kind and shows me where to hang up my coat. I leave my tote there too, just taking the notebook. That's not so bad, I decide. The receptionist shows me the ladies' room and I smooth down my hair and straighten my clothes and wipe off my shoes as well as I can. They'll be salt-stained when they dry, though.

The interview goes very well, I think, and I ask a couple of people for suggestions about neighborhoods they would recommend. One confides that she lives with her parents in West County and uses her brother's address in Soulard. "They don't check that carefully," she says. I think that I would be a nervous wreck if I tried that, but it's not an option for me anyway.

"Is Soulard nice?" I ask her.

"Well, it's the City," she says, with a shrug and a strong emphasis on "city."

"My brother's doing a gut rehab. What a mess."

I want to ask about a gut rehab, but I decide that can wait. The head of Personnel shows me out and says he'll be in touch soon.

I'm feeling good about the interview, so I stop at Famous-Barr and buy a briefcase-shaped purse that feels professional enough for future interviews and, I hope, a job. I look at wool dress pants and the sort of boots the women were wearing at the office, but decide to wait. My interview clothes are good enough for someone with no paycheck.

I take the bus back to U City, planning to sprint home and change. My interview clothes feel wrong for the Loop, and I don't want Richard to think I dressed up for him. The bus is late, though, so I stuff my tote bag into the Famous-Barr bag and walk into Blueberry Hill looking a little more formal than I'd like.

Richard comes in a minute later and we find a table and order. I'm starving and get fries with my burger. When the waitress leaves, I start by asking if there was any more fallout from the first article.

"Some of my friends were concerned about some of those letters to the editor," I tell him. "There weren't any threatening ones, were there?"

"Oh, they don't tell us, unless it involves some error we made, the reporter made, I mean. Or a threat to one of us."

"You get threats?"

"Sometimes. Okay, I haven't, but a few people have. Nothing ever came of it, though, as far as I know. I think it's the Mafia coverage they worry about, not something like this."

We talk about Mafia car bombings, which are ugly but not really a concern for either of us. We eat our burgers and I tell him that I've just had a job interview with the LRA, which seems to interest him. I jabber on about that for a while, since it's very interesting to me. After a while, though, I feel a little guilty.

"I guess this isn't getting you anything for your story about the Loop, though, is it?"

"Oh, well, my editor isn't that interested anyway. I just thought something might come up if we talked. Something you ran across but didn't cover maybe?"

"I'm sure there's another DeBaliviere out there, or another Loop. Or maybe I'll find something if I get this job." And then I have another thought. "You might look at Kinloch. The Campus Y at WashU has a tutoring program there. It's not part of the Black migration up through North Saint Louis and North County. It's actually been a Black city from way back."

I get a look that says he's not interested, so I tell him I have to get going, I've got one more thing on the calendar tonight. He raises his eyebrows, like he might want to tag along, so I tell him I've got a shift at the food co-op and I've got to change and make some calls first. He's a reporter, so he's savvy enough to see that he can't get past all that, so he thanks me for my time, pays the bill, and says he'll be in touch. I tell him I'm happy to have lunch any time and he gives me a business card. In the space of a day, my collection of business cards has gone from one to five.

The hall party that night is a smashing success. Michelle has begged tables and lamps and chairs from the other first-floor residents, and I've brought along and hung up some new Big Art. Someone sets up a record player and Michelle decides to haul her couch out into the hall. This prompts the others to bring out comfortable chairs and someone else rolls out a rug. Of the twelve apartments, ten of us show up, and I'm sorry to find that the two missing ones are both on my floor. All ten of us are in grad school or working in our first or second jobs. I finally meet the tenant in 3C, who works in Clayton and spends a lot of time with her boyfriend, who lives in Maplewood. After a few glasses of wine, we elect Michelle mayor of the building and decide to have monthly parties, next time on the second floor.

When the party winds down, I help Michelle move furniture back into her apartment, but we decide to leave the Big Art. "More where that came from," I tell her.

"I wish I had thought to do this last year," I say as we wrestle my old sofa through her doorway. "But you know, I have never even seen anyone in 3B or 3A. Did you ever get in touch with anyone there?"

"No," she says, a mischievous look in her eyes. "No one ever answered the door, and no response to the note I put in the mailbox. By the way, did you ever notice—no names on their boxes or buzzers. But I kept checking, and I did see lights go on and off sometimes, so I think someone lives in both of them. We could make up a really great story about how they have a secret door between the apartments, and another secret door into the locked stairwell at the other end of the building."

"It's locked? I never tried it. I thought that was a fire escape—we have to be able to get out at least."

"Nope, locked inside."

I think about calling the city about that, maybe when I can risk getting thrown out, like when I have a job.

"Oh well, thanks for doing this. I'll do the notices next month if you like."

"I'll do it—you all elected me mayor, remember."

On Saturday morning I work my shift at the food co-op, which has moved into a sort of storefront on a side alley off Delmar.

It's not as clean as I'd like, so I set to work sweeping when I'm finished filling orders.

"Let's put 'clean the windows' on the job list," I tell Rick when he comes in for his shift. He looks around and shrugs.

"We're not Schnucks," he says.

"Okay, the windows can wait, but we really should be careful about cleaning up spills—don't want mice in here."

"That reminds me, have you seen the cat lately?" Rick asks.

"No, I thought it was mostly at your place."

"Well, if you do see him, bring him in. Mice patrol, just in case."

I'm not sure the health inspector will agree, so I keep sweeping until all the rice, nuts, seeds, and flour are cleaned up. I like the idea of the co-op more than the reality, I think. Or maybe others are run a little better than this. I decide I can put in some extra shifts while I'm looking for a job.

CHAPTER 64

Two weeks later I sweep out the co-op again and clean the windows between customers. On the way home, I walk by the Coalition for the Environment and stop in to see if David needs help with anything. He's cleaning out his desk.

"What's up? You're not moving out, are you?"

"Oh, it's my last day—I got this great job at the Saint Louis Land Reutilization Authority as a planner/analyst. I guess they had a lot of applicants—it took two interviews. I'm really excited about it."

He goes on to tell me about doing his PhD in Urban Planning and his dissertation on urban renewal strategies. By the time he takes a breath, I'm over my shock and happy for him. He's obviously a better candidate than I was anyway. I wish him well and go home. My thanks-but-no-thanks letter from the LRA is in my mailbox and I add it to my collection.

But also in my mailbox is a letter and a contract from *Saint Louis Today* wanting to publish my article and pay me for it. Not a lot, but enough to cover rent for a month. An edited copy of the manuscript is enclosed. I read through it, make myself put it aside, read it again. They have punched it up, made some of my carefully couched statements into firm statements, and drawn my conclusions more forcefully. I wait another day and call them, thanking them profusely and asking them to tone down some of their changes.

"Are the changes untrue?" the editor asks.

"Not necessarily, but I can't vouch for them absolutely. I don't know that there is a concerted, coordinated effort to move the Black population out of DeBaliviere. It's possible that it's only about money and not about race."

"Okay, got it. I'll take care of it. Otherwise, we're okay to print? We just lost an article for the April issue, so this was perfect timing. We just need the contract back by day after tomorrow, so if you could drop it in the mail this afternoon, that would really make my day."

I sign and seal and practically skip to the post office.

When I get back, the phone is ringing. Lulu is wondering if she can stay with me for the summer so she can work at the housing office again, instead of going back to Mom's and looking for a job. I've been expecting this, so I agree. But then she puts on her kid sister voice.

"What about next year? Do you think I could stay there for next year?" I don't answer and she adds, "We could save a lot of money."

"But you have enough financial aid for housing, don't you? Did something happen?"

"No, that's all fine, I just thought it would be good to, you know, have some extra."

This doesn't sound like my sister.

"Extra for something in particular?" I ask, and it comes in a rush.

"Well, there's an intercession class that I really want to do—it's a trip to England and France and my friend Annie is going, and it would be really good for me. Really."

I hate to crush the dream, but I'm reluctant to agree to sharing my space, too.

"Maybe you could be an RA next year—that gets you a free room. And you know that I might find a job out of town and be gone, even by May."

"Oh, I hope not!" she says, and then realizes what she's said. She starts to apologize, and I tell her I understand and then tell her about the article in *Saint Louis Today*. She gets excited about that and goes off to tell her friends about her famous sister, and we let the apartment topic slide for the moment.

CHAPTER 65

I continue to apply for jobs and get some interviews but no offers. The last week of March, the April edition of *Saint Louis Today* is published, and my five free copies arrive in the mail. Right on the cover is a photo of the boarded-up DeBaliviere Street businesses and a headline "Out of the Loop—Race and Relocation in DeBaliviere."

That seems a little strong. I open to page five and there it is, my byline and my face. I wonder how they got my photo—it's my student ID picture, pretty grainy but obviously me. I read through the story, getting worried as I go. It seems to be exactly like the proofs they sent me, not toned down at all. Finally, at the very end, there is my statement to the editor: "I don't know that there is a concerted, coordinated effort to move the Black population out of DeBaliviere. It's possible that it's only about money and not about race. But I think it's about both." There is also a large sidebar with statistics that support that statement, although they are not my statistics. I see a tiny note at the bottom of the box that says "Source: City of Saint Louis Public Records."

I read it again, slowly, and I decide that everything it says is true, even if the academic in me would not state things so strongly. Nor would the coward in me. I call Lulu and tell her it's out, then drive over to give her a copy. We go to DeMun for chocolate sodas to celebrate.

The first call comes two days later, the first day the magazine is on newsstands, just after dark.

"Bitch," a voice says, and hangs up. I can't even tell if it's male or female. I hope it's an April Fool of some sort.

The next evening, the same thing happens, just the one word. I'm pretty sure it's a man's voice. When the phone rings the next day, again just after dark, I don't answer. It rings a long time. The day after that, I bake a cake and flee to Leland, where I tell them what's going on. They tell me to sleep in the hole that night, and a debate rages for a few minutes because someone else is staying there. I sleep on the couch in the living room that night and decide it will have to get a lot scarier at home to make me sleep there again.

The next call comes in the middle of the day and it's more of a tirade, not entirely clear, but clear enough. I'm accused of being a hoity-toity know-nothing and a Negro-lover, although that's not the exact word he uses. I quietly hang up. I'm not really scared, not too scared, not yet, not enough to go back to the past-its-expiration-date sofa on Leland. Not scared enough to bunk with Lulu, either, not that she's got space for me.

I can't change my phone number with all those resumes out there, and my address is in the phone book. I take another look at my photo and decide to switch to a tucked-under French braid. I get out my leather hat, which looks ridiculous now that the weather is warming up. I drive to Molly's shop and ask her advice.

"You know," she says, "I think pulling your hair back in the braid is enough. That and big sunglasses. Just hold your head up and look confident. It helps that you live in a twelve-unit. Harder to pinpoint exactly where you are. Although I guess the building address is in the phone book, so that's out there no matter what." She sighs heavily. "But these guys are cowards. I think you're safe."

There are plenty of places to buy sunglasses on Delmar, so I walk home trying them on and find a pair I like—dark but not showy, not memorable. I buy a second pair, big blue ones, just to change my disguise. In the bright sun, it seems more like a game now. I'm admiring myself in shop windows when I remember that I drove to Molly's, and I nonchalantly turn around and go back for the car.

A few days later, Betty calls and asks if I want to work a few hours. Both her student workers have bolted, freaking out about term papers and finals coming up in May.

"And by a few," she says, "I mean about twenty hours a week."

Typing is the last thing I want to do with my new master's degree, and it's not feeding monkeys or tending bar—but then it's also not feeding monkeys or tending bar, so I say I'd love to.

Working at the Y turns out to be a lifeline, giving me income, occupation, and distraction. I worry about missing phone calls about jobs and spend all of my non-working hours in my apartment. Evenings and weekends I come and go at different times each day, sometimes exiting toward the street and sometimes toward the alley. The crank calls come less often but now I'm getting mail. They tend to rant and rave, mostly about taking our city back, and they go on about crime and drugs and shiftless people, but they don't actually threaten me, so I don't do anything about them. I put them in a folder marked "Hate mail," though, and leave it on my desk, just in case.

On May 1, I pick up a copy of *Saint Louis Today* and turn to the letters section. They've published one rebuttal to my article, which is coherent and nothing like the letters I've been getting. And they've published a letter thanking the magazine for publishing my article. I read it, feeling good about myself again, and laugh when I get to the end: It's signed by Adela. That letter is followed by a strongly worded call for a thorough investigation into the demise of the small businesses on DeBaliviere. It's signed by Mrs. Como. I feel good all day, although by evening, I start to wonder if Adela and Mrs. Como are now going to be hounded too.

When I start down Wingate, I see flashing red lights, and as I get closer I see they are parked in front of my building. Michelle is among the crowd on the sidewalk, and I sidle up to her.

"What's going on?"

"You'll never believe it. See that guy in the back of the cop car? *That* is 3A. And see that woman talking to the cop over there? *That* is 3B!"

"What happened? They didn't really have a door between?"

"No, nothing like that. He just went over and broke into her apartment. Just smashed the door in. She wasn't there, thank goodness. It sounds like he didn't do much, just took a TV and some records back to his apartment."

"That's creepy, isn't it?"

"That's his dad over there by the cop car. He was saying he thought his son was better, that he was ready to live alone again, something like that. It was easier to hear when they were inside; out here I can't catch the details. There was something about being scared by a cat."

I look at the guy, who is maybe thirty and very overweight and sad-eyed, staring at his lap. I can picture him sitting in his apartment day after day, so silent I didn't know he was there. I wonder if he's a Vietnam vet with some sort of shellshock.

"Did you hear anything about the woman—who she is, why we never see her?"

"It sounded like she's been gone a really long time, like a year. Hard to imagine paying rent when you're not here, but maybe she had a grant or something."

I leave Michelle to glean whatever she can and go inside and upstairs. The hallway is a mess where he shattered the door, just smashed right through it. Thank goodness I wasn't here for that; I would have assumed it was a hate-mailer looking for me. I can see where he plowed back through the mess to his own door. A cop is there, but he says I can go in my apartment as long as I stay away from the taped area.

"I guess these doors are a little flimsy," I say, opening mine.

"This was an unusual situation," is all I get out of him.

He gives me his card in case I have any questions, and I add it to my collection, pretending it's no different from any of the others. I close my door and flop down on my couch, and a black cat hops up onto my lap.

"DB?" I ask, and he meows back. "Hey, were you the scary 3C cat?" He nestles down and closes his eyes, purring. I am too full and too tired to lie awake rehashing the day's events. I listen for crazed burglars for a while, but I sleep long and well and wake to a ringing phone.

CHAPTER 66

"Novelle, are you there? Dr. Stone would like to see you today if you have a free half hour."

It's the secretary in the Economics department, and when I get my voice working, I ask her when would be convenient.

"This morning, if you can make it. He's leaving around noon for a conference. It sounds like I woke you up—I'm sorry, but he's anxious to talk to you today."

"I can be there in an hour—wait, what time is it now?"

"It's nine, so ten would be just fine. I'll let him know."

She hangs up before I can ask what it's about, which may be why she got off the phone quickly. But she sounded upbeat and anyway I've stopped worrying that my thesis will somehow be rejected ex post facto. At ten sharp, hair still damp but braided, I knock on Dr. Stone's door.

"Novelle, come in, have a seat. This is Bill Jones." He motions to a chair and to a white-haired man all in one gesture.

I say hello to Mr. Jones and shake his hand before I sit.

"Dr. Jones is from the National Center for Economic Studies. You know it, of course."

I nod. I have heard the name, but I can't really distinguish it from a dozen other organizations I've researched in looking for a job. Why didn't he drop that name in his message so I could have taken a quick look in Olin before I got here? Not that I really had time for that.

"You sent them a letter of interest for a research fellowship, back in January." Dr. Stone says this firmly, with a look that says I did and I should acknowledge it. I am at least 90 percent sure that NCES was one of the many recipients of my January correspondence, so I can say just as firmly, "Yes, that's right."

"Dr. Jones here has been checking your credentials and then last month he saw your article in *Saint Louis Today.*" He looks at me and adds quickly, "Probably because I sent it to him. But I'll let him finish."

"We have a clipping service, so it got to me that way also. Along with the responses published in the current issue. You've raised some hackles." He looks at me with a smile, but I can see he wants a real response, not just a nod.

"I have," I start slowly. "And while that wasn't my intent, I have to say I was glad to see the responses, good and bad." Dr. Jones is waiting for more. "That taught me that economics can be more than reporting and forecasting." It's only taught me that as I was saying it, but I now know it's true, so I go on. "It taught me that economists, at least some of us, have a role in . . ." I pause, because the phrase that is on the tip of my tongue is "shaping policy" but that sounds banal even to me. I take a breath. "We have a responsibility to dig in, to look at more than statistics. At the very least, we need to look at statistics we don't ever consider, maybe that don't exist yet." I'm warming up now, but Dr. Jones stops me.

"Were you scared?"

That has to be the last question I expected. No point in lying, though.

"Well, yes, a little." I leave it at that.

"Good, that makes you a realist." He smiles at me and turns to face Dr. Stone. "I guess we should stop grilling her and tell her what this is about."

"Novelle, Dr. Jones is here to see his sister, who lives in Clayton. But he thought he would deliver the news in person that NCES is offering you a fellowship."

My first thought is: Is it the paid kind? Instead, I thank him and say something about being honored. He opens his briefcase and hands me an envelope.

"The details are in here: pay, housing allowance, length—it's twelve months. You can think about it and let us know within a week if you can, or at least let us know if you need more time."

With that, he stands up, says he must run and will see Dr. Stone at the conference, and then turns to me again.

"I really hope to see you in Cambridge," he says, shaking my hand, and it takes me a minute to realize that he means Massachusetts, not England. Apparently, it's important to distinguish between Boston and Cambridge. I'll have to remember that.

I want to tear into the envelope and find out if this is a real job or a minimum-wage resume filler, but I stay cool.

"Congratulations," Dr. Stone says. "This is a big deal. I had given up on it—I knew that you were a long shot because of the hard-core economics-is-numbers people at NCES. But I also knew they were concerned about all the internal turmoil in the '60s and the impact of that on the economy. They've been taking an interest in stretching their ideology since then."

"Am I going to be fighting the status quo every day then?"

"Well, if you are, you're the one to do it. That's why he asked if you were scared. Good thing you owned up to it. Leave a message if you have any questions."

I savor the moment all the way home and wait until I'm upstairs to open the envelope. The stipend is generous, and the housing allowance is twice my current rent and utilities, but I know that just means that Cambridge is expensive. The rest of it doesn't matter, at least not at the moment. Meanwhile, I look around at the apartment. I'll be gone in three weeks. The couch, the cat, the Big Art, David Black's bed. It will be here, and I will not. I need to tell someone, so I call Lulu, who is a little surly because she has one more final tomorrow.

"Of course you got a great job, you always do everything right," she says. "Boston's a long way, though."

"Yeah, and cold too."

"Hey, you'll be moving to Boston for a year! I can have your apartment. That's so perfect. You'll get back when I graduate. It was meant to be!"

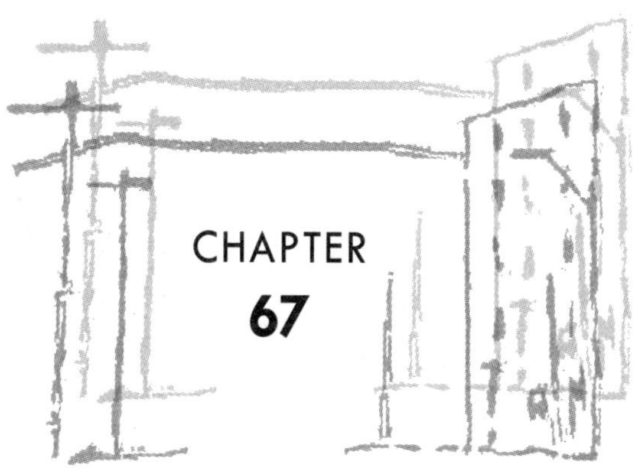

CHAPTER 67

Lulu moves in the next week, and we both ignore the question of what happens at the end of my year in Cambridge. Who knows where either of us will end up in a year? I tell her all about the phone calls and mail and my concern about her living at my address.

"I'll put a fake name on the mailbox and a different fake name on the door up here," she says, stroking DB, who seems to have moved in along with Lulu.

On the last day, I want to take the bus to the train station, just for symmetry, but Lulu won't hear of it, and I have too much luggage anyway. We drive all the way down Delmar in silence, me musing about how Delmar became the perceived border between north and south, Black and white, dangerous and safe. Between nothing and everything. Through the windshield, both sides look the same.

I hug my sister, find my seat, and will the train to go faster, toward my new job in Cambridge. But my eyes tear up as we cross the Mississippi and north Saint Louis appears along the river beyond the Arch. In my mind, I look all the way up Delmar to the Loop, to my north-of-Delmar apartment.

"You'll be back."

Startled, I look around. A woman smiles at me from the aisle seat one row back, a little girl in a pink dress and cornrow braids next to her, peeking over a large picture book. The woman nods her head a few times and says it again. "You've got something there, and you'll be back to do it." She smiles again and turns back to the child and the book.

I give Saint Louis one last look and turn to face Cambridge. I can't wait to get there, but I know the woman is right. I will be back. I can hardly wait.

ACKNOWLEDGMENTS

When I started writing this book, I was like Novelle on the Delmar bus: heading into the unknown, with not much more than a location and dream. But once I got my footing, I let the story go where it wanted. I followed Novelle through the Loop in University City to my own grad school apartment and then let her live her own, very different life.

The story is set in 1976, a watershed year in America. The '60s were finally gone. No incoming freshmen had worried about the draft or protested the Vietnam War or lied about going to Woodstock or the Summer of Love. Tie-dye was out, the boys had all cut their hair. The three assassinations that defined the '60s were faded nightmares, as were Nixon and Watergate. The Civil Rights Act had passed, the Equal Rights Amendment was just a few states from ratification, Roe v. Wade was firmly enshrined, and closet doors were creaking open as anti-homosexuality laws were slowly going away. Nuclear war was off the table. We had changed the world and made it safe for . . . for what? Disco? Only we hadn't, as Novelle finds out.

Although this is a work of fiction, most of the places are real, or were in 1976 and 1977, when the story takes place.

The Loop, DeBaliviere Place, Blueberry Hill—all are fixtures in Saint Louis. The issues Novelle finds herself immersed in were real too. Were and still are. Every city has its version of the Delmar Divide. The story, however, is a complete fabrication. It illuminates history without retelling it verbatim.

- Ray Nesbitt was inspired by Ray Nesmith, who was a long-time director of the WashU Campus Y, although his unexpected death occurred earlier in 1976 than it does in the book. He did indeed teach yoga and stand on his head. He was a campus legend, truly beloved and long remembered.

- The Campus Y was and still is in the basement of Umrath Hall, although brides no longer use it for dressing—rooms are now available for that in Graham Chapel's own basement.

- Joe Edwards was inspired by the real owner of Blueberry Hill, who has been key in making the Loop what it still is today.

- Wingate Avenue is a pseudonym, but figuring out the real street name is child's play for anyone with a map.

- Paul's Books is gone, and Left Bank relocated to the Central West End years ago, but Subterranean Books has taken root in the heart of the Loop.

- Pratzel's Bakery was opened downtown around 1914 and gradually moved west with the Jewish population. It was indeed a late-night stop for generations of students and other locals in the Loop from 1931 to 1978.

- The jeweler on Delmar was inspired by the one who repaired my watch in 1976. And yes, the real jeweler had a tattoo from a German prison camp.

- Lee Sherman was inspired by Les Sterman, who directed East-West Gateway for twenty-six years and was instrumental in the development of light rail in the bi-state area (although the study Novelle works on is pure fiction).

- Delmar Boulevard is actually a combination of Delaware and Maryland, in spite of what the fictional Dr. Stone says on page 196.

ABOUT THE AUTHOR

Photo credit: Amy Sullivan

Ellen Barker grew up in Missouri during a period of demographic upheaval, and she returns there in her novels. She has a bachelor's degree in urban studies from Washington University in Saint Louis, where she developed a passion for how cities work, and don't. She lived in the Loop in University City for several years and began her career as an urban planner for East-West Gateway in Saint Louis. She then spent many years working for large consulting firms, first as a writer-editor and later managing large data systems. Her volunteer work involves years of pet-assisted therapy with children in "the system," both foster care and prison. She is the author of three earlier novels: *East of Troost*, *Still Needs Work*, and *The Breaks*. She and her husband live in Los Altos, California, where they can indulge in hiking year-round.

Ellen loves to hear from her readers, who can contact her through her website: www.ellenbarkerauthor.com—where you can also read about all her other books. She also loves it when readers leave reviews of her books on Amazon, Bookshop.org, Goodreads, or any other reader-oriented website.

Looking for your next great read?

We can help!

Visit www.shewritespress.com/next-read or scan the QR code below for a list of our recommended titles.

She Writes Press is an award-winning independent publishing company founded to serve women writers everywhere.